FEAR

JEFF ABBOTT

sphere

SPHERE

First published in the United States of America in 2006 by Dutton
First published in Great Britain in 2007 by Sphere

A CIP catalogue record for this book
is available from the British Library.

ISBN-13: 978-1-84744-015-0

Typeset in Sabon by M Rules
Printed and bound in Great Britain by
Clays Ltd, St Ives plc

Sphere
An imprint of
Little, Brown Book Group
Brettenham House
Lancaster Place
London WC2E 7EN

A Member of the Hachette Livre Group of Companies

www.littlebrown.co.uk

Jeff Abbott graduated from Rice University with a degree in History and English, and worked in advertising for many years before turning his attention to writing. He lives in Austin with his family.

For more information on Jeff Abbott visit: www.jeffabbott.com

Praise for *Panic*

'*Panic* is a sleek, smart thriller that combines a family tragedy, international intrigue and the redemptive power of love into one of this year's best books. There is no question: Jeff Abbott is the new name in suspense' Harlan Coben

'*Panic* is a hottie, a real who, why and what's happening novel' *Independent on Sunday*

'*Panic* is an instant classic, immediately full of questions – who, what, why, how – that have answers you won't see coming' Lee Child

'Fast and furious, this is a thriller you won't want to put down' *Sunday Express*

'Jeff Abbott gives us an exciting roller-coaster ride from Texas to Washington and the Everglades via London, and the pace, not to mention the furious action, never lets up' *Guardian*

'*Panic* is a ride down the roaring rapids. Jeff Abbott has put together a hell of a page-turner' Michael Connelly

'Abbott has fashioned another burst of white-knuckled suspense that's extremely hard to put down' *Publishers Weekly*

'A near-perfect thriller that may indeed result in physical distress akin to panic for anyone trying to put the thing down before the last bullet flies. Fans of Harlan Coben, Lee Child, Joseph Finder or John Grisham – anyone who enjoys a wild ride on a bumpy road – can cheer the arrival of our latest master of the fine art of the page-turner. Highly recommended' *Booklist*

'Thrilling and relentless' *Time Out New York*

Also by Jeff Abbott

In memory of my brother Danny

Canst thou not minister to a mind diseas'd,
Pluck from the memory a rooted sorrow,
Raze out the written troubles of the brain,
And with some sweet oblivious antidote
Cleanse the stuff'd bosom of that perilous stuff
Which weighs upon the heart?

– William Shakespeare, *Macbeth*

Tell me, if you can, what is courage.

– Plato

FEAR

JEFF ABBOTT

ONE

I killed my best friend.

Miles stared at the words, black in their clean lines against the white of the paper. First time to write the truth. He put the pen back to the pad.

I didn't want to kill him, didn't mean to kill him. But I did.

'Baring your soul fixes nothing.' Andy sat against the edge of the kitchen table, watching him write. 'She'll just hate you.'

Miles said, 'No, she won't.'

Andy lit a cigarette, exhaled a blue cloud over the confession as Miles wrote. 'You've lied to Allison for weeks . . .'

'Lie's a bit strong.'

'Not as strong as murder. Telling her what you did isn't going to make you better.' He watched the smoke dance from the cigarette's tip.

'Shut up.' Miles finished writing out his confession. Andy wandered to the kitchen, rummaged in the refrigerator, found an early-morning beer.

'Priests say confession is good for the soul, but this is an exceptionally bad idea. Even for your soul. We had a deal, Miles.'

'This doesn't affect you.' Miles signed his name – his real name, Miles Kendrick – at the bottom of the page. Allison had never seen his true name.

'You tell her what happened, it very much affects me.' Andy slapped his hand on the table. 'Let me read what you wrote.' Miles slid the paper across the table to him, then went to the kitchen counter and poured black coffee into a cup. He usually drank his coffee first thing, but this morning he'd wanted to write the confession before he lost his nerve.

Miles went to the bathroom, splashed cold water on his face. Stared at himself in the mirror.

I used to be someone, he thought. *I used to be me, a regular guy, the anybody American with a home and a business and a life, and now I don't know who I am anymore. The old me died. The new me doesn't want to be born.*

'Lies!' Andy called from the kitchen.

Miles wiped his face and stepped back into the kitchen. 'I'm telling the truth.'

Andy slapped at the confession. 'The truth you remember. Not the truth of what really happened.'

'It's all I remember.'

'You didn't save those cops.'

'You know I did.'

'And I think about the high price every day, Miles.'

Miles stepped around Andy, took the paper, folded it, slipped it into an envelope. 'I have to be honest with her.'

'You're breaking our deal.'

'The only deal we have is in your mind. I have to go. Don't be here when I get back.'

'I don't want to get ugly, Miles,' Andy said, 'but you give her that confession, and I'll kill you.'

4

Miles stopped by the apartment door. He yanked on his coat, slid the confession into his coat pocket.

'I will, Miles.' Andy's voice was low and it prickled Miles's skin as if an ice cube ran along his ribs. 'I'll slip a gun into your mouth. I'll pull the trigger. I'll settle the score.' Andy paced the kitchen floor, arms crossed, glaring.

'You go ahead and try.' Miles shut the door behind him and leaned against it. Then he hurried down the steps, past the comforting cinnamon smells of the bakery on the ground floor of his apartment building. He stopped right outside the building's front door, craned his neck out an inch, scanning both ways up the narrow streets, eyeing every car and pedestrian.

No one waited to kill him. No cars idling on the road, full of assassins to mow him down before he took five steps. He started his walk to Allison's office. He didn't drive anymore because he was afraid if the Barradas found him, they'd wire a bomb to his car's ignition. They'd blown up the last two people who had testified against them, scattering engine and glass and flesh across a driveway in Hialeah and an office parking lot near Miami. The center of Santa Fe, where he now lived and worked, was territory he could cover on foot. Santa Fe was so much smaller and quieter than the constant revving hum of Miami. He walked through the Plaza at the heart of the old city, past the Native Americans spreading turquoise and silver jewelry across black felt mats. He headed up Palace Avenue, past a beautiful young mother pushing a stroller with twin girls under a pink blanket, tourists ambling along an architectural route, joggers huffing in the crisp gray of the mountain morning. *Jogging*, Miles thought, he should try jogging. Good healthy exercise to heal all the rot inside him.

He glanced over his shoulder twice to see if Andy was following him. No Andy, although it wouldn't take him long to catch up if he decided to press his case.

The confession, inside his pocket, made a soft crinkling sound as he walked, and he smoothed the paper straight with a slide of his finger.

The paper would change everything in his life, once again.

He walked past the stone grandeur of Holy Faith Episcopal Church and the elegant Posada Hotel and Spa. Most of the homes along this stretch of Palace Avenue had been converted into office space. Allison Vance counseled in an old brick Victorian that stood out from the more common adobe-style buildings, its yard dotted with spruce pines and cottonwoods. The hum of a saw roared through an open upstairs window. The landlord was refurbishing the empty top two floors while Allison refurbished people's heads.

Miles went up to the house, glancing over his shoulder. Andy stood on the bricked sidewalk, huddled against the cold, his tropical print shirt and khakis out of place in the morning chill of a Santa Fe spring.

Go away, Miles mouthed at Andy.

'If you give her that confession,' Andy said, 'it changes nothing. It doesn't hurt me, it hurts *you*. You got me, Miles?'

Miles gestured at him to go.

'This ain't done.' Andy tossed the cigarette onto the street, marched back toward the Plaza.

Miles found his breath and went inside. The door to his right read ALLISON VANCE, M.D., PSYCHIATRY. He opened it,

6

stepped inside, rested his head against the door as he closed it.

'Good morning, Michael,' Allison said to his back. 'I'm glad you made it this morning.'

'Made it early,' he said. Certain days he couldn't face the appointment, the idea of sifting through the black sand of his memory, afraid of what he might unearth. 'What's the matter?' he asked.

'Nothing at all,' Allison said, and her tense expression faded. 'Would you like a cup of green tea?'

He hated green tea but said, 'Great, thanks.' He took off his jacket, hung it on a hook – the confession still in its pocket – and sat down in the fat, worn leather chair across from hers.

She poured a steaming cup of tea and handed it to him.

'Thanks,' he said.

'You look tired, Michael.' It was his new-life name, one conjured up by Witness Security.

'I'm not a morning person.' He sipped.

'You probably worked a lot of nights, being an investigator.' Attempt number one to get him to talk. His being a former private investigator was one of the three nuggets of truth she knew about his old life.

'Nighttime is the right time,' he said. 'Cheating spouses often burn the midnight oil.'

'Is that who you shot? A cheating spouse?'

Attempt number two, based on nugget number two. The dance remained the same; she would try to get him to talk about the horrible instant when his old life died, glean details he couldn't remember, and he would duck and run, hiding behind jokes and chatter. 'No. I never carried a gun.' The words came out like molasses dripping from his lips. *Get up and give her the confession*, he told himself.

7

Andy stood behind Allison. 'What's wrong, Miles? Lose your nerve? Go ahead, tell pretty lady exactly what you did to me.'

Miles froze. His skin felt like it had been slathered in ice. Andy had never set foot in Allison's office before. Miles glanced at his coat, where the confession lay. He looked at Andy. Andy grinned and shook his head.

'Michael? Is something wrong?' Allison leaned forward with a frown.

Miles hid behind a long sip of his tea. Steadied his breath against the rim of the cup. Looked up again. Andy made a gun of his fingers, fired it at Miles.

'Michael, every time I mention the shooting, you freeze up.'

'I know.' He set the tea down. 'I don't want . . . to not remember what happened anymore.' The words felt thick in his throat. 'I need you to help me.'

She sat across from him. 'Of course, Michael. This is a major step. Wanting to heal yourself – it's a critical element that's been missing from our work together.'

'I don't want you to hate me,' he said.

'I couldn't. Never.' She offered a thin smile. 'I think I understand you better than you know.'

'Wait till you find out what I did,' he said. 'I don't even remember all the details of it – I can't.'

'Your willingness to talk about your trauma is all that matters, Michael.'

'I know I haven't been cooperative with you, but I want to be sure . . . I stay your patient. You're the only one who can help me.'

'I'll take it as a welcome compliment, thank you, but—'

He held up his hand. 'Don't give me the shrink line about every therapist is good, blah blah blah. And I don't want you sending me to a hospital; I can't, I won't, go to one of those places, they're not an option.'

An expression of surprise, or of disappointment, he couldn't tell which, crossed her face, then vanished with her nod. 'No hospitals. And I welcome the change in attitude toward your therapy. Where would you like to start?'

Prep her for the confession, he decided. 'I keep seeing the person I shot. I can't live this way, I can't have him on my shoulder all the time, so it's either get fixed or go even crazier.'

Her expression might have been cut from steel. 'Is he here now?'

'Yes. He's a fever I can't shake. He told me this morning he wanted to kill me.'

'What's his name?'

'Andy.'

Behind her, Andy crossed his arms. 'I really resent you bringing this do-gooder bitch between you and me, Miles.'

'Let's talk about the shooting,' Allison said.

'I told you, I don't remember all the details.'

'We'll go slow. Start with where the shooting happened.'

The first word caught, a stone in his throat, but he coughed and said, 'Miami.'

'Your home?'

'I grew up there. So did Andy.'

'Where in Miami did the shooting take place?'

'A warehouse. No one there but me and . . .' He stopped; he couldn't look at her. Handing her the confession now seemed impossible. He steadied his breath; the burn of panic inched along his bones.

'Me and two policemen and Andy . . .'

'The knife that's in the kitchen drawer,' Andy said.

'Wicked sharp. I'll put it in your hand, I'll help you draw a nice hot bath, and then you can slash your wrists, and we're cool again.'

Miles stopped. 'I want to be healthy again, I want my life back . . .' He stood and he paced and put his face into his hands.

'Let me help you. Go back to the story.'

'But I can't remember, I can't remember, how can you help me if I can't remember?'

'Small steps. You shot this Andy.'

'Yes, yes.'

'Why?'

The pictures crossed his mind, a jumble, photos dropped at random on a floor. 'We're laughing. Then – Andy freaked. He pulled a gun. Aimed at the head of one of the cops.'

'And you shot him.'

He sank into the chair. 'Yes. But I don't remember it.'

'Doesn't pretty lady deserve the truth,' Andy whispered, 'before you give her a letter full of lies?'

'Let's not try to remember,' Allison said. 'Let's just talk about what you visualize if you think about the shooting. That's different from the memory itself.'

He sipped the green tea and wished the cup held bourbon. 'I remember the laughing. But then the laughing stops and I raise the gun. I see Andy start to speak but I can't hear what he says. I pull the trigger. He shoots me.'

'He shot you?'

'Yes. In the shoulder. I see him fall. I . . .' The scar on his shoulder began to ache, throbbing like a heartbeat. Sweat coated his palms, the close air of the building tightened in his chest – the smell of the paint, the faint hammering two floors above him faded and suddenly the

10

office disappeared, the chill of New Mexico that pressed through the windows replaced with the humid blanket of Miami, the gunfire boomed a ceaseless roar in his ears, echoing in the cavernous warehouse, drowning out Andy's scream, his own voice filled with shock and horror, the *chock* of the bullet hitting Miles's flesh, a cannonball of pain.

'Michael?'

'Oh, Jesus, please.' Miles ran his hand along his forehead. He felt feverish, sick. He steadied his hands, pressing them against the soft leather of the chair. He was here. Not there. He could not go back there. Never.

'Michael. Michael.'

Michael wasn't his name and he didn't want to answer to it and then he remembered, yes, he was Michael now and forever. If he wanted to live.

'Yes,' he said.

'You were having a flashback. You're safe. No one will hurt you.'

'I'm safe,' he repeated after her. He blinked.

She cleared her throat. 'Tell me about Andy.'

His hand wanted to reach for the confession, just give it to her, but he didn't want his hands to shake when he gave her the envelope.

'I want . . . Michael, are you listening to me?'

He put his gaze on her. 'Yes, Allison. But I don't want to remember any more. I'm sorry. I can't.' *End it*, he thought. *Tear up the confession, walk out. Never come back. Have Andy as the perpetual roommate until you die.*

'You took a forward jump today. You said you want your health back, your life back. Fight for it, Michael.'

'It's too hard.' He found his breath again. 'Let's talk

about my mom and dad. Did I tell you my dad gambled a lot?'

'I don't think we can shy away from what you're facing with Andy. I want to introduce a new element to our therapy.'

He heard, behind him, the door to her office opening.

Miles spun up from the chair, covered the five steps to the door, grabbed the man's neck, and pushed him hard against the wall. The man matched Miles's height and he closed a strong hand over Miles's hand, tried to wrench Miles's grip from his throat.

'Michael! Stop!' Allison yelled. 'Let him go!'

Miles released his grip. The man had blond hair, blue eyes, a heavy build under the tailored suit. He gave Miles a cool stare.

'I dislike people coming up behind me,' Miles said.

'Clearly,' the man said.

'Michael. This is Doctor James Sorenson. I've known him for many years. He's done amazing work with people suffering from severe post-traumatic stress disorder.'

'Then he should know not to sneak up on people,' Miles said. 'Sorry.'

'I apologize . . . if I frightened you,' Sorenson said. For a big man, he had a soft voice, raspy, as though he felt few words pass his lips. He smoothed his suit lapel.

Miles didn't care for the underlying tone of Sorenson's voice, the slightly superior way in which he'd said *frightened*. He returned to his seat and faced Allison.

'I don't want another doctor,' Miles said. A hot anger surged in his chest. This wasn't how a doctor as caring as Allison behaved, springing another doctor on him. It was wrong. It wasn't her.

'I know. But Doctor Sorenson is running a new program

I believe could help you. Could give you your old life back.'

The confession. It would stop this shift, keep this other doctor out of the picture. *So get up out of the chair and give her the confession and stop being petrified of what she will think of you.*

Andy, standing behind Sorenson, said, 'It's not about what she thinks of you. It's about knowing exactly what happened when I died. That's what you don't want to remember. How you killed me.'

'My old life . . .' Miles shook his head at Allison, then at Sorenson. 'I don't want my case discussed with anyone else.'

'You don't need to worry about confidentiality, Michael,' Sorenson said. 'Your secrets are safe with me. I only want to help you.'

Miles knew he could get up and leave. He didn't want to hand the confession to Allison, not with Sorenson here. Potentially reading what he wrote. No. Not now.

Sorenson seemed to study the indecision on Miles's face, and said, 'I want to help. Your memories – whatever they are – must be very terrible to you.'

'Less terrible than dying.' He couldn't say, *Andy died and I loved him like a brother. Best friend since I was three years old. He died and I killed him, God help me, God forgive me. I didn't mean to kill him. I didn't want to kill him. I was trying to save him.*

Sorenson leaned forward and Miles saw muscles bunch in the man's big shoulders. His expression was flat and cold. 'There's a theory about traumatic memories. Our most terrible memories take the deepest root. Because they're not like regular memories. After a trauma, we constantly dredge up the results of our worst, life-altering

13

experiences. We examine them, we dissect them. What could I have done differently, what choice could I have made to avoid the tragedy? Leave for school two minutes earlier and my car doesn't crash into a truck and kill my child. Keep a more careful eye open and my friend doesn't get gunned down in a battle.'

Miles waited.

'The traumatic memory is walled off from "regular" memories, as it were, and fails to integrate with other memories. It's never processed as a nonthreatening memory would be – filed and put away, to borrow an office metaphor. So the terrible memory becomes more deeply rooted and so does the trauma associated with it – the nightmares, the crippling fear, the paranoia that fate will strike a deadly blow again. Even when you don't remember specific details, the memory is there, an engine for the trauma. It's a vicious circle.'

Miles tucked his hands in between the armrests and the cushion of his chair in case the trembles returned.

'If you could forget the worst moment of your life – would you?' Sorenson asked.

'No one can forget.'

'But if you could, would you? Forget all the trauma associated with killing this Andy person.'

'Yes,' Miles said. 'Yeah, I would.'

'Won't happen,' Andy said, now sitting on the chair's arm, leaning close to inspect Sorenson. 'We're freaking inseparable.'

'Well, I can't wipe your brain clean, but I could lessen the trauma of the memory.' Now Sorenson smiled. 'Think of it as a shot of mental Botox, as it were, to smooth out the wrinkles in your memory that cause the pain.'

Picturing Andy dying, with no guilt, no pain, no fear,

no horror. No guilt. Miles looked at Allison. 'This is for real?'

'I want to enter you in a special program for trauma victims. Allison thinks it might be helpful to you.'

Allison studied her hands in her lap.

'Is this program what you think I need?' Miles asked.

Allison, wordlessly, nodded. She glanced at Sorenson and Miles saw this was why she'd been tense when he arrived, this other doctor hidden in her office. Waiting for him.

It all seemed – wrong.

'Will you let me help you, Michael? Allison is recommending two other patients of hers for the program. We're meeting here tonight at eight to discuss it. I hope you'll join us. Your case fascinates me.'

'Thanks for the offer. I'll give it serious consideration.' Miles stood. Session over, even though twenty minutes remained on the clock.

'You made real progress today,' Allison said. 'I appreciate your listening to and talking with Doctor Sorenson. Thank you for – understanding.'

'I'll make my decision and let you know.'

'Decision made, you asshole,' Andy said to Sorenson. 'He's not coming anywhere near you.'

Sorenson shook Miles's hand with an iron grip. 'I hope we can, together, make your pain go away.'

'Speaking of which,' Allison said, 'here, Michael.' She pressed a white plastic vial of pills into his hand.

'What's this?'

'A very mild sedative to help you if you have another flashback.'

'Not necessary.' He disliked pills and hated taking the antidepressants she prescribed for him. Swallowing each pill reminded him of his failure to be strong.

15

'Dosage directions inside,' Allison said. 'Call me if you have questions. I really hope we'll see you here tonight at eight.'

Miles slipped the pills into his jacket. He heard his confession crinkle against the vial. He left, closing the office door behind him. Sweat coated his palms, ran in a trickle down his ribs.

Andy lounged by the entrance. 'I knew you couldn't go through with it. Just tear up the confession and let's go home.'

Miles said, 'I'm going to work and forget about you.' He stumbled outside. The bracing air slapped against his face.

'Sorenson,' Andy said, 'calling your case interesting, it made my skin crawl. I'm a lot more than a case.'

'You're right,' Miles said. 'I don't like him either.' He spoke low, into his cupped hand, as if he were warming his skin with his breath.

'Good, then, you don't need his dumb-ass program.' Andy slung an arm around his shoulder. 'My favorite part of the confession was when you said you were trying to save me. That's rich. You don't save me, you don't get to save yourself, that's only fair, Miles.'

Miles stopped. Closed his eyes, hunched his shoulders against the cold, counted to one hundred, listening to the distant hum of cars driving on Paseo de Peralta. He opened his eyes and Andy was gone.

Would you forget the worst moment of your life?

I can't go on this way, he thought. *I can't.* He'd join the stupid program, let Sorenson take apart his brain if it would banish Andy. If Allison believed going under Sorenson's wing would cure him, fine.

He touched the confession in his pocket, realizing he'd

16

been rubbing at it like a praying man fingering a rosary. Tonight at eight. Tonight he'd give it to Allison as a show of faith, listen with an open, if broken, mind to Sorenson's proposal to fix his head.

'But I might kill you before tonight,' Andy said, back again, leaning in close. 'Make you step out in front of a speeding car. Put a gun in your mouth. Walk you up to the top of a tall building and right off the edge—'

Miles ran.

TWO

Dennis Groote was late to visit his daughter because he had to kill the last of the Duartes.

He'd tracked the man – an accountant who'd managed to duck under the police radar after the Duarte gang collapsed – to a meeting Monday night in San Diego at a luxury hotel near the beach. Groote had spent Monday night camped in an unoccupied room next to the target. He had slipped inside it at nine that evening using an illegal scramble card. If any late-arriving guests showed up to claim the room, he would simply send them back down to the front desk, claiming a mistake had been made, and leave. The kill would wait for another day. Patience meant success; patience meant life.

The accountant arrived shortly after nine-thirty Monday night, but wasn't alone. Groote heard the accountant and a woman, talking in awkward tones, then the accountant's laughter, hearty, trying to be macho. Then the unmistakable sounds of kissing, of clothes sliding along skin, of movement on mattress.

Groote played solitaire on his PDA during the love-making, yawning once, waiting for the accountant to be done. He could simply pick the lock on the adjoining room door, walk in, shoot them both, and not miss a second of visitation time with Amanda. But he did not see why he should kill a woman who simply had selected the wrong sexual partner for the evening. He hated the idea of an innocent person suffering needlessly. He waited and hoped that the target's girlfriend wouldn't stay the night.

But she did. Groote listened to them continue their intimacies until midnight, then they fell asleep. He gave them another hour, hoping the woman would rouse from the post-coital slumber. Still the sound of silence, of light snoring from both the accountant and the woman. Then Groote dozed himself, waking in the thin light of Tuesday morning.

He listened at the door. Hushed, steady snoring. But he heard a soft step, heard the shower next door rush to life.

Now. He could be done and gone while the woman showered, out of harm's way. Groote jimmied the lock between the door linking the two rooms, eased it open. The accountant was fortyish, tall, barrel-chested. He didn't look the part of a bean counter; more like a laborer, with his rough face and heavy jaw.

'Hi,' Groote said.

The accountant's eyes opened in sleepy confusion and he said, 'Uh, hi.'

'You helped destroy my family. Just so you know.' Groote shot him with his silenced gun, twice between the eyes.

He heard a scream from behind him, over the hiss of the shower. Damn, she'd started the hot water but hadn't stepped under the spray. He grabbed the woman, shoved her hard against the wall, covered her mouth with his hand. She was older than the accountant, in her late forties. Groote recognized her; a concierge at the hotel. Groote had noticed her last night; he'd noticed and taken account of

19

every person in the lobby during his walk-through. She'd had a welcoming smile for him then, glancing up from her computer, and he had nodded in return.

Now Groote jabbed his gun against the woman's throat. 'Answer me and I'll let you live.'

The concierge closed her eyes, shuddering underneath his touch.

'You understand?'

She nodded.

'Why are you here?' Groote took his hand a centimeter off her mouth.

'Here?' The concierge sputtered in her terror. 'Oh, my God, oh, my God . . .'

'Yes. Here. With him.' *Wrong place, wrong time*, rattled in Groote's head, but he hated the phrase. He heard Cathy's final words: *I'm taking your car, more room for junk in the trunk.*

'He invited me. Please don't kill me. Please don't.' The concierge tried to back away from the gun barrel pressed into her throat, but Groote kept a hard grip on the woman's hair.

'Does he stay at this hotel often?'

She nodded a yes.

'Did you know him before tonight?'

'Yes.'

A predetermined choice then, not the random love-making of just one night. 'You know what kind of man he is?'

She shuddered with fear. 'He – he's just a CPA. For a boating company . . .'

'He had a different job before. His actions helped kill my wife, maim my daughter. He paid out the cash that bought the guns that destroyed my family.'

She shivered under his touch. 'Boating ... company ...'

'You should be more discerning about your friends, miss,' he said gently.

'Yes, okay, I will, I promise ...'

'I'm very sorry for the inconvenience.'

And he shot the concierge once between astonished eyes.

He took I-5 North to Orange. Staying up most of the night, generously giving the concierge the chance to leave, taking the time to check the accountant's laptop and files for anyone else connected to the remnants of the Duarte crime ring who needed killing, setting up the scene to appear like a robbery, battling the morning traffic sludge, made him late for his morning with Amanda. But at least he knew now he had not been unfair.

Not like Amanda or Cathy, who had never had a chance.

At ten – almost an hour late – he screeched into the heart of Orange, zooming past the restored Orange Circle with its charming shops, down past Chapman University and its sparkling new buildings. Orange was a nice town; he ought to move here, be closer to Amanda. Hit man of suburbia – the idea nearly made him laugh. He drove a few more blocks down to a cluster of brick buildings that suggested the quiet ambience of a modern prep school. Except with bars on the windows. At the gate at Pleasant Point Hospital, he gave his name to the guard at the post. He drove up to the main building, parked his Mercedes, hurried across the lot. He knew he needed a shower, a shave, but he had not wanted to waste another moment. A group of the children played outside in the morning sunshine, a few others standing, staring off at the sky or the ground or their hands. He didn't see Amanda.

He hurried into the building, checked in at the front desk. Today's nurse was Mariana, his favorite.

'I'm late,' Groote said. 'Terrible traffic.'

'Amanda's in her room,' Mariana said.

'Thank you.' Groote signed in and hurried down the hall to Amanda's room. He heard the plaintive notes before he reached her door, stepped in slowly so she could see him, not be startled. She remained jumpy, months after the horror.

Amanda lay twisted on her bed, knees drawn close to her chest, her right cheek pressed to the pillow. Patsy Cline, her mother's favorite singer, drifted softly from the speakers. 'Walking After Midnight.' Too sad a song for a bright morning, too sad a song for a sixteen-year-old. She ought to be listening to those boy bands, snapping her fingers, singing into a hairbrush, dancing before bathroom mirrors. At home with him, where she belonged.

'Amanda?' He stepped over to the CD player, turned the volume low. 'Amanda, it's Daddy.'

Now she opened her brown eyes, looked at him, through him.

'Hey, Amanda Banana.' He drew a chair close to the side of the bed. 'How are you?' He kept his voice gentle and soothing.

Amanda didn't answer. The frown on her mouth, the way her stare cut through him as if he were mist, told him a bad day loomed for her. And for him.

He took her hand. 'You want to get up and go outside?'

She barely shook her head. One of the scars on her face – the small star-shaped one near the corner of her mouth – jerked and he thought she would say good morning. But she went still.

'I'm so sorry I'm late, pumpkin, I had a work project this morning I had to finish.'

Now her eyes focused on his face. She said, slowly and carefully, 'Mom came to see me.'

'Ah. Did she?'

'Yes.'

'What did Mom say?'

'She wants me to hurt myself.'

'Oh, no, baby, she doesn't. She doesn't.' Groote tried to take one of her hands in his but she kept her hands twisted into claws, tucked tight against her chest.

'She said,' Amanda whispered, 'that I should cut off my face.'

'No, baby,' Groote said. *The drugs, the lame-ass therapy's not working, she doesn't even remember Cathy's dead.* 'She wasn't here.'

Now steel crept into Amanda's tone. 'She was. She comes nearly every day.'

'Baby. It's all in your head.'

'She was here!'

He stopped trying to argue with her. He wanted her calm and talking, not shrieking and screaming and cutting his visit short. There was so much necessary ugliness in the world, she was his pocket of beauty. He touched the scar at the corner of her mouth; another scar bisecting her eyebrow; the wriggled thread of tissue beneath her ear. The outward souvenirs of bullets smashing through glass, of a car tumbling down a rocky canyon. He kissed each scar. He whispered in her ear: 'Mom would never tell you to hurt yourself.'

He smelled a raw, metallic odor. Familiar. The smell of

23

blood. He leaned back from her, searching her face, running fingers along the bed. 'Amanda!'

She folded her gaze back into herself.

He yanked the covers off her. She lay in soft pants and shirt and he groped along her limbs and her torso for injury. Nothing. He pulled her cheek up from the pillow; her skin lay smooth and unbroken. His hands hurried at the back of her head and stickiness gummed his fingers.

She began to scream, thrashing against him, screaming for him please to take her face off.

'I don't understand,' Groote said, 'why she hurts herself.'

'The reasons are many.' Doctor Warner was a heavyset man, florid face under carrot-red hair starting to gray. 'She blames herself for the accident.'

'She shouldn't. It wasn't remotely her fault.'

'She still blames herself.'

'Well, I blame you for her state of mind,' Groote said in a voice of icy calm. 'My daughter is cutting her scalp open, for God's sakes. Your staff let her get hold of a safety pin.' And that had been her shrieked explanation as he summoned help: *Taking my face off has to be done from the back, Dad, it's easier.*

'It won't happen again.'

'I want you,' Groote said, keeping his control but nearly hissing through his teeth, 'to help her.'

'We've tried art therapy, medications, group therapy. All the standard treatments to process unintegrated, traumatic memory. Amanda is simply not improving.' Warner tented his hands under his jaw. 'The mental damage she suffered, trapped with her dead mother for so long, it may not be reparable.'

'If it's broken, it can be fixed,' Groote said.

'Amanda is not a dish to be glued back together,' Warner said.

Patience, he reminded himself. *Deep breath*. 'When I say fix, I mean . . . give her enough health to have her life back. To want to live again.' Groote thought, *I'll find out if you have a family, Doctor, because if you don't help my daughter you won't be able to help your own. You can get a real sense of what pain is.*

'Amanda had problems before the accident. Her biological father abused her.'

'Yes.' Groote didn't care to be reminded of the sad details, and he felt Warner was saying, *Sorry, buddy, your daughter was damaged goods before you brought her here.* But Groote had taken care of the rotten, no-good deadbeat father as a secret favor to his new wife and daughter. He never experienced hate when he killed, except when he'd put ten bullets into that worthless scum. He had not known he could love Cathy and Amanda so much; the idea of love had seemed like a rumor, never real until he found them.

And now Cathy was gone, and Amanda needed him. She only had him to protect her.

'Obviously the loss of her mother is devastating to her. But the conditions in which she lost her mom, they're much more damaging than her mother dying in a hospital bed of cancer, or even dying instantly in an accident. In a way, Amanda experienced her own death when she experienced her mother's. Think of it as a compound fracture against her mental health. It took her straight over into complex post-traumatic stress disorder.'

'You're not helping her,' Groote said in a low tone. 'She's trying to take her face off. If she hurts herself again I will hold you personally responsible and you'll learn an entirely new meaning of the word *consequences*.'

Warner smiled. He was a smart man, Groote thought, who knew very little. 'Threatening me doesn't help your daughter, Mr. Groote.'

'I'm sorry. But I need you to fix her. To make her right again. Please. Please.' And then salvation came, in the form of his cell phone ringing. Only the hospital and his clients had this number. He opened the phone; he didn't use voice mail, it carried too much risk. 'I'll have to call you back,' he said instead of hello.

'Please do,' a smooth voice answered. 'This is Quantrill. I have the perfect job for you. It could even help your daughter.'

Groote drove over the speed limit all the way to Santa Monica. Oliver Quantrill's house, a fusion of steel and glass, stood in a wealthy neighborhood. Quantrill sat on his expansive tiered deck, drinking mineral water, tapping on a laptop. He was tall, gym-club and protein-diet gaunt, in his early forties. He closed the laptop as Groote approached him.

'How did you know about my daughter?' Groote cooled his rage – *No, be honest, it's not rage, it's fear* – down to a simmer.

'Calm down, Dennis. I had you checked when I first hired you. It would have been foolish not to, given your past. I mean Amanda no harm.'

'Talk. What job could I do for you that helps my kid?'

'Do you know exactly what I do, Dennis?'

'You sell information. I don't know specifics.'

'Here's a specific. I've acquired medical research designed to help people suffering from post-traumatic stress disorder. People such as Amanda.'

Groote's legs went weak. He sat down. 'Research.'

26

'Abandoned research. It didn't work the first time. I've had my team make improvements. Now it works.'

'Works how?'

'It's a drug that makes PTSD controllable. Possibly curable.' Quantrill sipped at his orange juice. 'Would you like your daughter back, Dennis? What would that be worth to you?'

Groote opened his mouth, then closed it.

'Everything, wouldn't it?'

'Sure,' Groote said. 'I would want it for my daughter.'

'You and many, many other people. Experts estimate that up to ten percent of the American population, ten percent of the European population, suffers from a form of PTSD. That's many millions of potential patients. And then we have all the soldiers coming back from the Middle East fresh from war, with as many as forty percent with traumatic memories. Huge cost, right there. And the civilian populations in the war zones. Add in all the other horrors of life that can haunt us: hurricanes, assaults, rapes, car crashes, accidents, terrorist attacks ... well, you can see fighting trauma is a growth market.' Quantrill took another sip of his juice, poured a glass from the carafe for Groote, handed it to him.

'I haven't heard of any drug research along these lines, and I follow anything that could help my girl.'

'The research and testing has been done, well, under the table. So I can sell the research to a pharmaceutical and they can claim it's a product of their own development. I get an ongoing percentage. Sooner that's done, sooner Amanda and everyone who needs the drug gets it.'

Groote's mouth went dry. 'Why's the research got to be secret?'

'Not your worry. But I do need you to worry about a

woman in Santa Fe. Her name is Doctor Allison Vance. She's been working with the patients who've tested the drug in a psych hospital I own there. My research director's worried that she might blow a whistle on me to the FDA. She does that, no miracle drug for anybody. Including Amanda.'

'I already dislike Doctor Vance intensely,' Groote said. 'I'm sure she's a truly awful person.'

Quantrill grinned. 'I knew you were the right guy for this job. Go to New Mexico on the next available flight. Bring back the research materials to me. I know they'll be safe with you. And if Doctor Vance becomes a problem, then I need you to introduce her to a very serious accident.'

THREE

Pull yourself together, Miles told himself. Andy quit following him as he ran along Paseo de Peralta and turned the corner onto Canyon Road. *He's fighting you because he's afraid you really will make him go away.*

Miles stopped running, stuck a hand in his pocket, closed his fingers around the pills Allison had given him. No, he wouldn't take one yet; he wanted his mind sharp at work. As sharp as it could be. If Andy reappeared . . . then down the pill. But Andy didn't seem to enjoy the gallery much and Miles walked on surer footing inside its walls.

The exercise calmed him, but he couldn't shake Sorenson out of his thoughts. The man had seemed ready to take a swing at Miles; he didn't carry the soothing air of a psychiatrist easing a startled patient. Miles played the odd session back in his head. Just springing another therapist on him was wrong, dead wrong, not the sort of thing Allison did. A therapist wasn't supposed to do the unexpected. Life rattled his cage enough most days.

Right now the gallery beckoned as his refuge.

Miles had had only two job interviews in his whole life. He'd always worked for his dad at Kendrick Investigation Services, in its strip-mall office between a

29

pawnshop and a vintage-clothing store in a Miami neighborhood. When Andy brought Miles to meet the Barradas two days after his father's funeral, his first job interview had been decidedly one-sided: *Your dad owed us three hundred thousand off greyhounds and ponies, Miles, and he put up the agency as collateral. So we could take your business right this minute. But thanks to your buddy Andy, we're offering you a deal. We need a man to be our own personal spy, Miles. We need you to steal information for us. Get the incriminating evidence on other rings – find out who their dealers are, their suppliers, where they're stashing and cleaning their money. We have that, we take them down, we take over their business. You can give us leverage, give us a competitive advantage.* Mr. Barrada enjoyed reading the latest business-book best sellers and adapting their ideas to mob life. *You do that for us when we ask for the next two years, our debt's settled.* And, scared to the bone, he'd had no choice but to say yes.

The interview with Joy Garrison had been equally difficult. He'd walked through the gallery, his Witness Security inspector contemplating the paintings and their high price tags, and followed Joy upstairs to her private office. She was a petite woman, fiftyish, attractive, and at first he thought she was the stereotypical Santa Fe hippy-dippy, in her billowy pants and her silver-and-turquoise jewelry. But as soon as he sat across from her he recognized a toughness in her eyes that rivaled that of Mr. Barrada.

She studied him for an agonizing minute. He forced himself not to fidget in the chair.

Finally she said, 'You really want this job.'

'Yes, ma'am.'

'But you don't know shit about art, do you, honey?'

'Not much, ma'am. But I—' And he stopped because Andy stood in the corner, arms crossed.

'What's the matter? But what?'

'I wanted to go to art school. Learn photography. I didn't get the chance.'

'Parents disapproved?'

'Yes, ma'am. Said they wouldn't pay for a waste of money.'

'My parents said the same thing. They were right, I couldn't draw a straight line. But being an artist and selling art are two different skill sets.' She laughed. 'This gallery pays for Mama and Daddy to be in a real nice retirement village.'

'I'm a hard worker, ma'am. I can move the art for you, lots of those paintings and sculptures must be pretty heavy.'

'I need brain more than brawn. Inspector Pitts says you're handy with computers. I sell to collectors all over the country but my Web site's crap – I need a much more effective one. I also need help tracking inventory.'

'Yes, ma'am. I can build you a database, build or manage a Web site, run and fix your computers, make your systems more secure, whatever you need.' He didn't want to see Andy, so he kept his gaze locked on his lap. 'You tell me how to sell art, I'll sell art. I'll do whatever you need.'

'Hon, look at me when you talk to me.'

He looked up.

'We'll go slow on you selling, until you can look people in the eye.'

He swallowed. 'That's probably a good idea.'

'You're not my first federal witness to hire. They sent me an embezzler two years ago. She did just fine for two months, then she stole five thousand from my ex-husband.' Joy shrugged. 'Better him than me.'

'I won't steal.'

'You understand I'm the only one here who knows you're a witness. Inspector Pitts didn't tell me your real name, or where you're originally from. Just your new name, and your criminal record and your past work skills as reported to WITSEC.'

'I don't have a record, ma'am.'

'That's why you have the job, honey.'

He remembered to breathe. 'Thank you. You won't be sorry.'

She leaned forward. 'I can imagine you've been through a real ordeal, walking away from your life. I want you to know, Michael, that you can trust me. No one else at the gallery will know you're in the witness protection program. I will never, ever betray that trust.'

'Thank you. I hope to earn your trust, Mrs. Garrison.'

'Call me Joy. You start tomorrow.'

She stood and he stood and shook her hand, and he'd loved the job for the past two months.

The door to the Joy Garrison Gallery jangled as he opened and closed it. The gallery represented fourteen artists who were growing in repute among collectors. Most of the paintings and sculptures were priced at two thousand dollars or more, and Miles wished he could have made a living creating calm beauty on canvas. Miles nodded at Joy and her son Cinco as he stepped into the back office where he and the staff worked. She sat at a sales rep's desk, jotting on a sticky note. She raised an eyebrow; Cinco stayed on the phone with a New York collector, praising a new painting as a must-have.

'You're not scheduled today, hon,' Joy said.

'No, ma'am, I'm not. I just wanted to catch up on my work for a couple of hours. You don't have to pay me.' His voice stayed steady, his hands didn't tremble.

'Are you okay, hon?'

'I just need to keep busy.'

'Well, if you're so eager to be of use, could you call and find out when that new computer's arriving? You can see the way I've been replacing e-mails today.' She held up the sticky-note pad. 'And I need a bunch of photos taken of the new Krause sculptures and posted on the Web. Then I need you to update the Web site with a new price list.'

'No problem.'

'You make me look bad, Michael,' Cinco said, hanging up the phone. 'Don't you need days off?'

'I get bored easy.'

Two women who were friends of Joy's were now at the door, bearing lattes and gossip, and Joy laughed and called to them, and they headed to Joy's office, upstairs at the back of the gallery. Miles carried a small painting Joy wanted to show them.

He came downstairs; two tourists browsed in the front, and Cinco answered their questions about a sculpture of a leaping ram. Miles refilled his coffee mug and decided to call his WITSEC inspector to ask for a vetting on Sorenson so he could join the treatment program if he wanted. But he stepped into the back office and found Blaine the Pain sitting at his desk, drumming fingers. From the office doorway Miles shot Cinco a desperate frown; which Cinco answered with a grin that said, *Sorry-you're-screwed, I got customers, he's your problem.*

'Hi, Mr. Blaine.'

'Don't hi me, Michael. Are you rotating paintings today?'

'Tomorrow, sir.'

'Is *Emilia Stands in the Sun*' – his most recent work, a beautifully shaded portrait of a young Latina among high grasses – 'getting shoved to a back corner?' *Emilia* had worked the walls for four months but remained unsold.

'No, sir, I don't think so.'

'Because if *Emilia* doesn't get prime wall space, well' – and he issued his favorite threat – 'I'll bolt to another gallery. I have offers. Constantly.'

'You bolting would break our hearts, Mr. Blaine. I promise you we're trying our best to find the right buyer.'

'I just want it to sell. *Emilia* needs a good home.' A tinge of desperation edged his voice.

'We won't let her be orphaned.'

'Good. I have to go to Marfa today.' Marfa was a town in the West Texas desert, reborn from its background as the shooting site for the film classic *Giant* and emerging as a junior Santa Fe, a thriving arts colony with lower living costs. 'I might move there, a friend's driving me there to check it out for a couple of days. I just wanted to be sure *Emilia* didn't get stuck in the back. Would you call me if she sells?' He scribbled a number on a note and handed it to Miles.

'Yes, sir.'

Blaine the Pain left. Miles closed the office door and dialed DeShawn Pitts's pager number. He entered his identification code and hung up. Less than a minute later the phone rang.

'Joy Garrison Gallery,' Miles said. 'Michael Raymond speaking.'

'It's Pitts. What's up?' The voice sounded young but deep, slightly distracted, and Miles could hear the rustle of paper shuffling on a desk.

'Not on the phone. Lunch. Can you drive up here?' DeShawn lived in Albuquerque; he was the WITSEC inspector for federally protected witnesses hidden in northern New Mexico. He was responsible for helping Miles protect his new identity, finding him work and settling him into his new life, keeping him safe.

'Give me a hint, man.'

'My shrink wants to bring in another doctor to work with me, and I'm concerned about him.'

'I'm sure Doctor Vance wouldn't recommend a quack. What's his name?'

'James Sorenson.'

'Why do you need another doctor?'

'He's running a project for PTSD patients.'

'Did you ever tell Doctor Vance you're a witness?'

WITSEC had told him he was permitted to tell his psychiatrist of his status as a protected witness – it was considered crucial for successful therapy, given the enormous mental ordeal relocation was for witnesses. But he'd never told Allison he was in witness protection. She knew only that he'd been involved in a shooting and exonerated by the authorities. WITSEC requested he specifically not tell Allison his real name or where he'd originally come from, unless it was critical to his therapy. All those details were in the confession he'd been too afraid to give her today.

'No. I never told her I'm a witness.'

'Group therapy's not a good idea for you, man, since you got to be circumspect. But we can talk about it at lunch. Meet me at Luisa's. Twelve-thirty.' And DeShawn hung up.

Joy hurried back in, grabbed a file off Cinco's desk, a rich smell of espresso rising from her coffee cup. She hurried back onto the sales floor, calling out to her visitors, and the aroma of the coffee made the world swim before his eyes. Cuban coffee. Rich and heady. A screech of laughter from one of Joy's friends. The smell and the scream cut straight through to his brain. The gallery transformed into an empty warehouse, shafts of light cutting through the gloom, and he stood in the warehouse and the four men drank the heavy coffee. Miles tried to hide his trembling hands. The two undercover FBI agents, Miles, and Andy talking at the table, Andy about to get the best news of his life, and then Miles spoke, just a few words, and then tried to laugh.

The words he spoke? He couldn't remember the words.

Andy stared at him, standing behind the two undercover agents, who sat at the table pouring themselves refills of coffee. And then it all went wrong as Andy reached for his gun, Miles grabbing for his own gun in reaction, horrified, saying, 'Andy, don't.'

He heard the shots, the triple echo. Opened his eyes. Back in the gallery, the bloodied floor of the warehouse gone. He sank to the floor, next to the copier. He leaned against the equipment and his finger twitched, jerked once against a ghost trigger.

Awful silence, darkness, as if the world had swallowed him whole.

'It's pointless.' Andy knelt next to him. 'This is your life now. Me. You. Never parted. Give up trying to change.'

Miles shook his head.

'You'll die trying,' Andy whispered.

Then he heard laughter. Joy's warm, honeyed laughter. The gallery, its wonderful quiet, surrounded him. Miles forced himself back into the chair at his desk. He took deep breaths, trying to ward off the pain and the fear.

He couldn't live this way.

'So don't. End it. I'll help you,' Andy said.

Miles groped at the weight of the pill bottle in his pocket. Allison's pills. *A very mild sedative to help you if you have a flashback*, she'd said.

He fished the vial of pills out of his pocket. Plain plastic bottle, no label. He twisted it open. The pills were white capsules.

Folded among the pills lay a note.

He pulled out the piece of paper. He spread the note flat on the desk with his fingers.

Dear Michael: I need your help. I need your services as a private investigator. I'm in real trouble. Come to my office tonight at 7 and I'll explain. Don't tell anyone. I'm depending on you, see you at 7 P.M. Allison.

FOUR

Miles stood in line at Luisa's Drive-Thru, a Mercedes in front of him, a homeless man who smelled of dollar wine next to him, and a pickup truck loaded with truant high-school kids behind him, gunning the motor.

When he'd first arrived in Santa Fe, Miles had crafted a careful series of policies and camouflages to keep people from realizing he was Dealing With Issues. Don't answer Andy in public, resist jumping at sudden noises, close his eyes and stand still when a flashback invaded his mind. He didn't want to stick out, be noticed, devolve into the street-corner crazy raving at ghosts. Because if you acted crazy, you landed in the asylum.

Today his fit-in-with-the-normals policy was in the toilet.

Luisa's Drive-Thru was an entirely accurate name for the tin-roofed, simple establishment on a curve of the busy Paseo de Peralta. It offered no counter service; customers used the drive-up window or nothing. So a man who walked everywhere stuck out, standing in line between the cars. On the stroll over he had spotted a gaunt street person he knew named Joe, a man in his late fifties, laid waste by alcohol. He figured Joe received few invitations to dine, so he'd said as he walked past, 'I'll buy you lunch at Luisa's if you want.' And Joe, without a word, had followed him.

The federal witness and the homeless drunk stood between the two cars, having spoken their orders into the microphone, and now were waiting patiently in line to reach the order window.

Behind him, the pickup's engine revved in motorized machismo. Miles heard the laughter, hollow and cruel, of stupid children.

'Hey, losers!' a girl called. Miles glanced over his shoulder. The girl sat close to the driver, a thick-necked kid with a shaved-close head. Miles saw the girl was the brain, the boy the brawn. She was beauty-queen pretty but an ugly, taunting sneer slashed her face. Three other kids crowded the cab.

'Hey, losers!' Beauty Queen yelled again. She wore a cocky confidence born of her loveliness and her knowledge of how to use it. 'Get a car, why don't you?'

The pickup jolted an inch closer to his leg. He ignored it.

'They'd leave you alone if I wasn't here,' Joe said in his low, beaten whisper.

'No, she wouldn't,' Miles said. 'An ass is an ass.'

The girl, secure in the presence of her personal grizzly bear, laughed. Loud enough to be sure that Miles heard. 'It's a drive-through. Not a walk-through. What's the matter with you?'

Miles thought he looked normal. Not mental. But he wondered, in the sidelong glances he often earned, if there was a mark on him, a shock in his eyes, that announced damaged goods to anyone seeking a victim or a mark. Joe walked in slow retreat to the other end of the lot, eyes riveted to the pavement. The pickup jerked closer, barely nudging the back of his knee. Miles stood his ground.

The Mercedes in front of him pulled away from the order window, revved out into the traffic along the loop of Paseo de Peralta.

Miles didn't walk forward to claim his order.

The pickup's horn blared. 'Hey! Move it along!'

Miles stayed still. Andy, next to him, said, 'What's your damn problem?'

'Retard! Move it along!' Another long honk. The bumper edged into his leg again, forcing him to take a step. Laughter.

Slowly, Miles walked up to the order window. Luisa, the owner, worked the window and she filled a plastic bag with Miles and Joe's meal, beef and chicken tacos wrapped in thin foil, cups of beans and rice.

'Hey, there,' she said. 'How are you? What's all this honking?'

'Just kids,' Miles said.

'Asshole!' Beauty Queen leaned on the horn. Now Miles looked at them; the football player grinned. 'Move it along, Two Wheels,' the boy called.

Miles handed Luisa the money, in exact change. He noticed she kept the napkins, the salt, and the homemade salsa packages and the sugar packets on a shelf.

'Just a second, Luisa, and I'll be back,' he said, grabbing several sugar packets and a straw. He walked around the pickup, shaking the sugar packets at the football player and Beauty Queen.

He popped the gas cap open and wedged the first sugar packet in place to shove it inside when the driver's brain cells clicked in unity and his door flew open, the kid staring at Miles in shock.

'I'll beat your ass into the ground!'

'Not another step,' Miles said, 'or you'll have one sweet ride.'

The football player stopped. 'Don't, man!'

'Then drive off,' Miles said. 'Why do you want to be an asshole?'

'What's the matter?' Beauty Queen pushed on the boy's broad back. 'Just go beat his ass.'

'Sugar in the tank. Ruins the car,' Football Player said to her in a low, strained voice.

Miles suspected it wasn't enough sugar to do real damage, but Football Player didn't know that. 'Etiquette lesson for today, be nice to people who don't have a car. I dump the sugar, the no-car group includes you.'

'Smack his ass, Tyler,' Beauty Queen yelled.

'Yeah, Tyler, try to smack my ass. Maybe you'll win or maybe I'll show you how to respect your elders. But one more step, it's definite you'll be truckless.'

Tyler froze with indecision, stuck between Beauty Queen's braying enthusiasm for violence and a sureness that Miles would poison the gas tank before Tyler reached him.

'Tyler. Kick his ass!' Beauty Queen screamed.

'Tyler, use your brain.' Miles started whistling 'Sugar, Sugar'. He saw DeShawn's sedan wheel hard into the lot, pull into a parking space.

After a pause of five seconds, brain won. Tyler got back into the truck, peeled away. Miles could see the girl hollering and gesturing at the boy.

Miles walked back to Luisa's window, put the sugar packets and the unopened straw back on the counter. 'I cost you their lunch business,' he said, sliding her an extra twenty. 'Please accept my apology and this as payment. And three Cokes, too, please, Luisa.'

She got him his food and the Cokes without a word.

He walked a bag of tacos over to Joe, who stood with hung head and shamed frown.

'Here you go,' Miles said.

'Thanks,' Joe said. 'Sorry I left you alone. Them kids. I just can't take it. The meanness.'

'No worries. They're gone. You come see me at the gallery if they bother you.'

'I set foot on Canyon Road, the fancy-asses call the cops.'

'Not if you come see me, okay?'

'Thanks.' Joe took the bag of food and the Coke, gave a polite nod, and walked down the street.

Miles got into the Ford sedan and handed the taco bag to DeShawn. Pitts was a big-built guy, an ex-college football player, with a shaved-bald head. The sedan fit him like a too-tight suit. He wished he'd read Allison's note before he called DeShawn, because he wouldn't have asked the inspector to have lunch with him.

She wants your help. Not anyone else's, so keep your mouth shut. Don't bring DeShawn into this. You can be the man you once were. Help her, on your own.

'Thanks, man. But feeding bums and fighting with kids?' DeShawn said. 'You know, bud, the idea is to not draw attention to yourself.'

'Good to see you too.'

DeShawn handed him a chicken taco, snagged a beef one for himself. They started to eat. DeShawn demolished the first taco, wiped his mouth clean. 'First things first, Miles. I did a quick check. There's not a psychiatrist or a medical doctor or a psychologist licensed in New Mexico named James Sorenson.'

Miles swallowed soda. 'I don't understand.'

'Maybe you got his name wrong.'

'I . . . must have. I haven't been sleeping good, I must have misheard.' He didn't know what else to say. 'I tried

42

to call Allison back this morning, to find out more about the program, but she's not answering her phone.' That part was truth; he'd tried to reach her, repeatedly, after getting her note. But he'd only gotten her voice mail, and he just asked her to call him back. But Sorenson wasn't a doctor – why had she introduced him as such?

Why had she lied to him? Why had she let Sorenson lie to him?

Because Sorenson had forced her to lie.

I'm in real trouble.

DeShawn chewed on his beans, sipped at his Coke. 'Therapy must not be sailing smoothly if she's bringing in a backup shrink.'

Miles was now frantic to get back to Allison. He stuck his unfinished lunch back in the bag.

'What's your rush?' DeShawn asked.

'I'm not in a rush . . . You don't have to worry about my therapy, I'll be ready to testify, DeShawn.'

'Man. The first go-round in court wasn't your finest moment, but you're going to be aces for Big Man Barrada's trial. I have faith in you.'

'Don't say that to me if you don't,' Miles said suddenly. He had broken down twice on the stand when cross-examined about the shooting, about the deal made with him to testify. The defendant – a junior Barrada member the feds had chosen to put on trial first in hopes of cutting a cooperative deal, which the guy refused – got a reduced sentence because Miles hadn't appeared, to the jury, to be an entirely reliable witness. 'I need people to have faith in me.'

I need your help . . . I'm in real trouble.

'Miles, m'man. Total faith from Big D. You not seeing folks who aren't there, not hearing voices again, right?'

'Right,' Miles lied. 'Only in my dreams, and everyone should have a crazy dream now and then, right? I'll get this doctor's correct name for you.'

'All right. But I want to know details of this program, Miles, before you agree to anything.'

'Sure,' said Miles. 'I don't work this afternoon. Would you mind dropping me off at my apartment?'

Miles hurried into his building with a quick wave to DeShawn. He ran upstairs, retrieved a tool he figured he might need. He ran down the stairs, thinking, *You take this step, you can't go back*. He headed toward Allison's office.

FIVE

'I'm not going on *Oprah*.' Celeste Brent put the small razor back under the computer mouse pad, where she kept it. She didn't need to feel the blade against her skin right now. 'I can't handle . . . being on television again.'

Victor Gamby's voice boomed from the speakerphone. 'I understand your hesitation. But think of the people we could help, sharing our stories with millions.'

'You sound like a commercial.'

'I'm selling an idea, Celeste. Being back on television might get you past your fears.'

'I'm not leaving my house. And I'm not having a media zoo here.'

'Do me a favor. Open your door, stand in the doorway. You don't have to step outside. Just try it.'

'No.'

'I could ask them to do a satellite link with your house when I'm on the show. That way we could both appear together. Celeste, we could get America's moms talking about post-traumatic stress disorder, make it a real health-care issue, encourage people to think about it the way they do depression or cancer. Please.'

'Victor, you go. You're an actual hero.'

'Oh, please.'

'I'm just someone who had a really bad fifteen minutes.' She leaned close to the plus-sized computer screen, read the words that a young girl half a country away had posted to Victor's online discussion group this morning: *Most days I'm so sad sadder than anybody should be and I just want to curl up & cry forever and the bite of the blade into my skin is the only way I can feel does anyone understand?*

'Celeste. Reconsider. Millions of people watched you on *Castaway*. They know you, they rooted for you,' Victor said. 'It's Oprah, for God's sakes. You cannot say no.'

'No.' Celeste reread the girl's words on the computer screen and thought: *I understand, sweetie, I truly do.* She clicked to the next message in the forum. Jared T, having soul-emptying dreams about the Battle of Fallujah. She wished she could give Jared T a hug. She swiveled the chair away from the computer screen. 'Did I tell you I got an offer for another reality show?'

'Celeste, that's wonderful.'

'Brace yourself, and imagine the possibilities: *Group Therapy*.'

'Please be kidding.'

'I couldn't make this up. They want me, and Denise Daniels, the child star from *Too Cool Kimmy* – she had a nervous breakdown last year – and that college basketball star who's supposedly bipolar, and a couple of other celebrities who have had mental illnesses, all living together in a house with Doctor Frank, the talk-show host, and, yes, it gets better, once a week a player gets booted out of the house.'

'*Castaway* for crazy people,' Victor said.

'Oh, no one says that,' Celeste said. 'They just think it.'

'But that's what we're fighting every day. This perception that people with traumas aren't really sick, that they just need to buck up and get over it. They wouldn't do a show like that for people who had cancer, would they?'

'No.'

'So stop acting like a person with PTSD and act like a famous person with PTSD. Let good come from your fame. Help me, Celeste.'

The sensor that alerted Celeste whenever anyone entered her front yard chimed and opened a video window on her computer's monitor. It showed Allison Vance, hurrying up the stone walkway. Odd. She didn't have an appointment scheduled with Allison.

'Victor. I have to go. I can't do the TV appearance with you, but I know you'll do a wonderful job.'

'Celeste—'

'I'll call you soon, Victor, take care,' Celeste said, and hung up. TV again. Leave the house? Or have strangers gawking at her? Or wanting to hurt her again? No, never. The doorbell buzzed. She pulled hard at the rubber band looping her wrist and let it snap against the tender skin. Once, twice, the pain brief and sharp but settling her nerves.

She went to answer the door. She unlocked it, released the dead bolts, said, close to the wood, 'It's open,' and took five steps back, just so Allison couldn't pull her out of the house and into the open air. Not that she would, but Celeste didn't take chances. Allison came inside, clutching a briefcase bag close to her hips.

'Hi. Did I forget an appointment?' Celeste asked.

'Not at all, Celeste, but I have a favor to ask of you, if it's not an intrusion. How are you today?'

'Extraordinarily stupid. I just declined a chance to meet Oprah,' she said with a tone of defiance.

'I'm sure it would have been exciting. But also a tremendous spotlight to be under.'

'You don't think I'm making it up?'

'You're famous.'

Celeste shrugged. 'Used to be.'

'We could up your antidepressants. It might make leaving the house easier.'

'Other than not wanting to leave the house, I feel okay. I don't want more pills.' Celeste toyed with the rubber band, popped it against her skin.

Allison pointed at Celeste's wrist. 'And how's the rubber band working out?'

'Saccharine when you want sugar.'

'But you haven't hurt yourself today.'

'No. Not today.'

'Great. And yesterday?'

'Once. Just once.' She fingered the thin slash on her arm.

'Have you eaten today?'

'I did. Bowl of cereal for breakfast, salad for lunch.'

'Wonderful.'

As if eating two simple meals and not slicing your skin meant sanity. Celeste twisted the rubber band tight. A spark of pain, nothing more, just enough to remind her she was alive and Brian lay dead and buried, shut up in a coffin, unable to see the sun, breathe the air.

'I'd like to borrow your computer,' Allison said. 'I know you have a really powerful setup, and I need a machine for quick number-crunching. It'll only take a few minutes.'

Celeste almost said, *No, no, and hell no*, she didn't

care for the idea of anyone touching her computer – her precious and only link to the rest of the world. But this was Allison, the twice-a-week bright spot of hope. So she swallowed and said, 'No problem.'

'My system got nailed with a virus this morning. Down and dead.'

'Bring it to me and I'll see if I can fix it,' said Celeste.

'That's kind of you. I just have research materials I need to compile for a report. I have the programs and the data I need on disk.'

'My computer's in the study. Would you like some coffee? Or a soda?'

'No, thank you. I really don't want to intrude.'

'You're not. It's down the hall to your right. The system's already on.'

Allison thanked her and headed down the hallway. After a few moments Celeste heard the click of the keyboard, the hum of the CD drive.

Suddenly she wanted the razor against her skin, to know its gentle bite. It hit her like a fire, smoldering, then bursting into fresh flame. *Sure you do*, she thought, *just because Allison's here and you'd get immediate attention. You want attention, call the television producers back and tell them you'll do that new reality sideshow. Now, that's attention.* She stretched the rubber band and it snapped in half. She dug in her purse for another, past the vial of pills Allison had given her the previous week, past the little razor she kept hidden at the purse's bottom. Her fingers closed around the razor case.

Just a nip of a cut. Just enough.

She closed her eyes and the world folded around her, and she was trapped in the sun-hot house, her and Brian's dream home, bought with her *Castaway* prize money, and she was bound and crying and begging the Disturbed Fan not to hurt Brian, to leave him alone, to hurt her please God not him and the Disturbed Fan blew her a kiss and bent over Brian, the knife bright in his hand.

Celeste sank to the chair. The memory tore into her worse than the razor, and when the flashes came she couldn't gouge her skin fast enough. But now she stopped herself, she caught her breath, the only pain the heat of grief at the back of her eyes.

'Celeste?' Allison's hand came down on her shoulder.

'Don't touch me.' Her voice didn't sound like her own, but lower and beaten.

Allison withdrew her hand. 'Are you all right?'

'Yes.' She stood up and the purse tumbled to the tile floor, spilling its contents in a clatter.

'Celeste. You were having a flashback.'

'Past tense. It's gone.'

'You're safe.'

'Yes, thank you, I know.' She wanted Allison gone, a flush of embarrassment creeping up her skin.

'What triggered it?'

'I think . . . the sound of you typing. I never hear anyone on a keyboard except myself and then I don't notice it. The Disturbed Fan – after he'd gotten into my house, after he'd tied me up, he got on our computer. He hacked my fan Web site.' Her throat felt rough as sandpaper. 'The first step of not having to share me with the world.' She shuddered.

'I'm so sorry.'

'I'm all right.' The urge to cut started to fade, from fire to smoke.

'I'll stay with you so you don't hurt yourself.'

50

'No need. I might cry. I won't cut.'

Allison nodded. 'You're making real progress.'

'I hope.' She hoped. Progress. Baby steps. She still couldn't imagine opening the front door and walking out into the grander world. Too much.

'I'm done with the computer. Thank you again.'

'It's no problem.'

'I don't mean to pry. I saw on your screen, you're logged on to one of the post-traumatic support blogs.'

'Yes. Victor Gamby's. I think I mentioned him to you. He's a friend of mine in Los Angeles – he's tireless about raising awareness of PTSD issues. He's the one who wanted me to appear on *Oprah* with him.'

'I hope you're strong enough to accept his offer.'

'God, are you kidding? No way. No way in hell.'

'Someday, Celeste, you'll leave this house. You'll want to.'

Celeste couldn't speak. Allison cleared her throat, blinked as though she were searching for the right words. 'Those discussion groups . . . it's good that you're reaching out to others.'

'I don't talk about myself. I just read what other people say.'

'But it helps to know you're not alone.'

'I've made an art of being alone.'

To her surprise Allison knelt among the scatterings from the spilled purse, fished out a fresh rubber band, stood awkwardly, and slid the band on Celeste's wrist. 'There may come a day you don't want to be alone.'

Celeste shrugged. 'Who'd want a basket case like me?'

'Oh, Celeste.' Allison shook her head. 'I have a second favor to ask.'

'Sure.'

'If anyone calls from the hospital – especially Doctor Hurley – you haven't seen me today.'

'Who's Doctor Hurley?'

Allison stuck out her tongue, rolled her eyes. 'My boss at my part-time job.'

'Shame on you, playing hooky,' Celeste said.

'We all need a mental-health day.'

'Or week, or month, or year.'

'I'll call you tomorrow, see how you are,' Allison said. 'Thanks.'

Allison left, and Celeste shut the heavy door behind her. She peered around the curtain, watching over the low adobe wall surrounding her yard as Allison got into her BMW and drove off. Celeste stood at the window, her hand against the reinforced pane of glass. Twenty seconds later another car shot by and then the mud road lay quiet, and Celeste listened to the wind rattle in the cottonwoods.

She went back to the computer – Allison had thoughtfully left it as she found it, the posting from the boy-soldier back from Baghdad front and center. She clicked on E-mail Reply and wrote: *It does get better, sweetie, be sure and find a doctor who really understands PTSD and will listen to what you tell him/her. Don't let them tell you it's just in your head or depression, don't let them use nothing but pills to numb you. Don't lose faith. If you were here, I'd give you a big hug if you'd let me.*

Then, to the girl cutting herself, Celeste wrote: *I wanted to cut today and I didn't. Lately I'm more able to resist the urge, maybe it's the change of the seasons maybe I'm just less 'crazy' today but we're not crazy we're broken and we are our own glue sweet girl know that we on the list care and if I were there I'd give you a big hug and tell you: You will, you will, you will be okay.* She

52

signed both replies 'ceebee,' the name from her initials she used on the group, because she dared not use her own. That would bring out the media vultures.

She pressed Send. She didn't want anyone else to suffer the hell that she did, she was only twenty-eight but here were these kids younger than she, already with savaged souls, and it broke what was left of her heart. Saying no to Victor, the flashback, reading other people's sadness, she needed a lift. She hunted for the antidepressants Allison had prescribed for her, kneeling in the jumbled spill from her purse. The razor. The rubber bands. Her wallet.

The vials of pills she kept in her purse were gone. White pills and blue pills. She took the blue if her mood sank low, like now, and she needed the comfort of an anti-depressant, the white pills right before a therapy session with Allison, to calm her, to make it easier to talk about Brian and the Disturbed Fan. But the bottle had just been there on the floor, hadn't it, when Allison got her a replacement rubber band?

She knelt, glancing under the chair and the coffee table, finally getting up and wandering the room. She went to her bathroom and found one bottle holding the sweet blue numbers. But no white pills. Where the hell had she put them? She should have asked Allison for a refill, but that was all right, she didn't have a session for two more days.

She downed a blue meanie, as she called them, and went and sat in front of her window. She observed the shifting sunlight of the day from inside her cage. The thought nagged at her. Those pills had been in her purse this afternoon, she was sure of it.

Perhaps Allison had taken the pills, palming them when she rummaged through Celeste's purse. But why, without telling her? And asking her to keep her secret for her, as if they were teenage girls, was downright odd. Actually unprofessional. Keeping a secret meant responsibility, and she wanted nothing to do with responsibility.

She got up and headed for the phone.

SIX

Miles slowed to a walk as he reached Palace Avenue. He scanned the office's parking slots. Allison's silver BMW wasn't in the lot.

But he saw Sorenson walking through the front door, into the building. He carried a fat briefcase, the kind Miles had seen government lawyers use to haul massive files into the courtroom.

Miles ducked close to a cottonwood, counted to thirty, then went up to the steps and into the building.

Allison's office was closed. He risked a quick listen at the door; he heard the softest tread of foot on floor. The hallway air reeked of paints and solvents and he heard voices upstairs, workmen discussing the renovations, the quiet voice of a woman asking when the work would be finished, she planned to relocate here from Denver and, damn, she needed an office before the rents went up. The painters laughed and agreed with her sense of urgency.

Keep them occupied, lady, please, Miles thought. Knock or wait? Confront Sorenson – but with what? That he wasn't licensed? He considered the oddity of Allison's request, a note tucked into his medication. She presumably couldn't ask for help in front of Sorenson. So Sorenson was her so-called real trouble. She couldn't call and ask for help, which might mean that Sorenson was going to be around her a lot. Or monitoring her calls . . .

That sounded ridiculous. Paranoid. But she'd said Sorenson was a doctor, and he wasn't. So what was he?

He stepped away from the door toward the office across the entryway from hers. The door stood open, the beige paint on the walls fresh. The workers upstairs must be refurbishing these rooms as well. They could return at any second and he didn't want to be forced to explain his presence. But he eased the office door shut to an inch, where he could still see Allison's door.

Two minutes later, Sorenson stepped out from Allison's office, locked the door with a key, and left the building through the front door. No briefcase in hand.

Miles watched Sorenson step out of his line of vision and ten seconds later the door he was hiding behind slammed into his face.

'Jesus, mister, sorry,' the painter said, peeking around the edge.

'My fault,' Miles managed to say. 'Sorry.'

'These offices are already leased,' the painter said. 'The ones upstairs are available.'

'Okay, thanks, sorry.' Miles fled into the hallway, then into the bathroom. Washed his face, counted to thirty. He heard, after a minute, the heavy tread of the painter's feet going back up the staircase.

Miles hurried to Allison's door. He fished the lockpick he'd brought from home out of his pocket. It resembled a Swiss army knife set, and he pulled a blade free and eased it into the door. He hadn't picked a lock since he'd stopped his spying for the Barradas, since he'd walked into a meeting with the feds to help bring the Barradas down. Lockpicks were part of the world he'd left behind but when he got to Santa Fe, he'd bought a basic set of picks off the Internet. He had assembled, and hidden in a rented locker at the bus station, a cache of equipment and money in case WITSEC couldn't protect him, in case he had to vanish on his own terms. Because, until he lost his mind, he'd always taken care of himself.

He wondered, as he bit his lip and worked the mechanism, if picking a lock of a person who'd asked him for help was a violation of the Memorandum of Understanding WITSEC had required him to sign. He wasn't supposed to commit a crime. It wasn't a contract, but the MOU laid out, in clear black and white, his responsibility as a freshly minted law-abider, and the government's duty to protect him. If WITSEC found out he'd jimmied her locks, they could boot him from the program, and then he was dead.

He was crossing a line not drawn in ink or sand but in trust. But she wasn't answering her phone and Sorenson – who wasn't a doctor and had lied about being one – came and went at will from her office. He was afraid for Allison.

The lock clicked open.

He stepped inside, shut and locked the door behind him. He checked the office.

She wasn't here.

Okay, then, he thought. *She's not here. He comes in with a large briefcase, he leaves without it, which means he left it here. And what's inside tells me who he is.*

He searched the closet; it stood empty, except for a hooded sweatshirt, a raincoat, an umbrella, a sealed cardboard moving box marked MISC, and a box of spare office supplies. He peered under her desk. Empty. There weren't that many places to stash a large briefcase. He went through the office methodically, telling himself he should leave, he wasn't a private investigator, he wasn't the Barradas' spy anymore.

'I don't think she'd appreciate you being here,' Andy said.

Miles paid him no attention. No sign of the briefcase. Now it was more interesting; now it was an item Sorenson didn't want found. But he'd run out of hiding places.

The phone rang. He let it ring. Five rings and then Allison's voice-greeting on the machine, simply asking the caller to leave a message. A woman's quiet voice came on: 'Hi, Allison, it's Celeste Brent, um, the medicine you gave me last week seems to have vanished, the white pills, and I guess I need to get a replacement.' Pause, but he could still hear the woman breathing into the line. 'And I'm not really comfortable keeping secrets for you. It's nothing personal, I think we're just crossing a line that we shouldn't. So, please, don't put me in that position again. If I'm being a bitch, I'm really sorry, call me and we'll talk.' The woman hung up.

Celeste Brent. The name sounded vaguely familiar, but he couldn't place it. The fact that the name was familiar bothered him; he'd have to be sure and find out who she was.

Then he heard a voice in the hallway, heard the key slide back into the lock.

He stepped into the closet, eased the door closed so he could see a sliver of the office, and heard the door open, then shut.

The thought of Allison catching him here made his chest nearly burst with shame. But Sorenson hurried past the two chairs where Allison always sat with Miles, into her office. He couldn't see Sorenson but he heard the creak of a chair, he heard fingers tapping on a computer keyboard for several minutes. Miles stayed still, careful to breathe silently through his nose, a panic surging up and down his spine. Jesus, what if Sorenson stayed here until Miles was supposed to meet Allison? The thought made his legs ache, his mouth wither dry.

The typing stopped. He heard Sorenson say, apparently into a phone, 'The action's loaded. Dodd doesn't know.' A laugh, a pause. 'Tonight. Yes. Her house. No problem.' Then silence.

Miles strained to hear. What did that mean? Who was Dodd? The silence was awful. He imagined Sorenson walking straight to the closet.

Then he saw a flash of Sorenson's blazer, crossing the narrow viewpoint, then the rattle of a file cabinet opening, a few seconds' pause, then the file cabinet closed with a slam. He heard the click of a lock engaging in the cabinet.

Then feet crossing the floor, the office door opening, shutting, locking again.

Miles remained perfectly still. Frozen. He counted to three hundred. Then he counted it again. Slowly he unfolded himself from the closet, hands shaking. He inspected the file cabinet. He could pick the lock – but, no, he couldn't peruse her patient files. Too much of a betrayal. He unlocked the door. He relocked the office door and left, pocketing the lockpick.

He glanced up and down the street. No sign of Sorenson. Nothing made sense, Sorenson mucking about on her computer, going through her files, hiding a brief-case in her office. He hurried back down Palace, toward the Plaza. He dug his cell phone out of his pocket and tried Allison's number again.

'Allison?' he said when she answered.

'Yes. Michael?'

'Please tell me what's going on. What trouble are you in?'

She didn't answer right away and he heard the rumble of an engine; it sounded as though she was in a car. 'Can you come at seven?'

'Yes.'

'I can explain then. Before Sorenson comes at eight.'

He risked a shot across her bow. 'Is Sorenson really a doctor?'

An awkward laugh. 'Very good. No, he's not.'

'Why did you lie to me?'

'Because I didn't want him to know . . . that you could help me.'

'Who is he? Is he threatening you?'

'I'll tell you all tonight. I can't talk now.'

'He's planning something tonight at your home.'

A pause. 'How do you know?' A tinge of shock in her tone.

He decided to wait. See her face to face. 'I just know. I'm – I was an investigator, I find out things.'

'Is that how you've spent today – investigating?' She sounded surprised.

'Yes. I used to be good at it.'

'I don't doubt it at all. I know I can trust you. Come at seven and I can explain it all.'

'All right. Allison – who's Dodd?'

But she had hung up.

He tried her phone again. No answer.

As he walked, the wind began to gust and the air carried the raw scent of storm. He ran up the stairs to his apartment. The rooms were too warm; he opened a window a couple of inches, let in the chilly air. WITSEC had offered to rent a house for him but a house meant too much space and quiet, too much room for Andy to roam free.

Exhausted from his close call, he collapsed onto the bed.

He read Allison's note again. He shook one of the pills from the bottle into his palm; a tiny white slug of a capsule. He'd decided against taking one after the flashback in Joy's office, not wanting to talk with DeShawn while medicated. The pill was light as a feather. He fingered the capsule; the casing dented under his fingernail. Pushed harder. The dent went deep.

He pulled apart the two halves of the capsule – empty.

She'd given him a vial of fake pills. Odd on top of odd.

He lay down on the bed, contemplating the ceiling. The burden of responsibility – of helping her, of making a decision to do rather than just to be – pressed on him. The lack of sleep from the night before, restless and frantic as he considered writing the confession, made his eyes hurt. What if he couldn't help her, if he was unequal to the task? He touched the confession in his pocket and closed his eyes to try to think.

SEVEN

'Does it work?' Groote asked. He nearly held his breath and thought: *This is it, Amanda, here's the miracle that saves you and makes you all right again.* He had flown out from Orange County to Albuquerque, then sped the hour north to Santa Fe. His exhaustion from the long night of waiting to kill the accountant evaporated. 'Does it really work?'

And in the hospital conference room, Doctor Leland Hurley smiled at him and his hopes and his question. Hurley started talking again about lessening the vivid emotional toll of the most horrifying of memories, rattling off a glossary of brain chemicals: epinephrine, propanolol, super beta-blockers, adrenergic receptors. Hurley spoke of giving patients back their normal lives and all Groote could think was, *Does it work, does it work, does it work?*

Doctor Hurley gestured at the elevator. 'Let's go to the top floor.'

The top floor meant Frost. The medicine.

Most of the patients were in their rooms after an early dinner, small but comfortable cubbyholes. At the end of the floor's main hallway stood an expansive group room where they could talk and gather.

'Here's a treat you won't see every day,' Hurley said, leading Groote through a door that read VIRTUAL REALITY TREATMENT. QUIET, PLEASE.

The room was dark, separated in half by a glass screen, a jumble of computers loading the walls. A young man, on the other side of the glass, dangled by four elastic cables from the ceiling. A strange helmet covered his eyes and ears; he wore a tight white bodysuit, webbed with wire and tiny gadgets that Groote guessed were recording heartbeat, breathing, and other functions. The patient hung, almost motionless, jerking now and then as he reacted to the scenes playing out of the goggles. On a screen, what appeared to be a computer-animated movie showed a darkened alleyway, wet with rain, three men walking close. One held a chain, the other a blade.

'What are those scenes?' Groote asked.

'We re-create their traumas for them,' Hurley said with a thin knife of a grin. 'We do extensive research and inter-views to get the details of their individual traumas, then we construct a computer-generated scenario that matches those details. We watch it onscreen – he sees it on the goggles, as though he's immersed in the scene. You see it's like a rough cut of a video game, except it's tailor made to help them face their worst fears. It helps those who aren't yet willing to talk consistently about their experiences process the memories, so they can discuss them and the medicine, Frost, can weaken the bad memories. This sub-ject was attacked and nearly murdered in a vicious gang mugging in Washington. So he's experiencing a re-cre-ation of the mugging.'

'Virtual reality,' Groote said. 'But it's not required for the medicine to work, right?'

'For us, it serves as camouflage for Frost. Every patient

here believes they're testing the effectiveness of the virtual-reality treatment – they don't know they're being dosed with Frost.'

Groote frowned. 'They don't know they're test subjects.'

'No. We couldn't let them know. It's important we not publicize the research, since we'll be selling it to a pharmaceutical that'll claim the research for their own.'

The young man jerked against the suspension cables, started to gasp and plead for help as, on the screen, the computer-generated thugs attacked him with chains and knives. A technician sitting on the same side of the glass as Groote and Hurley spoke quietly to the patient through a microphone, reassuring him.

'I understand your stepdaughter suffered an interesting trauma.'

Interesting? Nice word; this guy was a lab-rat freak. 'Daughter. I adopted her. She and her mother were driving on a canyon road when another car fired shots at them and drove them off the road. They were pinned in the wreckage. My wife died a few hours later, my daughter lay trapped in the car with her mother's body for another thirty-six hours before they were found.' Tightness filled his chest. He was surprised at himself, sharing his family's horror with a near-stranger – but he knew this was *it*, clear and present hope for Amanda, the promise of a future for her beyond tiled hallways and sedatives and twenty-four-hour care. 'The doctors haven't been able to help her. She tries to hurt herself.'

'Her brain is dealing with this constant recalling of the traumatic memory. The memory strengthens – and so does the trauma associated with it – the nightmares, the fear, the paranoia,' Hurley said. 'In your daughter's case, everything becomes a reaction to the power of the memory; I suspect she's afraid to ride in a car, or thinking of her mother sends her into a dissociative state where she flashes back to the trauma itself, or she hurts herself because she believes she should have died with your wife.'

'Yes,' Groote said.

Hurley pointed at the man in the virtual-reality chamber. 'Most of the research about dulling the traumatic memory – we can't wipe a memory out, after all – has revolved around introducing beta blockers to the patient, which help keep the memory from forming. When we have a frightening experience, our brains activate stress hormones, neurotransmitters, and peripheral beta-receptors – I call the whole mix "fear juice."' Hurley smiled. 'Those chemicals enhance the memory of the traumatic event. Conceivably we can interfere, right away, with the formation of a traumatic memory if we introduce beta-adrenergic antagonists such as a beta blocker called propanolol – so the memory of the trauma never gets the power of the fear juice, to put it simply.'

Groote nodded. 'I did take chemistry in college, I can handle a technical explanation.'

Hurley smiled as if he didn't believe him. 'Of course. A traumatic memory consolidates in regions across our brain – it doesn't just exist in one set of brain cells that we can zap away. But the moments when the patient recalls the memory, as our boy is doing right now, are also the moments when the memory is at its most chemically fragile. It's the best opportunity to weaken the memory, make its impact less debilitating. You pull the memory up out of the bed of your brain; it's like loosening a rose from its bed of soil. If you don't treat the memory, it takes root again, harder and deeper. But if you chemically weaken the memory after it's pulled up, you can strip the thorns, so to speak. The problem was, with earlier experiments, you had to introduce the beta blockers very soon after the trauma; there was nothing to help those suffering from long-term trauma. Until Frost. It's a cocktail – well, "a combination" sounds better – of drugs that combines several approaches: a synthetic, super beta-blocker to undermine the fear juice and powerful new brain enzyme blockers to keep the fearful memories from getting their thorns back.'

On the screens one of the animated attackers delivered a vicious kick to the man's chest, held a knife to his throat. The patient stayed still in the cables, tilted his head as though a scene only mildly interesting were playing out of the screen.

'You're saying Frost could let this guy eventually forget this attack?'

'Not entirely. But Frost strips the trauma of the attack, keeps the fearful memory from strengthening. Frost can make his memory of being beaten almost to death toothless – so that the recall of it produces no effects of post-traumatic stress disorder.' Hurley tapped a pen against his bottom lip, grinned with pride. 'This man suffered his trauma two years ago. Four months ago seeing the computer-generated re-creation practically drove him into a dissociative state. But now, after treatment with Frost, his heartbeat's slightly elevated, he's nervous, but not frightened.'

'It's a cure.'

Hurley grinned. 'It works. As long as it's used in combination with therapy that brings back the traumatic memory – such as our virtual-reality room or regular psychiatric therapy – while medicated with Frost. Come with me.'

Groote followed him out of the VR room and down the hall to Hurley's cluttered office. Hurley sat down at his desk and tapped on the computer keyboard. 'All forty-six patients dosed with Frost were suffering from severe PTSD, with extreme flashbacks, pronounced anxieties, and often maladaptive behavior. All of them have shown steady improvement in the lessening of their trauma through usage of the memory drug when compared with the control group of forty-six patients who got a sugar pill. A small sample, but enough to interest the pharmas in our sale.'

'And this Allison Vance knows about the program.'

'She doesn't know about Frost – only the VR side of the project here. But I believe she's gotten suspicious about whether we're dosing the patients. I caught her trying to take a blood sample from the lab; she said she thought the patient might be HIV positive and that we should get it tested.'

'That's not completely implausible.'

'It suggested to me she thought there was a story hiding in the blood samples,' Hurley said. 'If she got hold of Frost, or she knew about the auction of our research to the drug manufacturers, she could make trouble.'

'The drug companies wouldn't develop this themselves?'

'Think how many ads for drugs you see. Their marketing budgets are much more than their research-and-development budgets. We'll make a mint, so will they.' Hurley turned back to the computer.

Groote crossed his arms. 'Where'd Quantrill get Frost?'

'I don't know.'

'He steal it? He's a thief, even if you put a fancy consultant title on him.'

Hurley didn't answer.

Groote leaned forward. 'Here's my theory. He doesn't want the drug companies to know where he got Frost from, does he?'

'I couldn't say, Mr. Groote.'

'Why have Allison Vance involved?'

'She's fairly new to town, not plugged in to the local psychiatric community. She keeps to herself. I needed a doctor to handle assessments. She was affordable and efficient. Patients liked her.'

'She could sneak out a Frost sample and get it tested.'

'I administer all the doses. None are missing.'

'How do you check them?'

'Counts.'

'Are these solid capsules? Could she replace any with fakes?'

Hurley's face grew red. 'You're giving her far too much credit. She wouldn't resort to thievery. She'd simply call the authorities if she had a concern.'

'So we buy her off if she raises a stink.'

'Allison's not the type much motivated by money. She's altruistic. Always blathering on about how the patients come first.'

'Why not just bring her in, sit her down, and question her?'

Hurley gave a nervous laugh. 'I'm not a strong-arm type of guy. That's why you're here.'

'But she hasn't run to the authorities about your setup.'

'Allison would never make a sudden or ill-placed accusation. Spend five minutes with her and you can see she's simply a careful person, as most psychiatrists are.

You can see how she is, we have videos of her interviewing the patients . . .' He unlocked a desk drawer, opened it, froze.

'What's the matter?' Groote asked.

'I have backup DVDs of all our research – I keep them in here. They're gone.'

Frost. Gone. The tightness came back to Groote's chest. 'But they're only backups. You have the originals on the hard drive—'

'That's not the point. If Allison wanted to expose us, she's got the proof on those DVDs.'

'Maybe you simply misplaced them.'

'No. I do a daily backup here, lock them up tight. I have the only key.' Hurley's voice rose in panic.

'Is Allison here now?'

Hurley moused and clicked on his computer screen. A video window opened to show the three entrance and exit points from the hospital; it also displayed a log that recorded the usage of the staff's electronic passkeys. 'No, she's not.'

'Where might I find her?'

'Probably at her office. On Palace Avenue, close to the Plaza.'

'How long ago did she leave?'

Hurley clicked on the keyboard; two of the video windows stayed open, one showing Allison Vance walking out of the building; according to the timer, at ten that morning. The other video showed a young man, in patient scrubs, glancing over his shoulder, heading out a door. The timer read ten minutes ago.

'Who's that guy?' Groote asked.

'A patient. Nathan Ruiz. What the hell's he doing with a pass-key? It's showing him because the key he's using is the same code as Allison's . . . The guards must not have seen him leave.'

Groote drew his sidearm from under his jacket.

'I don't know how he got past the doors up here,' Hurley said.

'He's the thief.'

'Not this guy, he's a total fuckup, and the patients don't know about Frost,' Hurley said. 'I'll handle him. You find Allison and see if she has those files.'

'It's not the end of the world, right? You still have the original research.'

Hurley's tone was tight and frantic as he started to head down the hall, Groote following him. 'Don't be an idiot. Whoever took the research, they could give Frost to the FDA and blow us out of the water. No medicine for us to sell.' He shook his head. 'No medicine for your kid.'

Groote bolted past him.

EIGHT

Thunder boomed and Miles opened his eyes, sweaty, sour mouthed, jerking away from the fading dream of Andy pulling a gun from the back of his pants as Miles tried to say, *Don't don't don't*, of Andy collapsing on the grease-spattered concrete, Miles collapsing across from him, the floor dusty against his cheek. He blinked again.

Night had slid into the room.

He read the soft gleam of his clock. Six fifty-eight. He'd be late to meet Allison. He grabbed his coat and ran out into the cold drizzle.

He ran down two streets, then across the Plaza, then up Palace Avenue. The rain faded to a mist and he could see the lights aglow inside her office. Allison, still waiting for him.

Miles ran into the parking lot and he spotted Allison's BMW parked at the back of the lot. Then as he turned his face toward the building the blast cracked the world and slapped him backward through the mist, hitting the pavement shoulders-first, the afterimage of the explosion a fiery blot against his eyes.

He threw his arm up over his face and heat hooked into his pants, his stomach. He rolled over once, wriggling, knocking the burning debris away from his clothes. He staggered to his feet. The building's front collapsed but he heard nothing but an awful ringing in his ears. Flames burst from Allison's building, a fiery fist raised toward the sky.

He ran into the wall of broiling air surrounding her building; he retreated with a low moan humming in his throat. Where her office had been – right-side front – a heart of hell burned. Miles stood, numb in shock.

Sirens wailed as two fire engines pulled close in the street. Pain began to creep along his arms, his hands. He probed at the blood on his skin and his hair, felt it drying in the heat.

He stumbled backward, dug out his cell phone, punched in her pager number, frantically keyed his number for a reply, thinking, *She's not here, maybe she walked to dinner because I was late.* He tried her cell phone; just voice mail.

Another fire truck roared to a stop, the fighters moving into position with practiced speed and grace, water jetting quickly from their hoses, a perfume of destruction drifting through the rain-cleaned air.

Miles dodged the firefighters, went back across the street, sat down on the curb among the crowd that had poured out of the Posada and along the street. He heard a firefighter ask a kid in a Posada valet uniform what had happened. The kid said, 'Gas explosion, man, big huge boom.'

Not a gas explosion, Miles thought with horror as the shock cleared his head. *No. Sorenson. He carried a case into her office. A case I didn't find.* The action's loaded, he had said. *A bomb, Jesus, he planted a freaking bomb in her office and I didn't find it when I could have, this is my fault my fault my fault . . .*

'Sir?'

Miles raised his head. Another firefighter stood over him.

'You okay? You're injured.'

'No. I'm okay. I was walking' – he almost said *to* but he caught himself – 'past the building. Suddenly it just blew.'

'You're cut. Come with me.'

Miles followed the paramedic, shuffling. The office building shuddered again, fire tearing upward through the remnants of roof now, spouting fresh flame into the sky. A tremendous crash sounded as the broken innards of the building collapsed. He thought of the refurbishment going on inside, the solvents, the paint, the lumber, all fueling the inferno.

A crowd – from the residential streets nearby, from the church, from the hotels – formed and he walked through the mass of people, searching for her face, listening for her voice.

I need your help. I'm in real trouble. See you at seven.
He had failed her.

Sorenson. Sorenson had done this. What else had he said? *Tonight. Yes. Her house. No problem.*

Her house.

He stopped following the paramedic toward an ambulance; he cut back through the crowd. He walked away, unable to look at the fire.

No one stopped him as he left.

Miles half walked, half ran to Allison's house, ignoring the pain in his scraped hands, the ringing in his ears, the trickle of blood winding down his neck.

'You should have died with her,' Andy said, running alongside him.

'Shut up,' Miles said, throwing a punch toward Andy, who sidestepped Miles's fist, laughing.

Miles kept running.

Her home lay up the long curve of Cerro Gordo on the far east side of the city, up a hill thick with chimisa and piñon. Cerro Gordo cut through the side of the climbing terrain, lined with adobe homes and stretches of scrub. The road went from paved to unpaved. The thunderstorm, now more rumble than rain, wandered to the east. The clouds hung low and gray, darkening the mountains, shrouds for the day.

He shouldn't know where she lived; she would have understandably considered it an intrusion. He had not followed her or found her in the phone book; she was unlisted. But once, she was leaving after their session and when they walked out of the building a bill tucked in the side of her purse fell. He picked it up and gave it to her but saw the address, and he'd trained himself in his earlier life to memorize addresses, account numbers, phone numbers, with a single glance. He had walked by her house only once, when he knew she was at her office. Just so he would know the route. Because he feared if Andy got too loud, too insistent, that if Andy slipped a gun into Miles's hand, guided it toward his temple or his mouth, he would need her and not find her by pager or phone before Andy squeezed the trigger.

He needed to know where to run for help.

Off Cerro Gordo, private driveways split from the main road and snaked farther into the hills. He took the driveway for the group of five houses that included hers, ignoring the NO TRESPASSING sign, walking past the open adobe gate. Hers was the second house. The road stood empty, gravel lined with scrub. He hurried past the first house, its windows black.

Her house stood dark. No car in the driveway. He ran to the front door. He gently tested the doorknob. Locked.

The house remained still.

'She's gone,' Andy said from the adobe wall that lined her driveway. 'Gone, gone, gone.'

Miles hurried to the rear of the house, following a stone path. He squatted down to study the lock. No dead bolt shot. If an alarm system wailed, he would melt back into the night.

Miles tested the knob first. The back door swung open as he pushed.

He eased inside, shut the door behind him. He stood in her bedroom. In the dim glow from a bathroom light he saw the room's details: wicker furniture painted a soft rose, a turquoise throw rug with twisted geometric patterns, a bookcase filled with worn paperbacks, a queen-size sleigh bed. A bureau, with a mirror crowning it. The mirror was cracked from side to side, in a single fracture, and two of himself stood in the bedroom.

He walked into a kitchen. Dishes were stacked in the sink. A forgotten glass stood on the tile countertop, a swallow of soda puddled at the bottom. Next to it, a container of aluminum wrap lay open, a strip of foil dangling free in a jagged tear. As though she'd just stepped away to run an errand or answer the phone.

He went through the kitchen and into her den. The barrel of a gun eased against the back of his head.

'Freeze,' a voice hissed.

NINE

'Her office is gone,' Groote yelled into his phone. He stood at the end of Palace Avenue, watching the burning building.

'Gone?' Hurley spoke as if he didn't understand the word.

'Destroyed, burning like a goddamned torch,' Groote said. 'There's a crowd, I heard people say there'd been an explosion.' He'd driven down from the hospital to Vance's office, stopped as the traffic snarl formed, left his car when he saw her building consumed in flames and smoke. 'What the hell is going on?'

'I don't know. I don't understand.' He sounded dazed. 'Allison's office is on fire?'

'Someone's screwing us over hard,' Groote said. *And screwing with medicine that could help my kid, and God help them when I find them.* 'This isn't coincidence – a patient Allison Vance worked with breaks loose and her office gets incinerated. Did you find the guy?'

'No. His name is Ruiz. He's violent, dangerous.'

Christ, Groote thought. He'd been in town barely an hour and the entire operation he'd been sent here to protect was collapsing. 'I suppose we can't call the cops.'

'Um, we'd prefer not to.' Hurley cleared his throat. 'If

Allison's dead, hopefully the research files were blown up with her. That means we can't be exposed.'

'I don't like it,' Groote said. 'Suppose she wasn't at her office. Where does Allison live?'

TEN

'Hands on top of head, palms up,' the voice ordered. 'Now, asshole.'

'I understand,' Miles said. 'No problem. Calm down.' He tensed his arms, his legs, thinking, *He gets his arm close, I can yank the gun past my head, before he reacts.* But if Allison was a captive, fighting might endanger her; and he couldn't escape and leave her behind.

'Allison!' he yelled.

'On your knees, prisoner,' the voice ordered.

Prisoner? Miles sank to the brick floor, thinking, *Some head shots are survivable, but not where he has the gun, right in my temple.* He knew how much it hurt to be shot, the blinding pain.

Fingers probed for his wallet. 'Michael Raymond,' the voice said.

'Yeah.'

'You'll give complete answers to every question.' Trying to sound commanding but the tone betrayed inexperience. *He's just as scared as I am.* But scared was not good. Scared meant nerves pulled tauter than wire, with a finger tightening on a trigger of a gun aimed at Miles's head.

He forced calm into his voice. 'I'm looking for Allison Vance. Put the gun down.'

'You with the other guy?'

'Other guy.'

'The first guy who came.'

'I don't know what you mean . . .'

Hands hauled Miles to his feet, steered him into the bathroom. Sorenson lay in the tub, a wicked, bloody bruise on the side of his head, his feet and arms bound with a sheet. Miles could see Sorenson breathing shallowly; he was unconscious.

'This man blew up Allison's office,' Miles said.

'What?'

'Her office is burning down . . .'

'You're lying.'

'No, it's the truth. I'm a patient of hers. I had an appointment with her tonight. I can prove it. Put the gun down, please.'

'You're not even a good liar. Her patients are all at Sangriaville.'

'What's Sangriaville?'

The voice ignored him. 'You said her office was burning.'

'Look at my face. My hands. I was in her office parking lot. There was an explosion—'

'No.' Sharp, short, shot with shock. 'No, no, no . . .'

'She was in trouble. She asked me for help. This guy was in her office earlier today, I think he planted a bomb. Why is he here?'

The voice trembled. 'He came in the back door . . . I hit him.'

'He was empty-handed?' *If he's blown up her office, why not her house too?* Miles thought.

'Yes.'

'Let me wake him up.'

'Get away from him.' The guy pulled Miles away from the bathroom, shoved him hard onto the tile of the den floor. 'Leave him alone; I don't need to be outnumbered. What have you done to Allison?'

'Nothing.' Miles kept his voice steady and calm. 'Her office burning isn't the kind of lie that works for long. I'm not sure you can see from here, but if you walk down Cerro Gordo you can see the glow from the fire.'

The man's hand shook, making the gun against Miles's head tremble. *Keep him calm*, Miles thought.

'Stand up,' the voice ordered, and Miles got to his feet. The man pushed him along, keeping the barrel of the gun nestled in Miles's hair.

Miles pushed open the drapes. Opened the balcony window, which faced onto the sideways spill of the hillside down to Cerro Gordo.

In the quiet, the sound of sirens carried on the wind.

The man behind him made a choked noise in his throat. 'They got to her. They killed her.'

'Who's they? Sorenson?'

Silence from the man. The barrel of the gun pressed hard against his scalp, as though a decision had been reached.

Miles's guts turned to water. 'I promised to help her,' he said. 'I have a note from her. Asking for my help.'

'Sure.'

'Right pocket. Pill bottle. Read it for yourself.'

'I can read it once you're dead.'

'Then you'll have made a terrible mistake.'

The guy jammed the barrel hard against Miles's ear, found the vial, popped it open, read the note in the dim light that bled in from the bedroom.

'It's her handwriting,' Miles said.

Seconds stretched into eternity. Miles waited for the shot. Finally the guy said, 'Allison – was at her office tonight. She told me to wait for her. She would be here soon.'

'Okay, then, we're on the same side.' Miles found his voice. 'Take the gun off me, please.'

'No one can know I was here. They'll stick me back on the top floor.'

'I won't tell,' Miles said, unsure of what the man meant. 'I promise. Put the gun down. I can help you hide.'

'You. You're nothing. I'm a certified hero, you understand me?'

'Absolutely. You sound like a tough and smart guy. I need your help if we're going to catch whoever hurt Allison,' Miles said. 'You already took out Sorenson, and I think he's the bad guy. Let's make him talk.'

'Unless you killed her, and the guy in the tub's the good guy, and you're not. How do I know?'

'But I have the note, and he doesn't,' Miles said.

The guy considered. 'You said you're a patient. What's the matter with you?'

'Nothing much.' His standard answer, given before he could think. The gun stayed close to his skull.

'Define *much*. Tell me how crazy you are.' He prodded Miles's temple with the gun.

'A dead guy follows me around,' Miles said. 'I killed him. By accident. I didn't mean to. But I can't shake him.'

'I'm not crazy,' the voice said with pride. 'Not at all, not anymore. They fixed me.' The gun's barrel came off Miles's head. 'I'm better than you, I'm made of iron now—'

Miles lashed out hard with his hand, caught the guy solid in the chest. He stumbled back and Miles tackled him low, hit him hard in the guts twice. The guy bent in half, collapsed. Miles pried the gun from the guy's hands, stepped back, keeping the Beretta trained on him. Miles fumbled for a lamp, flicked it on.

The gunman was just a kid, in his early twenties. His hair was military short, a dark burr, a face crafted of angles – sharp nose, razors for cheekbones, a pointed jaw. Two light patches of scarring scored his cheeks, the bridge of his nose bent slightly from an old break. He gasped for breath, glared at Miles with dark, scared eyes.

Miles aimed the gun at the kid's legs. He hadn't held a gun since he shot Andy. His hand started to quiver and he steadied the gun with a double grip. He concentrated on the weight of the steel in his palm, heard Andy's snicker behind him.

'Goddamn,' the kid said. 'Are you going to cry?'

Deep breath. 'Stand up. Hands on top of head,' Miles said. His voice cracked like a teenager's. He couldn't freak now, he couldn't lose it now.

The kid obeyed, swallowing in air.

A step at a time. Miles patted down his pockets and jacket. The kid wore jeans and a denim jacket that still had the store tags on them. He wore slip-on sneakers, navy-colored. No wallet, no money in his pockets. No other weapon. A bracelet ID, the kind used at a hospital. Miles stepped back, kept the gun level. 'Take off the bracelet. Toss it to me.'

The kid, with humiliation hot in his eyes, wrenched the bracelet free and threw it at Miles's face. Miles caught the bracelet. It read RUIZ NATHAN, carried a nine-digit number on it, the term FROST-C.

'Shoot him if you want,' Andy said from the corner of the room. 'Build yourself an entourage.'

'Shut up,' Miles said.

'I didn't say nothing,' Nathan Ruiz said, his breath back in his lungs. 'Man, you better shoot me now because I'll kill you when I get the chance.'

'You're a very angry person.' Miles lowered the gun, aimed it away from the kid, ejected the clip, cycled the round out of the chamber. He put the clip and the bullet into his pocket. Now his voice sounded calm.

'That was stupid,' the kid said. 'You should have killed me. You don't want to piss me off.' Hot, hard fury was in his eyes, but a waver in his voice hid behind the bravado, and he didn't charge at Miles.

'I'm not going to shoot you and you're not going to shoot me. You're her patient, too, I think.'

He stepped back, bumped a coffee table, moved around it. He noticed a lipstick-red cell phone sitting on the table.

'I went through his pockets.' Nathan jerked his head at the bathroom. 'He had Allison's phone.'

That didn't bode well. Miles jiggled the broken bracelet. 'What's Frost?'

'I don't know. I don't sit around pondering the meaning of my ID bracelet.' But Miles didn't believe him; the kid's gaze returned to the floor.

'Why are you waiting for Allison in the dark with a gun?'

No answer.

'I can haul your ass straight down to the police, Nathan.'

'I took it from that guy – you said his name was Sorenson. Hit him over the head when he came in the back door.' Now he stretched an empty hand toward Miles. 'Give me the gun and the clip back and we'll part ways.'

83

'No. We're going to talk to Sorenson. Together. Find out what he did to Allison—'

Then they heard a click from the front door lock. Not a key sliding into it; a pick, working the mechanism. Miles knew the subtle difference in the whisper of metal forcing metal.

Someone was breaking into the house.

ELEVEN

'Allison?' Nathan turned toward the door.

'It's not her,' Miles said. Jesus, he'd unloaded the gun, that was stupid. He knocked over the lamp, fumbled for the clip in his pocket. 'Get in the back bedroom. Lock the back door.'

Nathan Ruiz muttered, 'The guards can't find me, they can't know she helped me—' He spun on his heels, ran out onto the balcony, jumped over the railing. Miles grabbed at him and missed. Ruiz tumbled fifteen feet, landed in dirt and gravel, slid into the piñon trees, scrambled down the hillside that led to Cerro Gordo. Making a panicky, noisy escape.

The front door opened. Miles saw a tall figure in the spilled light from the toppled lamp, male, thickly built. Miles, retreating against the railing, saw a gun tracking his path.

Miles vaulted off the balcony. He heard the awful *vroot* of the silencer; the heat of the warped bullet passed above his shoulders, jetted near his scalp. He screamed.

He landed, twisted into the gravel, tumbled down against a piñon trunk, wrenched himself free. He sat on his butt and skidded down the rest of the way, down from the private driveway and the house onto the unpaved stretch of Cerro Gordo.

He heard the sound of a second muffled shot in the blackness above his head. To his left, feet pounded gravel; Nathan, panting as he ran. *Follow him, and maybe they catch you both.* So Miles bolted to the right, running hard and clean, zigzagging on the darkened road.

He heard a pursuer following him off the balcony, sliding down the pebbled slope. To his left lay a patchwork of houses, yards, undeveloped land. He jumped over an adobe wall, fell down into a side yard, ran past a kitchen window where light gleamed and children pleaded for chocolate ice cream for dessert. Over another fence, down a strip of driveway, the sound of his pursuer drawing closer.

Miles vaulted over a few more fences, then he ran into an open stretch of darkness. Armijo Park, he'd noticed it on the hike up Cerro Gordo. Flat, plenty of room for dogs to frolic, kids to run and play tag and football. He ran across the parking lot, caught his leg on a chain that fenced the park, sprawled on the grass. He could hear the pursuer and now a searchlight sparked from an approaching car, sweeping across the park.

He got up and ran, hard, not in a straight line, trying to dodge the circle of light that hunted him past the fence, past the playground, past the swings and slides. The clouds covered the sky and the gurgle of the Santa Fe River rose in the breeze. Usually the river ran dry or with the barest trickle, but now it surged with the recent heavy rains and snowmelt.

Get across the river, hide in the neighborhood, hunker down . . . Then his shoes hit the smooth glass of polished stone and he remembered the river still had to be across the street and *below* him, at least fifty feet, and he skidded into empty air.

Dead. Dead in a straight drop to rocks and then he crashed through a web of tree limbs. He grabbed at a cottonwood branch that smacked hard into his back, missed, fell, hit another one, rolled along its edge, arms flailing, fell again, thinking in a crazy jag, *This'll smash out my brains and I'll be fixed.*

But the next branch caught his weight, held, then cracked with a slow groan, and he let his weight slide down the creaking bough. Listened. No sound of a man still giving chase. The spotlight danced above him, a car driving into the park itself, searching. Hunting him.

He scissored his legs out over empty air. The branch snapped again. He let go.

The land rose in a sharp shift and Miles hit the ground after a ten-foot drop that jarred his ankles, sent him sliding. His legs caught a cactus, the spines needling through his thin khakis, and he howled. But he stumbled to his feet, navigated through a maze of trees, and saw a car driving by, its headlights painting the night.

East Alameda. He ran out onto the road, eased himself down the shallow bank, forged the thread of river in a few steps, the cold water soothing against his tree-and-rock-scored hands. He clambered up the side of the bank, glancing over his shoulder. No gunman. No police car. Nobody.

Across the street, the river, up the hill, the spotlight winked out, like a giant's eye closing.

He wandered into the riverside neighborhood and ran through the spiderweb of streets. A dim orange glowed against the cloud bottoms to his right – Allison's office, or the building next to it, still burning.

'You still got the gun?' Andy asked him, walking beside him, unruffled.

He groped along his belt. No. The Beretta was gone, lost in the tumbles he'd taken. But jammed deep in his jacket pocket, he touched the crumpled confession he'd written for Allison.

'Losing the gun's for the best,' Andy said. 'It would make my killing you a lot easier. What now?'

Miles didn't answer. He walked, steering clear of Palace and the fire engines. He could smell the smoke on the wind. He stumbled across the empty Plaza – Santa Fe rolled up early most nights – and along the side streets until he reached his rooms. He washed his hands and face clean of dirt, sprayed antibacterial lotion on his palms and on his cheek. The bleeding from his head had stopped, clotted in his hair. He dumped his wet clothes in a pile, extracted a trio of cactus spines from his leg. He sat on the edge of the bed, wondered what Sangriaville meant, who was Nathan Ruiz, who was the man who had tried to kill him, why Sorenson had come to Allison's house, and tried not to imagine Allison vanishing in a ball of flame.

The red cell phone on the table. Hers, he'd seen her use it before. She'd left it at her house. He tried her cell phone again. Two rings. The phone clicked on. But silence.

'Hello?' Miles whispered. Then against all hope: 'Allison?'

'You and I both know she's not here.' A man's voice. Low, gravelly.

'Where is Allison?'

'All burned up. I think you know that, mister, because I think you and Ruiz were part of her plan.'

'I don't know what the hell you mean.'

'I heard your voice,' the voice said, 'on the other side of Allison's door. So don't pretend you weren't the asshole with Ruiz that ran away from me.'

Miles sat on the bed. 'Okay, I won't pretend. Who are you?'

'I don't like names.'

'Did you kill her? Do you work with Sorenson?'

'I don't know who the hell that is.'

'You're lying,' Miles said, but the voice talked over him: 'Allison took property of mine and I doubt it coincidentally got blown up with her. I'll pay you for the research. We can reach a deal. But you're going to give it back, or you're dead.'

Miles counted to ten, thinking, trying to figure out how to play the shooter. 'I can't give you what she took if I don't know what exactly it is . . .'

A long silence. 'Listen, you stupid bastard. I don't believe you were an innocent bystander at Allison's house tonight. You and Ruiz, you're in on it with her, and you're going to return Frost, or I'm going to kill you. Simple.'

Frost. The same word on Ruiz's bracelet.

'The man in her tub . . . Sorenson. I think he hid a bomb in her office today. I don't know anything else.'

A pause and Miles could hear the man's heavy footsteps on tile. 'What man in what tub?'

'There's a guy in her tub . . . knocked out.'

A pause. 'There's a bunch of sheets wadded up on the floor, and that's all.'

Sorenson must have escaped between the time the shooting started and when the shooter returned to Allison's house – presumably to search for whatever this Frost was.

'She's dead, you can't sell the research, I told you I'll pay you. Last chance,' the shooter said.

You want answers, tell this guy you've got what he wants. Draw him out, catch him. You couldn't save Allison

89

but you can find out what the hell happened to her. Except if he did that, he was drawing a giant bull's-eye on his back, and an attack could come from any direction.

Miles closed his eyes. 'I don't have . . . Frost . . . but I might know where you can get it.'

'Where?'

'Not now. I'll – have to be in touch with you later.'

'There is no later. You got right now. You tell me what you know, I'm going to let you live.'

'You don't even know who I am.'

'I know what you are. Greedy. Stupid. In over your head. Listen, jackass, I hunt for a living. I'll find you, I promise.'

Miles kept his voice steady. 'You give me a number to reach you at, and I'll call with Frost when I have it.'

'Unacceptable. I made you a one-time offer. You're declining. Suffer the consequences, asshole.'

A cold rage gripped Miles's chest, stomach, throat. 'I'll make you suffer instead.'

When the shooter spoke, his voice was barely a whisper. 'When I'm done with you, you're going to think having your face ripped off is a walk in the goddamned park.' And the shooter hung up.

Miles closed his eyes, saw the house burning, him late for the most important appointment of his life, Allison dead and gone.

She asked you for help and you failed her. He had failed her, failed her as he had failed Andy. *I was supposed to save you.* He'd wasted his time with her, parrying her therapy, playing smart guy, never letting her within distance of the truth, when all she'd wanted to do was help. He felt her absence in the world like a hole punched into his chest.

90

But he didn't have to curl up in a ball. He could make the people who had killed her pay. He got up from the bed, weighed his options.

Ruiz. Had the shooter and his people with the search-lights caught Ruiz? Nathan Ruiz knew his name was Michael Raymond now. Or worse, maybe his cell-phone number had appeared on Allison's cell. It gave the shooter roads to finding him. The apartment was rented to Michael Raymond, and the shooter could trace the billing address of the number to this apartment. He couldn't stay here.

But he couldn't run again, he couldn't fail Allison again. The man thought Miles had something Allison had stolen. Why? What was Frost? This involved Sorenson, clearly – he'd shown up at Allison's house after the blast – presumably hunting for Frost as well. But all that mattered right now was getting the hell out of here and hiding before the shooter came calling.

Miles grabbed a bag of clothes, called DeShawn's number, got no answer. He tried to calm his thoughts, decide what he was going to say. He had to hide from the shooter, but at the same time, he couldn't let WITSEC move him from Santa Fe. If that happened, he could never nail the shooter, nail Sorenson, nail Ruiz, whoever had killed Allison.

'Is that the idea?' Andy said, sitting on his bed. 'Avenge her – a charming concept – and you're well adjusted again and I vanish. You're kidding yourself, Miles. You and I are a team. Forever.'

Miles took his bag and walked alone in the dark to a modest motel off Cerillos that catered to starving artists and hikers. The clerk didn't ask for ID when he put an extra twenty on top of the night's rent.

The room was plain but clean. He lay down on the bed and switched on the TV. The local news was all about the terrible explosion in Santa Fe. The fire was out. Firefighters had found badly burned remains in the rubble. The deceased had not yet been identified, but investigators believed it was the body of the woman who rented the office space, a psychiatrist. The reporter, standing before the fire trucks and the ruined shell of the building, said investigators were not ready to comment on the cause of the explosion.

The deceased. Allison was dead and gone, and in the smoke-kissed night beyond the grimy window was the lying Sorenson, and a shooter determined to kill, and a screwed-up kid named Nathan Ruiz, and they held the answers he needed.

Now all he had to do was find them without getting killed.

'It's going to be fun, seeing you lose it all again,' Andy said.

TWELVE

Groote ordered the two security guards to dump the kid on the bed, fasten the restraints to his arms and then to the railings, then told them to get out. They left and shut the door behind them. He clicked the call log back open from Allison's cell phone that he'd taken from her home. A cell-phone number from the man who had called, coded in Allison's cell phone as MR.

MR was the walking dead.

He tucked the phone back in his pocket and dumped a pitcher of water on the kid. Nathan Ruiz sputtered to consciousness with a jerk.

'Hi,' Groote said. 'You've had a field trip tonight.'

'I – I . . .'

'You're at a loss for words. Probably because you were expecting to see Doctor Hurley. Well, he's not suited for this kind of therapy, Nathan.' Groote sat down next to him. He lit a cigarette, although he hadn't smoked in ten years, puffed deep enough for the fire to catch hard, blew the smoke without a cough. 'It's just going to be you and me.'

Nathan blinked.

'You're back where you belong.' Groote tapped his own temple. 'You're not getting out again.' He let five seconds drip by and said, 'Your friend took off without you. Guess he didn't care.'

'Who?'

'His initials are MR. You give me the rest of his name, we're cool, you and I. Cool is good.' He held up the smoldering cigarette. 'Hot is not.'

The boy's expression hardened past the grogginess. Groote could see him summoning up what stray courage remained in his gut. 'I don't know his name.'

Groote jammed the cigarette into Nathan's wrist.

Nathan screamed. Groote withdrew. 'I'll do the other wrist, then I'll do your tongue. Then your eyes. It'll be incredibly gross.' He thought: *Please don't make me burn you bad*. 'What's MR's name?'

'I really don't know who he is – he wasn't supposed to be there.'

Groote decided to deal the boy a bit of rope. 'Then who was supposed to be there?'

'Allison.' Nathan gritted his teeth against the pain. 'She gave me a passkey to get past the door . . . told me to meet her at her house.'

'And do what?' He leaned back, as though getting comfortable for their nice chat.

'Leave here.'

'Why?'

'She said . . . I shouldn't be at Sangriaville anymore.'

'Your insurance hasn't expired, Nathan, so why did she want you to check yourself out?'

'She said Doctor Hurley wanted to kill me.'

'Gosh, Nathan, and he only speaks highly of you.'

'I don't know anything else.' Fear clenched his eyes shut.

Groote considered, put himself in Allison's shoes. You

suspect illegal drug testing. You steal the research as evidence. But you also want a patient who's been guinea-pigged as a show-and-tell for the FDA. Given that, wouldn't you concoct a better scheme to get him out of the hospital? No – not if you were pressed for time, if you knew Quantrill was ready to move on Frost, shut the operation down now that the testing was complete. 'Where's Frost, Nathan?'

'Frost?'

'Allison took some DVDs, the kind you use in a computer to store big files. They had information on them for a project called Frost. Tell me where those DVDs are.'

'I don't know. I just did what she told me, please don't hurt me no more.'

'Oh, I don't want to, Nathan. Seriously. But I have a problem. Those DVDs Allison took, they're not in her house. Could be they blew up with her at her office. But it's awfully convenient, you see, and I don't believe in that convenient a world. She takes something of great value, she gets obliterated, and then there's a group hug at her house. It changes the equation.' He smiled at Nathan. 'I read your file while you were napping. You're quite a special case, Tin Soldier. Maybe you made Allison go boom-boom.'

Nathan shook his head in horror. 'No, man, I wouldn't, I couldn't ever . . .'

'You tell me what happened from when you ran.' Groote rotated the cigarette in his fingers, studied the smoke, reheated the tip with a deep drag.

'She left an electronic passkey for me. Told me to run at six-thirty, told me how to get to her house. She left a change of clothes for me. She had told me to sit and wait in her bedroom until she came in, but there was a big mirror in there, I don't like mirrors, don't do mirrors, no mirrors.'

'You may like them less when I'm done,' Groote said quietly.

Nathan kept on: 'So I went into the den, stood near a window so I could see her come. But a man came. He drove up past her house, left his car, came back down. No sign of Allison. I got scared. He came in and I hit him on the head with this Indian carving she kept on the mantel. I tied him up with sheets and dumped him in the tub. I didn't know what else to do . . . I figured Allison would tell me.'

Groote frowned. That matched MR's story. 'He wasn't there when we found you, Nathan. Who was he?'

'The other guy . . . said the first guy's name was Sorenson.'

The name meant nothing to Groote. 'And you had no idea who the other guy was?'

'No.'

'But him you didn't crack on the head, him you didn't tie up. Why so nice to him, Nathan?'

'I wanted him to talk – tell me what was happening.'

'Did he?'

'No. He didn't know . . . He said Allison's office was bombed.'

Groote considered. It bothered him, deeply, that an apparent bomb had killed Allison Vance. Bombs were not built on a whim. Bombs were complicated and technical and a pain in the ass. Guns and knives and rope were far easier ways to accomplish the goal of shutting up one person. Bombs meant resources, expertise, time to plan. Bombs meant an enemy who might blow Groote's ass out of the water.

'I – I don't think this guy you want killed her,' Nathan said.

'I don't have a lot of suspects.'

'That Sorenson guy—'

'— could just be a story you and your friend hatched to throw salt on the trail if either of you got caught. No, Nathan, I think MR's the answer to my prayers.'

'I don't know anything about MR . . . I'm sorry, I don't.'

Groote dropped the lit cigarette at the bottom of the water pitcher. It hissed and died. 'I'm sorry, Nathan, but cigarettes are too slow.' He pulled the screwdriver from his pocket, held it up so Nathan could see. 'You need the right tools for the right job.'

'Please. Please don't.'

'Custom-made for me in Hungary. Precisely balanced. I keep the edge cleaner than an angel's ass.'

'I don't know him! I can't tell you.'

'I bet you liked word problems in math class. I mean, launching missiles and shit in the army, you must have gotten at least a C in geometry.'

'Word problems?' Nathan, trembling, shook his head.

'If you've got an inch of flesh covering your bones, and the screwdriver can penetrate two centimeters at a blow, how long before the screwdriver reaches bone? I threw in the metric angle because I know you're just a mathematical genius.'

Nathan fought the restraints. 'Please . . . don't. Don't.'

'Don't? Don't? Well, sure, Nathan, I won't. It doesn't have to be the hard way, not one bit, if you don't care for math.' He made his voice soft and intimate, brought the screwdriver close to Nathan's wide eye. 'Lots of sick people need Frost, Tin Soldier, you included. Someone I love included. Talk or I work out the word problem on your flesh and bones. Which is it?'

'I can't tell you . . . what I don't know.'

'I respect your heroics. Truly.' Groote gave Nathan an affectionate pat on the cheek. Then he stabbed the screwdriver deep into Nathan's arm.

THIRTEEN

Wednesday morning at 7:00 A.M., the cell phone rang next to Miles's head. He came awake instantly, panic settling in his guts, trying to be fully aware before answering the phone and talking to the shooter.

'Hello?'

'Where the hell are you?' DeShawn sounded pissed.

'I met a woman . . .' Miles lied. 'I spent the night at her place. That allowed, Mommy?'

'I need you back at your apartment, Miles. Right now, please.'

'What's wrong?'

'I got bad news. I'll pick you up. Where are you?'

'It's not far. I'll walk,' and he hung up before DeShawn could argue. Miles didn't want to go back to his place, with the shooter likely to be tracking Michael Raymond, but he couldn't act afraid to be at home; DeShawn would relocate his ass out of Santa Fe in ten seconds flat, and no way he was leaving now.

Miles washed his face, changed into a clean shirt, jeans, and sneakers. He left his duffel in the room and locked up; he'd head back here before the gallery opened and retrieve his stuff. He walked back to the apartment, but no shooters jumped out to blast flesh off his bones. DeShawn's car wheeled over to him and Miles got in.

'Doctor Vance is dead,' DeShawn said.

'I saw it on the news this morning.'

'You okay?'

'I'm upset.'

'You understand, Miles, this has anything to do with the Barradas, you're moved in five seconds.'

'It doesn't.'

'You sound very confident.'

'They wouldn't kill my shrink. If they found me, they'd kill me. And probably not with a bomb off their own turf – too hard to transport. They'd just put bullets in my head.'

'You know anything about this tragedy, Miles?'

'No.'

'What happened to your face?'

'Got into a fight last night.'

'Man, wooing and fighting, you had quite an evening.' A tone of disbelief tinged his voice.

'Where are we going?' Miles started to ask, but then they were there. DeShawn inched the car past Allison's burned building. Yellow fire-scene tape haloed the lot; a group of firefighters were sifting the ashes toward the rear of the building, a couple of news stations from Albuquerque had parked their satellite wagons down from the wreckage. A spill of people stood along the sidewalk, gawking at the ruin. The lot was empty, Allison's car towed away.

Miles pointed at the firemen shaking a sifter, ashes tumbling at their feet. 'They're searching for the door's lock, to see if it's locked or not. A firefighter friend in Miami told me it's one of the first items of evidence they search for.' His voice sounded dead to him. 'I heard on the news they found her. Do you think she suffered?'

'No, Miles, she didn't. There was . . . very little left of Doctor Vance. They've only found, um, pieces. I'm sure she died in the force of the blast, she didn't burn to death.'

Miles put his face in his hands, forced his emotions back under control. He could have stopped it, if he'd found Sorenson's hidden case. He missed it and she died. 'Oh, goddamn.'

'I'll miss her,' Andy said from the backseat.

'I'm sorry, man, I know you said she'd been a great help to you.' DeShawn put a hand on Miles's shoulder.

Miles kept his voice neutral. 'Do they know what happened?' He was going to catch Sorenson, or whoever was ultimately responsible for Allison's death, and drag them in front of DeShawn, like a cat dropping a dead mouse at its master's feet.

'I talked to the arson investigators. They can't search the front of the building, where the floors collapsed, until they get heavy moving equipment in from Albuquerque. They got to do chemical tests, see if it was a gas explosion or see if it was a bomb. Don't know yet.'

They drove away from the burned hulk.

'I have to ask again, Miles, did she know you were in witness protection?'

'No. I never told her. I was going to – but I didn't want her to know. I was ashamed.'

'So her records, no way they survived the blast and the fire, and even if they did, they couldn't disclose your witness status. That's our number-one concern,' DeShawn said.

'Not that my doctor's murdered,' Miles said. 'Really, it's nice y'all care.'

101

DeShawn pulled the car over, parked, gave Miles a hard stare. 'Do you know for a fact she was murdered?'

'I know this has nothing to do with the Barradas.'

'But it's got to do with something, doesn't it, Miles? You tell me another doctor, who I can't find a record of, wants to help Allison with your therapy and that day she's dead.'

'I must have gotten his name wrong. Sorenstam, Sorengard, I only met him for a minute. Allison said she used to work with him.'

'If the arson team finds this was deliberate, you're answering their questions.'

'I understand. How soon before they know?'

'Well, the investigators got to get deep into the building once it's safe, run those chemical tests, check with the gas company to see if an undue amount of gas fed into the building. But I think it's got to be a gas leak. All the renovations going on in that building, a worker damaged a pipe, started a leak. Why would anyone bomb a shrink in Santa Fe?'

'Be a Boy Scout,' Andy said from the backseat. 'Tell him nothing but the truth.'

Instead he wondered what else DeShawn might say, if Miles didn't make a big deal out of the question: 'Is her house okay?'

DeShawn raised an eyebrow. 'What do you mean, okay?'

'I assume the police or the arson investigators have gone to her house to look for her.'

'Yes.'

'It wasn't, I don't know, burglarized or anything?' He kept his gaze fixed on the window. 'People rob dead people's houses all the time.'

'Miles, what aren't you telling me?'

102

'Nothing. I don't know why anyone would want to hurt her.'

'Far as I know, her house checked out just fine.'

So. The shooter had cleaned up before he left, didn't want anyone unduly suspicious about what had happened at Allison's house. The shooter had talked about paying Miles for research, which he called by the name Frost – a code name, Miles guessed, since it had also been inscribed on Nathan's medical bracelet. Research could be either big bulky files of paper or computer disks or both. Easily hidden, but also easily found and moved.

Miles said, 'Let's cut to the chase. Are you all going to move me?' He reckoned Washington bureaucrats were at work figuring the calculus of his life's worth, wondering if moving him was warranted just because his doctor had died in an unusual way. But he couldn't tread water and stay in the Michael Raymond life; not if the shooter tracked him through Nathan's knowing his name or through the cell call. He couldn't hide in his new life and he couldn't run.

'Not if there's no real chance your identity was disclosed. But I'd feel better if we put you up at a hotel for a few days under a different name. Until the arson investigation's done.'

'Fine. Can I go to work now?' Miles asked.

'Are you up for peddling art? I know you cared about Allison . . .'

'Work's the best thing for me right now.' But Miles didn't mean updating the gallery's Web site or moving sculptures. I need dirty work, he decided, the kind I used to be good at, bringing secrets to light.

The gallery was not yet open, but Joy was working the phone at a sales rep's desk, sweet-talking a deal with a collector in Boston. She wiggled fingers at him in a friendly wave, frowned at the scrapes on his face. He gave her a thumbs-up and suddenly wanted never to lose this job.

He unrolled the morning paper and scanned it. Nothing that DeShawn hadn't already told him. Investigations continuing, the building a loss, remains recovered in such bad shape that DNA testing would be required. The article said Allison had lived in Santa Fe only a few months longer than Miles had; it surprised him she didn't have deeper roots here. He checked the police report section: not a word about responding to any disturbances along Cerro Gordo. Maybe Nathan had gotten away.

Miles sat down at his desk, fired up the management software that the gallery used to track sales, contacts, artists, and works. He sorted through a list of incoming paintings to process, saw Joy's note to craft e-mails to three major collectors interested in one artist's seventeen new paintings that the gallery had received late yesterday. He needed to take digital photos of all the new paintings, load them onto the Web site, and enter them into the system so they could be tracked. Then a schedule to rotate paintings: hang selected new arrivals (all landscapes and portraitures of the high desert), ship the unsolds back to the artist or see if the staff could sell the works from the back room. And Joy's new computer had arrived yesterday afternoon; he needed to hook it into the network and load it up with software. A long day. But he had his own mission to perform.

Joy hung up. 'Good morning. What happened to you, hon?'

He touched his face. 'It's not an interesting story.'

'I figured you were going to say you'd been out drinking with Cinco.' She frowned. 'Did you hear about that fire over on Palace?'

'Yeah, I did. Awful. If you don't mind, I'll get your new computer set up first thing this morning. It just may take more time to get it hooked into the network. New operating-system protocols.' Sweat showed its guilty face on his arm, in his hair, on his lip. He really hated lying to her. But no one could know what he was doing. Joy's eyes glazed as soon as he said *protocols*.

'Well . . . go do your voodoo.'

'Okay.' He startled at the jingle of the back door. Joy's son Cinco, holding a massive cup of coffee, came in, yawning.

Miles asked, 'Has either of you heard of a place called Sangriaville?'

'No. Is it a new bar?' Cinco asked. 'Because new bars are officially off my list.'

'I don't think so. I thought it might be a town with a mental hospital.'

Joy blinked. 'There is a private mental clinic way up the road, near where Canyon dead-ends, called Sangre de Cristo.'

Sangre de Cristo. Sangriaville. 'Maybe it's one and the same,' Miles said.

Joy said, 'I don't know, honey. But then, I don't know any crazy people.'

FOURTEEN

Upstairs, Miles closed the door to Joy's office so no one could surprise him. He unboxed and fired up the new computer, hooked it up to the gallery's wireless network, and downloaded a free open-source Web browser that he would delete when he was done; he didn't want to leave a trail for Joy to find.

He Googled for a Web site for the Sangre de Cristo mental hospital in Santa Fe. There wasn't one. Odd. A modern hospital without a Web site. Didn't they need to provide information to the medical community or to potential patients? He found the hospital in the Yellow Pages; just a simple listing, no advertisement for their services.

He found a directory of New Mexican hospitals – Sangre de Cristo was listed, and licensed. Owned by the 'Hope-Well' Company. He Googled 'Hope-Well'; no Web site.

Someone didn't want to be found. Time to dig into the old bag of tricks.

He called the hospital, using his cell phone. 'Hi, this is Steve Smith, I'm doing a story for Associated Press on the doctor who died last night, and I need to get information on your hospital.'

'What doctor?'

'You don't read papers? Allison Vance.'

'I'm afraid you're mistaken,' the receptionist said. 'We have no doctor by that name.'

'May I speak to your public relations officer?'

'We have no comment.' And she hung up.

He did a Web search for Nathan Ruiz, adding Santa Fe as an additional search term. There were two Nathan Ruizes in town: one owned a restaurant on the south side, one ran a community center. He clicked through the sites. The restaurateur was in his fifties; definitely not the young man who'd held a gun to his head last night. He phoned the number for the other Nathan Ruiz.

'Corazon Community Services, Nathan Ruiz speaking.'

'Mr. Ruiz, hi, this is Fred George with the State Insurance Board. I'm sorry to bother you but we're conducting an investigation into insurance fraud and I'm hoping you can assist me.'

'Um, sure.'

'We're tracing patterns of fraudulent claims. There have been a number of claims filed in your name for care at the Sangre de Cristo Hospital in Santa Fe and I'm calling to see if those are legitimate.'

'I've never been to that hospital in my life,' Ruiz said. 'Am I liable for these charges? My insurance company hasn't said a word.'

'No, sir, you're not liable at all. There may be a patient there with a similar name, but we're finding that inaccuracies in filing protocols are causing claims to be misapplied to other people with the same name,' Miles said in a rapid, officious tone.

'It's not me and I don't know another Nathan Ruiz,' the man said. 'Do I need to call my insurance company?'

So no relative with the same name. 'No, sir, you've been a big help. Thank you for your time,' Miles said, and hung up. He went to the search engine, broadened the 'Santa Fe' to 'New Mexico', searched again.

He found a Nathan Ruiz in Los Alamos who had earned the honor of Eagle Scout, a Nathan Ruiz who had died in Clovis the previous month at the age of thirty-seven, a Nathan Ruiz who had been hurt in the Iraq war and come home to Albuquerque.

He clicked on the news story. This Nathan Ruiz had been a technician with an army battery squad, a team charged with firing missiles in the opening rounds of the Iraq invasion. His team had been accidentally bombed in the chaos of the advance toward Baghdad, misidentified and attacked by a U.S. jet as an Iraqi Republican Guard missile unit; four of the team had been killed, the others badly injured. Nathan Ruiz had been sent home.

If he was at Sangre de Cristo, coming home hadn't gone well.

His father, Cipriano, was quoted in the story about Nathan's homecoming. 'We're just so proud of his bravery, of his service, and we just want him back home with us.'

Cipriano Ruiz. Miles switched over to an Albuquerque phone listings site and found the number.

He dialed. A woman answered on the fourth ring. Her voice sounded dejected, as though each day were simply a series of disappointments. 'Hello, Ruiz residence.'

'Mrs. Ruiz?'

'Yes.'

'My name is Mike Raymond. I knew your son Nathan in Iraq.'

Silence.

'I haven't talked to him since he came home. I wanted to see if he's adjusting okay.'

Silence.

'Mrs. Ruiz, may I speak with Nathan?'

She said nothing for five seconds and he wondered if she'd hung up when she spoke. 'No. He doesn't live with us.'

'Is there a number where I can reach him?'

'He – he's in a hospital.'

'Is he all right?'

'No, he's not. He's at a special clinic. For when you have problems after war, you know. He . . .'

'I don't mean to pry, Mrs. Ruiz. I just wanted to see how he was.' He paused. 'If he's at a clinic, is it Sangre de Cristo up in Santa Fe?'

'Oh, yes.' She breathed a sigh of relief. 'You've heard of it?'

'Yes, ma'am, just that it's very good.'

'Oh, yes, I hope they take good care of him. Because . . .' and she stopped. 'I don't understand.' She paused again, as though wrestling with the words. 'You tell me, why he doesn't just get over it . . . the sadness.'

Miles's stomach tightened. 'What do you mean?'

'He survived. Those other boys died. He should be grateful he didn't die. Why isn't he happy? He's alive.'

'The post-traumatic stress disorder, ma'am, it's' – he struggled with a way to describe it – 'it's not a lack of willpower. It . . . affects the way the mind works, the way he reacts to everything. It's a fire he can't put out. You think the fire's out, it's gone, then it burns again.'

'Then get an extinguisher.' She sounded beaten. 'He wants to cry and jump at shadows and have bad dreams forever? Mister, I had a baby die. Nathan's older brother, he was only three weeks old and he died in his sleep. Crushed my heart. But if I didn't get over it, I don't have Nathan. I don't have a life. Where's his strength?' Her voice wobbled.

'He still has his strength, ma'am, I'm sure.'

'Last time I talked to him, leaving him at the hospital, I said, *Have hope, baby,* and he said, *Mama, all my hope's dead because I'll never forget.* I say, *Don't forget, just deal with what happened,* and he shakes his head at me like I'm crazy.'

'How long ago did you see him?'

'When he went to the hospital, six months ago. I miss him terribly. We get him home, out of danger, and' – her voice broke – 'but he's not doing well, it hurts my heart.'

'I'm very sorry, Mrs. Ruiz. Would it be possible, do you think, for me to see him?'

'No visitors. Not even family. The doctor said it's part of the therapy.'

'That seems really unusual. Who's his doctor there?'

'Doctor Leland Hurley.'

'Well. I'd like to write Nathan a letter, then.'

'No contact. At all. The only way to clean out all the pain from his mind, they said.'

He inched onto thin ice. 'That must be expensive. I didn't think the government would cover a private clinic.'

'I'm not supposed to talk about the program,' she said suddenly. 'What was your last name again?'

'Michael Raymond. I'd really like to talk to Nathan when he's back home.'

'You leave me your number, I'll give it to him.'

He left her his cell-phone number. 'Thanks, Mrs. Ruiz, I hope Nathan is better soon.'

110

'I hope so too. Before he hurts himself, before he hurts somebody else. Good-bye.' She hung up.

I'm not supposed to talk about the program. No contact, that's what the doctor said. Weird. He didn't know what was considered cutting edge in PTSD treatment, but surely isolating a patient from his loved ones wasn't typical.

Allison said Sorenson ran a special program. Sangre de Cristo offered a special program. So was it one and the same, and was the shooter connected to the program?

The next name on his list was Celeste Brent, the woman who'd left the message on Allison's phone. He Googled her name combined with 'Santa Fe' and got an avalanche of results. The first was a headline: 'Reality TV Star Moves to Santa Fe after Tragedy.'

TV star?

A knock sounded against the door. Miles closed the browser.

'The computer working yet, sweetie?' Joy asked, sticking her head inside.

'Having trouble getting your e-mail running,' he fibbed, 'but I'll figure it out.'

'We need to rotate a few pieces, can you please come help me?'

'Sure,' he said. He could read the rest about Celeste Brent later. But he realized with a cold shiver, if he was to find the truth, he had to get inside that hospital, Sangre de Cristo, find out what was going on there.

A mental hospital. His worst nightmare.

'The crazy guy,' Andy said from the other side of the room, as Miles hung a new painting with Joy's guidance, 'breaking into the asylum. This I have to see.'

111

FIFTEEN

First the fists, then the rubber hoses, then finally the screwdriver, brought back into the act for a virtuoso encore, won Groote a name from Nathan's battered lips. Groote derived no pleasure from hurting others; agony was a means to an end. But two hours into the torture – really, Tin Soldier had done an impressive imitation of a hero, holding out far longer than Groote had figured he would – he'd screamed out a name for Allison's shadowy partner: Michael Raymond. The MR in Allison's cell. Five minutes later he got a physical description as well: about six two, strong build, brown hair, brown eyes.

Groote called a friend immediately back in California – a friend who made his living piercing firewalls, to test the security of the cell-phone provider. His friend, assured of a generous payment, spent the day hacking and then late Wednesday afternoon gave Groote a home address and a work number for the account. Groote dialed the work number, got a woman's voice welcoming him to Joy Garrison Gallery on the world-famous Canyon Road, listing the employees and giving a number to reach their voice mail. 'For Michael Raymond, press four,' the computerized voice intoned.

Groote hung up. *Gotcha, asshole.*

Groote stood in the compact kitchen on the Sangre de Cristo's top floor and drank a glass of ice water. He dumped the ice into the sink and scrutinized his hands. Nathan's blood had crusted underneath Groote's nails and he needed to give them another hard scrub.

He shuddered. You did what you had to do. For Amanda. For all the other poor sick bastards out there who need to be unchained from their nightmares. Even if Nathan Ruiz was one of those same poor bastards.

Doctor Hurley – sleepless, frazzled, a scared rabbit in a forest full of foxes – unlocked the door, stepped inside the kitchen, locked the door back behind him. 'Quantrill's on the phone. He sounds unhappy.'

'Imagine.'

'This isn't my fault. Not at all. I asked Quantrill for additional security and he balked. He should have sent you earlier. I won't be held responsible—'

Groote hit him, not hard, but enough in the stomach to shut his mouth. He sagged to the floor, vomited up a splash of coffee.

'I can hit you next time, in the nose just so, Doctor Hurley, and send a splinter of bone right into your brain. It's no sweat off my back. You understand me?'

Hurley nodded, real fear in his eyes.

'So shut up. I'm in charge now, you're not. You don't have to worry your overstuffed head about responsibility. But I can't abide whining.' He helped Hurley to his feet.

'You – you should take his call in my office,' Hurley said in a daze.

'I'll do that.'

He walked back to Hurley's office and thumbed the phone's button. 'Groote.'

'Tell me you have Frost back.'

Groote kept his voice calm. 'Cut the drama. If I had it I'd have already called. I need you and Hurley to keep your heads on straight, you got me?'

He heard Quantrill take a calming breath. 'So what's the situation?'

'I have a theory. She takes on exposing you, it's natural to assume she had help, and Nathan says she asked this Michael Raymond guy for help. Raymond works at an art gallery, which doesn't make sense in terms of how he could help her – but say Nathan's telling the truth. Michael Raymond realized your drug was going to go for a premium price. So he uses Allison to get Frost. Then he gets rid of Allison.'

'A bomb . . . who would use a bomb?' Quantrill's voice held a sudden fear in it that replaced the impatience of a minute ago.

'We don't know it was a bomb. Could have been he rigged a gas explosion. We don't know shit about this guy except his name and he works in an art gallery.' He paused. 'Both mentioned another name. Sorenson. Nathan and Raymond claimed Sorenson was a guy who came to Allison's house after she died, but I never saw him. So either there's another player working here, role unknown, or they're lying to me. I got to go with what I know.'

Quantrill considered in silence.

'Mr. Quantrill,' Groote said, 'I need you to be honest with me. You got enemies, I'm guessing, other than this woman who might have been a whistle-blower. Who knows about Frost? Who might try to steal it from you?'

'A pharmaceutical. Another information broker.'

'The drug company so they could produce it. The broker so he could sell the research.'

'Or,' Quantrill said slowly, 'Michael Raymond might want a financial payment. He doesn't blow the whistle the way Allison would. He sells me back the research copies for a price.'

'But then when I spoke to him he didn't want to set up a meeting. He seemed . . . confused. But he did say he knew where Frost was, it would take time, but he'd call me back.'

'Then he's wanting us to squirm to drive up the price.'

'If he goes public . . .'

'No drug company could produce a medication based on illegal testing,' Quantrill said. 'We have to bury how Frost was tested. It would kill the research in its tracks. Years before anyone would touch it again or bring it to market.'

Years Amanda didn't have. 'Then the money has to be his motivation. Otherwise he would have gone public already.'

'Find him. Say you'll pay him five million for Frost. You'll have to make sure he hasn't passed the information on to anyone else. Obviously you can't leave him alive.'

'I'll get out the screwdriver.' He hung up and Groote checked his gun and his watch. First try the gallery for Michael Raymond, then try the apartment. A gallery. It didn't fit a guy who Allison Vance would ask for help. And that bothered Groote. He didn't like walking into the unknown.

He fitted his gun into his jacket holster and headed for the parking lot.

SIXTEEN

Groote walked into the gallery. He surveyed the art on the walls with indifference: portraits of Navajo and cowboy, landscapes of burnished New Mexico desert and wild-flower-dotted fields. He read the price tag on one landscape of a stone-choked creek. Eleven thousand dollars. He'd killed a man for less once.

He stopped and listened with care. He guessed there were two people in the gallery, from the murmur of voices. A woman, a man, talking softly from the rear of the gallery. He left his sunglasses in place – no need to be easily recognizable. He went back to the door, flipped the OPEN sign of engraved, polished metal to CLOSED, turned the dead bolt. He hoped he didn't have to kill everyone in the building. He'd prefer to get Raymond out of the building, get him alone. But better to be prepared.

He headed for the back office, listening to the man's voice, unsure if it was Raymond's. He scanned the floor plan. Two exits off the hallway, a set of stairs going up to another display room of art, three more rooms to his left, a short hallway and a set of French doors to his right.

He stopped at the back office's door. A fiftyish woman, brightly pretty, and a man in his thirties stopped talking and both smiled at him, ready to part him from his money for one of the paintings outside. They were clearly mother and son; the family resemblance was striking. There was a third desk in the corner, empty.

'Hi, may I help you?' the woman asked.

'Yes, ma'am, I need to see Michael Raymond. I promised to buy a painting from him.'

The woman seemed to freeze for a second, then said in a rush: 'Well, I'm sorry, Michael's not here this afternoon. I'm Joy Garrison, the owner; this is my son Cinco. May we assist you?'

Groote glanced at Cinco, who opened his mouth as though to interrupt the woman, then shut it.

'Mom—'

'Cinco, it's fine,' Joy said in a tone that brooked no discussion. The phone rang; Cinco picked it up, said hello, and started answering a question about the gallery's operating hours.

'Which painting were you interested in?' Joy asked.

The woman must want to scoop the commission, Groote thought. 'The landscape by the front door. How odd. Michael told me he would be here today. But I'd like to talk to him about it, make sure he gets the commission.'

'Of course. I'm sorry he's not here.'

'When's he expected back?'

But then she snapped her fingers. 'Oh. Wait. You're right. He will be here today. Around six, right before we close. Picking up his paycheck. I forgot he told me.'

Groote nodded. 'Okay, then, I was sure I'd lost my mind.' He laughed politely. 'I'll check back with him around six.'

'Did you want to leave a name, sir?' Cinco hung up the phone.

'Jason Brown,' Groote lied, because to refuse a name would be suspicious.

The phone beeped and Joy Garrison punched a button. 'Yes?' she said. 'Of course I can get you that painting, sir, yes . . .' and started to nod, jot words down on a notepad.

It still seemed wrong, but he heard a rattling at the door, another customer testing the knob in surprise at the early closing, so he went back to the door, flipped the sign and opened the lock, keeping his back so Cinco and Joy couldn't see what he'd done. He said, 'Excuse me,' to two turquoise-bedecked tourists, slid past them, headed for his car. Time for Plan B – go to Michael Raymond's home address, see if he was there, and if not, search the place for an idea of who he was. Then come back around six for a private talk with Michael Raymond.

Groote was ten blocks away when he realized his mistake, and he powered the car hard around in a screeching U-turn.

SEVENTEEN

Miles, coming out of Joy's office up on the second floor, saw the man, saw him flip the sign and lock the door, and thought: *He's here for me.* He took four silent steps back from the railing, ducking behind a sculpture of a crouching cougar and wondering if this was the man who had chased him from Allison's apartment. The shooter.

Then the man spoke to Joy and Cinco, asking for him by name, and Miles was sure.

He had no weapon, but he grabbed a small sculpture – an iron figure of a Sioux warrior. The rider rose high above the horse, a spear thrusting forward, and Miles decided he'd hit the shooter in the temple, where the bone and flesh were weakest. He couldn't let the man hurt Joy and Cinco.

But then, God bless Joy, who said he wasn't there. Cinco played along. Miles listened to the conversation, heard her parry with and then lie to the guy. Then he crept back to the office, thinking, *He won't kill anyone if he thinks they're on the phone.* So he lifted the handset, punched in the extension for Joy's desk, heard it give off its internal buzz; Joy, smart, acted as if she'd gotten an outside call and Miles said to her, 'Get busy, he'll leave.'

Then a rattling on the door, and he heard the footsteps

119

of the shooter leaving, heard him offer a polite excuse-me to a customer at the door.

He counted to ten, started down the stairs. Joy rushed past two women, possibly ignoring a buyer for the first time in her life.

'Who was that?' she said.

'You lied to him,' Miles said in surprise.

'I didn't like him. The sunglasses, the way he asked for you. I know trouble when I see it. You don't do sales. So I knew he was lying.' She grabbed his arm, hurried him to the back, told Cinco to go deal with the browsers. She slammed the door behind her. 'Could a bad guy from your old life be hunting you?'

He knew she meant the Barradas but it was easier not to explain. 'Yes. Listen to me. Close the gallery right now. Leave. In case he comes back at six. And I'll make sure he leaves you alone.'

'I'll take you wherever you want to go.'

'No. I'm not involving you further. Just go. Now.' His face burned. 'Thanks, Joy, for being my friend, you don't know how much you and this job meant to me. Don't tell Cinco about me, okay?'

'I'll make up a good story.' Tears in her eyes, she tip-toed up and kissed his cheek. Then she opened the door, announced to Cinco and the ladies that they were closing immediately, nicely shepherded the two women out of the door, told Cinco to go home.

'What the hell's going on?' Cinco demanded.

'Get your mother home,' Miles said. 'Now.'

'Would you please tell me why we're all panicking?' Cinco asked.

'Michael, let us give you a ride . . .'

'No. Go, Joy, please.'

Joy squeezed his hand and then she hurried Cinco to her car. They drove off in a peal of tire.

The shooter knew his name. Andy, seated on Cinco's desk, said, 'Game's over, Miles.'

Miles ignored him, grabbed a University of New Mexico Lobos baseball cap from Cinco's desk, pulled it low on his face, and then ran around to the back of the building. He needed to get back to his hotel. The gallery next door was owned by three potters – and he remembered that one always biked to work. He'd call her and tell her where the bike was later. He still had his lockpicks in his pocket and he worked the bike lock open in ten seconds.

'Reduced to being a bicycle thief,' Andy said. 'Shame on you.'

Miles jumped on the bicycle, awkwardly – he hadn't ridden one in ten years – found his rhythm, then sped around the building's corner, out onto the lot, onto Canyon Road.

And saw the shooter behind the wheel of a car, heading back up Canyon, veering straight toward him in a scream of rubber.

EIGHTEEN

The buzz instead of a ring. It was a setting on office phones. The call Cinco took when Groote first walked in gave off a ring; Joy'd gotten a buzz for that second call, but she'd pretended it was an outside call. His instincts told him the woman had been lying. The idea of Michael Raymond coming back at six was just to get him out of the gallery.

So he veered hard, ignoring the horns laid down around him as he narrowly missed clipping a truck, vroomed back down Paseo de Peralta, and took the hard right onto Canyon.

And right ahead of him, an idiot on a bike, a baseball cap practically covering his eyes, riding and balancing awkwardly in the middle of the street. Groote just missed him as he steered the car hard into the parking lot for the collection of galleries.

Groote saw the CLOSED sign hanging crooked in the Garrison Gallery's door. He ran up to the door, tested the knob. Locked. He broke the pane of glass closest to the knob; an alarm wailed. He opened the door, drew his gun, ran through the gallery, upstairs and down. No sign of anyone.

The police would arrive within minutes. He tucked his

gun into his holster under his jacket, went out the back, saw a woman standing with hands on hips, frowning at the noise.

'I'm a friend of Joy and Cinco's,' he said to her before she could speak. 'Is something wrong?'

'My bike's gone.' She gestured toward the gallery door, the shrieking whine. 'Is it a break-in or a false alarm?'

The guy on the bike. Outmaneuvered by an art hippie lady and a guy on a fricking bike. He ran past the woman and hurried to his car.

Groote bolted onto Canyon, then Paseo de Peralta. Had to choose and took a hard right. He drove two minutes, running red lights, looking for the guy on the bike. Wheeled hard around and went the other way, cursing. He backtracked, tore up side roads at eighty miles an hour. His heart caught in his throat, he pounded the steering wheel in fury.

I was this close to him. To finding Frost.

No bike on the street. No bike anywhere. Michael Raymond was gone.

NINETEEN

Miles carried the stolen bike up to the hotel room with him, washed his face. The cache of money and equipment he kept at the bus station in case he ever needed to flee town on his own – now was the time to go fetch it. But if the shooter was prowling the roads of central Santa Fe, riding the bike was a risk; he couldn't outrun a car.

A fist pounded his door. DeShawn, ordering him to open up.

He answered and DeShawn pushed in, frantic-faced, slamming the door behind him. 'We're moving you to a new city, getting you a new identity. Right now. Grab your bag.'

'Why?'

'You've been disclosed, Miles. Your cover's blown. The police found a laptop in Allison's car trunk. It contained a scanned copy of your entire psychiatric file from Allison. Including the fact that you're a federal witness and your real name.' He shook his head. 'It omitted the fact that you lied to me, of course.'

DeShawn's urgency had nothing to do with the shooter's appearing at the gallery.

'I—'

'You're done in Santa Fe. Let's go.'

Miles rocked on his feet, the news a punch in his gut. 'How would Allison know my real name?'

'You sure you didn't tell her?'

'No. I never did.'

'I don't believe you. You told me you didn't even tell her you were a witness!' DeShawn's voice was cold. 'You lied to me, Miles. She knew your name, she knew where you were from, she knew what you were, and now she's dead.'

'I never told her.' The confession – signed with his real name – was still in his pants pocket. 'You said a scanned file? Like a paper file scanned for a computer?'

'Yes.'

Sorenson, opening and closing the file cabinet yesterday afternoon. He'd taken something. Miles's file. But it had apparently been full of information he'd never given Allison. 'Jesus and Mary,' Miles said.

'You done lying, Miles? Your face. You weren't in a fight. You were close to her office when it exploded.'

'No.'

'You tried to call her pager right after the explosion – I got the records. Explain that timing.'

'She wanted to talk to me . . .'

'You were supposed to be there when the office blew, Miles, weren't you. You were supposed to die with her, don't you see it?'

'No.'

'You told her who you were. And then she started digging into your past, to understand you, to help you, and she tipped off the Barradas. Maybe by accident. But if you'd kept your mouth shut that you were Miles Kendrick, she'd be alive right now.'

Miles shook his head. 'I never told her my real name! And even if I did, why kill her? Why hurt her?'

'You dumb shit!' DeShawn yelled. 'Do you know how many people want you dead? The Barradas, sure. Then all the crime rings you screwed over spying for the Barradas, they want your ass: the Razor Boys, the Duartes, the GHJ ring . . . Miles, she knew and she died and she left behind a record of your old name. That's all that matters. You're compromised. Welcome to your next exciting new life.'

Miles went and picked up his bag. His mind raced. No, he couldn't leave now, he couldn't get on that plane. 'What if I say no to relocating?'

DeShawn's voice went cold. 'Now I speak as your inspector. WITSEC's voluntary, Miles. You can walk away from our protection anytime you want. But as your friend, you're dead meat if you stay. The press will get hold of this, eventually, her death is too big a story here. As your friend, I'm worried you're not thinking straight, that you remain mentally unbalanced and unable to make a cogent decision, and I will knock your ass out and put you on a plane to save your life. That's all off the record, of course.'

'Of course. I—'

'Nothing to keep you here,' Andy said from the corner. 'She's dead and gone. Quit being helpful, Miles. People get killed.'

'What's the matter?' DeShawn said.

'Nauseous.' Miles went to the sink, jetted water into a glass.

'First you fail her, now you run,' Andy said. 'You're an A-one piece of work, Miles.'

Miles drank his water, ignored DeShawn and Andy both. No. He wasn't going anywhere, not until he knew the truth about Allison's death. She needed him. He had failed to help her in time, he had failed to be the man she needed him to be. What had living a lie gotten him?

Nothing. He'd lost this new life as easily as he'd lost his last one. The decision was clear and strong in his head, crowding out his fear, silencing Andy's murmurs.

Escape was the only answer. He had to avoid DeShawn, at least for a few days. Hide out in Santa Fe, find the shooter, uncover the truth. The WITSEC higher-ups might very well boot him out of the protection program for running; but he thought they might not. He was a mental patient and critical to their remaining cases against the Barrada ring. He had saved two FBI agents from certain death. But he was breaking a cardinal rule of WITSEC. Disobeying an inspector, running on his own.

'I'll go with you. But first I need to talk to Joy. Please,' Miles said.

'You can call Joy from your new location.'

'I want Joy and Cinco protected.'

'Did you tell them your real name too?'

'No.'

'I guarantee you they'll be safe.'

'Make the call now. I want deputy marshals staked at Joy's house, at Cinco's, at the gallery.'

DeShawn saw it was Miles's price of compliance. 'Okay, man, I'll make the call.' He dialed, spoke softly into the cell phone while Miles shoved his few belongings back into his bag.

DeShawn clicked off the phone. 'The Garrisons will be protected. My guarantee.'

'Thank you.' Miles hoisted the bag onto his shoulder. 'Let's go.'

DeShawn walked ahead of him, opening the door, and Miles drove hard into him.

'Miles, don't try it!' DeShawn yelled as he slammed into the door. He howled in pain, his hand caught between

127

the frame and the latch. Miles hammered a fist into the back of DeShawn's neck. Once, twice, and then DeShawn got his feet anchored, freed his hand from the door's trap, and cannonballed into Miles.

'Major mistake,' DeShawn said, drawing back his fist. A hard punch to the chest, to the jaw, two hard blows to the stomach, left Miles heaped on the bed.

'Goddamn, you hurt my hand.' DeShawn stood over him, shaking the sting out of his fingers. 'What the hell got into you?'

Miles didn't answer, closed his eyes, told himself to ignore the pain. He made his breathing labored.

'Assaulting a federal officer,' DeShawn said. 'Never mind you were supposed to be my friend.'

Miles kept his eyes closed. He heard the soft clink of handcuffs.

'Quit playing possum,' DeShawn said, grabbing Miles's wrist. 'Open up your eyes and stop—'

Miles pivoted and kicked out with both feet, hard. One foot caught DeShawn in the nose, the other in the throat, and he staggered back. Miles spun off the bed, pain fueling him because he couldn't lose now, DeShawn would rightly beat him senseless.

He grabbed DeShawn's hurt hand and twisted.

Two finger bones popped and DeShawn sucked in breath and cussed. Miles reared back and punched him hard, twice, grabbed the hotel-desk alarm clock and brought it down hard on the back of DeShawn's head. Once. Twice. DeShawn went down to his knees, trying to pull Miles close to get him in a neck lock, and Miles swung the Lucite clock again, into DeShawn's temple. DeShawn went down, eyes closed.

'I'm sorry,' Miles said. 'I'm really sorry.' He knelt

down, checked the pulse. Present and steady. He wouldn't be down long and he'd be real pissed when he woke up.

Miles ripped the cables from the TV, from the lamp. He bound DeShawn with them, took a sheet from the bed, tied it to the two cables holding DeShawn's hands and feet, immobilizing DeShawn. Miles tore a pillowcase, tucked a wad of it into DeShawn's mouth, careful not to block his breathing. He took DeShawn's car keys from his pocket, left his badge, gun, and wallet alone. He put DeShawn's cell phone on the bed. Then he gently dragged DeShawn into the closet, closed the door, jimmied the desk chair hard up under the knob.

His face and his ribs hurt; DeShawn had pulled his punches but Miles ached as if he'd been sideswiped by a car. He had, at most, a few minutes. Most likely DeShawn had logged that he'd been heading to pick up Miles at the hotel, and if he didn't report back in a few minutes, WITSEC and the FBI would start calling and come straight to the hotel.

'I'm sorry, DeShawn,' he said to the closed door. 'Please forgive me. But I've got to make things right.'

He hung the DO NOT DISTURB notice on the door and walked away from life as Michael Raymond.

TWENTY

Miles hoped Andy would stay behind in the hotel room, haunt it as a ghost, keep DeShawn company. But no. Miles was Andy's haunted house.

And now he had to drive.

Fear pounded his stomach, a fist burrowing past skin and muscle to braid his guts. The Barradas were famous for wiring the ignitions of those they hated and Miles told himself as he walked toward the car that the fear was false, the Barradas would not be able to wire DeShawn's car, wouldn't be able to find DeShawn.

'Of course they could wire DeShawn's wheels.' Andy hurried to walk beside him. 'I mean, Allison knew your name. The Barradas could know DeShawn was coming to fetch you, they'd just need a few seconds to attach the bomb—'

'No,' Miles said. 'Shut up.'

'Blow up you and DeShawn together. That's justice to the Barrada boys. Wire up the ignition while you're fighting with DeShawn upstairs.'

Miles kept walking toward the car.

'You don't *seriously* think you're driving, do you?'

Miles stopped. Andy danced ahead, jumped atop the hood of DeShawn's car, did an improvised twist. 'I better be careful, I might set the fucker off!'

He's not there, there's not a bomb. It's perfectly safe. You're just adding theft to your crime load today.

'Too scared to drive.' Andy dropped down to the hood, rested his feet on the bumpers.

Miles ran, unlocked the car, sweat pouring down his back. His hand trembled as he shoved the key into the ignition, twisted it.

'Ka-boom!' Andy screamed from the other side of the windshield, twisting his face into a contortion, pressing hands and lips against the glass.

But the engine didn't explode; it just started.

Miles gripped the wheel.

'Better stop!' Andy said. 'Better stop. Right now.'

Miles shot him the finger, gritted his teeth, and jerked the car forward. Andy fell off the hood and then started his low whisper again from behind Miles. 'This isn't going to work,' Andy said in a low hiss.

All I need, he thought, *a backseat driver.*

'You killed me, and now you've killed Allison,' Andy said. 'Who will die next for your sins, Miles?'

The scar on his chest burned, he closed his eyes, slipped into the steam of a Miami morning. Andy smiling at him and then a shocked Andy pulling his gun in sudden resolve, aiming it, the bullet hitting Miles, and then he was in a hospital, under heavy security, the government telling him he couldn't be Miles Kendrick anymore.

Why was there this blot of snow in his memory, in his head? The sting went wrong – Andy reached for his gun, Andy knowing that Miles had gone government. A blot where he couldn't see the past. He could hear the voices of the two undercover agents, saying, *You did the right thing, man, you're a hero.*

But he didn't know why.

Now. Focus on now. The cache of money and a gun at the Santa Fe bus station in case he needed it. He rooted in the duffel's side pocket and found the locker key.

He drove over to the bus terminal on St. Michael, slowly circled it twice.

If WITSEC knows I rented the locker . . . would they routinely check on such things when they settled a witness in a new city? See if he rented a mailbox or a locker or a storage unit?

Would WITSEC look for me here?

Worse – would the shooter? No major airport in Santa Fe, you want out of town quick and got no car, you take the bus. He would have to risk it. The shooter wouldn't know or guess he didn't have a car.

Unless he spotted you on the bike.

Plan B. He drove back to Paseo de Peralta, searching for homeless Joe. He'd give him a twenty to retrieve the duffel; the shooter would ignore Joe, and the feds, if they knew about and surveilled the locker, would grab Joe but let him go when it was clear he knew nothing. But no sign of his friend on the streets, so Miles reluctantly wheeled back to the station.

He had to take the risk.

He walked inside. The terminal was busy on a late afternoon, a departure to Albuquerque and El Paso booming over the loudspeakers. He glanced around; no sign of the shooter, no one who stood with the iron spine of a federal officer. He grabbed the green duffel out of the locker, shouldered it, hurried back down the street to his car.

Miles opened the duffel. His worldly possessions now, in addition to his few clothes, consisted of the ID and credit card in his deceased father's name, a loaded Beretta, and a thousand in cash, hidden in the duffel's false bottom.

'Think you're smart,' Andy said next to him.

Miles stopped. 'Yes,' he said slowly, in a whisper barely above a breath, 'I do. I'm smarter than you. You're dead and I'm not.'

Andy went silent.

Miles needed a place to hide. He drove fast, sticking to side roads, until he got to Blaine the Pain's house off Old Santa Fe Trail. He parked DeShawn's car behind the house, next to Blaine's car, and knocked on the door. No answer. Blaine the Pain was still in Marfa with his friend, reigniting his painter's inspiration.

He fished around in the flower pots on the porch of the adobe and in the third one his fingers found the shape of a key. He slid it home in the lock, unlocked the door, praying Blaine was still gone, praying there was no beeping chime of an alarm system.

He slipped inside, closed the door, listened to the silence.

Home sweet home. For now.

TWENTY-ONE

Thursday morning Miles watched, from behind a heavy curtain, Blaine's neighbors driving off to work. Then he drove DeShawn's car to a grocery parking lot and abandoned it, unlocked and keys dangling in the ignition, and hiked the mile back to Blaine's house.

He had slept atop the covers on Blaine's bed, his mind cracked with exhaustion. And when he woke, he realized trying to find Nathan Ruiz was the wrong tack.

He'd sooner be able to find Celeste Brent, who had left that strange message on Allison's recorder about keeping her secret.

Blaine the Pain apparently had taken his laptop with him to Texas. Miles found a Santa Fe phone book, scrambled through the alphabet, ran a finger down the listings. No Celeste Brent. No C. Brent.

Okay. She was a TV star. Fame was a critical currency in Santa Fe. He'd seen several celebrities who stopped by Joy's gallery on their jaunts through town.

It gave him an idea. He dug into his bag and searched the pockets of pants he'd worn Tuesday – he still had Blaine the Pain's cell-phone number, scribbled on a note. He picked up the phone and set it down. Blaine's cell would likely show him calling from Blaine's house. Using his own cell phone was a risk – the feds could trace your location if the phone was on, he'd heard. But he couldn't use Blaine's phone. So he took the risk.

He flipped open his cell phone and dialed.

'Yeah?' Blaine answered, sounding his usual grumpy self.

'Hi, Mr. Blaine. It's Michael Raymond at the gallery. I may have found a buyer for *Emilia*.'

'Oh, man, Mike, that's great.' Blaine sounded happier than he ever had, and Miles's chest twisted in guilt.

'Well, sir, nothing's set. I have a woman who indicated serious interest, but she didn't leave a phone number – I guess she forgot. She's local, and she's famous, so I thought you might know her. Her name's Celeste Brent.'

'Yeah. I don't know her, no one *knows* her, but I know who she is.'

'I guess I don't.'

'Well, I never watched *Castaway*. I prefer PBS.'

'What's *Castaway*?'

'That reality show where they dump a dozen people on a godforsaken island and they compete to be the last one standing for five million dollars.' He snorted in disgust. 'A popularity contest on steroids.'

Miles now recognized the show's title. Most of his work for the Barradas had been done at night, so he didn't follow many television programs. But her name had sounded familiar and a drop of the show's incessant coverage must have seeped into his brain. 'She was on this game show?'

'Won the five million. A couple years back. Fifteen minutes of fame for running around in a lime-green bikini. A vicious, backstabbing game and she was the Queen Bee on the island. I'd be surprised to know how she saw the *Emilia*. She's a total recluse. She makes a hermit look like a social butterfly.'

'Why?'

'Her husband was murdered and she went – how do I say it kindly? – nuts.'

'That's awful,' Miles said. 'Nuts how?'

'Agoraphobic – is that what it's called? She won't leave her house, not even to go into the yard. But she must be recovering, if she's out hunting art.'

'She's unlisted, and now I see why,' Miles said, improvising. 'Do you know anyone who'd know her address? She asked in the voice mail for me to bring the *Emilia* by for a private viewing.'

'And she didn't leave an address or a number for you? That's weird.'

'Sir,' Miles said, 'if she's been a recluse for so long, she might not be smooth in her dealings with folks.'

'True. Let me make a couple of calls and I'll call you back at the gallery.'

'Actually, call me on my cell phone.' He gave Blaine the number. 'I'm not at the gallery but I can run by there as soon as I know where Ms. Brent's address is.'

'Okay. I'll call you back in a few. Thanks, Michael.'

'Yes, sir.' Miles hung up.

Nuts. Maybe post-traumatic syndrome, just like him. Two minutes later his cell rang and Miles answered.

'I called the top realtor in Santa Fe,' Blaine said. 'She knows everyone of a certain net worth. Celeste Brent lives on Camino del Monte Sol.' He gave him the street number. 'She sold Celeste the house. She said Celeste never leaves it. I mean never ever. She has a woman who does all her shopping, runs her errands. She doesn't have any visitors inside, unless it's her doctors or this caretaker. Isn't that the craziest thing you ever heard?'

'Yeah. Crazy. I guess she found the *Emilia* on the Web site.'

'Crazy money is still as good as sane money.'

'Okay.' He felt real regret about the necessary trick he was playing. 'Don't get your hopes up, Mr. Blaine.'

'Let me know what happens. Talk to you soon.'

'Thank you, sir.' Miles clicked off the phone and started thinking about how he might talk his way into a total recluse's house.

TWENTY-TWO

The sheet felt cool on Celeste's face. She lay in her bed like a corpse in the morgue. The crying was done; no tears left inside.

Allison was dead. The past twenty-four hours had been full of numbing grief, shock, denial. Celeste kept a gun in the house and she'd gone and picked it up twice and then eased it back into its drawer. *I can't, Allison would kill me.* Then she'd cry and then she'd laugh, the good memories of Allison plowing through the grief.

She slipped out from under the sheet and sat at her vanity in the bathroom and, very lightly, touched the razor. She could cut herself, just a tiny nip. She knew cutting was a slide backward. She'd felt stronger in the past week, more sure of herself, than she had in many months. The razor's edge gleamed; a perfect line. Like the line drawn in her life before Brian was murdered, before she died on the inside and she didn't know how to resuscitate herself.

She pressed the tip down into the flesh of her upper arm, the pain kicked, up rose a bud of blood.

What are you doing? Allison's voice rang in her ears. *You really want to have a sharp edge be your answer to pain?*

She put the razor down, stared at the blood, saw the dead face of her husband, the dead face of his killer in the crimson bubble.

Allison would be ashamed of her. She stopped the blood, dabbed antiseptic on it, covered her weakness with a bandage. She put the razor back in its sheath, tucked the sheath between two folded twenties in her purse's billfold, and slid a fresh rubber band onto her wrist. She called it her cutting condom, the bit of rubber that was supposed to ease her off an addiction to pain. She started snapping the rubber hard against her wrist, again and again, until fatigue seeped through her and nausea claimed her stomach. But the urge to cut was gone. She curled back under the sheets.

Call the police. And say what? The afternoon before my doctor died, she showed up, acted odd, used my computer? Well, so what? All it would do would be to bring the media's attention swinging back toward her, a blinding, inescapable light. She could imagine the headlines: 'Former TV Star Linked to Shrink Death.' She knew nothing; there was nothing to tell.

She stayed in her room when Nancy Baird, who did all her shopping and errands for her, came by with the twice-a-week grocery run.

'Celeste? You okay?' Nancy called from the kitchen.

'Yes. I've got a cold, so I'm just staying in my room.'

Nancy opened the door. 'I ain't scared of no cold germs. You want me to run to the pharmacy and get you medicine?'

'No,' Celeste said from the sanctuary of the sheets.

Nancy, fiftyish and no-nonsense, came into the room and put a hand to Celeste's forehead. 'Not hot or clammy.'

'No. It's in my throat.'

139

'Let me see.'

'Oh, honestly, Nancy, let me alone.'

'You got too much leaving you alone,' Nancy said. 'Get up and out of bed, girl.'

'Just leave me alone!' Celeste screamed. 'Just unload the groceries and go.'

'There's no need for shouting,' Nancy said, unruffled. 'You want me to call Doctor Vance?'

'No,' she said, not adding, *She's dead, you must not read the papers.* 'No. I'm just . . .'

'Sad and lonely,' Nancy said. 'You want to come home with me, have dinner with me and Tony?'

An invitation, always extended.

'No, thank you.' Celeste fought back fresh tears. 'Nancy, Doctor Vance is dead.' Shock blossomed on Nancy's face. Celeste told her the news accounts.

'My God.' Nancy sat on the edge of the bed.

'So the paper said it might be a gas explosion, but what if it wasn't, what if someone wanted to kill her?' Celeste got up out of bed, started pacing the floor. *She showed up unexpectedly, she acted weird, she asked me to keep her secret. From the hospital.* But she couldn't tell Nancy about Allison's request – Nancy would call the police, they would come, then the press . . . no. Never again. But she should call the authorities . . . tell them what Allison had said. What if it was important? What if Allison had been murdered? That thought, one she'd been keeping at bay, rushed at her like an avalanche.

'Honey. Listen to me.' Nancy put an arm around her. 'It was an accident, I'm sure, no one would want to hurt Doctor Vance.'

'She works with crazy people. We're dangerous.' Celeste paced the floor.

'You're not crazy, dear . . .'

'Yes, I am, I am crazy, Nancy.' Celeste stumbled to the curtains, leaned against the wall. 'The price I pay for not saving my husband . . .'

Nancy steered her back to the bed. 'Did you stab Brian?'

'No . . . no . . .'

'Then you didn't kill him. Banish that thought from your mind. You're not responsible.' Nancy shook her head. 'You're not nuts. Nuts is thinking that how you're living is normal, and you know it's not. Now. You're not going to hurt yourself, are you?'

'No,' she said, 'I won't.'

Nancy glanced at the fresh bandage on Celeste's arm. 'I better stay tonight.'

'No. You have a life. Go live it.'

'I'm staying.'

'I won't hurt myself. I'd rather be alone. Really. Please. I'll call you if I need you.'

'You're alone too much. Have you eaten today?'

'Breakfast. Before I saw the news.'

'Then I'm going to make you a pot of vegetable soup before I go. I'll get you a plate of cheese and crackers to snack on while it's cooking.'

'Stop being so nice.'

'Stop acting like you don't deserve it.' Nancy gave her a hug and Celeste let her, although she didn't much like being touched.

'Thanks, Nancy.'

'I don't mean to sound insensitive to Doctor Vance,' Nancy said, 'but it might be wise to find another therapist.'

'I don't think I can face a new psychiatrist right now.'

'Doctor Vance wouldn't want your therapy to end.'

'You're right.' She wiped the tears from her cheeks. 'I think I'll go check my e-mail.'

'You spend too much time on the computer. One day I'm gonna unplug that monster and wheel it to the street. Might get you out of the house.' Nancy squeezed her hand and went off to the kitchen.

Celeste sat down at the computer. Allison had sat here; she'd seemed nervous. Skittish. Now she was dead, under extraordinary circumstances. Maybe one didn't have anything to do with the other. Just because you had a weird day, then you died, it didn't necessarily mean anything.

But the day Brian died had been off kilter. The coffeemaker broke; it gurgled in protest and wouldn't brew. She dropped the egg carton pulling it from the refrigerator, spilling shells and yolks across the tile. So Brian said, *I'll run to the store and I'll swing by Starbucks, babe*, because now she got recognized everywhere she went in Atlanta, there was a checker there who always wanted to make a big deal about seeing the winner from *Castaway*. So Brian was gone when the Disturbed Fan she believed was a friend knocked on the door with his easy grin and she let him into the house because she trusted him, he was her fan club's president, and then he pulled the knife and the gun and told her she and Brian were going to die, just as soon as Brian got home with the dozen eggs and hot coffee.

She closed her eyes, steadied herself in the chair. Brian walking in, her tied up and the Disturbed Fan starting to tuck the fabric between her lips, Brian calling, *Babe, I got Sumatra, I hope that's okay*, and then it all ended, her life wadded up and thrown away.

She swallowed past the mountain in her throat. She hit

the space bar on the keyboard, awakening her computer from sleep. She could dig around the system, see what Allison had done. Before Brian died, Celeste had been an accomplished programmer; now her computer was her only friend, aside from Nancy.

She checked the Sent Items folder in her e-mail program. Nothing unusual there; Allison hadn't e-mailed anything from Celeste's account. Next she dived to her Web browser and checked the history.

The list of sites the browser had visited yesterday scrolled down the screen. Odd. Celeste had spent much of Wednesday morning on Amazon, shopping for new books on PTSD, and those pages were cleaned from the browser's history. But the sites she'd visited after Allison's visit: Victor Gamby's blog and discussion board for PTSD sufferers, CNN, and eBay, those sites' addresses remained in the history list.

Which meant wherever Allison had gone on her Web browser, she'd then erased the entire history. She hadn't wanted to leave a trail.

Celeste opened the various Microsoft Office programs, surveying the listing of recent files, to see if there was a file name she didn't recognize. None. So Allison had not opened a Word document or spreadsheet, or she had cleaned out the history of files opened in those programs.

What had Allison said? Celeste frowned, trying to remember: *I have all the programs I need on this disk.*

'Celeste, your snack is ready,' Nancy called. 'Come sit in here with me while I finish making your soup.'

'All right.' She wondered if there was a way to recover the cleaned-out history file. She'd have to research that once Nancy left.

The kitchen smelled of broth and chiles and she sat

down to a plate of wheat crackers and grapes and Havarti cheese. Food. She needed this more than hours of crying in bed, although Allison deserved grieving. 'Thank you.'

'You're welcome, sweetie.'

'You're right about finding another therapist,' Celeste said. 'Allison mentioned a Doctor Hurley at Sangre de Cristo. I'll call him and set up an appointment.'

Nancy told her that was a good idea and took her leave. Celeste ladled out the simple soup into a bowl. It tasted wonderful; hot, spicy with green chiles. She ate two bowls of it and felt better.

She opened the Yellow Pages, found a number for Leland Hurley. She dialed the hospital, got connected to his voice mail, and left a message, asking him to call her regarding a doctor to take over her therapy. Then she added: 'Allison acted ... oddly the day she was here, Tuesday, and I need to talk to you about it.' She felt disloyal but she knew Nancy was right; she couldn't let her therapy stop. She wanted distraction, so she flopped on the sofa, powered on the TV, settled in to pass the time with an old Bob Hope comedy.

The doorbell rang. She clicked the TV to the channel that fed into the security camera on her front door. She didn't know the man standing at her porch. He held up a sign to the camera, handwritten in block letters on white cardboard. It read I KNOW ALLISON'S SECRET.

She gaped at the screen in disbelief. The man gave the camera a polite wave.

She pushed the intercom button. 'Who are you?'

'Hi. My name is Miles Kendrick.'

'What do you want?'

'I believe you may have information relevant to why Allison died.' He never let his eyes drop from the camera.

144

'I don't talk to people,' she said. 'Go away.'

'I know you prefer to be alone. I understand. But I believe you'll want to talk to me.'

'How did you know Allison?' she finally said.

'She asked me for help.' He produced another note, held it up to the screen. She read it; she knew Allison's tight, neat handwriting.

'How do you know what information I have?' she asked.

'Because Allison told me,' he said, 'that she was in trouble and that I could trust you.'

She studied his face for five minutes. Her hands trembling, Celeste got her gun, its weight unfamiliar in her hand, and opened the door.

TWENTY-THREE

Groote didn't want to use the screwdriver again, but he didn't have a choice.

Michael Raymond hadn't run home, he hadn't run back to the gallery, he wasn't answering his phone. Wednesday night Groote had called the MR number listed on Allison's cell, using a hospital phone; but there was no answer. He'd left a message that simply said, 'You and I need to talk, Mr. Raymond, I'll call you when your phone's on.' He'd called every hotel in town, checked flights outbound from Albuquerque. He had found where Joy Garrison lived and driven twice past her house. A Santa Fe police car sat outside. No help there. He drove on both times to avoid attracting notice.

Of course Michael Raymond might have abandoned his bike and left town by car. But – and the thought nagged at Groote – if the guy had killed Allison and taken Frost, had the research worth millions in his pocket, why stay in town on Wednesday, working at the gallery? He'd stayed a full twenty-four hours when he should have disappeared if he had the drug research. But the dink had gone back to life as normal.

He must have had a damned good reason to stay in town. *I don't have . . . Frost . . . but I might know where you can get it*, Michael Raymond had said. Perhaps the guy hit a delay in putting his hands on Frost.

Nathan Ruiz might know the reason.

Groote found Nathan heavily sedated; he steered Hurley to Nathan's bedside.

'I need him talking,' Groote said.

Hurley pulled his arm away from Groote's grip. 'I need him not screaming his throat raw. The other patients can hear him.'

'Who gives a crap? Tell them he's having a nervous breakdown.'

'We've got another avenue to pursue,' Hurley said with an irritating level of confidence back in his voice. 'I got a phone call from one of Allison's patients – Celeste Brent. She used to be famous, she won a reality TV show.'

'A PTSD patient?'

'I think so, given her recent past.' He gave Groote a brief background on Celeste Brent. 'The news accounts after she moved here say she's agoraphobic, has made her house a fortress. She said Allison visited her Tuesday afternoon, acted oddly.'

Groote considered. 'Presume she took the research Tuesday when she left. Allison either hands off the research to someone else or hides it; she wouldn't leave it in her office, because there and her home are the first places you'd search. Say she hid it, and Michael Raymond knows she hid it but he hasn't found it,' Groote said, 'then it's the best explanation for why he hadn't left town yesterday.'

Hurley nodded. 'So where would she stash it?'

'Put yourself in her shoes. She had the research. She didn't take it straight to the FDA or to the press, so she had a reason to keep Frost secret, at least for a few hours.

147

Best if she could hide it in a place where she could get access to it but others couldn't, at least not easily. Perhaps Mr. Raymond's problem is one of access.'

Hurley saw where his idea was going. 'She wouldn't leave it at a patient's house.'

'But hiding something at a recluse's house – where only you and a couple of others have regular access – is an interesting idea. You said she lives in her house like it's a fortress. We need to talk to her.'

'This is all speculation.'

'I used to work in speculation all the time.' Groote didn't add that it had been part of his job at the FBI, trying to figure out connections between players to build the bigger case.

Hurley blanched. 'You can't go over there and bully her. She called me – I can find out what she knows.'

'All right. Go.'

Hurley left.

Groote checked his watch. California time was close to four, Amanda would be in her room. He dialed the number; the nurse got Amanda and brought her to the phone.

'Hey, Daddy.'

'Hey, sunshine. How's your day?'

'I'm not sunshine today.'

'What's the matter, Amanda Banana?' He realized he talked to her as if she were a small child, but he couldn't help himself. The undamaged child was the daughter he saw in his mind's eye, not this broken, sad teenager who needed more than he could give her.

'I miss you.'

His heart tightened. 'I miss you, too, angel, but this is an important trip for Daddy.' Dare he raise her hopes?

Hope was the greatest medicine of all, if it wasn't dead in her heart. 'Daddy's working with nice folks that have a new way to help you.'

'What way?' She sounded suspicious.

'It's a pill, honey. A magic pill.'

'Magic pill,' she said dully. 'Oh, please, Dad.'

'It kills all the bad memories in your brain. But a very, very bad man stole the magic pills, and Daddy's going to catch him.'

'You're making this up,' she said.

'No. I got to go slay dragons now and get that magic pill back. I think he hid it under a hundred mattresses a princess sleeps on.'

Now she laughed, indulging him, the sweetest music in his world. 'You're such a geek, Dad.'

'I love you, Amanda Banana.'

'I love you, Dad,' she said after a pause, as though she had to find the words, recognize the emotions. 'Go slay a dragon for me.'

'I will, baby, I will.' He clicked off the phone, pinched the bridge of his nose, took a deep breath. He couldn't fail her, he couldn't let her rot in that hospital. Not when she could be fixed.

Groote went back down to the soundproofed room where Nathan Ruiz lay handcuffed to the bed. He wore a bloodied scrubs shirt and underwear. Four vicious gouges dotted his leg, where Groote had made his cuts and twisted his screwdriver. Groote closed the door behind him. Nathan opened his eyes and cringed.

He leaned over to Nathan's face. 'You're gonna tell me the truth now, you're gonna tell me everything you know about Michael Raymond. You tried to protect him, you went all those hours without giving me his name, which

149

suggests to me that you know more than you've told me so far.'

Nathan spat at him, but the glob just landed on his own nose and lip.

Groote gently wiped the spittle from Nathan's face. 'Nice defiance. Piss me off and we're moving on to power tools.'

'I'm – I'm not afraid of you,' Nathan said.

'I know fear. You're drowning in it, son. But you're about to be drowning in pain instead.' He lowered his mouth close to Nathan's ear. 'Where did Allison hide Frost?'

'I told you, I don't know anything about her taking your stuff.'

Groote didn't want to go through hours more of torture; he wondered if the boy's relatively strong courage was proof that Frost worked on him. So change tactics. 'I don't have to hurt you if you help me. Celeste Brent. Tell me about her.'

'Who?'

'She was one of the last people to see Allison alive.'

Nathan closed his eyes. 'Don't know her.'

A knock on the door announced Hurley; Groote noticed he didn't look at Nathan. 'What am I supposed to do if Allison did leave Frost with Ms. Brent?'

'Call me. I'll deal with her. People commit suicide when they lose their therapist sometimes,' Groote said. 'Unfortunate, but it happens.'

TWENTY-FOUR

Miles heard six soft clicks: dead bolts unlocking. Then the door opened. 'Put the note down,' a voice whispered. 'Step back ten steps from the door. Count the steps aloud.'

He did as he was told.

The door creaked open another few inches, a hand reached out, swept the note inside. The door slammed closed. He heard the locks turn.

Three more minutes. He peered up at the moon showing its face from behind a heavy cloud, its light silvering the wildflowers that graced the beds. The dead bolts, all six of them, clicked and the door opened again. Now the hand held a gun, a sleek Glock. He could see her, only part of her face visible, standing there in a T-shirt with a Batman logo, faded jeans, her hair pulled into a thick ponytail.

'You can come in,' she said.

'Guns make me nervous.' He'd left his own in the car.

'Everything makes me nervous,' Celeste said. 'Explain why she wrote you a note. Why not just ask for your help?'

He saw no reason to lie; she might slam the door in his face, but she might equally decide to trust him. 'She didn't want another person in the room to know she was asking for help.'

'Who?'

'A man named Sorenson. He said he was a doctor but he's not. She passed me the note in a vial of pills.'

'Pills? White pills?' Her voice rose.

'Empty shells. No medicine in them.'

Ten seconds passed. 'We'll talk. But by my rules. Hands on your head. Step inside.'

He obeyed. She eased back, keeping a healthy ten feet between them. Neither her voice nor her hand holding the Glock was particularly steady.

'Shut the door,' she said. 'Don't lock it – keep your hands on your head. Just shut it.' He did, easing the front door closed with his elbow. He waited.

'Okay,' he said. 'Can we talk?'

'Sit.' She gestured with the gun to a heavy armchair in the corner. He sat, she remained standing on the other side of the room, the gun trained on him.

'I understand your caution, but that's not necessary.'

'Why did Allison turn to you?'

'I used to be a private investigator. She believed I could help her.'

'Used to be.'

'I'm retired.'

'She gave you pills. Were you a patient?'

'Yeah.'

'What's wrong with you?'

'I'm Dealing With Issues.'

'Don't be vague. I don't leave the house. What do you do?'

He swallowed. 'A friend of mine tried to kill someone. I killed him. He follows me around.'

'I prefer my life to yours,' she said.

'Allison asked me for help, she asked you to keep a secret, she got killed. We should compare notes.'

'It's too late to help her.'

'I can't walk away from it. I can't. May I put my hands down?'

'No.'

'I'll tell you why Allison was in danger if you tell me her secret.'

'Why should I care? She's dead.'

'I can see you care. You've been crying. But, Mrs. Brent – Celeste – you might be in danger the same way she was.'

A sick, sad frown twisted her pretty face. 'I've already survived attempted murder. It's generally a once-in-a-lifetime experience.'

'Me too. But you and me, we're beating the odds.' He told the events of the past two days: meeting Sorenson, Allison asking him for help, finding out Sorenson wasn't a doctor, the confrontation and chase at Allison's apartment, the shooter coming to the gallery looking for him. He left out that he was in WITSEC and hiding from the authorities. He didn't want to scare her.

She listened without interruption.

'This man that's hunting me, he thinks I've got this research that Allison stole. I'm wondering if she gave it to you or talked about it to you.'

'Backtrack a minute. You're saying Allison was a thief.'

'I know how it sounds. But she's dead. Nathan Ruiz has been in this hospital, and if he's telling the truth, she was helping him escape. He was part of this Frost research . . . he had FROST on his hospital bracelet. Allison was trying to get him away from the research.'

'Nathan Ruiz could be lying.'

'People chased and shot at us.'

After a moment, she lowered the gun and he found it

153

easier to breathe. 'Fair enough. But why would she bring this research here?'

'Because if they were suspicious of her ... she could only go places where she could be expected to go. She stole something of great value. She can't keep it in her house or her office – this man, or this Sorenson guy, might be after it. She needed another hiding place, one that she can reach easily yet doesn't arouse suspicion.'

'And you think she hid this secret in my house.'

'How long since you left your house?'

'That's none of your business,' she snapped.

'You're right. But say she had to hide it in a hurry. If she showed up, unexpected, she could be sure you were home. Because you're always home.'

Celeste started to argue but saw his point. She crossed her arms under the Batman logo. 'This is crazy.'

'Whatever Frost is, it's got to matter hugely to these people.'

'But what would it be?'

'This man she seemed afraid of, Sorenson, he mentioned a new therapy. Said it could deaden the effects of traumatic memory. Maybe Frost relates to his project.'

'But you said Sorenson's not a doctor. How does he connect to Sangriaville?'

'I don't know. But Nathan said they'd *fixed* him. If you forgot your trauma, or it didn't ruin your life anymore ... would you say you were fixed?'

'You can't just make trauma go away.' Anger in her voice.

'If he was helped by a new therapy, let's say for the sake of argument, and Allison was sneaking him out of the hospital ... it suggests to me that she needs to show he's better.'

'To support the research she stole. He's human proof.'
He saw from her frown she was considering his theory
from different angles.

'You think this is about drug tests?'

'If so, they're secret tests. Or illicit.'

He noticed a rubber band circled her thin wrist and she
snapped it slowly against her skin, an unconscious twid-
dling of thumbs. She seemed to be trying to make a
decision, gauging him.

'You've got two facts on your side you don't know
about. Or I'm as crazy as you are.' She let out a tense
breath. 'The day she died. She came by to borrow my
computer, hers was on the fritz. After she left I couldn't
find a bottle of white pills she gave me a couple of weeks
ago, to take before our sessions, and they were missing
from my purse. I had the insane idea she'd taken them,
but I couldn't really believe it.'

He remembered the message she'd left on Allison's
office phone. 'You took these pills before your therapy.'

'Yes. She said it would make it easier for me to talk
about my trauma.'

'I wasn't a cooperative patient,' he said. 'Could you
talk about your trauma freely with her?'

Celeste ran a tip of tongue along her lip. 'Yes. Much
more so lately.'

'Are you . . . stronger, or less affected by the memories,
since you started taking the pills?'

'I . . . don't know. I cut myself.' She kicked at the floor.
'But I've been cutting less . . . but that doesn't prove she
fed me experimental medicine.'

'What'd she do on your computer?'

'There's nothing new on my system . . . but she erased
the Internet history logs.'

155

'Let me see.'

'I have a question first. You find out what she stole or why she died, what then?'

'We blow these people out of the water. Expose what they've done, that they killed Allison. Get Nathan away from them, if they still have him. If they know that Allison came here on the day she died, they might come for you.'

'Oh, shit. I called the hospital today. Told them I needed a new counselor, that Allison visited me the day she died, acting weird.'

'Have they called you back?'

'No.'

'We may not have much time—' Miles started, and a beep sounded.

'My front-yard sensor,' Celeste said. The doorbell rang.

'You expecting anyone?' he whispered. The door was still unlocked, he remembered she insisted he not lock it when he first came inside.

She shook her head. 'No one but my friend Nancy, and she's already left.' She aimed a remote at the TV; clicked on the camera view of her front porch.

A man, wearing a white lab coat over a rumpled suit, stood on the stone tiles, peering up at the camera.

'You know him?' Miles asked.

'Never seen him.'

'Talk to him on the intercom. See who he is.'

'I don't take orders in my own house, Miles.'

'Sorry. Please.'

She pressed a button on an intercom. 'Yes?'

'Ms. Brent?'

'Who are you?'

'I'm Leland Hurley. I'm an associate of Doctor Vance's

156

from Sangre de Cristo. You called me and I wanted to be sure you were all right. May I come in?'

Miles stood close to Celeste. 'He could tell us what we need to know.'

'What, he just spills the beans? Or let me guess, you go all nuclear on his ass.'

'Neither. But he can't see me or know I'm here; I can't risk he knows what I look like if they're hunting me. I can hide and listen and you can talk to him. I won't let him hurt you.'

'No, I can't.' A sudden terror strained her voice.

'You can,' he said. 'Please, Celeste. Please help me. For Allison.'

She put her hands over her face as the doctor blinked uncertainly at the camera.

TWENTY-FIVE

'A man is here to see whoever's in charge.' The guard stood in the fourth-floor hallway, swallowing, looking at a point to the left of Groote's shoulder.

They're afraid of me, Groote thought. A pleasant discovery, like learning a woman thought you were attractive. 'I don't see anybody.' He'd closed the door behind him, but he wondered if the guard had spotted Nathan.

'Said he had absolutely to see whoever was in charge.'

'What's this guy's name?'

'Sorenson.'

Interesting and unexpected. Groote kept a poker face on for the guard. 'Is he a suit or is he trouble?'

'Trouble. Big guy. He knows how to handle himself.'

'I'll talk to him downstairs, in the conference room. You stay close, outside, in case I need backup.'

The guard complied. Groote went back into Nathan's room. He lay there, listless, staring at the ceiling.

'Your buddy Sorenson's here,' Groote said.

Nathan looked at the ceiling.

'So I'm supposed to think you and Michael Raymond were telling me the truth now about this third guy.'

'I told you . . . I didn't know why he came to Allison's.'

'He's downstairs, we can ask him. If you capped him

on the head, I'll invite him to bash you in return. Describe Sorenson again.'

Nathan repeated the description and Groote took the stairs down to the ground floor. It gave him time to think. He had been convinced that Sorenson was a ruse, agreed to by Michael Raymond and Nathan, to put suspicion on a nonexistent third party. But maybe the two guys had told the truth and this Sorenson, he was Allison's real partner. Maybe.

Groote went out into the lobby and found Sorenson waiting. The man matched Nathan's description: big, blond, with a well-cut suit and a rough face that preferred shadow.

'I'm Groote, director of security at the hospital.' He offered a hand.

Sorenson shook it but Groote saw that he braced himself, as though he suspected Groote might try to yank his arm, throw his balance. Sorenson jerked his head at the guard seated at the reception desk. 'I need to talk to you privately. Regarding Allison Vance.'

'What's your interest?'

'That's best discussed alone.'

Groote led him back to a quiet conference room on the first floor, shut the door. He decided not to say he'd heard the man's name before – let the guy talk, spin his web, see what story Sorenson had to peddle.

'I acquire projects for Aldis-Tate.'

Groote knew the name: a big international pharmaceutical. 'And?'

'And we were interested in buying research from Mr. Quantrill that he's testing at this hospital.'

'I'm just a security guy . . .'

'I think not,' Sorenson said. 'You were at Allison

Vance's house on Tuesday, shooting at people. I observed you from the bathroom door. You missed them. I made you for a much better shot.'

This was a guy he could deal with. Groote raised an eyebrow. 'I'll be damned. They told me the truth.'

'They?'

'Ruiz and Raymond. They said you were at her house, I didn't believe them.'

Sorenson shrugged. 'I went there to talk with Allison Vance. I woke up badly tied with sheets, sitting in a tub, with a migraine that I'm still nursing.'

'Why are you here, Mr. Sorenson?'

'Allison Vance approached one of our research directors, a college friend of hers, about a prototype drug being tested here called Frost.'

'I don't think I could comment . . .'

'She offered to sell the Frost research to us. I think now she must have made that offer under the table.'

Sell it? Quantrill had been worried she'd publicize it, destroy their chances of getting it to market. The bitch had been a mercenary. It almost restored his faith in human beings as creatures of profit.

'Did you accept her offer?'

'No.'

'So why are you here now?'

'Because we've received another offer to buy Frost,' Sorenson said.

Groote said, 'Those would be stolen goods.'

'I suspect so. Goods that Allison Vance was murdered for.'

Michael Raymond had killed her for Frost and this was it, confirmation of his theory. 'So why not just buy it from him, why come to me?'

'Because we're not going to buy stolen research. Mr. Quantrill, despite loving the shadows, is a known quantity. And I believe, knowing that Aldis-Tate's coming to you with this information, we can strike an accommodation on the pricing of Frost. Before the auction.'

'Auction.'

'Yeah,' Sorenson said. 'Whoever took the Frost files from Allison is staging an auction in four days. I told Quantrill this yesterday. Didn't you know?'

Heat built in his face, in his chest.

Sorenson noticed. 'Odd. I figured your boss would have told you. I've been told the opening bid is half of what Quantrill would have asked. It's going to gut him, the thief selling Frost at cut rate.'

'But the drug would still get produced, right?'

'If Aldis-Tate acquires the research, Frost would be the top priority for us. I don't know about the others. There's a certain amount of smokescreening to be done, to cover up the research's origins. But if we work directly with Quantrill's team, as opposed to buying it from a murderer and a thief with whom we could never consult on matters of research or testing, Frost could be produced faster.' Sorenson shrugged.

'You want me to make you a deal for Frost.' A year or two of life for Amanda.

'We're willing to pay Mr. Quantrill quite well for Frost. But he cancels his auction, you close down this thief's auction, and we're the exclusive buyer.'

'You're a real humanitarian.'

'Patients will get it sooner. And I prefer not to deal with a murderer like Michael Raymond.'

'How do you know so much about him?'

'Allison identified him as a patient who was helping her

in acquiring the research. I got the impression he was a very dangerous man.'

A patient; it wasn't what Groote had expected to hear about Michael Raymond. 'But your deal's worthless if he's conducting an auction.'

'Mr. Quantrill puts the word out to the other buyers that the research is flawed. The buyers lose interest. The deal is then between us and Mr. Quantrill. Michael Raymond needs to be dead so he doesn't tell the media or the FDA Frost's dirty secrets, but I expect you can drop him. I can help you. I could arrange a meeting. You could show up in my place. Michael Raymond solved.'

Michael on a plate, Jesus, that sounded sweet. 'Let's you and me make a deal of our own, Mr. Sorenson. You want Frost. I want a reputable drug company that will get Frost on the market. I don't want to put my life on the line anymore just to make a bigger profit for Quantrill and Hurley.'

Sorenson kept an amused expression on his face. 'I'm listening.'

'I'm just tossing out an idea. I'll deny it if you take it to Quantrill. But if you help me make sure Michael Raymond can't blow the whistle on the testing here, Aldis-Tate gets Frost. I'll give you the research myself if Quantrill won't play.'

Sorenson smiled. 'You're a bad boy, screwing over your boss, but I like you, Mr. Groote.'

'When Aldis-Tate starts the legitimate testing . . .' Groote lost his voice for a second, coughed his throat clear. 'There is a person I would insist be involved. If you can guarantee she gets Frost, not the placebo, not a damn sugar pill.'

Sorenson nodded. 'I'll consider your proposition and

I'll keep it private. One request, while I'm here. Might I see Nathan Ruiz?'

'Why?'

'Allison was supposed to provide him as an interview subject to our researchers.'

'Forget he attacked you. He was scared.'

'I don't wish him ill. But I'd like to examine a patient who's benefited from Frost.'

'All right. He's upstairs. He ran from us but got roughed up, so he's not the picture of health right now.'

'Let me,' said Sorenson, 'be the judge of that.'

A knock sounded on the door. Groote opened it. The front-desk guard stood there, frowning, leaning close in worry.

'You have another visitor. His name is DeShawn Pitts and says he's a federal marshal, and he won't leave until he speaks to someone in charge.'

The feds. He glanced at Sorenson. 'Wait here for a minute.'

Sorenson stood. 'I don't need the hassle of the feds. I'll leave.'

'Wrong. They'd come in force if they were in arrest mode. This is one guy. Let me find out what he wants and I'll be back in a few.'

Sorenson gave the slightest of nods and Groote closed the door. He knew he was double-flipping on a tightrope, cutting a deal without Quantrill, and now a fed showing up after business hours. He sauntered into the lobby, hand out for a hearty shake, saying, 'Hi, I'm Dennis Groote, ex-FBI, I'm the security director. What can I do for you today?'

TWENTY-SIX

Celeste answered the door, telling herself, *Pretend you're back on the island, playing the game. Get him to open up. You can do it. Find his weakness and play against it.*

'Hello, Ms. Brent,' he said. 'I'm sorry to show up without warning, but I picked up my phone messages while I was close to your home and thought I'd stop by.'

'I appreciate it.' Celeste nodded. 'Come in.'

He stepped into her fortress and Celeste gestured him to the sofa; let the shrink sit on the couch for a change. She settled in a leather chair; she wanted the power position in the room. She put on a blank smile; Celeste Brent had played dumb and helpless while manipulating her fellow players across a sand-strewn chessboard, letting the alpha males thump their chests and strut their way out of the competition, letting the bikini-clad nubiles claw each other, spicing the competition with rumor and innuendo that never caught up with her, rising above the backbiting to win the votes necessary to walk off with five million dollars. She wanted to put a gleam in her eye, show her guts, show her resolve, but not now. She wasn't sure she could play the game, fool this capable man. She forced herself not to look toward the bedroom, where Miles was listening.

'How are you?' he asked.

'Shocked by her death but coping.'

His neutral expression didn't change. 'I'm sure the last thing Allison would want is for your treatment to be adversely affected by this tragedy.'

'Do the police know what happened yet?'

He shook his head. 'It takes time. I suspect a gas leak.' Hurley leaned forward with an air of grave concern that was designed, she decided, to steady her. 'You were one of the last people to see Doctor Vance. We found her appointment schedule on her computer at the hospital. Did you make that appointment, or did she?'

Celeste decided on the truth. 'She stopped by here. On her own.'

'Is that an expectation you have of a therapist – impromptu visits?'

'No. She wanted to check on me.' She decided to put Miles's theory to the test. 'We've been trying a mix of new ideas in my therapy and I seem to be handling the stress of my memories better.'

Naked surprise crossed his thin face and then he blinked and it was gone. 'That's great, Ms. Brent. What was she trying in your therapy?'

'I hate taking pills,' Celeste said, 'but she had me on a new antidepressant before our therapy sessions and the new pills definitely helped.'

'Wonderful. And she came by to monitor your progress with this new medicine?' A chill filled his voice.

'I suppose. She took the pills back from me.'

'Did she say why?'

'She said I didn't need them anymore,' Celeste lied. 'Then we talked, sort of an abbreviated session.'

'Did these pills have a name?'

'She called it some kind of compound, but I don't recall the name.'

He took a deep breath, Celeste guessed, to collect his thoughts. 'This will sound odd, but did she seem nervous, or frightened?'

'Well . . . she wasn't herself.'

'I wonder if she might have asked you for a favor.'

'What kind?'

'This is awkward. To keep information safe for her. Perhaps on a computer disk.'

Celeste forced herself to frown in surprise. 'Why would she?'

'That day Allison removed sensitive data from the hospital.'

'What kind of data?'

'I'd rather not say.'

Celeste let two beats pass. 'I can't see Allison doing anything unethical.'

'Allison might have gotten involved with very bad people – they might have forced her to take the data.'

She lobbed a test at him. 'Then call the police.'

He failed. 'We'd prefer not to—'

'Of course. Hospitals hate scandal. They hate dirty laundry.'

He gave her a frown that suggested he'd underestimated her. 'Sangre de Cristo has nothing to hide, and we've already reported the theft,' he backpedaled.

'If she stole it, what reason would she have to leave it here? I don't think you've thought this through, Doctor Hurley.'

He leaned back from her, pride clearly stung – he was not a good poker player.

'May I call you Celeste? I feel as if I know you from

your TV days.' He dumped sugar in his tone now. 'I must know if she left anything with you. For safekeeping. You're not betraying her trust if you help me.'

'No. She brought nothing but her briefcase.' Celeste kept her voice steady. 'She sat in the same chair you're sitting in and we talked and she left.' Celeste decided to play the trump card, see how he reacted; it would either prove or disprove Miles's theory. 'Wait. I was finishing up a late lunch when she stopped by, and she asked to borrow my computer. She was expecting an important e-mail and wanted to check her account on the Web.'

'Were you with her?'

'I don't stand over people's shoulders while they read their e-mail. She was alone for about five, ten minutes, while I finished eating.'

His face paled, his lips tightened, and he seemed to be steadying himself for an unwelcome task. 'I appreciate your honesty, Celeste. But I suspect I have unwelcome news. Those pills she took back from you. Were they white?'

'Yes.'

'I'm afraid you'll need to come to the hospital with me.'

'No. I'm agoraphobic. I don't leave my house.'

'You were given medications that could have interacted badly with your other meds,' he said. 'We need to get you tested.'

'No.'

'I can sedate you, if you prefer. But I must insist. For your own good.'

'No.'

A shift in his eyes and she was afraid of him, now; he wore the simmering glare of a child unused to refusal. He stood, tented his hands. 'Celeste. This is a medical emergency, and I can compel you to come with me . . .'

'I said no.'

'You can't take care of yourself at home. You're not better, you're worse. Just imagine' – and he took a step toward her – 'you started cutting yourself again, really bad, and just imagine I found you, bleeding, suicidal . . .'

And then the soft click of a gun. Miles stood behind Hurley, Celeste's gun at the doctor's head. 'And just imagine you sit down and start talking.'

Hurley froze.

Miles shoved Hurley back onto the couch. 'Do no harm is supposed to be your motto. It's sure as hell not mine.'

'You're making a mistake,' Hurley said.

'It doesn't feel like a mistake,' Miles said. 'You okay?'

Celeste nodded.

'If you're interested in the white pills,' Miles said, 'I can help you.'

Hurley said, 'I hope we can work out a deal.'

'The deal is you answer my questions, I don't blow your brains out,' Miles said. Celeste got up from the chair, retreated toward the kitchen. 'That's the deal, Doctor Dolittle.'

'You already have Frost, if you're Allison Vance's partner,' Hurley said. 'I'm not sure what else you can negotiate for.'

'Tell me the truth about Frost.' He put the gun close to Hurley's head.

'Medicine to tranquilize those suffering from PTSD. It makes the trauma bearable, so therapy can be more effective.'

Miles glanced at Celeste. 'These white pills, they make you sleepy?'

She shook her head. 'Not sleepy. Calm.'

'Allison had you take one before therapy, right?' Hurley said.

Celeste nodded.

'That's right. It dulls the traumatic memory so that the person can talk about the trauma more easily.' Hurley said.

'But Celeste and Nathan Ruiz didn't know they were being tested.'

Hurley didn't answer and Miles prodded him with the gun. 'No one knows. I didn't know she was giving it to Celeste.'

'Where is Nathan Ruiz?'

'He – he escaped from us. We've had no word from him. I suppose he's hiding. Or dead.' He raised an eyebrow. 'He's dangerous, you know, to himself, to you if he gets a chance.'

'The medicine's not helping him?'

Hurley shrugged.

'Who's the guy who's hunting me?'

'I'll tell you,' Hurley said, 'if you give me Frost. Listen, you want to take down that guy, I'll give you a bonus. He's crazy. No offense.'

'None taken,' Miles said. 'You're trying to tell me he's not on your side.'

Hurley nodded. 'I'll help you so you can get rid of him. I'll set it up. But you give me Frost.' Hurley attempted a smile; an awful, frightened flex. 'He's not going to let you walk. He'll kill you for it.'

'I don't have Frost.'

Hope lit Hurley's eyes. 'Were the files burned up with Allison?'

'I don't know. What's on these files?'

'All the research notes, the chemical formulae, videos of the patients during the testing, everything to prove Frost is effective.' Hurley shook his head. 'If you really don't have Frost, then you played the wrong bluff with him. He's sure you do.'

'Who is he?'

'I don't have a reason to help you now.'

Miles frowned. 'Celeste. Please go into the other room. Close the door. I'll use the silencer. It shouldn't be too bad.' He winked at her.

Her eyes wide, Celeste shook her head. 'Don't kill him. Please. Don't.'

'Have to. He won't tell me what we need to know.'

She shook her head, not understanding his bluff. Then he winked twice again. And she got quiet. 'If you have to.' She hurried into the kitchen.

'You and I are not sitting across from a negotiating table, Doctor,' Miles said. 'I'm sitting with a gun at your head. Now. Answer my questions. Who's hunting me?'

TWENTY-SEVEN

'My name is DeShawn Pitts,' the tall man said, shaking Groote's hand. 'I'm with the U.S. Marshals Service and I need to talk to you regarding a person of interest.'

Groote noticed Pitts wore finger braces on his left hand – two fingers broken – and his bruised face announced he'd been on the losing end of a recent fight.

'Happy to help.'

'Where were you with the Bureau?' Pitts asked.

'Fifteen years in the Los Angeles office.'

'Now you're for hire.'

'The parent company of the hospital retained me.' He realized he was talking too much, but he always did when he was around other feds. Old habits. His colleagues had always made him nervous, hyperaware, as though they could see the shadow he'd become after Cathy died and Amanda got sick. He brought Pitts to Hurley's first-floor office, two doors down from the conference room where Sorenson waited.

'You said you wanted to talk about a person of interest.'

Pitts took a seat. 'Yes, and you'll forgive me if I skimp on details. A person of interest that we're trying to locate – his name is Michael Raymond – received a call on his cell phone from this hospital two days ago. I need to know who tried to call him.'

Groote kept his face impassive but thought, *Oh, hell. When I tried to call MR back again and got no answer.* 'Michael Raymond. The name's not familiar to me.' *Who is this Michael Raymond and why is he screwing everything up for me?* Groote cleared his throat and typed on the computer keyboard in Hurley's office. 'Let me check the visitor logs.' He collected his thoughts while he scanned the log. 'He hasn't visited us. I can e-mail the staff, ask if anyone knows him.'

'Not quite yet. His psychiatrist was Allison Vance. Have you heard about this explosion—'

He's a patient of hers. Nathan was telling the truth. 'Of course. It's a tragedy. And you thought he might seek help from us.'

'He's . . . delusional. He believes that he needs to "right" Doctor Vance's death.'

Groote raised an eyebrow. 'Does he believe he bears responsibility?'

DeShawn Pitts pointed to Doctor Hurley's nameplate on the door. 'Hurley's your psychiatric chief? I think I should wait and discuss this man's mental state with the doctor. You understand.'

'Of course. I didn't mean the question in a medical context but in terms of security. If this man is a danger to the hospital, I want to know what kind of threat he is.'

'I don't think he'd hurt anyone. But if he shows up, I want you to call me immediately, at this number. Detain him if you can.'

'Call you and call the police.'

'No. Just call me. It's critical that I locate him. Without a lot of public fuss.'

Groote raised an eyebrow again. 'I could be of much greater help to you, if I knew exactly who this man was.'

'I'm sorry, I can't go into details.'

Searching for a man but you can't say that you're searching for him. Interesting, Groote thought. *More than interesting. A situation with very few plausible explanations.* 'Is this man wanted by the Marshals Service? Is he a fugitive?'

'As I said, he's a person of interest, and we don't want to make a big production.'

This man knows the truth about my target, Groote realized, and he measured, on an internal scale, the risk of confrontation with Pitts. 'Your boy doesn't believe the fire was caused by a gas leak.'

'No.'

'And this investigation, it's part of his delusion?'

'Possibly. He's suffering from severe post-traumatic stress disorder.'

'You know, it's possible that your guy called Doctor Hurley. Hurley knew Doctor Vance; the psychiatric community here's not that big. Perhaps the call was Hurley returning a call from your guy.' He tapped fingertips against the table, pretended to think. 'Hurley mentioned an odd call the other day.'

'Then I need to speak with Doctor Hurley. You and he could help me bring this guy in.'

Groote seized the opening. 'I'm not in the business of laying traps for people. Legally, I'm in quicksand if Mr. Raymond shows up, I detain him, and call you and you have no just cause.'

Pitts clicked tongue against teeth. 'You said you were ex-FBI.'

'Yes.'

'Why'd you leave?'

'Family tragedy.'

DeShawn said, 'Excuse me, but I need to make a phone call.'

'Certainly. There's a private room next door.' He ushered DeShawn into the room – an interview room, used in consulting with patients.

'Walls are padded,' DeShawn said, a hint of distaste in his voice.

'Yes,' Groote said without comment, and closed the door. 'Hit the door twice when you're done.' Then he hurried back to the computer in Hurley's office, activated the hidden camera in the soft fabric of the wall. Every room had these cameras, ready for use when Hurley needed them. A mike paired to the camera and he snapped a window on the computer open, adjusted the sound.

'Jimmy, I need background on Dennis Groote. Former FBI field agent in Los Angeles,' Pitts said. The mike wasn't powerful enough to pick up the response. DeShawn waited on the phone. Groote already knew the answer would be glowing; his record was clean.

Pitts was asking, first, to ensure that Groote was who he said he was, and second, that – please, God, please – Groote could be trusted.

They want to find him but they don't want the locals to know a manhunt is on. So he's one of their fugitives, but he slipped the leash. Doesn't make sense. A fugitive wouldn't be working at an art gallery, wouldn't be seeing a psychiatrist regularly. No. Michael's not a fugitive. So what is he? A marshal hunts fugitives. But why hunt a fugitive and not let the cops know? Why protect the bad guy that way – protect. The word echoed in Groote's head. *Michael Raymond's not a fugitive – he's a witness.*

'Uh-huh,' Pitts said into the phone. He was now wearing the bored expression of someone getting a record read to him.

Meanwhile inspiration struck Groote. He opened another window feed on the room's camera, jumped back on the digital tape, watched DeShawn hit a speed dial. The number flashed on the phone's screen. Groote scribbled the number down on a Post-it note and slipped it into his pocket. He killed the second window. On the live camera DeShawn Pitts said, 'Uh-huh, okay,' three more times.

Groote picked up the phone and dialed the number. He got routed to another marshal, since DeShawn Pitts was already on Jimmy's line.

'U.S. Marshals Service.'

Groote made his voice a hoarse whisper. 'Jimmy – need Jimmy. Right now. Need help.'

'Who's speaking, please?'

'I'll only talk to Jimmy. Only to a WITSEC inspector. He's got to help me.'

'Hold on, sir,' and Groote clicked off the phone.

A witness. Michael Raymond was a federal witness. One they had lost, one they needed to find. *He's suffering from severe post-traumatic stress disorder. Find him without a lot of publicity.*

A witness who had run. But guys who walked away from the program were on their own. Except this one, who must still be of particular value.

On the camera screen DeShawn Pitts closed his phone. He pounded the flat of his hand against the fabric twice.

Groote went to the door, let Pitts out, led him back into the office.

'Everything okay?'

'Yes. You check out. Outstanding service record. Call Gomez at your old field office, he'll vouch for me and this operation. You won't be at legal risk.'

'Thank you.'

'Could you give me Doctor Hurley's number now? I want to arrange a meeting with him,' Pitts said. 'If you think he'll help.'

'He's very civic-minded,' Groote said. 'I'll call him for you.' He flipped open his own phone. Hurley would soil himself, trying to get Celeste Brent back to the hospital sedated and ready to talk, if a federal agent phoned him.

He dialed Hurley's number, smiling politely.

TWENTY-EIGHT

Hurley coughed, dried his mouth against the back of his wrist. 'The man's name is Dennis Groote. He's from California.'

'Who's he work for?' Miles jabbed the gun harder against Hurley's skull.

'A man named Quantrill.'

'Who's Quantrill?'

'He's my boss.'

'Where do I find him?'

'Santa Monica, California.'

'What's the connection with Sorenson?'

'I don't know any Sorenson.'

'Lying is a bad idea, Doctor. I shot a man. It's easier, I suspect, the second time.'

'Nice of you to share,' Andy said, leaning against the wall. 'Shoot him, Miles, he's useless. Kill again. It won't make you better or worse.'

Miles took his finger off the trigger but dug the barrel of the gun harder into the back of Hurley's head.

The pressure spilled the words faster from Hurley. 'I don't know any Sorenson, I swear to God.'

The cell phone in Hurley's pocket rang, playing a Bach toccata. 'I'm supposed to be checking in. I don't, Groote will come straight here.'

Miles believed him. 'You buy us time. Play dumb. Answer it.'

Hurley gently dug the flip phone from his pocket, opened it. 'Yes, hello?'

Miles kept the gun close on Hurley, knelt so he could hear. 'Doctor Hurley, it's Dennis Groote.'

'I spoke with Celeste Brent. She knows nothing.'

'Understood. There is a gentleman from the federal government in the lobby. He wants to speak to you about a patient of Doctor Vance's. A man named Michael Raymond. I know you're very busy right now . . .'

Miles prodded Hurley with the gun, mouthed, *Tell him no*.

'I can't see anyone,' Hurley said. 'Not now. Tomorrow.'

'I strongly suggest you should make time now, Doctor. This takes precedence. We could be of service to the authorities. They need to find Mr. Raymond.'

Hurley froze. Miles mouthed, *No*, again.

'Tomorrow,' Hurley said. 'Not today. I can't. My hands are full.'

A pause; Miles could hear Groote's frustrated sigh. 'All right. I'll set up a meeting for tomorrow.'

'Tell the officer thank-you for his patience.'

'Understood.'

'I have to go now,' Hurley said. 'Good-bye.'

'Bye.' Groote hung up.

Miles closed the flip phone. Celeste edged back into the room.

'I know you won't want to, Celeste, but you need to leave,' Miles said.

'Isn't that for me to decide?' she said quietly.

'These people are dangerous, you can't stay.'

'But I don't know anything. I don't have what they want.'

178

'Allison stole computer files, then used your computer. There has to be a reason. Might be she thought they were monitoring her system. But they're not going to leave you alone until they find out if you have Frost.'

Celeste sank into a chair.

'Your friend you mentioned. Could you call her, have her come pick you up?'

'And put her in danger? No. This is a matter for the police . . .'

'I have to do this, make it right for Allison . . . I promised her . . .'

Celeste stood up. 'Say she took the research and hid it on my computer. Or sent it to someone else, or to herself, in case she got caught. Or killed. There will be an electronic trace.'

'Up,' Miles ordered Hurley, jabbing the gun into his back. 'Celeste, please show me your computer.'

The two men followed Celeste down the hall. Pictures covered the walls: Celeste and a handsome young man on the beach, on a patio clicking margarita glasses together, Celeste giving the man a kiss on the cheek. And on the other side were a montage of photos, he guessed, from her brief television career: she and nine other people standing on a beach, her in a modest lime-green bikini, looking alternately pensive; crafty; overjoyed; chopping palm wood, hauling herself over a stone barrier. Holding a check for five million dollars, a dazzling smile as bright as summer.

He and Hurley followed Celeste into her study; her computer, a new, high-end number, sat on a maple table in the corner. The room smelled of cleanser and Celeste's tangerine shampoo, and Miles wondered if she washed her hair a lot, if she scrubbed her skin till it ached.

Cleansing herself of guilt. It had not occurred to him; Andy's blood seemed as permanent as a tattoo on his hands. The faint odor of antiseptic hung in the air like a woman's perfume.

Celeste sat at the computer and started to type.

'I want you to know I had nothing to do with Allison's death. Neither did Groote,' Hurley said.

'What about Sorenson? He planted a bomb there.'

Celeste paled. 'How do you know?'

'I'll explain later.' He put the gun back on Hurley. 'While she hunts, you tell me about Quantrill.'

'There are consultants – off the payrolls – who find promising research for the drug companies to develop further. Quantrill is one.'

'How long have you worked on Frost?'

'A year. The refinements to Frost are my ideas, you know, you're stealing *my* ideas.'

'I don't think she used an e-mail program,' Celeste said. 'She erased the browser's history file. Possibly she used an FTP program.'

'FTP?' Hurley asked.

'File Transfer Protocol. A kind of program used to upload files from one system to another. People use them all the time in building Web sites, moving the Web site's files from their computer to the host system. I've got one . . .' Celeste opened a folder. 'Here. Every upload creates a log entry. It'll list any files uploaded to another system from this computer.' Silence while Celeste hunted. 'She did use it. Here's a whole series of files uploaded to a remote Web server. Here's the address.' She hit a keyboard command; the printer spooled out the log for her.

'We need to find who has that IP address.'

Celeste went back to typing, querying the server's URL against an Internet database. 'It's registered to a Mercury Mountain Hosting, but there's no information as to where the server's located.'

'I know how to trace the server but I need additional software,' Miles said. 'You know Mercury Mountain, Doctor?'

'No. I've never heard of the company. But I'll make you a deal. We contact them, we get Frost back. Together. I'll get Groote off your ass; one word from me to Quantrill and he leaves you alone. You stay silent, you get the drug first. You get your heads straight. Forever.'

Miles jabbed him with the gun. 'I'm not shutting up.'

Hurley gave him the glare of a man emptied of patience. 'You aren't very smart at playing hero. You don't want to go there, not the two of you, not two fucked-up messes who can't talk without waving a gun in a face or don't dare step outside because your fear cripples you.' He practically spat his words at Celeste. 'I can give you your lives back. Free of the nightmares, free of the trauma. All we need is your silence.'

Miles thought of Sorenson's strange promise, echoing in his head: *What if you could forget the worst moment of your life?*

Hurley said, 'Celeste, I'm sorry I frightened you. But Frost could cure you. Isn't that what you want?'

Miles stepped back from him. 'Celeste. Is there any copy of what she uploaded to this remote server still on your system?'

'I'm searching the hard drive, but, no, not so far.'

'I don't want the good doctor to see anything else we find.'

'Okay.' Her voice was steady and she took her hands

off the keyboard. 'You say you won't be silent. Are you going to kill him?'

'No,' he said, then he added a lie: 'But I won't let him hurt us either.'

Hurley said, 'You're making a grave mistake, Michael . . .'

Surprise spread across Celeste's face. 'You said your name was Miles.'

'It is. He thinks it's Michael. Long story.'

'He's lied to you, Celeste. His name's Michael and there's a federal cop at the hospital asking for him,' Hurley said. 'You can't trust him. I've only tried to help you, to protect you . . .'

'How did you know my name?' Miles said. He thought back to Hurley's arrival – he had never spoken his fake name, or his real name, and neither had Celeste. Realization hit; Hurley had lied. 'You do have Nathan.'

'Yes.'

The fed wanting to talk to Hurley about Michael Raymond – why? What had Groote said? *We could be of service to the authorities.* What did that mean? One thing – setting a trap for Miles, one designed by the feds and executed by Groote. And Hurley had put Groote off for no real reason, and knowing how badly Hurley and Groote wanted Miles, Groote would be suspicious . . .

'Celeste!' he hollered. 'We got to go! We have to leave. Groote could be heading here right now.' So could the feds, but he didn't say that – she would argue to stay, and he couldn't leave her alone.

Celeste shook her head. 'No. I can't.'

'We have to go, now!'

She shook her head; her hands began to tremble. 'No, no, I can't, I can't leave . . .'

'I'll take you to my friend DeShawn,' he said. He got up and moved past Hurley. Screw this, he'd give himself up to WITSEC, he couldn't see her trembling and broken and hurt. They knew enough for the police to expose Allison's killers and this medical research she'd died to stop, he was crazy to think he could set the world back to rights for the lost Allison, for himself, for anyone.

A needle slid into his neck.

He wrenched his head away from Hurley. Miles tumbled over a chair, grabbed at his throat, fumbled fingers over the syringe, pulled it free from his flesh.

He fell back in the chair. Miles screamed as Hurley's thumbs gouged into his eyes with calm, surgical precision. He tried to kick away from the doctor but Hurley dug a nail into the soft corner of Miles's eyes, intent on popping the orbs from his skull. He tried to aim the gun past the agony in his face and one hand went from his eyes, seized the gun from his hand. Miles closed his hands around Hurley's wrists, lifted, and pushed. The barrel pressed against his lips in a cold kiss, as he heard Celeste screaming. Then the barrel jerked away from his mouth.

Miles pulled his knees between himself and Hurley with a mighty effort, kicked back, tore his face free of Hurley's claws. He couldn't see, his eyes blinded in pain, his head loose and light as a stringless balloon. Then the gun boomed, Celeste screamed, then sudden silence.

TWENTY-NINE

Groote didn't like the conversation with Hurley. Not a bit. It made no sense, passing up an opportunity to help find Raymond . . .

Raymond. Maybe Raymond was there, with Hurley. At Celeste's house. But how would he know about Celeste?

Because Allison had told him. Jesus, he had been in it with Allison.

He called Hurley's cell phone again. It rang. And rang. No answer.

Their plan was off the rails, and, crap, Groote had Sorenson in one office, this fed in the other, caught between them. Hurley would have to fend on his own for a few minutes.

Groote gave DeShawn Pitts a shrug. 'I'm sorry. You know doctors. They always leave you waiting. Doctor Hurley's dealing with a suicidal patient – he may not be available until tomorrow.'

'Then I'll check back with him in the morning.'

Groote walked the officer out with hearty handshakes and then stood at the window. Pitts's car remained in the lot; the officer sitting behind the driver's wheel, talking on his phone.

Just hurry up and go. Please. Finally Pitts drove away.

He tried Hurley's cell phone again. No answer. He went back to the conference room. Sorenson sat there, drinking coffee. 'Where's your fed?' Sorenson asked.

'Gone.'

'Why the visit?'

'It's nothing to concern you.'

'I still want to see Ruiz.'

'I have some other very pressing business to attend to, right now.'

'Our deal's based on me seeing Ruiz,' Sorenson said. 'I've helped you. You help me. It won't take but a few minutes.'

Groote decided. 'But let's make it quick. Follow me.'

THIRTY

'Brian?'

Miles curled on the floor, focus blinking back into his eyes. Pain speared his head and the voice was hardly above a whisper. He raised his head from the tile.

Scuffed leather soles lay inches away from his face. He blinked again, past the salt of the tears, jerked to his feet, forcing his eyes to stay open.

Hurley lay sprawled on the floor, throat an open wound, breath a gurgle. The sounds of the gunshot echoed in his bones, made him want to close his eyes, surged bile into the back of his throat – but Celeste was more important than his fear. Celeste lay crumpled before him, the gun in her hands. He spoke, and his tongue weighed like lead in his mouth. 'It's all right, Celeste. Give me the gun.'

'Brian, he won't hurt you, he won't hurt you anymore, I promise, I promise, I promise,' Celeste said. Miles crawled to Hurley, fumbled at the man's wrist. The pulse faded, then stopped.

'Brian. We're safe, all right, we're safe from him, I never should have let him in the house . . .' Celeste's voice, down to a trickle.

Miles lurched away from her, away from the dead man.

Leaned over the sink, threw cold water in his face. He tasted blood in his mouth and thought, *If he tore out my eye there would be more pain, right, or would I just be in shock?* His fingers probed at his face. Blood oozed in the skin between his eyes and the bridge of his nose. He rinsed it away. He managed to open his eyes, inspected his face in the mirror of a hutch that sat in the breakfast nook. His eyes were bloodied but both whole.

'Brian?' Now Celeste's voice rose again. She flinched at him as he came out of the kitchen, mopping at his face with a dish towel, holding out his hand.

'Celeste. I'm not Brian. I'm Miles. Remember? Miles.' He knelt by her and held out his hand. 'Give me the gun.'

She crawled away from the dead man. 'You're not Brian.'

'No. I'm Miles.'

'I . . . my house . . . my husband . . .'

'It's okay, Celeste. Let me help you. It's now. Not then.'

Celeste stopped shivering, nodded, put her face in her hands. 'He came into my house,' she said. 'He came into my house and he killed Brian. He made me wait with him, waiting for Brian to come home so he could kill him in – in front of me.' Her voice was low and guttural, as though it belonged to a shadow, not a person.

'I'm so sorry.'

She gestured at Hurley's body. 'I got the gun . . . to make him stop. Just to stop. But I really killed him.'

Miles picked up the syringe. Hurley must have had the injection in his lab coat – a perfectly good place to hide one. Probably to sedate Celeste, bring her to the hospital for . . . he didn't want to think. Hurley hadn't gotten the whole dose in him but enough to make him numb and sick and to clog his head.

'Celeste. Listen.' His voice sounded thick in the air. 'The man who hurt you, who killed your husband, he's not here. Hurley was trying to kill me, you saved me, do you understand?' He forced himself to speak slowly and calmly.

Now she nodded.

'Will you give me the gun?'

She clutched the gun close to her T-shirt. 'Never again, I swore. The cameras. The locks. Never again. Fort Celeste. I made this place Fort Celeste.' She wasn't listening to him.

'We can't stay here. Groote could be on his way. We have to go. Now.'

Celeste's voice started to break. 'I have a dead man on my floor. I want him . . . gone. I want you gone and my home back.'

'I know you do. But here you're a sitting target. Please, give me the gun.'

She handed him the pistol. Along her arms a web of paper-thin scars scrolled toward the elbows.

She saw him notice. 'I don't cut myself anymore,' she said. 'I'm better.'

'That's great, Celeste, that's wonderful.' He tucked the gun in the back of his pants, tried to think through the sedative haze.

'What are you going to do now?' she asked.

'I'm going to get you safe, and then I'm going to get Nathan Ruiz out of that hospital.'

'How?'

He went and searched in Hurley's pocket, found an electronic passkey, a set of regular keys. 'Walk in and take him.'

'Who is he to you?'

'The key to finding out the truth; but they still have him locked up.'

'But this Groote's at the hospital.'

'Not necessarily. He's out hunting for me. With the key and a gun I can walk in, get Nathan out.'

'That's absolutely crazy,' she said. She shook her head. 'And I can't leave the house.' She spoke as though he'd just informed her the world was flat.

'You were brave enough to help me. You're brave enough to walk through a door. It's just a door. Walk the hell out of it.'

'I can't . . .'

'I'll hold your hand,' Miles said. 'You can sit on the floor of the car, keep your eyes closed, stay away from the windows. Pretend the world's not there.' He closed his hand around hers. 'He will come here, he'll kill you.'

She crawled to her purse, dug out a bottle of antidepressants, swallowed one dry. 'I'll try.'

He slowly got to his feet, bringing her to her feet as well. She stepped around Hurley's body with a choked moan.

'Don't trust him, lady,' Andy called from the corner. 'Bad idea.'

Miles shot Andy the finger behind Celeste's back and opened the door for her. He leaned out, scanned the street first. Empty. 'It's okay.'

Celeste cringed at the world beyond the open door.

'There's my car.' He had found a set of spare keys and driven Blaine's car to Celeste's home. 'Forty steps. I'll walk with you, I'll count.'

'Just hold my hand,' she said, and she closed her eyes, and made the first step.

The spring breeze rustled in the cottonwoods. Ten

steps. She moaned. He kept his eyes fixed on the street, expecting a car to speed toward them and screech to a stop, carrying Groote, carrying death.

'You're doing great,' he said.

'Don't talk to me . . . like I'm a toddler . . . learning how to ride a freaking bike.' She started breathing in panicked hitches and he steadied his arm across her shoulders.

Twenty steps. The wind danced across her face and she flinched.

'You've done this before,' he tried, as a joke, not knowing what the hell else to say. Celeste kept her eyes clenched shut. 'Been outside.'

'I used to love the outdoors. Brian and I . . .' and she swayed on her feet.

'I've got you.'

She took another step. And another. Celeste made a low moan in her throat and walked faster, stumbling, her eyes clenched shut, and Miles guided her to Blaine's car. He had left it unlocked and she stretched out on the backseat. She folded her arms over her eyes.

He gritted his teeth and slid the key into the car's ignition. If she could get out of the house, he could drive the car again. At least the sedative shot made him less panicky; he just hoped he didn't drive the car into the ditch.

He started the car. No boom. He steered out onto the mud road.

'Where will you take me?' she asked.

'A friend's house . . . well, he doesn't know I'm hiding there. He's out of town for a couple of days.'

'Go to the hospital,' she said. 'I'll wait in the car. Now. For Allison's sake.'

He floored the accelerator, testing his reaction. The haze from the drug seemed to fade, overwhelmed by fear and adrenaline. He wheeled left onto the first street he passed, heading back toward the hilly rise leading to the hospital, praying that Groote was hunting him in the night, far away from Sangriaville.

THIRTY-ONE

Miles drove past a set of quiet homes, past empty lots, past the Sangre de Cristo Hospital, to Canyon Road's dead end: an Audubon Society complex. He U-turned at the Audubon gate and headed back down the road toward the hospital. He went past the clinic, giving it a curious scouting, wondering if eyes in the building were watching him. There was no security that suggested this facility housed anyone dangerous – no wire, only a high adobe-wall enclosure, no guard posted.

'Waiting for that next chess move,' Andy said. 'Show me the brilliance.'

He wanted to tell Andy to shut up, but he didn't want Celeste to hear him. He U-turned again, wheeled Blaine's car into the hospital's parking lot, parked near the back.

'How will you find him inside?' she asked.

'Nathan mentioned the top floor when I saw him at Allison's,' he said. 'So I'm going straight to the top. Can you drive?'

'Oh, sure,' she said. 'Driving's easy compared with shooting.'

'If you're approached – security guards, anyone – run. Go straight to the police, or a friend's house. Don't wait for me.'

'Miles,' she said, 'if Allison's giving me Frost, I think it works. I should be in a fetal position right now. I killed a man. I left the house. But I'm coping.' Nevertheless her voice shook and she swallowed, struggling to steady it. 'Maybe it's Frost. Hurley acted surprised when I told him she'd given me new pills.'

'Or you're just strong,' he said. She blinked at him. 'I'll be back as quickly as I can. Can you bear to sit in the front, keep the engine running?'

She nodded. She climbed over the seat, squirmed low in the passenger seat.

'I should get out more often,' she said. Trying to joke. She shivered.

'I'll be back in a minute,' he said. 'Run if you have to.'

She nodded.

'Celeste?'

She raised her eyes to his.

'Thank you. You saved us both.'

She swallowed. 'Go. Leave me your cell phone. If I have to drive off . . . call me, I'll come back for you.'

He shut the door, waited for her to click the locks, and headed toward the hospital's rear parking-lot entrance.

Every step made him want to run in the opposite direction. A mental hospital. The place he'd feared the most as his mind started to play tricks on him, as Andy began to chime into his days and nights. The place he was afraid Allison would send him. He kept walking toward the building.

If he could drive, he told himself, he could do this. Just walls, just floors, just people, it wasn't a horror.

'Introduce me to the guard,' Andy said. 'That'll get you in real fast.'

The main building was large, with an adobe exterior,

193

four stories tall. Two smaller buildings stood behind it, a gravel trail of roads snaking between them and the main house. It had the air of an exclusive club more than the clinical lines of a psych hospital.

He guessed there were cameras on him right now; surely they showed who came and went in the parking lot. He ducked his head down. Most of the main building's windows were darkened; lights gleamed in the windows on the first floor.

He held the electronic passkey up to the reader on the door; the panel light flicked from red to green and the door unbolted with a click. He stepped inside.

At the end of this short hallway was a door with a conventional lock, and he tried the three keys on Hurley's ring. The last one worked.

He expected to see a guard with a gun aimed at him when he opened the door.

Miles cracked the lock, went through the door, and closed it behind him. The hallway was empty, the lights dimmed. He took three deep breaths, trying to clear his head of Hurley's junk.

Late night in the hospital. His heart hammered in his chest. He pulled out his gun, stiff-armed it in front of him, watched the steady red light of a mounted camera eyeing him down the hallway. Despite the Sangre de Cristo's elegant architecture and immaculate grounds, he wondered if every asylum wasn't designed by the same cracked architect, immured behind bars deep inside one of his own creations. Locks at the end of every hallway, bends and twists to confuse anyone who might risk a run, light that had never been born of the sun – hard and white and ugly.

He turned a corner and a guard was waiting for him, ready, a baton swinging hard at Miles's neck. Miles jumped back – the baton smacked with bone-crushing force into the wall. The backswing caught his shoulder and agony burst up from the well of nerves at the joint. Miles fell to the floor and the guard – young, with heavy features – rammed the baton hard against his throat.

Miles closed hands around the baton's ends, tried to push back. The guard grinned and gritted teeth and shoved the baton, bolstered by his own weight, against Miles's windpipe.

Darkness danced on the edge of Miles's vision. But then Miles thought of staying inside this place, the doors closing and locking behind him, faceless men strapping him to a bed, confinement as sure as a coffin. Here. Forever. Locked up.

Fear surged in his muscles and Miles shoved back, using the floor as leverage for his shoulders and arms. The baton popped hard into the guard's mouth, then Miles hit him again in the nose. The guard reeled away from Miles. Gasping, Miles fought him for the baton. The guard wouldn't let go, made a choking yell for Jimmy and Dwayne past the blood coursing from his mouth and nose. Miles powered the guard's head into the wall, bit the fingers holding the baton. The guard let go; Miles dropped him with a blow on the back of the head. The guard collapsed to the floor, unconscious.

Miles glanced up and down the hallway. Deserted. He guessed these were offices and administration; no patients or caretakers here. A crackle and a buzz cut through the sudden silence, a voice calling for Robert. He leaned over the guard. An earpiece gleamed in the young guard's ear, cabled to a walkie-talkie clipped to the shirt pocket. Miles removed the earpiece and walkie-talkie and clipped them on himself.

'Robert? You got him?'

Miles thumbed the button and spoke in a whispery rush that might camouflage his voice. 'No, he broke free from me. Headed to the elevator.' He found the elevator, its doors open, pressed four – the top floor. Nothing. Four must be a secured floor. He waved the electronic passkey over a panel above the buttons and a green light lit. He tried again, pressing four, and this time the button glowed in answer. Then he stepped out of the elevator. The doors slid shut and the elevator started its climb.

'Robert?' the other guard's voice repeated through the earpiece.

'I think he's headed to four on the elevator.' The diversion might leave the fourth floor stairwell clear for him.

He headed for an EXIT sign, found the stairwell. Stairs were good, elevators were bad. The well was dimly lit. He headed up the stairs, expecting to see Groote on the landing or a guard who hadn't bought his story . . . but there was no one. Radio silence from the guards.

Sweat slid down his cheek, coursed down his back. He forced himself to take each step.

Andy stood at each turn of the stairs, smirking.

Miles's breath tightened in his chest. He reached the top floor.

Tried the door. Locked. He slid a key home, worked the lock. The door opened.

'Hello, Nathan,' Sorenson said.

Nathan opened his eyes. Tried to focus. 'Who . . .'

'My name is Sorenson. I'm a colleague of Doctor Vance. We met, oh, so very briefly, at Doctor Vance's house.'

Nathan said nothing.

'You hit me. It's okay. I don't think you realized I was there to help you. I'd like to talk to you for a minute.'

Sorenson took a step into the room. Groote followed him, a step behind.

'Are you better, Nathan, than you were when you first came to Sangriaville?'

Nathan nodded, glancing at Groote.

'That's wonderful to know,' Sorenson said, and in one brutal move he grabbed Groote's arm, wrenched it up while slamming Groote into the steel door. Groote yelled and Sorenson deftly twisted his arm. Groote screamed. Sorenson pounded his elbow twice into Groote's face, breaking the nose, hammering the back of his head into the steel door.

Groote collapsed to the floor. Sorenson kicked him once in the ribs, then in the jaw. Groote went still. Sorenson leaned down, seized Groote's gun, and raised it at Nathan. 'What have you told them?'

'I don't know what you mean . . . I don't know anything!'

'Ten seconds to rethink,' Sorenson said. 'What names did you give them?'

'I don't know what you mean, please don't!' Nathan yelled.

The soft buzz nearly made Miles jump out of his skin. Then he realized the stairwell door was set to give off a ping when opened. He closed the door quickly, aware he was without cover. But no one stood in the darkened hallway. No guards at the elevator, awaiting him. The lift had already arrived and the doors closed again and he saw on the digital indicator the elevator had returned to the first floor. Probably set to do so automatically. Maybe the guards on the floor had seen the empty elevator and ridden down to help the battered Robert.

He moved from the door, close against the wall, crouching low. He inched down the hallway, glancing through the wire-reinforced glass in the doors. Beds, with men asleep in them, mostly younger guys but a scattering of men in their fifties and sixties. None was Nathan Ruiz. Miles tested the doors; all locked in for the night. Or perhaps to keep the patients out of the line of fire when the guards stepped out and mowed him down. Two rooms held women, also asleep. An office with a computer and a set of cameras, empty, the screens showing more deserted rooms.

He heard a soft, choked cry from behind a metal door. It read VIRTUAL REALITY TREATMENT on the plate. He pushed the door. Locked. He tried Hurley's passkey and the door clicked open.

He started to push and a technician was at the door, reaching for the knob, the other hand pulling a headset off his ears, eyes widening in surprise as he saw Miles. Miles hit him a solid punch in the jaw, then another; the guy folded. Miles eased him to the floor, his hand stinging, glancing over his shoulder, sure someone had heard. He shut the door.

He stepped into a darkened control room, with a heavy pane of tinted glass. Beyond the glass a man floated, suspended in midair on white cables, jerking slightly, his eyes covered by a heavy, awkward visor, his ears hidden under sleek silver headphones.

On the screen a computer game played out – with sharp angles, with television-false colors, with a muted soundtrack of soldiers moving through narrow alleys and broad, dusty streets. He peered at the picture: men moving at night into an abandoned building, fake stars in a vault of sky above them, lights dimmed. Then bursts of light, the world gone in flame and dust, soldiers running and fighting, the blasts of rocket-propelled grenades painting the sky.

The man jerked on his tethers, a frown setting on his face, a cry erupting from his throat. The man wasn't Nathan: too short, too blocky.

War, Miles thought, *but not a game. What the hell was this place?*

He stepped backward and the cord closed over his neck.

The pressure was sudden and strong. Miles tried to work his fingers under the cable to give himself breath and couldn't. The technician twisted the cable tighter, using his weight to force Miles to stumble.

Black dots shimmered in the air before him; Miles drove his foot hard on the technician's instep and heard a howl of pain. He tried to lurch free of the cable's grip, kicked at the desk, hit a keyboard and a mouse as he struggled, trying to wrench the choking cord from the technician's hands. His injured shoulder throbbed as he fought for leverage.

The blank monitors above him blinked to life. Paused computer-generated tragedies began to play, similar to the war scene playing on the main monitor. A crashing car cartwheeling across an interstate, slamming into a big rig. A plane flying into the World Trade Center. A school bus erupting into flame.

Miles spun and jerked hard to one side, pulled the technician off balance. The technician lost his grip; Miles felt sweaty hands abandon the cord and grab at his neck. Miles kicked back hard, slammed the technician into the wall of screens. Miles threw back his head in a vicious ram, connecting with the technician's face. Glass shattered and the tech cried out in pain. The gripping hands around his throat eased and he jerked free. He dropped to his knees, grabbed the police baton he'd dropped when he'd tried to free himself from the cord. He swung the baton up and buried it into the tech's stomach. The technician collapsed and Miles carefully dealt him an extra blow on the back of the head. He steadied his breath, stepped away from the monitors and their looping horrors, bile climbing into his throat, a chill kissing his skin.

He tucked the walkie-talkie's earpiece back into place and heard the guards talking, searching the first floor, finding the unconscious Robert in a hallway. They'd be back here in a minute. He had to find Nathan Ruiz and get out, or they'd have him locked in here forever, hooked up to that machine, reliving his private hells. Horrible.

Miles stepped back into the hall, closed the door, then heard the brief, brutal sounds of a fight. The clang of a body striking metal. Then a scream: 'Please don't!'

He ran, the door was partly open and in the thin shaft of light he saw a man sprawled on the floor, another man standing, his back to Miles.

Miles opened the door.

Sorenson. With a gun. He started to pivot to fire and Miles tackled him, piledriving them both into the wall. Miles grabbed Sorenson's arm, slammed it hard once, twice, three times against the wall, trying to break Sorenson's grip on the gun.

He saw Nathan Ruiz with one arm handcuffed to a bed, trying to move out of the aim of the wavering gun. Miles fought street-dirty: he drove a knee into Sorenson's groin, leaned down, and bit hard on the bridge of

Sorenson's nose. Sorenson screamed again and clubbed Miles with the gun.

They toppled onto the bed. Nathan pounded Sorenson's head with his unbound fist; Miles wrenched the gun free from Sorenson's grip.

'Kill him!' Nathan yelled.

Miles put the gun on Sorenson's forehead. 'Who are you?'

Sorenson didn't speak.

'Who. Are. You.'

'I've read all about you, Miles,' Sorenson said. 'And I don't think you can shoot in cold blood. Not again.'

He knew his real name. Miles dragged Sorenson off the mattress and cracked Sorenson's head once against the tile floor. 'How do you know my name? Who the hell are you?'

'Your only hope of staying alive,' Sorenson said.

'Bullshit. You killed Allison. You put the bomb in her office. I saw you.'

'I didn't kill her. I can explain. But not here. This is Quantrill's turf.'

'I know what I saw.'

'You see a lot of things, Miles. You see Andy.' Sorenson grinned past the blood in his teeth. 'You don't need to fight this war, not alone. Let me help you.'

Andy. He knew about Andy. 'Who the hell are you?' he screamed.

Sorenson jerked a thumb at Nathan. 'Ask Mr. Explosives about who really planted the bomb.'

Nathan shook his head in horror. 'No . . . he's lying. I never hurt her . . .' He fell to the floor, still handcuffed by one arm, and closed his free hand around Sorenson's throat, tightened the grip. 'You're lying!'

201

Miles heard running in the hallway. He ran to the door, saw two guards approaching. He fired, high, and the bullet creased the ceiling, shattered a light, and the guards fell back to the elevator.

He heard the gasps of strangulation behind him; Nathan and Sorenson gripped each other's throat, Sorenson gaining leverage and Nathan's face purpling. Miles yanked Sorenson free from Nathan but kept his throat in a grip.

'Move and I'll shoot you.' Sorenson went still.

'Pull the cuff tight,' Miles ordered Nathan.

Nathan obeyed and Miles aimed the gun on the narrow length of chain, fired. The link shattered and Nathan ran for the door. He started kicking the unconscious Groote.

Miles hauled Sorenson to his feet, pushed him against the wall. 'Last chance,' Miles said. 'Who do you work for?'

'I can give you everything you want, Miles, everything you need. I'm not your enemy. Come with me and I can prove it.'

'Kill him,' Andy purred in his ear.

'I don't believe you.' Miles smashed the gun across Sorenson's face, threw him into the wall. The man collapsed, eyes rolling into whites.

Miles grabbed Nathan. 'Did you hurt Allison?'

Nathan shook his head. 'I didn't. I swear, I didn't. If I had I would have killed you when you stepped into her house. Who you gonna believe?'

Miles chose. 'I believe you.'

He heard the sliding hiss of the elevator doors. The guards. Trying again. The adrenaline surge was still high, warring with the pain the guard and the tech had dealt him, with the sedative Hurley had dumped into him. He fought down panic. 'How many guards?'

'Two or three. Most of the staff isn't allowed on this floor.'

Of course; the fewer eyes to see, the easier to illegally test drugs. And if there were only three, he'd already downed one. But two were still too many.

He risked a glance down the hall, barely putting his head into a possible line of fire, easing the gun out with him. A guard stood, five feet away, pistol out, leveled at Miles's head.

Miles ducked back as the bullet hammered into the door frame.

'Throw your guns down!' Miles yelled. 'Or I kill Groote and Sorenson!'

Silence for a moment.

'Slide the guns down the hall! Now! They got ten seconds . . . Ten. Nine. Eight.' He wondered what the hell he would do if they called his bluff.

A gun slid along the tile, stopped in front of him.

'Both of them!'

Another gun joined the first.

Hope they only had the two, Miles thought. He stuck his head out again; two guards stood in the dimmed hallway, murder in their eyes. Miles stepped out, collected the guns, flicked on the safeties, crowded them into the back of his pants.

'Come on, Nathan,' he said quietly. He kept his gun leveled at the guards. Nathan stepped out into the hallway. In his hands he held the police baton Miles had stolen.

'You're not going to get out, dumb-shit,' one guard said. 'We're in lockdown.'

'Then you're going to come with me and unlockdown it,' Miles said.

'I can't.'

'You'll damn well figure it out.' Miles grabbed the guard's arm, pushed him along.

'Mister, please, I got kids,' the guard said.

'Shut up.'

Nathan stepped past them and cracked the baton into the second guard's stomach. He bent double, vomited, moaned.

'They hurt me,' Nathan said in a distant whisper. 'Hurt me, hurt me . . .'

'We didn't,' the first guard said. 'Groote did. Not us. Okay? Not us.'

Miles could hear patients yelling and hitting fists against their doors, roused by the ruckus, screaming questions. Miles handed Nathan the passkey and Nathan bolted ahead, opening the stairwell door.

Miles hurried the guard past the doors and down the stairs at a run. 'Are the other patients in immediate danger?'

'I don't think so.' Nathan dashed ahead of him, leaping five stairs at a time.

'Get behind me,' Miles yelled, but the younger man paid him no heed, recklessly barreling down the four flights of stairs, Miles half sliding down the metal railings to keep up. The haze from Hurley's dope burned away; his fear fueled him but he didn't know how long the energy would last.

They hit the parking-lot exit door at the bottom of the stairwell. The passkey no longer worked. Locked. Trapped. Miles thought his heart would burst through his skin.

Sorenson shook off the pain and the dizziness and stepped out in the hallway. He saw the guard, still retching from the blow to his stomach.

He tightened his grip on his gun. He could kill the guard, kill Groote, but he didn't want to waste a moment or a bullet.

'Which way?' he asked the guard.

The hurt guard stopped heaving his guts long enough to point at the stairwell. Then he handed Sorenson an electronic key. 'It'll . . . override . . . locks.'

Sorenson grabbed the passkey and ran.

'How do we open the doors?' Miles yelled into the guard's face.

'Control panel – lobby.'

Miles shoved the guard through the hallway exit from the stairwell, all of them running, and as they rounded a corner into another hallway leading to the lobby, he glanced back and saw the stairwell door opening, then Sorenson in the dim light. Miles shoved Nathan and the guard forward and a bullet screamed from the doorway, hot as a devil's finger as it rocketed past the nape of his neck. He dived for the cover of the corner as a second bullet pocked the wall an inch above where his head had been.

The guard broke into a run for the lobby door. Nathan launched himself into the guard with all the grace of a zombie, a screaming, raving fury. They fell to the ground and Miles pulled Nathan off the man, shoved them both toward the door, keeping the gun trained on the corner.

'You unlock the doors!' Nathan screeched at the man, waggled his tongue and his fingers as though all sanity had abandoned him. 'Or I will kill kill kill you!'

The guard's face paled.

They ran into the lobby; Nathan shoved the guard to the computer. He, with trembling hands, entered in a key.

Miles heard the locks click.

Miles shoved the guard to the floor, told him to lie flat and be still. The guard obeyed. *Please, Jesus, let us out, be open*. His fear was like a fire on his skin. They hit the doors, stumbled into the brisk cool of the dark night, ran hard toward the parking lot.

Sorenson advanced carefully to the lobby, listened, heard only the rattle of breathing of the frightened guard. He stepped into the lobby.

'Front door,' the guard said. 'They went through the front door. There ought to be another gun in this drawer . . .'

Sorenson ran past the man, tested the door, decided they wouldn't be waiting on the other side to ambush him and ran after them. He saw them fleeing in the low gleam of the lights and ran as silently as he could, his pistol stiff-armed in front of him, keeping Nathan Ruiz's head in his sights.

'This way.' Miles pointed to the rear of the parking lot, and they weaved along, hunkering low.

Behind them an alarm shattered the quiet. 'You got a car?'

'Yes. We've got to be gone before the cops get here . . .'

'They won't call the cops,' Nathan said. 'Trust me . . .'

A bullet's whine pierced the air and Nathan fell, frantic, a scream choked in his throat. Miles whirled and saw Sorenson two rows of cars away, aim pivoting toward him. Miles fired in answer and Sorenson dropped.

But not like he was hit.

The parking lot was a maze of cars, some slots filled, others empty. Miles grabbed Nathan, who probed at his hair, at his scalp, for evidence of a hit, and shoved him below the line of car windows.

'I'm okay,' Nathan mumbled.

'Stay low.'

They worked their way through the cars, Miles panicking that Sorenson could simply step out into the row at the same time that they did and pick them both off. If Sorenson was close enough he'd hear them run into the parking aisle's open space, kill them with two rapid-fire shots.

And if Celeste saw them coming, if she stood next to the car . . . Sorenson could gun her down.

He put a hand over Nathan's mouth. Listened to the silence. The night's quiet fell on them. He fought back the surge of fear.

I can't let Sorenson just kill this kid. He forced himself to wait, to listen past the drumming of his own heart.

Eleven seconds later, he heard a scrabble of stone against a shoe, two cars to his right.

Miles dropped to the pavement, fired under the cars into the blackness. He heard a yell of fury, a body leaping onto a car in retreat.

Miles shoved Nathan and they ran. Miles turned and fired; he saw Sorenson drop off the trunk of a car, either hit or diving for cover. Miles stumbled but Nathan caught him, pulled him up to his feet.

Miles spotted Blaine's car.

In the low dazzle of the lot's lights, the car stood empty. Celeste was gone.

'Celeste!' he screamed. 'Celeste?'

The trunk opened. She peered out at him.

'What the hell?' he yelled.

'It's nicer in here,' she whispered.

'Out, now, now, now, we got to go.' And the crack of a bullet broke above him, demolishing a window in the car parked next to them. He whirled, saw dark figures – Sorenson and two guards – approaching. A blaze of fire from the barrel of two guns, bullets pocketing the trunk of the car next to him.

Shooting to kill, Miles dropped to a knee, trying to remember to breathe, aimed, his hand shaking, blinking past Andy's face and pulled the trigger. Once, twice, three times, laying down a round of fire. He heard himself screaming, a crazy man.

Behind him Blaine's old car roared into life. Miles flinched. But no bomb. Nathan was behind the wheel, Celeste ducking into the backseat.

Miles kept his wavering gun aimed at the darkness. He saw one guard running toward them. Miles shot out the window of the car closest to the man and the guard ducked and stayed down.

Miles followed Celeste into the backseat.

Nathan powered the car out of the slot; Miles fired at their pursuers until the clip emptied. They roared past Sorenson and the guards, through a sputtering hail of bullets, ricochets flying off the car roof. Miles covered Celeste with his body, protecting her. Nathan swung the car out fast and hard onto the narrow winding trail of Canyon Road. He hit sixty in ten seconds, crouched low next to the wheel. 'Who are you, man?'

'Miles Kendrick.' His old name didn't seem to fit him right anymore, like a shirt worn once, ill fitting and ugly, not to be worn again. He sat up, pulling up Celeste, looking behind him. No pursuit. Not yet.

'Your driver's license said your name was Michael.'

'It needs updating. My name's Miles. But I really am a

patient of Doctor Vance's. So is this woman. Her name is Celeste.'

Nathan's gaze flickered to Celeste in the rearview. 'Why'd you come get me?'

'I need you. I want to know the truth about why Allison died.'

'I'll drop you off but the car stays with me. I got to get far away from them.'

'Wrong. We should stay together,' Miles said.

'I don't like Nathan,' Andy said from the other side of Celeste. 'I like him even less than I like you. Go ahead and shoot him before he hurts you. You think you can trust this guy? You better find out what the hell Sorenson meant by Mr. Explosives.'

Nathan veered onto Cerro Gordo – the road that led past Allison's house – and Miles expected to hear the scream of police sirens. But nothing, and the road behind them was black and empty. The night lay quiet, closing its dark fist around the car.

'Stay together,' Nathan said. 'Why?'

'We can fight better together.'

'I don't want to fight . . .' he started, then stopped. 'But I don't want to hide the rest of my life either.'

'I have a place we can hide. Where we can decide how to stop these people.'

'Stop them from what?'

'Killing us.'

Nathan shook his head. 'I can't go to the police. My folks – they'll just send me to another loony bin. I don't need it anymore.'

'Neither do we. I don't know how Groote and Sorenson connect, but they'll be after us. We know what Allison stole from the hospital, and I think we know how to find it before Groote and Sorenson do. We do that, they can't hurt us.'

'There's another guy . . . Doctor Hurley.'

'We know. He tried to kill me. Celeste . . . stopped him.'

'Permanent stop?'

'Permanent.'

Nathan gave her a thumbs-up. 'Honey, I could kiss you.'

She shuddered.

'But don't worry,' Nathan said, 'I won't.' His grin, ecstatic at his freedom, went wide and manic. 'So where do we go, dude? We're free birds, free free free—'

Miles wondered, in helping Nathan, what dangerous genie he'd let out of the bottle.

THIRTY-TWO

'You hit, sir?' the guard asked.

'He missed me,' Sorenson said. 'Barely.' He imagined he could feel the heat where the bullet had just missed his ankle.

'I think I hit one,' the guard said, huffing for breath. He was the one who'd taken the blow to the guts. 'The window, I got him, we should—'

'You should have aimed for the tires.' He'd emptied his own clip too soon and was furious with himself. 'Is the alarm system keyed to the police?'

'Absolutely not,' the guard said. 'We're under orders not to call the police. Ever. Mr. Quantrill doesn't want them around.'

Not calling the cops made sense. Sorenson had no desire to bring unwelcome, official attention to the hospital; it had served its purpose. He turned from the guards without another word and headed toward his car.

'Hey! Mister, wait a goddamn second . . .' One of the guards caught him by the arm and Sorenson swiftly stopped, levered his arm free, brought his elbow back into the guard's face. The nose gave way with a sickening crack and the man collapsed with a howl.

Sorenson glanced at the other guard, who'd raised his

gun. 'Your clip's empty. So's mine.' He grabbed the broken-nose guard by the throat. 'He's a big boy but I can break the neck with a strong twist before you take two steps. So drop the gun, and I drive away, and then you go get your friend a doctor.'

The second guard looked into Sorenson's eyes. He slowly set the gun down, kicked it away without being told.

Sorenson kept his grip on the guard's throat until he reached his car, then he shoved the man to the asphalt in contempt. Groote knew he was an enemy now. And Nathan remained a threat, and he was with Miles Kendrick who, despite being mentally ill, had the skills and apparent guts to fight back.

Sorenson wheeled out hard into the night. Kendrick's car was gone.

He had to find Kendrick and Ruiz. Now. Or failing that, set a trap for them. One that they wouldn't see coming.

THIRTY-THREE

Nathan drove the car behind the adobe wall at Blaine the Pain's house. His hands gripped the wheel as though fused to the plastic.

'Nathan, be cool . . .' Miles started.

Nathan pulled trembling hands free from the wheel. Suddenly he seized the rearview mirror, tried to wrench it free from the ceiling.

Miles leaned forward and grabbed his arms. 'What the hell? Calm down!'

'Can we go inside now? Please?' Celeste shivered as though she'd fallen into snow.

Nathan aimed the mirror away from his face. Miles helped Celeste out, hurried her under the shelter of the porch. Nathan followed them. Miles opened the front door and held his breath, tried to imagine the explanation he would give if Blaine was back from Texas.

'Mr. Blaine? It's Michael, from the gallery,' Miles called. No answer. Blaine was still out of town.

Miles flicked on a kitchen light, leaving the other lamps doused. If the neighbors knew Blaine was out of town, he didn't want to increase suspicion.

Celeste collapsed on the couch, pulled her knees close

to her chest. Nathan scanned the room as if he were stepping on enemy territory.

Miles shut the front door behind him. 'We can stay here, at least for tonight.'

'Is it safe?' Nathan ran from room to room, as though he expected a shambling horror to lurch out from a dark corner.

Miles followed him. 'We're fine, I promise.'

'Is this your house? How many doors? How many windows?' Nathan went into the hallway bathroom and a few seconds later Miles heard a sudden, sharp crack.

He pushed past Nathan. 'What the hell?'

The mirror stood broken, a vicious crater in its center, cracks radiating outward. Nathan dropped a heavy soap dish to the floor.

'I hate mirrors.' Nathan retreated from the shattered glass.

'Why?' Miles took him by the shoulders, kept his voice calm. 'You can tell me.'

His jaw trembled; his eyes held a haunting fear. 'They – they look at me. From the mirrors. My friends.'

'Your friends that died in Iraq.'

'How do you know?' Nathan lurched away from him, running down the hall. 'I don't want them to see that I'm here . . .'

Miles caught him at the bedroom entrance, staring at a mirror atop a bureau. 'They can't see you. They can't.'

'But I see them. They went away for a while. But they're coming back, they live in the mirror and it's not my fault, it wasn't my fault . . .'

Miles steered him away from the mirror. 'We'll cover the mirrors, okay? Celeste, help me.' Miles took Nathan into the messy kitchen. Dirty dishes piled the sink, a sour odor rising from the trash. Nathan sank to the floor.

'Find towels, or blankets . . . cover every mirror you can find, please,' Miles said to Celeste. She seemed much steadier with four walls around her, and she nodded and left the room.

'Nathan. Pull it together, man, you've come so far tonight, you can't lose it. Stay steady.'

'It's like – withdrawal. I was better, now I'm worse.' Nathan startled with a jerk as a car rumbled in the street.

Frost. They'd been feeding him Frost, and probably he'd gotten his last dose on Tuesday. Maybe the drug's effects started fading without a daily dose.

Nathan shrugged Miles's hands off his shoulders, closed his eyes, steadied his breathing. Celeste ran back into the kitchen. 'I covered all the mirrors.' She knelt by them. 'You're bleeding. Your legs.' And Miles saw spatters of blood, dried and fresh, on the scrubs he wore.

Nathan ignored her. He reached a finger out toward her face and she flinched back. 'You were on *Castaway*. Holy smoke.'

She nodded.

'So you killed Hurley. He was a bad guy – bad doctor, bad breath, bad hair.' Nathan laughed, a broken giggle. 'You did a good deed, ma'am. Now if someone would kill Groote for me . . . if I don't get to do it myself.'

'No one's killing anybody,' Miles said.

Celeste reached for Nathan's face.

'No.' Nathan backed away from her. 'Don't touch me.'

'Just let me check.' Celeste spoke in a soft voice, quiet and reassuring.

He stopped his retreat across the kitchen. Nathan tensed while Celeste touched his jawline, inspected his

215

face. A swollen lip, a slight cut on the cheek with a bruise rising underneath it. 'They punched you.'

'Just once or twice.' His voice shook. 'Then hoses on my back.'

'Let me see.' Celeste eased up the back of Nathan's shirt: a quilt of vicious bruises covered his spine.

'Groote stuck a screwdriver against my bones. It hurt.' Tears came into his eyes and he shuddered. He shoved up his sleeves, pulled bandages off his arm, and showed them the constellation of welts; deep bloodied punctures. 'Cut down to the bone, jam the screwdriver against the bone. Then . . . turn. They did it on my legs too. Patch me up, then do it again.' He gritted his teeth.

'Oh, my God,' Celeste said. 'I'll see if there's a first-aid kit.' She ran from the kitchen.

'I can't go crazy again,' Nathan said in a hoarse whisper. 'I can't.'

'I won't let that happen,' Miles said, and Nathan laughed, a short broken giggle.

'You got spare sanity in your pocket?' Nathan asked.

'I know what you survived, Nathan,' Miles said in a low voice.

'You don't know anything, man, not a thing about me . . . you don't want to.'

Celeste ran back into the room, carrying gauze and Band-Aids and an antiseptic gel. 'Get the scrubs off.'

Miles helped Nathan stand. Grimacing from the pain, Nathan shucked the scrubs down to his knees. Purple dominated the back of his legs where Groote had whipped the hoses. Four brutal gouges marred his leg. Celeste medicated and bandaged the wounds. 'These wounds are deep. He needs a doctor.'

'No,' Nathan said.

'You're risking infection,' Celeste said.

'No,' Nathan said again. 'No doctors. We can't let Groote find us.'

Miles rummaged in the cabinet, found aspirin, poured a palmful into Nathan's hand, got him a glass of water. Nathan ate the aspirin like candy, a few at a time. He wiped the white dust from the tablets onto his shirt, finished the water. 'Thank you.' His eyes went glassy with exhaustion.

'When was the last time you ate?' Miles asked him.

'Tuesday.'

Miles rummaged in Blaine's nearly bare refrigerator, found a fancy-seeded bread and jam, cracked open a new jar of peanut butter, and made them all sandwiches. Nathan devoured his dinner in seconds, shivering with hunger.

Miles sat on the floor across from Nathan. 'You know what Frost is.'

'Yes. Allison told me it's medicine to cure your trauma. She told me when she got me the passkey, said I had to run.' Nathan wiped a hand across his mouth. 'At first I thought Frost was the code name for the virtual-reality treatments they give us.' He explained how the VR treatments worked – confirming what Miles had seen in the tech room.

'They made you relive the bombing,' Miles said.

'Bombing?' Celeste asked.

'I'm a war hero.' Nathan sat up straighter. 'Iraq. I volunteered after 9/11. I wanted to fight the good fight, protect the country I love.'

'Brave of you,' Celeste said softly.

He ducked his head in embarrassment. 'During the invasion, I was with a battery company, thirty miles out of

217

Baghdad. We launched our missiles, right after midnight, on target for a palace of Saddam's, but a U.S. jet pilot got confused, got bad info, he believed we were Republican Guard, he fired a heat-seeker' – he paused, swallowed, kept his gaze on his feet – 'killed four of my buddies. Nearly killed the rest of us.'

'I'm sorry, man,' Miles said.

'Parts of my friends hit me. I got a broken nose from a leg flying into my face.'

Miles and Celeste said nothing, because words had no power now.

'I got hurt in the blast, just burns' – he pointed to the peppering of scars on his cheek and nose – 'but it messed me up inside. I couldn't – I couldn't do my duty anymore.'

'PTSD,' Celeste said. 'It's not your fault.'

'Pathetic Terrible Stupid Disorder,' Nathan said. 'That's what I call it. I got freaky. I'd go nuclear in two seconds flat. Beat up an orderly at the psych ward in Germany they sent me to. But I got the honorable discharge, got the medal for standing ten feet further away from the battery than my friends.'

'And then you ended up at Sangriaville,' Miles said.

'When I didn't get any better. My folks were good to me, but after a couple of years, they're saying, *Nathan, get over the sadness now. Stop whining. Stop seeing dead people in the mirrors. Stop being this freak, be our son again.* Tried selling furniture at their place in Albuquerque; went from supporting missile systems to futons.' He tried to laugh. 'I wasn't good at moving the merchandise off the floor. I punched a guy when he couldn't decide between two recliners. Jesus, it's not a life-or-death decision. Pick after thirty minutes of shopping and sitting and fricking reclining. So the folks found a vets' program in Phoenix that got me free treatment – then my folks found out about Hurley's program and moved me to Santa Fe.'

'I read about those virtual-reality treatments,' Celeste said. 'But they're considered promising, and they don't involve drugs.'

'I didn't sign up to test drugs, none of us did, I signed up to test the virtual-reality treatments.' Nathan closed his eyes. Miles put a steadying hand on his shoulder. The trembling stopped. 'I didn't know about the drugs till Allison told me.'

'It's all cool. Just tell us what you know about Allison's death,' Miles said. 'Start at the beginning.'

'Sorenson – he's lying.' Nathan took another bite of sandwich. A dribble of strawberry jelly lay near his lip. 'I didn't kill her. You got to believe me. I would never . . .'

'I believe you.'

'Th-thank you. For getting me out of the torture chamber.' He clenched his fists, pressed them into his face. 'I thought I was fixed but now I feel worse than ever. Allison was the only person who helped me—'

'I swear I'll help you, Nathan,' Miles said. 'But you have to help us.'

'Help you what?'

'Find justice for her.'

Nathan laughed. 'How high and mighty. Justice.' Nathan cleaned the jelly off his chin with his thumb, the way a child would, sucked the jelly off the nail.

'She was our friend,' Celeste said. 'Our doctor.'

'You can't help a dead person,' Nathan said. 'They're dead, end of story.'

'Not end of story. She tried to help you,' Miles said.

Nathan's mouth went into a thin slash. 'I want to know

what I'm getting into, I still don't know why you use two names.'

'I'd like to know why, too, Miles,' Celeste said quietly. 'Which name do you prefer?'

He could unfold the confession he kept in his pocket, let them read it. But he wouldn't. He needed Nathan to trust him, but he wasn't sure yet he could trust Nathan. He knew the attitude was wrong – when he preached cooperation to a scared, beaten kid – but he couldn't help himself. So he kept the explanation edited. 'My dad died. He owed three hundred thousand dollars to a crime family in Miami. They forced me to work with them to pay the debt. They had me spy on their rivals. I finally cooperated with the feds, testified, and went into the witness protection program. The government moved me to Santa Fe and named me Michael. But I'm not in witness protection anymore.'

'Tell them the whole story,' Andy hissed from the kitchen table. 'I'm waiting.'

Celeste, as though she heard Andy's whisper, put a hand on Miles's arm.

'That's your trauma?' Nathan said. 'Jesus, that's fricking nothing, man.'

'Stop it,' Celeste said. 'This isn't a competition.'

'I'm just saying I don't see how being in witness protection would drive you nuts,' Nathan said.

'I killed a man,' Miles said suddenly. 'He tried to kill me and two undercover cops who had infiltrated the ring. I shot him.'

'What caused him to go postal?' Nathan asked.

'I don't remember,' Miles said. 'We were just talking to him and he pulled his gun and he tried to kill me.'

Nathan glanced at Celeste. 'Be careful what you say.'

'Don't joke. You owe this man your life,' she said.

Nathan shut up.

'There's my truth, Nathan. Your turn. Finish your story. Allison was getting you out.'

'Yeah. I was supposed to get to her house, wait for her. We were going to disappear, go where no one could find us, she said. She said we had to run Tuesday night. I don't know what made Tuesday special.'

'What about Groote?' Miles asked.

'Never saw him, or Sorenson, before Tuesday.'

'You ever hear of a man named Quantrill?' Miles asked.

'No.'

'Allison should have just called the state board on Hurley and Quantrill,' Miles said. 'Why run? Why hide? She could have simply gone to the police. She asked me for help. She sounded like she was making a stand to fight. But then she tells you she was running.'

Nathan said, 'Maybe she wanted your help in hiding herself and me. Since you know all about it.'

Miles shrugged. But the explanation didn't ring true to him, part of the story was bent, a piece was missing.

Nathan creaked to his feet with a wince, washed his face in the sink.

'If Frost was fixing you, why would you want to leave?' Celeste asked.

Nathan dragged a finger across his lips. 'Allison said Hurley was going to do extra experiments on me. Because my trauma was so bad. Eventually – take apart my brain to show how Frost worked on it.'

Celeste said, 'Oh, God, they'll kill all the patients?'

'No, they couldn't risk so many people dying without explanation. But I was supposed to meet with an accident,

Allison said.' Nathan put a hand across his eyes. 'I need to sleep.'

'Answer one more question. Do you really think Frost helped you?'

'I used to not be able to function at all. But I can now. So I guess I'm better. But lately, I can't always think straight. I get panicky.'

'Same with you, Celeste?' Miles asked.

She shrugged. 'Nathan, do you feel—'

'I don't want to talk anymore!' he nearly screamed. He threw his plate into the sink. 'Please. Just . . . I need to sleep. Let me sleep.'

Miles helped Nathan walk upstairs to a guest bedroom. Nathan eased himself down on the sheets, grabbed Miles's arm.

'If you try and hurt me while I'm sleeping, I'll kill you.'

'Dial it down a notch, man. I saved you. We're on the same side.'

'No,' Nathan said. 'No one's on my side.'

Nathan fell asleep in five minutes. Miles stood in the doorway, watching the slow rise and fall of Nathan's chest.

'He's dangerous,' Andy said. 'You can't trust him.'

'You're one to talk,' Miles said and went back downstairs. Celeste had brewed a pot of decaffeinated coffee and sat at the kitchen table.

'Do you believe him?' she asked.

'Yes and no. We know she stole Frost and sent it to this Mercury Mountain host. Allison doesn't use her own computer, or one at the hospital, or a public one in an Internet café or a library. She uses yours. She takes the pills she tested on you.'

'She told me Frost was an antidepressant. Medical

222

samples so I didn't have to bother with a prescription, since I don't – didn't get out much. I don't much like being a guinea pig.'

'She might have been giving you the pills purely to help you, if she was sure they would help,' Miles said. 'And then she took them back to protect you in case the hospital got suspicious.'

'It's unethical.'

'I won't disagree. But you're out of your house, you're functioning.'

'True. I don't doubt Allison's good intentions.'

'But I don't understand why Allison didn't go straight to the police, especially if Hurley planned to carve into Nathan's brain.'

'He's lying,' Celeste said.

'You think?'

'I do. But I don't know which part of his story isn't real. I just get the vibe he's not being entirely honest.'

'I get one vibe from him. He wants to be a soldier again. Strong. Capable. Confident.'

They sipped coffee in uncomfortable silence.

'I killed a man today,' she said. 'The words don't fit right in my mouth.'

'*Killed* is ugly. You saved me.'

'Did I? You're a big, strong guy. You kicked Hurley away, into me, the gun fired. It wasn't as though I fortified my courage and aimed to kill. I could have waited. If you stopped him with your fists, no need for my gun.'

'You did what you had to do.'

'Yes,' she said. 'That's the problem.'

Andy sat across from him at the kitchen table.

Celeste caught his quick squint at empty air. 'Your invisible friend. He's here?'

223

Embarrassment flooded him. 'No.'

She took a bird's sip of coffee. 'You told me you killed your friend. You didn't say he tried to kill two cops too.'

Miles shrugged. 'It doesn't change the fact that I killed him.'

'If you saved lives, you did the right thing, no matter how devastating.'

'I disagree with her,' Andy said. 'What does she know?'

Miles was quiet, not wanting to listen to either of them, tired to his bones.

'We have to have a plan, Miles. We can't hide here forever,' Celeste said.

He put down his coffee cup. 'We find Frost. It's the only way, first to prove we're not crazy and, second, to exonerate what we've done. Me running from witness protection, you shooting Hurley.'

Celeste hugged herself, as if cold. 'I'll like jail. Since I love being indoors.'

'You'd hate it.'

'Have you been?'

'No. But WITSEC, when they take you into the program, they put you in a facility where you can't leave for several days, you don't see other people. No bars, but it's jail.'

'I did the same thing you did,' she said. 'Walked away from my life. Put myself away from the world.'

The silence between them grew awkward and he said, 'I need to tell you about what I found in the hospital. Sorenson had beaten the crap out of this Groote guy and was trying to kill Nathan. He suggested Nathan killed Allison, that he knew about explosives. Now, maybe he was just trying to create doubt in my mind, but Nathan was in the army, and we don't know details of his service . . .'

'But why would he kill Allison when she was helping him?'

'Don't know. Let's say Allison stole Frost, then Sorenson stole it from her or killed her. I understand why Sorenson would face off against Groote, but why would Sorenson attack Nathan? How is Nathan a threat to him? He pretends to be a doctor, he kills Allison, he then tries to kill Nathan. I don't get how this all connects.'

'We'll get Nathan talking tomorrow. Right now I'm going to find a bed to sleep in.' She got up, pulled a knife from a storage rack.

'What's that for?' he asked. 'You don't need to cut—'

'It's not for me,' she said. 'For protection. In case the bad guys come in the night.'

'I'll stand guard.'

'You can't, Miles. You got drugged, you've been through hell. This isn't a horror movie, sitting around the campfire, waiting for the boogeyman to jump out. We bring our boogeys along with us.' She thumbed the edge of the knife. 'Good night, Miles.'

'Good night, Celeste. I'm sorry I brought all this trouble to you.'

'You didn't.' She went up the stairs.

Miles put his hands flat on the table. My God, he just wanted his old life back. His imperfect, dumb, but wonderful old life, him and his dad running the private investigation agency, no Andy gone mob, no crime rings extorting him to work off his father's debts, no reasons to hide, no hallucinations.

He drank another cup of coffee. *Choose a next step.* His head buzzed with a dozen questions, trying to fit together the mismatched pieces of the jigsaw that was the battle for Frost. But he knew with clarity that the only way to beat Groote, to beat Sorenson, to take the fight to them, was to locate the stolen Frost research. The bad guys didn't want it public; their fear was their only weakness he could exploit. He would find Frost and destroy them with it. So the next step was to find Mercury Mountain, Allison's recipient of the stolen research. If he couldn't find anything out from that angle, then he had to find this Quantrill guy in California – he was the chief, the money behind Frost. Follow the money; it had been his one rule in spying for the Barradas, and it never failed him. Except he'd never had to bring two innocent people in tow when he followed the money. His stomach twisted at the responsibility of protecting them; but he had no choice. He would simply have to keep them safe and try not to think about how he had failed Andy and Allison.

'I'll make it right,' he said to himself, to the empty air, to Andy.

He fell asleep across Blaine's unmade bed, the Beretta under his pillow, the way he had slept in Miami a lifetime ago.

THIRTY-FOUR

A camera eyed him under the eaves of Celeste Brent's porch, and Groote frowned. He had on his sunglasses and a cap pulled over his battered face to fend off the early light of Friday morning, but he didn't like his picture being taken. He yanked the camera loose from its mount and smashed the lens under his heel.

Reaching up to grab the camera made his arm hurt – hell, his whole body ached. His left arm throbbed, his head pounded, his broken nose was taped. He looked as if he'd been in a car crash.

Frost was gone. Sorenson had betrayed him; all the deal making was for nothing, the man had just wanted a shot at killing Nathan Ruiz, for whatever unfathomable reason. Nathan Ruiz and Michael Raymond had vanished. Hurley was missing. A fed named Pitts had nipped at his heels the previous night. Life was bad.

But if he thought of Amanda, he could push on.

He tried the doorbell. No answer. Knocked. Waited. If Celeste Brent was a psycho-level recluse, she might not answer the door.

He slid a lockpick into the door, tested it, eased the tumblers.

The door opened. No alarm chimed. He stepped inside, closed the door behind him. He left the lights off.

He nearly tripped over Hurley's body, sprawled on the floor.

'Dumb-ass,' he said under his breath. He drew his weapon, borrowed from an off-duty guard at the hospital, with a grimace of pain. Did a search. The house was empty.

He checked Hurley without touching him, but he didn't need to touch him to see that the man was dead. The man who had been a pain in the ass but could have helped his Amanda.

'I told you I should have come with you,' he said to the dead body.

He searched the house. No one there.

If the cameras ran constantly, they could tell him a story. He found a computer in the bedroom, with a massive external hard drive attached and video cables that fed into the walls. He fired up the computer. No login password. Not a surprise: no one ever used this system other than Celeste Brent. He searched the external drive; she kept the cameras' images in digital form for only a few days, then reused the drive's real estate. He accessed the video files, starting with yesterday's. The camera was motion-activated, saving frames when people neared the front door.

An older lady, matronly – probably a caretaker. Arriving, letting herself in with a bag of groceries, letting herself out. Then Michael Raymond showed up. Held up a sign.

I KNOW ALLISON'S SECRET.

Holy Mother of God. Groote's stomach churned. He fast-forwarded. Michael waits, then steps in. Nothing.

Then Hurley arrives, waits. Goes inside. More nothing. Then Michael and a woman – clearly frightened, as though she were unexpectedly walking on the moon – sticking close to Michael, stumbling out of frame. Damn. No sign of a car, no plates to trace.

He jumped back to the video files from Tuesday, the day Allison died. Fast-forwarded through the day until Allison appeared on the doorstep. Fast-forwarded until she left. Nothing else.

Celeste Brent had been in league with Allison Vance and so had Michael Raymond.

I KNOW ALLISON'S SECRET.

Four words to chill the bone.

He had to figure out where they had gone – because from the date/time stamp on the image, he guessed they had gone from here to the hospital. But first deal with Hurley. He couldn't leave the body. Celeste Brent was a has-been celebrity, but she was still a known name to many people; a body found inside her house would earn national attention. The caretaker woman might come back tomorrow; Hurley dead might be more of a problem than Hurley missing.

He stripped apart the computer system; maybe there would be helpful information on the hard drives to tell him where Miles and Celeste might run. He carried the hard drives out to the car, put them inside the backseat of the rental. Now. The trunk for Hurley, then the desert.

He closed the door and there, on the other side of the low adobe wall that separated the yard from the dirt road, stood DeShawn Pitts.

'Hello,' Groote said. Calm. *You can talk your way out of this, man, you have to, for your daughter.*

'What happened to you, Mr. Groote?'

'An accident at the hospital. My own fault, I slipped and fell down a flight of stairs.'

'You okay?'

'Yes. How'd you find me here?' He put a laugh in his voice.

'I parked down near the hospital. Wanted to grab Doctor Hurley for a talk. Saw you leaving, saw your face all beaten. Made me curious. Followed you.'

Too much suspicion from the guy. It saddened Groote.

'This your place?' Pitts asked.

'I wish. No, it's a patient of Doctor Hurley's.'

'That's Doctor Hurley's car parked there. His plates. I checked. He normally spends the night with his patients?'

'No, but last night was a special case.'

'I get the feeling Hurley's avoiding me. Is he here or not?'

Groote weighed the options, life or death.

'I really have to insist, Mr. Groote. At the least Doctor Hurley can step outside and talk to me for five minutes.'

Groote decided, with regret. He slammed the car door closed and tried to seem embarrassed under his bandage. 'Hurley talked to your person of interest; Hurley was the one at the hospital who called him. He's been calling all of Allison Vance's patients. A mild form of ambulance chasing.'

'Excellent.'

Groote jerked his head toward the house. 'Why don't you come on in and we'll talk?'

THIRTY-FIVE

Miles awoke to screams.

He lurched out of bed, unsure if he had actually slept. He had no morning aftertaste of nightmares: no Andy dying crumpled on concrete, no cries of horror echoing in the dreamy cave of his brain, no office of Allison's blasting into flaming rubble. The screams were from another's throat, thrashing cries of terror.

He ran up the stairs. Nathan lay in a tangle of bedsheets, fists clenched against air, kicking in a rage of shock.

'Nathan. Wake up. Wake—' and Nathan's fist closed around his throat, fingers of iron digging into Miles's windpipe.

'I didn't I didn't I didn't break it!' Nathan screamed. His voice crumbled into a ragged moan. 'I fixed it I fixed it I swear!'

'Nathan!'

Nathan jumped up from the bed, drove Miles hard into the wall, staring into his face.

'It's Miles. Let go,' he managed to say, sucking in the scarce oxygen.

'Nathan, stop it,' Celeste ordered from the doorway.

Nathan released Miles, stumbled back wordlessly, and sat on the bed.

'Bad dream,' Miles said. 'Just a dream, man, you're okay.'

An anger close to hate gleamed in Nathan's dark eyes. 'I don't dream.'

'Dream and scream. I been there.'

Nathan went into the bathroom – the mirror shrouded with a towel – and splashed water onto his face. Miles saw Nathan's hands were shaking.

'I don't dream,' Nathan said again.

'Whatever.' Miles rubbed the finger marks out of his throat.

'Screw you. I served my country, I was a soldier. What were you? A mobster, Miles, so don't talk down to me.'

Miles said, 'I won't, as long as you don't try to strangle me more than once a day.'

Nathan started rummaging in the guest closet for spare clothes. 'Miles. Listen, thanks for getting my ass out of the hospital. Appreciate it. But you and me, we're settled, I told you everything I know. Time to part ways.'

'Where do you think you're going?'

'Don't know yet.'

'I need your help.'

'Help.'

'We believe Allison sent the Frost research to a Web hosting company called Mercury Mountain. Probably to hide it from Sorenson, or to give it to someone else who could access the Web server. We need to find out where this server is.'

Nathan stopped at the door.

'Groote and Sorenson will want you dead. They'll want us all dead. Our only chance is to get Frost, prove what they've done to the world.'

'You do expose them, you ruin any chance for you or

Celeste or me, or anyone else with PTSD, to use Frost to get better. You think any drug company's going to produce a drug that the world knows was based on illegal experiments? Hell, no. You expose Frost, then you cut our own throats, man, we'll be broken forever.' His fists clenched. 'I agreed to the VR testing because I wanted to help my fellow soldiers. That matters more to me than some sad, pointless revenge.'

'We get Frost, we can help every soldier coming back from the war. Every child that's traumatized by abuse. Everyone who needs Frost,' Miles said. 'A legit company could do the research ethically, build on what Hurley did. There's nothing unethical about the chemical formula of Frost.'

Nathan nodded his head.

'But Groote and Quantrill and Sorenson, they'll be hunting us, Nathan, they will kill us if they find us. We can't recover if we're dead. And Allison asked you, and me, and Celeste, in different ways, to help her. I'm not inclined to let the people who killed her get away with murder.'

'Are you kidding me? You're a mobster, the feds are hunting you, not just Groote. And she doesn't want to step outside.' Nathan gave a jagged laugh. 'I can do plenty to get it back, but I can't have the two of you tripping me up. I suggest you guys lay very low for the next few days.' He turned to leave.

'You want to be a hero. Then be one,' Miles said quietly. 'We shouldn't work apart. Work with us.'

Nathan took five steps, then stopped. He rested his head against the doorjamb. 'I'm not good with people. You don't really want me around.'

'You can't have a life on the run alone, Nathan. No

money, no prospects, no help. We don't even know what the long-term effects of Frost might be. You can't run off on your own. Help us. You knew more about what Allison was planning. I know you must have trusted her. Cared about her.'

Nathan weighed the words for several moments. He dropped his bag on the floor, raised his head, nodded. 'All right. I'm in. So what's the next step?'

'Find Frost,' Miles said, 'and take the fight right back to these bastards.'

Breakfast was stale bagels, made edible through toasting and a thin coating of jam, and a pot of industrial-strength coffee. Normal morning routine. Except their routines usually included antidepressants, precious pills that they didn't have, and Miles wondered if the three of them would lose focus, the power of clear thinking, without their meds.

'So you just look up this Mercury Mountain on a computer and call them?' Nathan asked around a mouthful of bagel.

'I don't think we call. We go see whoever has access to the IP address where Allison sent the research.' He glanced at the clock: 6:00 A.M. He needed a computer on which he could make an online purchase and install new software, and he figured he wouldn't be able to do that on a coffee-shop computer.

But he could on the gallery's computers, if the locks hadn't been changed. Joy was in early often, but six in the morning was too early for her. He wondered if there would still be the police protection at the gallery he'd asked DeShawn to provide.

'We'll all go,' Celeste said.

'You don't have to, you can stay inside.'

'No. Let's all go,' she said quietly. 'I'll be okay.'

They found a pair of ill-fitting jeans and a flannel shirt for Nathan, along with tennis shoes. Celeste put on dark glasses and a ball cap and a windbreaker. She took the windbreaker's hood and pulled it over her head; too big for her, it shielded her face.

'You gonna be okay?' Miles asked her at the door.

'Yes. Let's do it.'

The three of them drove to the gallery, Miles driving, more confident behind the wheel. The lot was empty; no police car. Miles hurried them to the gallery's door, noticing a plywood cover where a pane of glass had been. He tried his key, fed his code into the alarm system. The red light changed to green.

Celeste slid the windbreaker's hood from her head, stepped inside, shivering. She and Nathan examined the art on the walls.

'What lovely pieces,' she said.

'Touch nothing,' he said, giving Nathan a hard look. Nathan shrugged. They followed him upstairs to Joy's office.

Miles fired the computer up, opened a browser, hunted in Google for the name Mercury Mountain. No Web site for a hosting service – so not a hosting service that wanted customers, just a name to attach to a server. Miles jumped to a software vendor who sold IP address tracking software, dug out the VISA card he'd opened in his father's name for emergencies.

'I used this software when I had to track for the mob who really owned certain porn sites,' Miles said. 'It's gotten a lot harder to find out who has certain Web domains, they could be bought with a stolen credit card or

235

paid for ten years with a money order. But I'd find which of my bosses' rivals owned porn sites, and my boss hired hackers to bring down the sites, cut into the rivals' profits.'

'You knew all the charming people,' Celeste said.

Miles bought the software, entered in his VISA number, prayed the transaction would go through. Waiting. And then he got a confirmation.

'Thank God,' he said. He downloaded and installed the software, entered his license key, and entered in the IP address Celeste had found on her system. A map of the United States displayed, tracking the IP address, and finally pulsed on a location in northern California. Miles clicked: the IP address belonged to a server in Fish Camp, California, owned by an Edward Wallace.

'Google him,' Celeste said. Miles did, conscious now that they might only have minutes left. Joy – at DeShawn's request – could have put an alert on the alarm system to let him know if the gallery was accessed after hours, just in case Miles came back. He hoped not.

Most of the Google results offered links to articles written by Edward Wallace – a few years out of date – mostly on post-traumatic stress disorder, and the gist seemed to be that the government was moving too slowly in addressing the growing problem of traumatic stress, especially among soldiers. He clicked through them; Edward Wallace was a neurobiology researcher in PTSD, affiliated with a university in San Diego. At least he had been four years ago.

'She sent it to Edward Wallace for analysis, maybe,' Celeste said.

Miles clicked on the next-to-last link. It summoned a local news story in a small-town paper from Fish Camp,

California. An Edward Wallace of Fish Camp had been injured in a hiking accident. He was new to town – recently relocated from Fresno. His wife, Renee, was on an extended teaching fellowship in psychiatry at a medical school in the United Kingdom, so he had been hiking alone when he fell.

'Odd. They don't mention the name of the school,' Celeste said, leaning over his shoulder. 'Where exactly in California is Fish Camp?'

Miles clicked and searched and found a map. 'Just a couple of miles south of Yosemite National Park.'

'We should call him. Say we know Allison and need to know how he's involved,' Nathan said.

Miles clicked on the last link, an archived notice from *The Fresno Bee*.

There was a wedding picture of Edward – bookish and tall – and his bride, Renee, smiling, intelligent, confident, blond hair pulled back in a ponytail.

Renee Wallace was Allison Vance.

THIRTY-SIX

Groote cleaned off the screwdriver under a jet of water.

At his feet, on the kitchen floor, lay DeShawn Pitts. Groote believed a man bent, broken, and without hope was a tragic sight.

Groote ran a finger along the edge of the screwdriver. He'd learned the technique in Laos from a morals-challenged detective when Groote briefly worked with their police force on an exchange program: make a slight cut where the skin lay shallow over the bone, drive the screwdriver's tip to the bone, twist and shred the flesh, let the subject hear the sound of metal grating against their own skeleton. Keep the subject gagged and you had quiet and a minimum of mess.

'One last time,' Groote said. 'Or we'll let Mr. Screwdriver explore fresh new territories. Above the eye socket. The pubic bone. Base of the spine.' He lowered himself down to DeShawn's eye level. 'Listen. Why protect this guy? He screwed you over. He ran. Didn't give a thought to your career, your professional standing.'

'My job,' DeShawn managed to say – his voice was barely above a whisper – '. . . to protect him.'

'I'm not with the piece-of-crap drug dealer you're hiding him from,' Groote said. 'I don't give a rat's ass what he did before. I'm a now kind of guy. I need to know how to best bring him to the surface.'

DeShawn closed his eyes.

'Where's he from originally?' He started to undo DeShawn's pants.

'No, please. No.'

'Tell me. This isn't pleasant for me either.'

'You'll kill me.'

'I have no quarrel with you. My quarrel's with Michael Raymond, who ran away from you.'

DeShawn closed his eyes. 'Never.'

'*Never* is such an outdated concept,' Groote said, reaching for the knife, imagining a blue surgeon's line in his craftsman's eye on the tender skin.

It took twenty more minutes, and his answers came in a broken flood as he played the knife's edge against an open nerve: 'Miles Kendrick – Miami.'

He knew the name. Jesus. He'd heard the guy's name before, talking with a couple of other old FBI hounds, talking about the Barradas' clever spy. He'd never seen a picture but he'd heard the name. *No telling how many crime rings that guy put a fucking dent in, man, the Barradas' own CIA, who ever knew mobsters would get creative and get themselves a spy?*

'Thank you, Mr. Pitts,' Groote said. 'Mr. Kendrick hurt a lot of criminal organizations. Do you know if he ever struck at the Duartes in southern California?'

DeShawn nodded. 'He ... helped take ... them down ...'

Yeah, but not down enough. They'd still had the strength to come after his family, blame the Grootes for their misfortunes. 'How did he take the Duartes down?'

'Think he ... stole spreadsheets ...'

'When?' And God help Miles Kendrick, Groote thought, if it was before the attack on his family.

DeShawn didn't answer, sliding toward unconsciousness. Groote controlled his sudden rage. Focus on what mattered now. 'What do you know about Frost?'

'What?' There was no deception left in DeShawn's eyes.

'Where would Miles go? Back to Miami?'

'No.'

'How hard is Witness Protection and the Bureau searching for him?'

DeShawn passed out and Groote slapped him awake, repeated the question.

'Hard,' DeShawn managed.

'Now. You've been very helpful. I really appreciate it. Thank you. I need to consider my options.' Deciding about how Pitts made the best bait, alive on the hook or limp in death. No reason for Miles Kendrick to care about this dumb-ass. Groote stood, checked his gun, tucked a plastic trash bag under DeShawn's head, fired once between the half-open eyes; the head jerked as the bullet funneled through bone and brain.

Groote tried to step into Allison's head. She planned to run with Frost's secrets, expose Quantrill and Hurley's illegal testing. She was going to vanish from her life, and who better to help her than a man who'd already vanished from his own? A man who stole secrets, as she'd stolen Frost. Except the plan went wrong for Allison. You couldn't tempt a criminal, a mobster, with a drug formula worth millions. Meat before the wolf, and he'd killed Allison for Frost. Groote was sure of it now. He'd thought first it might have been Sorenson, but he believed Sorenson was just a hired muscle for a pharmaceutical, making an attempt to steal the drug. Maybe Nathan, in league with Allison, knew about the deal and Sorenson wanted his tracks cleaned.

The evidence suggested Miles Kendrick had Frost. He was keeping it for his own gain, and he was keeping it from Amanda, and all the other people it could save.

He turned off the water, flicked the last drop free from the flat edge. Now he knew his enemy's face, his name, and he believed he knew how to defeat him. There was a calmness in the knowledge. He'd thought killing the Duarte accountant was the final step in justice for Cathy and Amanda; but no. Fate and its engine of revenge had brought him full circle, brought him to a man who could mean justice for his lost Cathy and sanctuary for his lost Amanda.

So Miles Kendrick needed Nathan Ruiz as an example of the drug's power, to bolster the case made in the research files. See Nathan, on video, barely able to speak when he starts taking Frost; see him, after months of it, able to effect an escape from a mental hospital and take part in a conspiracy. See, folks, this stuff works and works good, step right up, buy a bottle.

Miles Kendrick was running, crazy, with two other loonies weighing him down, and Groote was going to find him. And get Frost back.

The second auction for Frost – if Sorenson spoke truth, and he would have to confront Quantrill with this information – would be in three days. Kendrick had to be setting it up already, pressed to profit from all of Hurley and Quantrill's hard work. So he had three days to find Kendrick.

The answer was in Celeste Brent's computer. It had brought Allison here, it had brought Miles here. So start there. And find them, and kill them.

His watch said seven in the morning. He had time before sunset to take the bodies out to the high desert and dispose of them.

His phone buzzed. He answered.

Quantrill. Sounding tense, sounding bitter. 'I'm on my way to Santa Fe. We seriously need to talk.'

'That,' said Groote, 'is the understatement of the year.'

'This is a goddamned disaster—' Quantrill started.

'Not on the phone. Just tell me where you want to meet.'

Quantrill did, anger still in his tone. Groote clicked off and the phone buzzed immediately.

It was his hacker friend who had found the Michael Raymond address off the cell-phone account. 'I kept at that Michael Raymond problem for you. Nabbed a peek into the caller records. Finally wormed my way in.'

'Do tell. I'd like to know who he's been calling.'

'He made only one call on his cell phone yesterday. To a cell phone owned by a guy named Grady Blaine, there in Santa Fe. You want Blaine's address?'

'I most certainly do,' Groote said.

THIRTY-SEVEN

'It can't be her,' Celeste said. 'It can't be.'

Miles traced his finger over the photo. A woman, smiling shyly into the camera's lens, a casual photo taken during a run or hike outside. She wore an athletic top and shorts, stood atop a mountain, full of vitality. The kind of informal engagement photo favored by active couples. The photo credit printed sideways next to the picture read 'Edward Wallace.' It listed their degrees – Edward a Ph.D. in neurobiology and Renee an M.D. in psychiatry. She'd previously worked at both a university and a military clinic in San Diego to help veterans recover from post-traumatic stress disorder. She and her husband had moved to Fresno to establish a similar clinic.

'Maybe it's not her.' Nathan sounded distant, dream addled. 'You can't see her face quite clearly.'

Miles swallowed the bile creeping into his throat. *You were supposed to help me in becoming a new person; I had no idea you were already an expert.* 'It's her,' she said.

'She lied to us,' Nathan said. 'That bitch.'

'Don't talk about her that way,' Celeste said.

'She lied!' Nathan gritted his teeth and Miles saw tears of fury rising in the young man's eyes. Nathan staggered to the office door.

'Let's go.' Miles closed the browser, shut off the computer, and, at the door, reset the alarm. They followed Nathan out the gallery door and Miles locked up. The lot remained empty. He hurried them into the car and drove out of the parking lot.

'She lied,' Nathan said, 'and it caught up with her.'

'There has to be a reasonable explanation,' Celeste said.

'People always say that,' Miles said, 'when they're about to get totally screwed.'

Nathan frowned. 'Names aside, she stuck the research on a server. Could we access it?'

'Not without the password,' Miles said. 'So we talk to her husband.'

'You're all idiots,' Andy said from the backseat. 'Why don't you all deal with your real problems? Celeste killed a man, Nathan's a walking meltdown, and you, Miles, you're a friend killer. Charming group. Truly.'

'You can't stand it,' Miles whispered, 'when you think I might win.'

'Excuse me?' Celeste said, and Nathan said, 'What?'

'I'm talking to myself. Not you all. Sorry.'

'Your friend?' she asked.

'Yes.'

'Jesus, you talk to him?' Nathan said.

Andy laughed. Awkward silence and Miles thought, *I'm the one who didn't get Frost, they think I'm crazier than they are.* He steered into Blaine's driveway.

'So that's why you used two names,' Nathan said. 'Multiple personalities. Hey, how many voices you got inside your head?'

Miles ignored him as he helped Celeste hurry back inside Blaine's house. 'Shut up and let me think.'

'Were you speaking to me?' Nathan said. 'I can't listen to this crazy bastard carry on a conversation with an imaginary friend.'

Miles closed the door behind them. 'Shut up and realize what we're facing. Allison went to enormous trouble to set up her life in Santa Fe. That wedding announcement said she went to Oregon for her degrees. The degrees on Allison's wall were from Rice and Stanford and UCLA. She had to create a new history for herself, and you can't easily fake a medical-school transcript, a medical license, a new Social Security number, a past spun of nothing. It takes resources and time, trust me. She didn't do it on her own.'

'So who helped her?'

'Someone with money and serious motivation. Why fake an identity? Why couldn't she be in Santa Fe as Renee Wallace? She didn't do this alone. She had to be working for someone.'

Nathan shook his head. 'Man, this just got to be a bigger can of worms than I want to deal with. You all should just hide. Or go to the cops. We're done.'

'We need to drive to California,' Miles said. 'Find her husband.'

'Drive to California.' Celeste's voice cracked. 'You want me to ride in a car for . . . Several. Hours.' She turned and ran to the back of the house and Miles heard Blaine's studio door slam.

Miles – slowing down for considered thought – realized a car drive of hundreds of miles would be horribly frightening to her. He went to her purse, cracked open the bottle of antidepressants. Four were left. All the meds they had, and God only knew what kind of megadose Nathan needed to keep him calm. Not enough pills for all three of them. He slid the pills back into the bottle.

'I know how to get her moving.' Nathan flicked his fingers, made a whooshing noise.

'Let me talk with her.' Miles went through the house, to the studio door. Closed. He knocked. No answer. He opened the door.

Groote sat on a paint-splattered stool, one gun aimed at Celeste's head, another aimed at Miles. Celeste stood, lip trembling, not looking at the gun aimed at her.

'Tag,' Groote said. 'You're it.' His face was battered, his nose was taped, and his smile was cold and thin.

Miles shut the door behind him. *How the hell?* he thought. It didn't matter. He had to get Celeste away from this man.

'No. Call Nathan back here. Calmly. I want to talk with him too.'

'What do you want?'

'Frost.'

'We don't have it.'

'Where is it?'

'I don't know.'

'Don't lie to me. You were in league with Allison, both you and Mrs. Brent here.'

'No.'

'I just asked you not to lie to me. What part of that don't you understand?'

'Let her go, and I'll give it to you,' Miles said. Celeste looked up at him.

Nathan opened the door and boogied into the room. 'Problem solved. I lit a fire under you, Celeste, to get you going. Actually, under the curtains and—' He stopped and, frozen with fear, stared with shocked horror at Groote.

'Hey, Tin Soldier, how you doing?' Groote started, but then he saw what Celeste did, framed in the open door.

'Fire,' Celeste said in a whisper, pointing down the hall. 'Fire . . . he set a fire.'

Then the smell of smoke, sweet and awful and rising.

'You crazy bastard!' Groote yelled, standing up.

'You want Frost? It's upstairs,' Miles lied.

Groote put the gun's barrel on Miles's forehead. 'Show me.'

'Let them go.'

Groote hesitated. 'Out. Both of you. Just go outside. You run, he's dead.'

Nathan grabbed Celeste, steered her toward the back door. She started to scream as he pushed her into the yard.

Groote turned Miles, dug the gun hard into the back of Miles's head. 'Give me Frost. Now.' He strong-armed Miles past the hallway and up the stairs. In the kitchen, the curtains above the sink blazed. In the den, heavy draperies, a large cotton rug, the entire couch, burned brightly.

He'll kill me when he figures I don't have Frost, Miles thought. He fell as Groote pushed him on the stairs.

'Faster, crazy.'

'Don't hurt me,' Miles pleaded, and at the same time braced himself against the stair and dealt a savage backward kick. His foot caught Groote in the groin. Miles kicked again, aiming for the broken nose but catching the chin. Groote staggered, lost his footing, and tumbled down the stairs, landing in a heap on the tiles.

Miles grabbed the gun away from his hand, finding its fellow in Groote's jacket pocket.

Leave him. Run.

But the fire was spreading fast. He couldn't abandon anyone, not even a bastard like Groote, to die. He dragged

Groote into the backyard, dumped him into the cold water of a stone fountain. Groote gasped.

Miles put one of the guns to Groote's head. He dumped the clip from the other, put the clip in his pocket, tossed the second gun into the water. 'We're leaving now. Don't follow us. I lied to you. I don't have Frost. I don't know where it is. We're not a threat to you. We're just going away where no one will bother us and we won't bother anyone. Tell Quantrill. You understand?'

'I understand you're a liar.' Groote glared at him with hate.

'Stay in that fountain or I'll shoot you.' Miles backed away and ran. He jumped over a low-lying fence, headed for the front yard.

Nathan was coaxing Celeste once again into the car. Miles got into the front. He spun into the street and powered the car away from the burning house.

Groote was at the driver's window, trying to grab the wheel from him, and Miles floored it, broke free, roared down the street, and wheeled hard onto Old Santa Fe Trail.

'What – what do we do?' Nathan said.

'We don't stay here. We can't. We run.' He looked for Groote in the rearview, saw nothing. 'We go where Allison hid the files. California.'

Celeste started to moan.

Groote staggered down the street to his car. A couple of neighbors stood in the road and watched the flames popping from the windows, cell phones clutched to their ears. They stared at him and he ran down the road to where he'd left his car. Still with Hurley and Pitts dead in the trunk.

Think. Where would they go? Where would they hide? He had to change tactics, flush them out, figure their next step. But best not to be here when the fire trucks and the other authorities arrived. He had bodies to bury. A plan to make.

These crazy people were ruining everything for him.

THIRTY-EIGHT

Friday afternoon, Groote stopped at church on the way back from burying the bodies.

A shrine in Chimayo, north of Santa Fe, claimed that the dirt from its foundations could work miracles: smother the fire of AIDS in the blood, corral cancer cells, drive death into retreat. Groote drove past the cars lining the road that led to the old church, steering slowly past the camera-necklaced tourists, past an old woman in a wheelchair, past a kid about Nathan Ruiz's age with a fresh burr, crutches, and an empty camouflaged-pant leg, huffing himself toward the church as though he were competing in a race.

Groote parked and watched the kid and wondered if a dash of that Jesus dust would help Amanda. After all, salvation might be close at hand. Frost – in a form to fix his girl – still seemed miles beyond his reach.

All that, he decided, was about to change.

He got out of the car and walked along the outside of the church, toward the building's back.

Quantrill was waiting for him.

'My God, you're a horror,' Quantrill said, inspecting Groote's nose brace, the battered jaw.

'Thanks. How was your flight?'

Quantrill lit a cigarette. 'The peanuts were stale.' Ice in his voice. 'I'm not happy with the services you've provided so far.'

'I'm not happy with being lied to.'

'How have I lied to you, Dennis?'

'Tell me the truth about what Sorenson said – is there a second auction of Frost being set up?'

Quantrill blew out a frustrated sigh. 'Yes. I've heard about it from two of my contacts. Very unfortunate.'

'You could have told me.'

'I didn't want you distracted. Two of my contacts said they've been contacted by a guy willing to sell them the research – at half my asking price.'

He didn't give a rat's ass about Quantrill's money. 'I don't think Sorenson is behind the auction. I think it's Miles Kendrick.'

'Who?'

Groote explained what he'd learned about Miles's background. He left out that he'd let Miles and company escape; he wasn't about to admit his own underestimation of Miles Kendrick.

Quantrill considered. 'Then it's just a sick coincidence. The mobsters want him dead, they kill Allison, it has nothing to do with Frost.'

'That's what the feds are supposed to believe. But not us. Miles Kendrick had to know that when his shrink died in a bomb blast, his past might come to light and he'd be blamed for her murder. It covers up that he stole Frost, because he must have known we wouldn't run to the cops. I almost admire the guy; he built a brilliant plan.'

Quantrill nodded. 'You have to stop this second auction . . .'

'Do I? I want my kid to have the medicine. A drug

251

company buys the research cheap, they produce it faster. You're screwed, true, but I'm not.'

Quantrill didn't blink. 'But what if it's not Miles Kendrick running the second auction? What if it's Sorenson?'

Groote said, 'I don't get it.'

'And you say you admire clear thinking.' Quantrill tossed his cigarette an inch from Groote's toe. 'I think you actually hate Miles Kendrick, for a reason you're not telling me.'

'He's a goddamned mobster. I used to put people like him in prison.'

'And now you put them in graves.'

'A few might be in urns.'

Quantrill shook his head. 'Revenge won't make Amanda healthy. But Frost will, Dennis. Think, with a clear head, what we're facing. His threat is not that he'll sell Frost to someone. Consider what he's done and what that fed told you – Kendrick wants to bring whoever killed her to justice. He's killed Hurley, he's broken into the hospital. But the end result, each time, is to rescue a patient who was being tested with Frost. He doesn't want to sell it. He wants to expose it. What do you think will happen if Kendrick and his psycho buddies go public about Frost? Illegal testing of a drug on the traumatized, including veterans? No pharmaceutical will ever come near us, no matter the drug's efficacy. Even a worthy drug might be buried for years until the pharmas don't have to worry about lawsuits or bad publicity.' Quantrill lit a cigarette. 'I can derail the auction – doesn't matter if it's Kendrick or Sorenson. There are very few willing buyers to touch hot research. A few well-placed phone calls, a suggestion that the stolen research isn't complete, or if the second auction takes place I threaten to cut a plea bargain and name names for the FDA. It would be enough to stop the auction in its tracks. But if Miles Kendrick is intent on exposing us because he wants to avenge his doctor, then we're dead in the water.'

'He hasn't exposed us yet.'

'You have to stop him before he does.'

'All right.'

Quantrill jerked his head at the crowds heading toward the church. 'You see these people? Flocking toward dirt that, if you buy the freaking hype, cures every ill. Faith and hope are just commodities, and everyone buys them. And they'll buy Frost if you and I can silence Kendrick and his friends. We'll have a world where trauma never leaves its footprints.'

'You're wrong about faith,' Groote said.

'I'm not.'

'Everyone needs faith. In people if not God.'

'Profound talk from a killer.' Quantrill couldn't hide his smirk.

'You're not better than me, Oliver. I do what you're not willing to, what you're afraid to do. So don't talk down to me.'

'I won't.' The smirk tried to evolve into a steel-eyed stare, but Quantrill couldn't make it work.

'Here's what you need to do,' Groote said. 'Change medical records to show that Nathan Ruiz was released from the hospital by Doctor Hurley the day before Allison died. Then go back to California and put the brakes on the new auction.'

'All right,' Quantrill said. 'I'll have to report Hurley missing when he doesn't show for work on Monday. Hopefully drag it out until Tuesday. Plant an idea with the cops that Hurley was distraught over Allison's death – he fits the part of the heartbroken loner – and left town. You're sure they'll never find his body?'

'They won't.'

Quantrill crossed his arms. 'Good. So now for our other problem. Kendrick's got two loony tunes under his wing. He probably can't get far. He may even still be in town. Draw him out. Use Ruiz's family. They might be the first people Ruiz contacts.'

'When this is all said and done,' Groote said, 'my daughter gets Frost. First.'

'Of course, Dennis,' Quantrill said, 'but I can't do that, can I, if Kendrick stays a problem.'

'He won't. We done?'

Quantrill nodded.

Groote walked back to his car. He drove toward Santa Fe, starved for sleep – which he didn't see in his immediate future – for food, for a clear head. He had reserved a hotel room near the Plaza.

His cell phone rang. It was the computer technician at the hospital, who was examining Celeste's computer. 'I found evidence that files large enough to be the Frost research files were uploaded to a remote server via Celeste Brent's computer.'

'Where's the server?'

'I traced it to a location in Fish Camp, California, a server belonging to a man named Edward Wallace.'

The name meant nothing.

'Compare the files with Hurley's files. See if they're the same name, the same size.'

'I did already. She uploaded one extra file Hurley didn't have in his Frost database.'

'What's the other one?'

'It's a simple text file . . . it's called BuyList.'

BuyList. Buyers' list? Allison had gotten a list of the people lining up to buy from Quantrill, the under-the-table consultants who could filter Frost into a research department.

But why would that be in the research files? The buyers were Quantrill's business – not Hurley's.

'Get me an address for Edward Wallace.' He hung up. He dialed Quantrill.

'Before you run back to California,' Groote said, 'did Hurley have your list of contacts for your sale?'

'No, of course not. Why?'

Either Quantrill was lying or Hurley had the list and Quantrill didn't know it, or, scariest possibility, Allison had gotten the list from somewhere else. Someone else.

'Groote?' Quantrill asked.

'Nothing. Just curious.' He hung up.

So she had uploaded the stolen data. Why? Why not simply hand it to Kendrick if he was her partner?

Because Allison was hiding the data from Kendrick. As insurance. She had good reason.

The second auction. She'd gotten the names of the buyers for the second auction, somehow, from Quantrill. How and why?

And his confusion over this angle brought forward a question that had nagged him through the night: Why would Sorenson even mention the second auction to him? Why risk alerting him?

Because he wanted to win your confidence, lure you in, get access to Nathan Ruiz, kill Ruiz, kill you. He can tell you anything if he's pretty sure you're going to be dead in ten minutes.

He didn't know why Sorenson wanted Ruiz dead, but, hey, it didn't matter, facts were facts.

He parked at the hotel lot, got out of his car, exhaustion making his head spin, his nose throbbing from the break. He needed sleep and a painkiller, but first he had to call Nathan's family, back up Quantrill's story about Nathan's release, see if the family knew where Tin Soldier was.

The cell phone chirped. 'I found your address for Edward Wallace.' The technician gave Groote the address.

Groote clicked off the phone, tented his cheek with his tongue while he considered this new data. He believed Kendrick had come to Celeste Brent's computer specifically to get this information. He could be racing to California to get Frost.

It was a chance Groote couldn't take. He could sleep on the plane.

He headed for the hotel and then he saw them, federal agents, he knew the stance, standing near the door's lobby on the inside, a blond talking on a cell phone, a bald man with his back to Groote.

Pitts must have logged in, mentioned that he was tracking down Hurley, following Groote from the hospital. And now Pitts hadn't checked in for hours. It wasn't a hard matter to call local hotels, find a room rented to Dennis Groote.

He couldn't let the officers stop him for questioning. Giving a statement might burn hours he couldn't lose – especially if Pitts had mentioned any suspicions of Groote's honesty to his team members. He retreated toward the car, walking normally, praying with each step that the men didn't spot him. If he drove to the Albuquerque airport and took a flight to California, the Bureau would quickly know where he went; and if he hid it would seem, well, like he was hiding. Neither was an appealing prospect. He needed to lie low, find Frost, then resurface back in Los Angeles, where he could claim that, his contract with the hospital having expired, he'd simply come home; he'd had no idea anyone was interested in talking to him.

Santa Fe, a wonderful city he would have loved to share with Amanda, had gone very bad for him.

You get Frost first, and no matter what, he told himself as he slid behind the wheel. *You get it for Amanda, even if they catch you.*

He got back into his car, started the engine, and the fingers tapped against the window.

'Mr. Groote?' The man had the clean-scrubbed, earnest face of an eager Bureau agent. He'd been the blond talking on the cell phone near the hotel entrance.

'Yes?' Groote powered down the window, put a polite yet questioning expression on his face. *Start lying,* he told himself, *and make it a great one and forget about the DNA traces the two dead men left in the trunk of the car, don't you sweat even a drop. So this bastard can't slow you down any more than necessary.*

'Hello,' Groote said, with the politeness of recognizing a colleague.

The man was equally polite; almost apologetic. 'Hello, sir. FBI. We need to talk to you for a few minutes.'

THIRTY-NINE

'"The Mental Defective League – in formation!"' Nathan said. 'Name that movie.'

Miles, having driven for the past twelve hours, didn't want to play. Celeste, sitting low in the backseat, wearing a heavy pair of sunglasses, wrapped in a blanket, and with a dose of Xanax in her, didn't answer. It was late Saturday night, the galaxy of lights of greater Los Angeles spread out on both sides of Interstate 5.

'*One Flew Over the Cuckoo's Nest*. After Nicholson gets bzzzzzzt, the shock treatments.' And he leaned into the backseat, jabbed Celeste's head with his finger, saying, 'Bzzzt, bzzzt, bzzzt.'

'They should have given you shock treatments,' she said. Now and then she stuck her head out from the blanket, a turtle taking a measure of air. But she seemed to be coping, Miles thought, certainly better than Nathan was.

'Don't need the voltage,' Nathan said, 'not when I got Frost. I saved our skins, don't forget.'

Celeste said, 'Let's break for the night. It's still hours to Yosemite.'

'I can drive,' Nathan said.

'Bad idea,' Miles said.

'Jesus, man, I know how to drive.'

'You seem slightly wound up,' Miles said.

'You're not going to let your imaginary friend drive, I hope.'

'Enough, Nathan,' Celeste said from the back.

'What do you call Mr. Invisible?' Nathan said. 'Guilt Trip? The Shadow?'

'His name is Andy.'

'Well, we can't have Andy distracting you from your driving.' Nathan made a playful half-grab at the wheel.

Miles veered into the right lane, earning a honk and a finger from a driver he'd nearly clipped.

'I'm not letting you drive,' Miles said, 'because the mirrors bother you. I don't want you to freak.'

A long silence. 'I don't freak,' Nathan said.

'Let's find dinner and a place to sleep,' Celeste said quietly.

'We need to keep going,' Miles said, even though exhaustion rattled his brain. 'We need to keep—'

'Please,' she said, 'please. I need four walls around me.'

Dinner was take-out McDonald's, comfort was a worn but clean motel in the northern stretches of the city, near Santa Clarita. Miles got two adjoining rooms. Nathan demolished three Big Macs, downed a soda, let out a satisfied belch. 'Excuse me,' he said.

Celeste kept her back to them, sitting on the edge of the bed, picking at a salad.

'You okay?' Miles asked.

'I can't believe I left my house,' she said. 'I ought to feel free. I don't. I hope Nancy didn't come to my house and . . . find the body.' She shuddered. 'I shouldn't have left.' She closed the salad box over the mostly uneaten mound of lettuce.

'The shouldn't-haves are the path to insanity,' Nathan said. 'You better eat that dinner, Celeste. Soldiers know you got to eat, sleep, and sh— um, go to the bathroom, whenever you have a chance, you might not get another.'

She opened the box, forced herself to eat again.

Miles finished his hamburger. 'We all need sleep. We'll get up early tomorrow, head out.'

'We should camp a day or two,' Nathan said. 'Let Celeste recover.'

'We go,' Miles said.

'You're not the boss of us.' Nathan wiped his mouth.

'I am until we get Frost. Until we know we're safe.'

'We're not responsible for each other.' Nathan stood.

'Funny thing for a soldier to say,' Miles told him. 'I would imagine you feel responsible, Nathan, toward your fellow soldiers.'

Nathan's hands tightened into fists. 'What the hell's that supposed to mean?'

'Just that we have to take care of each other . . .'

'Ah. Like they do in the mob.'

'I'm not a mobster. I never was.'

'So you say. Why should we believe you?'

'Enough, Nathan.' Celeste stood. 'Sleep. Then we go.'

Nathan sat down on the bed. Celeste retreated to her own room and shut the door behind her.

'There's no way to hang a blanket over the mirror. Just don't look at it,' Miles said.

'I won't,' Nathan said to the ceiling.

Miles washed his face, slipped out of shirt and jeans, crawled into the bed nearest the door, hid the gun under his pillow.

'You don't have to sleep with a gun with me around,' Nathan said.

'It's in case Groote finds us again.'

'Yeah, because I'm fresh out of matches.'

Miles didn't smile.

'I know you and Celeste are mad at me. But the fire turned out okay, it gave us an escape route.'

'You can't go setting houses on fire. I could have talked Celeste into leaving. What you did was terribly unfair to her.'

'Worked, though.'

'Well, maybe. So would a lobotomy, Nathan, but it's not the answer for any of us.'

'You're stashing that gun under your pillow to keep it away from me.'

'You could have a gun in your bag.'

'I don't. Forgot them in Santa Fe in the fire. Why'd you tell Groote you had the goods?'

'So he'd let you go.'

'That was stupid.'

'No more stupid than your fire, Nathan.'

Nathan said nothing for a moment, then asked, quietly, 'What are Celeste and I to you?'

'I – I just don't want either of you hurt any more.'

'But why?'

'I don't know, Jesus, just be grateful.'

'I am, Miles. Thank you.'

Miles switched off the lamp, buried his face in the pillow.

He was close to sleep when he heard Nathan say, 'Miles?'

'Yeah.'

'If we get Frost . . . could we take it to the Defense Department? I keep thinking . . . about all the soldiers, coming home from war, brains screwed into new shapes from seeing all the horrors. They need Frost. I want to be sure they get it. That was the whole reason I volunteered for the VR treatments – to help.'

'And you said we weren't responsible for each other.'

'I meant' – and he searched for words – 'we don't know each other. Why did you come back for me?'

'It wasn't to make you indebted to me,' Miles said. 'I get the sense you really don't want any responsibility toward anyone else.'

'When I'm better,' Nathan said. 'When I'm fixed, when I'm good enough to be around other people. Soon. It'll be soon.'

'You're good enough now.'

Miles listened to the young man's breathing slide into the steadiness of sleep, savored the quiet, the wonderful, see-nothing dark, sank his aching, tired body into slumber.

'Don't get comfortable,' Andy said from the darkness. 'We need to talk.'

Miles closed his eyes, shut out the voice.

'You think you help them, I go away now, is that it? You couldn't save Allison, so you'll save them.'

Miles mouthed, *Shut up*, into the pillow.

'You didn't worry about saving me. Jesus. Known you since we were learning how to piss standing up, and you worry about complete strangers.'

'I tried . . . Saving you was the whole point of the sting,' he said into the pillow, afraid to wake Nathan but afraid to not answer Andy.

'You shot me.'

'You shot me,' Miles whispered back.

'But it was all your fault,' Andy hissed, his voice sounding like flame. 'Should've kept your mouth shut. You killed me with a word, asshole.'

Miles pulled the blankets over his head, a child burrowing

into the soft sheets to escape a bad dream. Sweat coursed down his ribs. 'I didn't.'

'You didn't save Allison, you won't save them,' Andy said. 'You'll make another mistake, and boom, boom, they'll be dead too.'

After Andy's laughter faded, the silence of the room pressed hard against his ears. Finally he closed his eyes, prayed for the dreams to keep their distance, and slept.

Miles heard the door click shut. Total darkness.

He thought the sound was his imagination, the click of the knob the final word of a dream. *You killed me with a word.* He searched under the pillow for his gun, closed his fingers around the barrel.

Silence.

He sat upright in the dark, fear squeezing his chest, the gun out steady in front of him.

'Shoot into the dark,' Andy said. 'Great freaking idea.'

He closed his eyes. No sound of Nathan breathing.

Miles snapped on the light.

Nathan was gone.

The clock read 4:03 A.M. Miles pulled on jeans, heard the reassuring jangle of the car keys in his pocket. Nathan hadn't taken the car, at least. Miles pulled on his shirt, tucked the gun in the back of his pants, left the shirt hanging loose behind him to cover the gun. He eased open the door to Celeste's room; she'd left a bathroom light on for comfort, and he could see her sleeping the sleep of the exhausted. He shut the door gently.

He grabbed the room key, went out into the hall. Empty and quiet. To the right was the lobby, to the left was the parking lot. He headed for the lot. Nathan was walking, he decided, planning to hitch a ride.

But the lot was empty. He could hear the distant roar of scattered traffic on Interstate 5. He ran back down the hall into the deserted lobby.

Nathan stood at a pay phone, hanging up as soon as Miles came into sight. His expression was defiant.

'What are you doing?' Miles asked.

'I called my folks . . . I had to let them know I was okay.'

'You shouldn't have.'

'Listen, my folks don't have caller ID or nothing, man, they won't know where I'm at and I didn't tell them. But I had to let them know I'm okay. I've always been tight with them. They're used to hearing from me every week, man, they'd freak if I didn't call.'

No contact with him for six months, it's part of the treatment. Miles let the lie hang in the air between him and Nathan, wondering if another lie would follow.

'Okay,' Miles said. 'How are your folks?'

'Great. My mom, she understands me. Always has. She's always been real supportive of me.'

'You're lucky to have her.'

'Okay,' Nathan said. He stepped away from the phone. 'I'm sorry I upset you. I can't sleep no more. Let's wake up Celeste, get going.'

'You said we should stay, let Celeste have indoor time.'

'I was wrong. You were right.'

'Wow. Me. Right.' He wanted to say, *Stop lying. Tell me who you really were calling. Tell me why you were in such a hurry to hang up you didn't even say good-bye.*

'The diner down the service road's open in another hour or so,' Nathan said. 'If it doesn't have mirrors all along the walls – some of 'em do, you know – we could eat there.'

'Sure. Sure.' Maybe he had been calling his parents. 'But we'd better get up and get on the road.' *Or he's called the police, and in five seconds I'll hear the sirens.*

But there was only the quiet of the night, and they went back to the room, Nathan averting his eyes from the mirror that hung over the sink counter, stretching on the bed. *He wouldn't call the police, not from the lobby, not when I might catch him,* Miles decided. *He'd just run, get clear away.*

He let Celeste sleep another hour. The motel stayed quiet, still, until the sounds of showers rushing through pipes, coughs in the hallway, the distant thrum of a truck pulling out of the lot, announced the new day.

They walked to the diner in the morning chill. Celeste huddled close to him, and as they reached the glass doors he saw her face on the cover of the morning's *USA Today,* an old publicity photo from when she'd won the five million, grinning out at the world from a vending machine.

'Uh-oh,' Miles said.

'What?' Then Celeste saw herself, put her face into Miles's shoulder.

A couple coming out of the diner, chatting, smiled a good morning at them. Then the woman followed their gazes, riveted on the newspaper dispenser.

Miles steered Nathan and Celeste back toward the hotel. He peeled out of the lot, thinking, *Those people didn't see her face and the picture, they couldn't have,* but as they shot by the diner the couple were still standing there, studying the front page of the paper they'd pulled from the machine.

265

FORTY

Andy rode with them, talking, murmuring, all the way to Fish Camp.

The town lived up to its simple name. Highway 41 wound high into the mountains, and a few miles before Yosemite the town stood before them: a couple of modest stores, a wide fishing pond, a scattering of rental properties and modest homes, a couple of bed-and-breakfasts and restaurants on the mountain's side, a scruffy 1950s motel called the Yosemite Gateway on the narrow ribbon of highway. Tall pines covered the landscape; every trash can in the motel lots and along the roadside was metal, with cover mechanisms to keep the bears from foraging in the garbage. To Miles, who had spent his entire life in Florida before that life ended, the mountains and the forests reminded him of drawings from a German storybook he'd had as a child.

Miles checked them into the Gateway, two adjoining rooms with a connecting door between them.

'Where's my room?' Andy asked. 'Okay, I'll just stay with you all.'

He's angry because you're close, Miles thought. *Close to Frost, close to having a way to banish him from your head, once and for all.*

Nathan landed on one of the twin beds in his and Miles's room and stretched out. Miles noticed Nathan kept glancing at the digital clock.

'I think Nathan has an engagement on his calendar, Miles,' Andy said.

'Now what do we do?' Celeste asked.

'Find Edward Wallace. But first, we're dyeing your hair,' Miles said. 'We can't have anyone recognizing you from the newspaper, and if you're on the front page of *USA Today*, I bet you're on television too.'

'I don't think I can go out anymore,' she said. 'I need walls right now. I need – I need to cut myself.' She swallowed, braced her shoulder against the door frame.

Miles went down to the motel office and asked for a rubber band. He brought it back, went into her room where Celeste sat at the end of the bed, knelt before her, took her hand, slipped it on her wrist.

'We are so not engaged,' she said. 'But thanks. The urge passed.'

He wished he had a rubber band to drive away Andy. Then he heard the soft, deliberate crack of glass. 'Oh, goddamn.' He rushed back to his room. Nathan stood, his fist covered by the room's chipped and faded ice bucket, the bathroom mirror fractured, two jagged Nathans frowning back at him from the glass.

'Can't you control yourself for just one blessed minute?' Miles said.

Nathan let the ice bucket fall to the floor, walked past Miles, threw himself back on the bed. 'I'll remember that when you start talking to air.'

'We don't need trouble with the motel, we don't need attention, we can't have anyone *remembering* us. Do you understand?'

'Sir, yes, sir,' Nathan said into the pillow. 'But I can't calm down. I can't. I need my meds, man, now.' Desperation kicked in to his voice.

'Miles, take it easy,' Celeste said. 'He can't help himself . . .'

'I'm sick of it. Sick of being sick.' Miles stumbled outside. The air, in May, was still chilly, cooler than the high desert of Santa Fe, and fingers of snow hid in the shadows of the heavy pines and furrows of land between the rental cabins. The air was crisp in his lungs, against his face.

He walked away from the car, from the motel, from the intermittent swoosh of passing cars heading the final two miles to Yosemite.

I can't do this, he thought. *I can't keep them calm and straight and focused.* He had no real plan after finding Edward Wallace, and he didn't want to admit his uncertainty to himself or to the others. How did you expose a conspiracy and have anyone believe you? What if, in bringing Frost to light, he killed the medicine's chances for acceptance and production because of its illicit creation? What if they got caught just because they went to get food and a television fan recognized Celeste? The whole enterprise was tottering, ready to collapse in rubble and dust, burying him under what he thought had been an impulse, a need to Do the Right Thing.

He stopped at the motel's corner, leaned his head against the brick. He took a fortifying breath of mountain air. He could do this. He had to, he had no choice. Celeste needed Frost, so did Nathan. They needed help. They needed him.

'No one really needs anyone,' Allison said to him from the corner.

He raised his head and she was leaning against the

bricks, dressed in the clothes she had worn the last morning of her life.

His breath caught in his throat, he shook his head, closed his eyes. Counted to ten.

He looked again. She was still there, her arms crossed. 'I – I . . .' he started to say.

'Miles, your path is clear. It's simple. Load the gun. Find a private place. Leave a note if there's anyone you want to say goodbye to – such as DeShawn and Joy. They'd miss you' – and she shrugged – 'but they didn't really know you long enough to care about you.'

He tried to speak; nothing came but a harsh hiss of breath.

'No one blames you for not wanting to hear Andy bitching in your head for the rest of your life. Years and years of him talking.'

'No.'

'You're worried about failing your – friends. You worried over failing me. But I failed you, Miles, I gave you false hope.'

He clenched his eyes shut, ran his fingers along the even lines of the bricks. A man from another room walked by him and Miles felt the burn of his curious stare.

'And that's all Frost is,' Allison said. 'False hope. You don't really think Nathan is better, do you? He's not. It doesn't work.'

He whispered a prayer. 'She's not real, I know she's not real, even if she was she'd never say these things, it's the sickness.'

He opened his eyes and ran into the space where she'd stood, but there was only the Sierra breeze.

She was gone. He pressed his palms against the brick wall. Nathan and Celeste were real, they were his responsibility. He had to get a grip. If he stayed strong, Celeste and Nathan could stay strong. So they could get the drug. He craved it now; strange to want something you'd never had, but he needed Frost to be real.

So get moving.

He walked back to the room. Nathan sat on the bed, watching a celebrity poker tournament on TV.

'Nathan, I'm sorry I yelled.'

'I've got five hundred years of bad luck from mirrors,' Nathan said. 'You yelling doesn't scare me.' He shook his head at Miles with a dawning fear. 'I haven't had Frost in days, man, and I'm falling apart. I got to have it, man.'

'Be straight with me. Was it your mom you called?'

He nodded slowly. 'You don't believe me.'

'I was under the impression you didn't get to talk to your mom at all when you were in the hospital. So I know you didn't call her every week.'

'True. But I did call her last night. I told you she'd be expecting to hear from me because I didn't want you to freak that I'd called her.'

'Then I believe you. Try to rest.'

'Miles.'

'Yeah?'

'About your friend that died. You can't stand there and let someone shoot you. You just protected yourself.'

'There's a lot more to the story, Nathan.'

'How do you know if you don't remember?'

'I don't know.'

'Window dressing. Are you sorry you're alive?'

'No. I'm not.'

'There's your answer, then.' Nathan closed his eyes.

Miles went to the open door of Celeste's room, knocked on the frame. She came out of the bathroom, drying her face with a towel. He closed the door behind him.

'Sorry,' he said.

'Nothing to apologize for,' she said.

He wanted to tell her he'd seen Allison, but the words dammed in his throat and he swallowed.

'You wanted to change my hair before we go,' she said. 'Let's get it done.' She went to a bag; they had stopped in Fresno, bought clothing basics and knapsacks at a twenty-four-hour WalMart. She pulled out a pair of nail scissors. 'You cut my hair, then we'll dye it.'

'I don't know how to cut hair,' he said.

'I haven't set foot in a stylist's shop in forever.' Celeste ran a hand through the thick mop of dark hair. 'I'm not vain. Just cut it off.'

'I'll chop away.'

She grabbed his wrist. 'Cut, not chop. Big diff.'

So he wet her hair, because when he got a haircut the stylist wet it, and he started trimming off the length with hesitant snips, almost afraid she would scream in horror if he cut too much at once, taking it slow, loving the heavy dampness of her hair between his fingers. She sat on a chair, in front of the mirror, and he kept a wastebasket under where he cut off the lengths, moving the basket with his foot to catch the falling tresses.

'You're gonna bite through your lip,' she said.

He let his lip go from between his teeth. He cut off a series of locks of her hair, smoothed it back with his fingers, gently rubbing her scalp.

'That feels nice,' she said. 'Thank you.'

He stopped. A stirring awoke in his chest. His mouth went dry. 'How short do you want it cut?'

She watched his face. 'Most pictures of me, it's at least

shoulder length. It's how people remember me. Give it a pixie cut.'

'A what?'

'Cut it boy short. No worries, Miles. I won't get mad even if you shave me bald.'

So he cut it short, diving the scissors close to her scalp, leaving a couple of inches of growth, gentle around her ears.

'You're doing a good job,' she said.

'I'm getting hair everywhere.'

'You don't have to be perfect.'

'Why do you cut yourself?' He kept his eyes on the scissors, poised above her damp hair.

'Better that than seeing dead people,' she said, and then instantly added, 'I'm sorry. That was unfair.'

'It's all right. But I hate to see you hurt yourself.'

'I don't have an answer. I hate it. Allison said I cut so I would feel again.'

'I hate just a paper cut. Doesn't it hurt?'

'Yes.'

'Don't you feel anyway? I feel empty.'

'Yet you're not, Miles. You know that you're not. Because you'd be dead if you were empty and you fought to save me, to save yourself. You feel, Miles, but I bet it's not emptiness.' She studied him in the mirror. 'Did you leave a woman behind in Florida?'

'No.'

'Ever married?'

'No. I try not to be one for needing.' He smoothed out a length of her hair, trimmed the end of it.

She ducked her head out from under his hands. 'You've cut off enough of my mop,' she said. 'Absolutely horrible. I'm completely unrecognizable. Thank you, I love it.'

He dusted her threads of hair from his hands into the wastebasket, read the instructions on the hair dye, slathered on the gunk to make her auburn-haired.

'I wish you were giving me red-red hair,' she said. 'Like Lucille Ball or Carol Burnett. Never sad watching them on TV.'

He spread the concoction through her hair and she sat while he rinsed his hands.

'If we don't find Frost, or Edward Wallace,' she said, 'what do we do?'

'You and Nathan go back to Santa Fe and tell the police what happened. You can't hide forever.'

'What about you?'

'I'm out of Witness Protection. I guess I'll go make a new life for myself.'

'Do you have another trial to testify in?' she asked.

He raised an eyebrow at her.

'It's a logical question,' she said. 'Witnesses are witnesses because they testify.'

'Yeah, I'm supposed to.'

'So you're not done.'

'No. I still will testify.'

'Then WITSEC will have to protect you again.'

He would probably be in jail for fighting DeShawn, but he didn't want to admit it to her. 'I'm done with WITSEC. I broke their rules. I'll hide myself.'

'You can't hide.'

'You hid yourself. Just behind a wall. I'll do it behind a new identity. Or I'll go far away. Cyprus. India. Thailand. It doesn't matter.'

He sat on the corner of the bed; she stayed in her chair.

'When you killed that man,' she said, 'did you have your breakdown right away?'

He listened to the sound of his own breathing. The walls were painted an awful beige-green. From the other room he heard Nathan's soft snore. 'I only remember me speaking, him drawing his gun, me shooting him, him falling, me falling. That's it. No details. It's a silent movie with frames missing.'

'So how can you be sure it was so decidedly your fault? He drew his gun.'

'He tells me it was my fault. He told me I killed him with a word. I'm afraid to remember.'

'He's a figment of your imagination.'

'No. He's our disease, given life and breath and voice.'

'If we had Frost, right now, would you take it?'

'I – I don't know.'

'You don't know because you don't want to remember. It might be worse than what you think happened.'

The confession was still folded in his pocket.

'And you told me a minute ago you couldn't worry about what people thought,' she said. 'I'm people. Quit worrying.'

'I never saw your show.'

'You didn't miss much.'

'Tell me how you won the five million.'

'No. When this is all over we'll rent the Season One DVD. I don't want to give away the ending.'

'I know the ending. You win. Tell me.'

So she did, chewing up the thirty minutes with talk of secret blocs and voting and backstabbing, and he checked the clock and said, 'Time to rinse your hair.'

She stood. He jetted on the faucet and she ducked her head underneath while he cupped the water and rinsed the dye from her hair. She toweled her hair and made the wet cut spiky with her fingers. She looked different enough from the woman in the newspaper photos to pass a casual inspection.

'You can tell me about the shooting, Miles. I won't hate you. I couldn't hate you.' She turned and her face was inches from his. 'I couldn't hate you. Ever.'

'You should know,' Andy hissed in his ear, 'that I'm never going to let you get close to another person again.'

Miles flinched. 'We can talk about it later. Let's find Edward Wallace.'

He pulled the thin phone book from the side-table drawer. It covered the scattering of communities near Yosemite. He ran a finger along the residential listings. 'Edward Wallace. He's listed. Not trying to hide.'

'We could just call him and ask him about Allison.'

'No. I don't want him shoving us off. You and Nathan stay here.'

'I want to come with you.'

'No. It could be dangerous,' he said. 'Besides, I'm experienced at getting information out of people, you're not. Please.'

The hurt shone in her face. 'Well, sure, since you're so experienced. I'll just sit in my disguise and talk to myself.' She crossed her arms and sat down.

'I'll come back with Frost,' he said.

'Yeah, great,' she said as he shut the door.

Celeste stood at the window and watched him go. Then she went back inside and stood over Nathan, curled in quiet sleep. Gently she touched his cheek, as if to reassure herself that he was still there. Then she found Edward Wallace's address in the phone book and wrote a note for Nathan. She put it by his bedside and he opened his eyes and reached out and grabbed her arm.

'What are you doing?' he asked.

'I'm going to help Miles.'

'No, Celeste. Stay.' His voice was quiet; not jagged.

'Let go of my arm, Nathan.'

He didn't. 'You need to stay. This is over now, Celeste, and you'll be safe.'

'What do you mean?' She tried to free her arm; Nathan tightened his grip.

'I did it for all of us. He'll be here soon.'

'What have you done—' She wrenched free from him, hit him in the chest, spun for the door. She opened it and saw Groote – the man from Santa Fe – running toward the room from the motel office, his eyes lasered on hers. She slammed the door, fumbled to engage the chain lock, missing, and then Groote powered against the door with all his muscle and fury and she landed hard on the worn carpet.

He leveled a gun at Celeste's head.

Nathan threw himself at Groote, and Groote whipped the pistol hard across Nathan's face, cutting his cheek. He kicked Nathan, pile-driving him onto Celeste.

Groote closed the door, threw the dead bolt, aimed the gun at them.

'Hi, Nathan. Don't light any fires. Nice to see you again, Mrs. Brent. Don't scream.' His smile chilled Celeste's skin. 'We need to talk.'

FORTY-ONE

Edward Wallace's windows needed a scrubbing. The sides of the bungalow cried for a fresh coat of paint. But a gleaming Mercedes stood in the driveway, at odds with the tumbledown air of the home. Not a home; just a house where someone lived.

Miles remembered Allison's neat tidiness; he couldn't picture her at this house. But then, she'd lived a lie; he didn't know the real Allison at all.

Miles went up to the porch, knocked. He heard a shuffle of footsteps; the door opened a crack. Miles saw a sliver of face: blue eye, blond hair, unshaven cheek.

'Mr. Wallace?'

'It's Doctor.'

'My apologies. Doctor Wallace. We need to talk.'

'I don't believe in God or fund raisers.' He shut the door.

Miles leaned forward, spoke low against the door frame. 'Allison sent me. Or I guess you call her Renee.'

Four beats of silence. Then the door opened.

Edward Wallace matched the picture of the man in the wedding photo; tall with a thin, intellectual face and the lean build of a marathon runner. He held a sleek automatic pistol in his hand, aimed at Miles's stomach. It trembled in his grip.

'Who are you?'

'Miles Kendrick. I knew your wife. At least, I thought I did.'

Edward Wallace bit his lip. 'You're the federal witness.'

Miles kept his surprise off his face. 'Allison told you?'

'Yes.'

'Would you mind pointing your friend away from me, Doctor Wallace?'

Wallace lowered the gun. 'I would have missed. I don't know anything about guns.'

'I have about a thousand questions for you,' Miles said.

'Well, I have only one answer. You and I are both dead men,' Wallace said, 'unless we help each other.'

FORTY-TWO

'You gave me a chase, man.' Groote knelt down near Nathan, keeping the gun firmly aimed at Celeste's head. 'Now. No more fighting, okay? It only hurts us both.'

Nathan's mouth trembled. 'No. No.'

'Thinking about the time we spent together?' Groote said. 'I don't enjoy hurting people. But no pain for you, no gain for me. Talk to me, and I won't get out Mr. Screwdriver again. At least not on you.' He grabbed Celeste, who had wriggled free from under Nathan.

'Don't,' Nathan said. 'Don't hurt her.'

'Then help me, Nathan.' He ran the gun barrel along the top of Celeste's new haircut. 'But I want to know where Frost and Miles Kendrick are.'

'Miles is gone,' Celeste said before Nathan could answer.

'Where?'

'To get Frost,' Celeste said.

'You're cooperative, Mrs. Brent,' Groote said.

Celeste swallowed. 'I don't want you to shoot us.'

'When will he be back?'

'An hour. Not sure,' Celeste said.

'You were in a tear-ass hurry to leave when you came out of the door,' Groote said. 'I heard you loved the great indoors.'

'Nathan works my last nerve,' she said.

'He has that effect,' Groote said. 'But you're working my nerve. You people chose the wrong guy to screw with—'

The phone rang.

'Let it be,' Groote ordered.

'If it's Miles,' she said quietly, 'he'll expect me to answer. He'll wonder where we are. I don't answer, he'll be on his guard.'

Groote shoved her toward the phone. 'Answer it. You warn him, I put a bullet in Tin Soldier.' He grabbed Nathan's hair, jerked the young man close to him, jabbed the gun hard against Nathan's temple.

She picked up the phone. 'Yes?' She could not believe how calm her voice was.

No answer. She could hear breathing on the opposite end of the line.

'Yes, we're fine,' she said, not wanting to say, *Yes?* again, wondering, *Why doesn't Miles speak?*

'Is Groote there?' a voice she didn't recognize said. A man's voice, with the barest hint of a Boston accent.

'Yes,' she said again.

The line ended. 'All right, Miles, good-bye.' She hung up.

'What did he say?' Groote said.

'Letting me know how the search is going.'

'For Edward Wallace.'

'Yes. But Wallace isn't at home. Miles is going to wait for him, bring back food when he's done.' She sat down on the bed. Her skin prickled. *What the hell was that call, who was that man?* 'We haven't eaten for hours.'

'Poor you.' Groote scratched at the bandage covering his broken nose. 'I saw you on *Castaway*. My wife loved that show. I know you can be a tricky bitch.'

'I played fair and square.' She couldn't believe the sudden anger in her voice.

'Whatever. Your face is known. You're going to be a problem for me.'

Terror filled her. Now that Groote believed Miles would soon return with the precious Frost, he would have no use for her or Nathan. He wasn't going to let her out of this room. His gun wore a silencer and his hands were big enough to crush her throat. His eyes, smudged with exhaustion, over the grimy nose bandage, regarded her without mercy.

She could not sit in this grubby room and wait to die, not again, waiting, choked with fear, for a man to walk through those doors and watch him be murdered. Not again.

'Why are you doing this?' Nathan asked Groote.

'My boss wants his property back,' Groote said. He prodded Celeste with the gun. 'You. Tell me. Does it work?'

'What?' She looked up from her lap.

'Frost. Does it work?'

'Why would you care?'

'Just curious.' His voice was flat but she saw heat fire his eyes at her question.

'You mean does Frost work, so is it worth it to kill us? Well, I'm too scared to tell you.' She put a waver in her voice. 'If the panic hits me, I start screaming.'

'No screaming,' Groote said in a harsh bark. 'You scream, you die.'

She shoved her palms against her mouth, pretending to stifle a shriek. Two deep breaths and she lowered her hands. 'I need . . . my medicine. Please.'

Groote said, 'Forget it. Just shut up and sit there.'

'Let her have her antidepressant, man,' Nathan said.

Groote gave him a kick to the chest that floored him. 'I don't want to hear your whining. I am incredibly tired of you people.'

'My pill's in my purse. In the next room.' She slapped at her chest, as if she were beating back a howl climbing into her throat. 'I have sedatives too. For Nathan.'

In his frown gone straight, she saw Groote make the decision she calculated he might; he could force a pharmacy down their throats, keep them under control. Groote put the gun on Nathan, hauled him to his feet. 'Come on, Tin Soldier. Try anything and you get a bad dent.'

She walked to the next room, Groote and Nathan a step behind her. She walked to her purse.

'Wrong,' Groote said. 'Pick it up by the bottom, Mrs. Brent, dump it on the floor. No surprises.'

She did as he asked and her junk tumbled in a pile on the greasy gray carpet: lipstick, the extra rubber bands Miles had brought her, her money clip, a black notebook, an empty pill vial, wallet, her cell phone, switched off as Miles had ordered so the wireless company couldn't get a reading on her location. She crouched among the junk.

'Hands away from the cell phone. Kick it to me,' Groote ordered.

She obeyed. He crushed the phone under his heel, breaking the keys and the screen.

She cranked open the pill vial. Empty.

'Oh,' she said. 'I'm – I'm out.' But she fidgeted, put her knee over the money clip.

'Stupid,' Groote said. She stayed kneeling.

'Get up, Tin Soldier, on the bed, I'm tying you two up.'

She got up, closing her fist around the clip. She worked the money loose, let the clip drop to the floor. Between the soft, worn bills the sharp bite of her razor nipped at her finger. She folded it in her hand.

Groote didn't see. He shoved her on the bed across from Nathan. 'If one of you moves, you die,' Groote said.

Tie me first, she thought, *please*. Because Nathan could help her fight him when Groote drew close to her.

But he tied Nathan first, pulling the phone cord loose from the wall, securing Nathan's hands and feet together, ripping a pillowcase, jamming a near-choking length into Nathan's mouth.

She told herself: *Don't flinch*.

There wasn't another phone cord in the room, so he snapped loose the curtain cord and came toward her.

She knelt on the bed and stuck her hands out in front of her, as though prepping to be handcuffed, and before he could reach her she said, 'I have most of the five million that I won. It's yours. Just let us go.'

And because he thought she was about to beg, not fight, he paused. 'I don't give a shit about your money.'

'I can't be tied up. Because of what happened to me . . . when my husband died.' Not a problem to put fear into her voice. But she was more afraid of what would happen if she didn't stop him. 'Don't tie me. I know where Frost is. Right now.'

'Where?'

She raised her chin. 'I don't want Nathan to hear.'

She figured Groote would steer her into the next room but he was too eager, he leaned closer to her and she might not get close again so she slapped at him. Except the razor was tight and true between her fingers and the blade

283

scored a garish red thread across his face, along his cheek, close to the eye.

He stumbled back in shock and she swung at him again, but he clubbed her arm aside with a low animal grunt that rose into a scream. She darted the razor toward his throat. Groote belted a fist into her temple and she tumbled off the bed. He levered his foot hard on her wrist, forced her fingers open, and the razor slipped free of them.

'Date with pain.' His voice sounded broken. 'That's right, you cut me, bitch, it better not scar, it better not scare Amanda . . .' His voice stopped and she fought him, biting, kicking, his hands clamping over her mouth, and he carried her, headfirst, into the bathroom. He held her upside down; her feet brushed the plaster ceiling.

'Where is Frost? Where is it?'

'I don't know—' she started to say, and then she saw the open toilet rushing toward her face. She managed a startled gulp of air before he drove her face into the shallow water.

Celeste struggled but he pinioned her legs with his own, her hands with one of his massive arms, and held her head at a precise angle and her face rammed against the porcelain. *He's done this before*, she realized in shock.

'You know! Tell me! Where is it?' he yelled.

All she could do was keep kicking, make him fight to drown her.

The air exploded from her lungs as though seeking release and she choked, breathed the water, and then he let her go. She fell to the cold tile, spluttering, coughing, tasting her own blood from her lips.

'Mrs. Brent? Are you well?'

The voice from the phone. Above her stood a fiftyish man, hair dark as coal, skin pale, with the biggest gun she'd ever seen pressed against Groote's head.

FORTY-THREE

'Why are we both dead men?' Miles asked.

'We know too much. Or rather, people think we know too much.' Edward Wallace stepped aside and Miles walked into the house. He could see a back wall, dotted with photos. Of Allison. Wearing glasses, hair lighter in color, cut longer.

'About Frost.'

'Do you have it?' Cautious hope lit Wallace's eyes.

'No. You do.'

Hope changed to surprise. 'What?'

'Allison hid the files on a server here. The day she died.'

'Oh, Jesus. That explains it.' Wallace sank against the wall.

'Not to me, Doctor Wallace.'

'I don't have Frost.'

'But you could access this system where she put the files—'

'No. Listen, you have to go. Now. You can't be here when Dodd gets here.'

'Who's Dodd?' Miles remembered having heard the name when Sorenson spoke on the phone in Allison's office: *Dodd doesn't know.* And asking Allison who Dodd was as she hung up on him before she died. Dodd. The missing piece of the puzzle.

'You can't be here and you can't know who he is. Please. Just go.'

'No. Show me this system where she uploaded the files.'

'I don't have the Frost files.'

'You erased them.'

'No. I don't know what happened,' Wallace said. He set the gun down on the table, ran a hand through his hair, which stuck in clumps as though he'd run his hands through it in unending worry for the whole day.

'Your wife asked me for help, Doctor. I didn't help her in time and she's dead, and the only way to help her now is to make sure whoever killed her doesn't get away with it.'

Wallace's half cough, half laugh was a strange sound in the quiet of the bungalow. 'You. Stop them. I don't know which side killed her, but you won't stop them. Listen. Dodd could arrive at any time. We need to go.'

If you're so afraid of this Dodd, why haven't you already left? Miles wondered.

'Dodd wants Frost. Why? Who is he?'

'If I tell you – will you help me hide? Before they kill me the way they killed Renee.'

This didn't add up, but the fear on the man's face seemed real and defined. 'These people killed your wife. Why don't you just go to the cops?'

'I – can't go to the police.'

'Explain.'

Wallace took a fortifying deep breath. 'Dodd was in charge of the original Frost project.'

'Hurley and Quantrill didn't create Frost?'

287

'No. They built on our findings. I was on the original Frost research team,' Wallace said. 'So was Renee.'

'Why was she living as Allison Vance?'

'She had no choice – being Allison was her cover story. Dodd forced her. He's with the government.'

'What agency?'

'Dodd's group is code-named Shaman. But you won't see them listed on a congressional budget. They operate out of back rooms, with money cleaned through legit projects. He's in charge of clandestine scientific research for the Defense Department.'

It clicked. Frost would be an immediate benefit to soldiers mentally devastated by the horrors of war. 'So she was supposed to steal it for Dodd.'

'Returning his stolen property.'

'Why didn't she just send it to Dodd?'

'I don't know.'

'Why did she send Frost to your server?'

'I don't know. I'd had no contact with her since she went to Santa Fe. Dodd forbade it.' Wallace closed his eyes. 'The – the people on Dodd's team three years ago, we developed the initial version of Frost. I'm a neurobiologist – I worked on the beta blockers to prevent traumatic memories from consolidating. Allison was one of the psychiatrists. But our prototype drug didn't work unless administered within two hours immediately following the trauma. One soldier in the test group, he went psychotic. When his long-term trauma didn't go away . . . he killed the other patients in the testing. All of them.' Wallace's voice broke. 'We brought those people there to help them, to cure them, and they all were murdered, one by one, in their sleep. Dodd ended the project and killed the research. Renee blamed herself.'

'She knew about Frost. She knew what it was, from the beginning,' Miles said.

'After Dodd shut down the project, his team drifted into other work. Renee and I moved up to Fresno to open a PTSD clinic while I taught college and continued research. We kept a low profile, and then Dodd showed up at our house a few months ago. Quantrill had got hold of the original research – another researcher stole the original work and sold it to him – and managed to take Frost to the next level. Dodd found out – probably from the researcher who sold the data to Quantrill. Dodd can be . . . convincing. As in his way or it's your funeral. That researcher died in a car accident. I don't believe much in coincidence.'

Miles remembered the news account. 'You had a hiking accident a few weeks back.'

'Dodd forced us to quit our jobs and we moved up here for a lower profile. Renee went to Santa Fe to do Dodd's spying for him . . . She called me late one night on the phone from her office. She missed me. Dodd must have been monitoring her office line; he sent a message as to what happens when his rules are broken. He came, asked me to go on a hike with him so we could talk, gave me a shove off a ten-foot bluff. Just enough to hurt, to rough me up. A warning.'

'Nice.'

Wallace said, 'Renee blamed herself for the Frost patients' dying before; she never got over it. Dodd covered up the deaths, made the families believe the patients had died in a fire in the ward at a medical hospital in San Diego where we did the work.'

'So Dodd wanted a new and improved Frost back. He made Allison his spy.' She'd been a spy of sorts – just like him. Miles's chest tensed; he remembered her words the last morning he saw her: *I think I understand you better than you know.*

Wallace nodded. 'Memory research ... it's a small world. Quantrill couldn't know that she'd worked on the original team. She had to see if his version of Frost had promise, steal it if it did, and then she could be Renee again.'

'Why didn't Dodd just go to the authorities and let them handle it? Quantrill broke the law, buying government secrets ...'

'Dodd didn't want the original project exposed; the Pentagon was doing secret drug testing on veterans. I don't think Dodd has a shadow; the man doesn't see the light of day often.'

'Connect the other players for me. Sorenson. Who's he?'

Wallace sat down in the chair, mopped sweat from his forehead. 'He's a mean bastard. He worked security on Dodd's projects. He was supposed to go to Santa Fe and protect Renee, help her if she needed to bypass security systems to steal the Frost research.'

'Sorenson killed her.'

'What?'

'He planted the bomb that killed her.' He told Wallace about seeing Sorenson enter and leave Allison's office without his case, return and speak on the phone about Dodd.

Wallace paled, covered his eyes with his hand.

'Would Sorenson have access to explosives?'

'He used to be in covert operations for the Pentagon. He's Dodd's security guy. Dodd called me early this morning, in a panic, because he knew she'd sent the files to the server. I don't know how he knew ...'

'Early this morning?' Miles said. Oh, Jesus. His mouth went dry. Nathan, putting the pay-phone receiver down, a sheepish look on his face, a lie on his lips about a weekly duty to call his mother. A call he could not risk in the same room, even with Miles asleep. Dodd was connected to Allison; Allison tried to help Nathan escape. So maybe . . . 'I think I know who called him. Dodd ever mention a guy named Nathan Ruiz?'

'No.'

It didn't mean Nathan didn't know Dodd. 'So Dodd wanted the files she sent.'

'But they're not there. I use the server to run a small Web hosting business, and to hold my research database, run power-hungry apps I use in my work – I never saw any files, never knew they were there. You have to believe me.'

'Dodd doesn't.'

'I gave him the access codes, he checked it himself. Someone accessed the server this morning using the admin password Renee and I used and ran a wiping program to destroy all the data on the drive . . . everything's gone, totally overwritten. Nothing's recoverable, and I've already tried. The only other person with the administrative password who could have done that was Renee. Unless she gave the password to someone.'

Miles thought it through. 'Sorenson. Allison wasn't hiding the files from him – she was stashing them to deliver to Dodd. So the files would still be available to him or Sorenson if Quantrill's people caught or killed her. But she must have told Sorenson the code, or he found the password – people are always writing that stuff down – and he took the Frost research off the server, then wiped the server to destroy the files once he'd retrieved them.'

'Dodd doesn't believe me, he thinks I have Frost. He's coming. That's why I need to hide.' A tremble colored Wallace's voice.

The picture wasn't fully clear and Miles shook his head. 'Go back to Sorenson. Where's he?'

'Dodd said Sorenson went missing two days ago; Dodd thinks another man, a guy named Dennis Groote who works for Quantrill, caught up with him. Probably killed him.'

Probably after our escape from the hospital, Miles thought. 'This Nathan Ruiz I mentioned. He was a patient of Allison's. Sorenson went to a lot of trouble to try and kill him at Sangre de Cristo, but I don't know why.'

'I never heard of him.'

'But you've heard of me. She asked me to help her before she died. If Sorenson was supposed to protect her, she sure didn't need me. So . . . she must have suspected he was betraying her. He took Frost.' But then why give him the key to the hidey-hole for the files? It made no sense, unless she'd given the password before she suspected him.

'This is all Dodd's fault,' Wallace said. 'If he'd left well enough alone . . .'

'One more question. WITSEC vetted Allison, it did a background check on her.'

'So?'

'So Allison Vance isn't a real person; she couldn't have passed the check under false name.'

'Well, clearly, she did. Dodd would have handled ensuring her background was impeccable.'

Still, it bothered Miles. 'Why risk it, though? If she was there as a spy, why take on a client who might expose her?'

'She must not have known at first that you were a federal witness – but I don't know . . . Dodd ran her show. Listen, all I need is your help to vanish.'

'Ask Dodd.'

'No.' Wallace shook his head. 'No way. I want out. No more.'

Miles said, 'It's not right.'

'What the hell do you mean?'

'She died on Tuesday night. You say that the server was wiped today. Sorenson can't be dead – if he did the wiping.'

Wallace blinked, nodded. 'Well, yes.'

'How do you wipe a server?'

'Like you would any hard drive – you have to have the high-enough account level and then you use a specialized program that overwrites all the files on the drive.'

'So why didn't he clean it off on Tuesday? It doesn't make sense . . .'

'I don't know.' Wallace stood. 'I can't stay. We'd better go.' He paced the floor, talking to himself. 'Mexico. Not far enough. I had to learn French and German for my doctorate in science, so Europe would be good . . .'

Timing, Miles thought. *Days to notice the files, hours to run. Yet Wallace stayed, the fresh widower, the frightened lab geek, waiting for Dodd's vengeance.*

Wallace was lying, and Miles reached for the gun in the back of the pants just as Wallace seized his abandoned gun on the table and, with a runner's grace, spun toward Miles and fired.

293

FORTY-FOUR

'Mrs. Brent,' the man repeated, and Celeste got to her feet, shaking, leaning against the wall. 'My name is Dodd. Do exactly what I say and you'll be safe. Please untie Nathan. Go wash your face. Sit on the bed with him. Do not leave the room, do not make a phone call. Do not scream. I will help you. Am I clear?'

Stunned, she nodded.

Dodd shoved Groote out of the room, pushed him against the wall, started searching him. *His gun*, she thought, and opened her mouth to speak: *I kicked his gun under the bed.* But caution made her be quiet.

Dodd glanced back at her. 'Mrs. Brent. Do as I say, please, and everything will be fine.'

She worked Nathan's gag free. 'You okay?' he said.

She nodded and untied the knots binding Nathan's hands and feet. She was so glad to be alive she shivered, from head to toe, as though she'd plunged into freezing water.

'Sir,' Nathan said to Dodd, 'thank you. Thank you.'

'You're all right, Nathan?' Dodd asked.

'Yes, sir.' Crisply said, as though he were back in the military, ready to go fight the war all over again.

Celeste washed her face. Her lips were swollen and

she'd bled from her mouth and her nose, but not much. The soap smelled of lemon and she scrubbed her skin hard.

'Who are you?' Celeste asked as she dried her face.

'He's my boss,' Nathan said, a clear pride in his voice.

'Boss?'

Dodd finished searching Groote and shoved him face-down to the other bed, put the cannon close to his back. 'Answer my questions or your spine will be gone. You work for Oliver Quantrill.'

'Who?' Groote said.

'I admire loyalty but only to a point. Where's Sorenson?'

'I have no idea.'

'Don't lie, Mr. Groote.'

'Sorenson broke my nose – ask Nathan. If I knew where the bastard was I'd kill him. But I don't.'

'Interesting,' Dodd said. 'Mr. Groote hurt you, didn't he, Nathan?'

'With a screwdriver.' Nathan scrambled to the floor and retrieved Groote's gun, handed it to Dodd, and Celeste wondered, *What the hell is he doing?* She thought, too late, she should have retrieved the gun first.

'Want to take a screwdriver to Mr. Groote?'

Nathan shook his head. 'No.'

'Isn't Nathan a better man than you are, Mr. Groote?' Dodd asked.

'Apparently.' Hatred coated his voice.

'Nathan,' Dodd said, 'don't be alarmed by what I'm going to say to Mr. Groote. It's only because we live in desperate times.' He leaned closer to Groote. 'I have an offer for you. Quantrill's a dead end. You need to come over to my side.'

'Which side is that?' Groote asked.

'We're the people who invented Frost in the first place. Your boss stole it from me.'

'What—' Celeste started to say, and then Nathan silenced her with a subtle shake of his head.

'Let me tell you how we can help you, and help your daughter, Mr. Groote.'

'My daughter—' Groote said in choked shock, and Celeste saw real fear light in the man's eyes, real terror. 'You don't go near my kid, goddamn you . . .'

'Only fearful men make threats, Mr. Groote. Confident men make promises. Here's my first promise to you: I'm your new employer.'

'I don't recall looking for a new job.'

'Breathe a sigh of relief; you've had the shit kicked out of you since you signed on with Quantrill. Now you work for me. I'm buying out your contract.'

'I'm not for sale.'

Dodd produced a digital recorder from his pocket. 'I know your price.' He clicked the button.

'Daddy?' A girl's voice was quiet, drugged, blissed. 'Dad? Hi. It's me. I'm supposed to say hi to you first. They're moving me to a new hospital this morning. They said you were too busy to come see me during the move but that you'd visit soon.' A murmuring woman's voice sounded next, whispering to the girl to say good-bye. 'Yes,' the girl slurred. 'I love you, Daddy, come see me soon.'

The recording ended. Groote gasped in strained hitches and found his voice. 'I'll fucking kill you.'

'And what will happen to your Amanda then?'

Groote said in a torrent: 'Jesus, please, don't hurt my kid, God, where is she? Who the hell are you that you can move her without my permission?'

Celeste felt chilled by the fear on Groote's face, the smug smirk on Dodd's, the heartbreaking whisper of the girl's voice. She stood.

'Keep her still, Nathan, please,' Dodd said.

'What the hell is this—' Celeste started, and Nathan pulled her back to the bed, made her sit.

'Do what he says, he's the good guy.'

Celeste thought, *No he's not.*

Dodd said, 'Amanda's simply insurance. I just want to be sure you stay on my side. You're going to betray Quantrill for me, Mr. Groote, but I want to be sure you don't pull a double cross on me. Your daughter is perfectly safe. It's up to you to see that she remains perfectly safe.'

'The government,' Groote said suddenly. 'You're with the government.'

'*Government* sounds so large. Unwieldy. Inefficient. I'm more of a back corner,' Dodd said.

'Quantrill said Frost was abandoned research,' Groote said. 'You saying he stole Frost from the government?'

Dodd put his lips close to Groote's ear. 'Here's the deal. All you need to know is that if you get Frost and kill Quantrill and Sorenson for me, you get your daughter back safe and sound. Guaranteed. You're not prosecuted for any of your freelance activities. And, Dennis – may I call you Dennis? – your daughter gets Frost. Just like how Nathan gets Frost, and how Mrs. Brent will get Frost if she and I can come to an understanding.' Dodd gave Celeste a polite nod. She wondered if she could reach the door before he fired. Eight steps. Two more out the door. He'd mow her down, shoot her in the back, she had no doubt.

Groote swallowed. 'I'll do whatever you want.'

'Understand this. Amanda's safety depends on my

safety. You betray me, she suffers. No one wants an innocent girl who's already suffered so to endure additional
pain. Give me no reason to doubt you, Dennis.'

'I won't,' Groote said. Celeste could not feel sorry for
him but the confident killer who'd broken into their
rooms was gone, a confused hulk in his place.

'Sit up.'

Groote obeyed.

'You came here first?'

'Yes. I figured they would go for the cheapest motel.'

'You followed them all the way from New Mexico?'

'Of course not. I flew to Fresno this morning. I saw on
Celeste's computer the Frost files were transferred to a
server owned by Wallace.'

'But you haven't been to see Doctor Wallace?'

'No. I got delayed in Santa Fe answering questions
from the FBI. About Kendrick. The Bureau's looking for
him.'

'Because he's a missing witness?'

Groote nodded.

'You think Kendrick has Frost?'

'I believed he did.'

'Did you kill Allison?'

'Hell, no.'

'Did you kill Sorenson?'

'No but I would if I could.'

'They – and Nathan – all worked for me. At least they
did. Sorenson killed Allison, tried to kill Nathan, ran off
with Frost, I suspect,' Dodd said.

'To sell it,' Celeste said, and they all looked at her.
'None of this is about helping people, it's just about the
money. It's always money.'

'Mrs. Brent,' Dodd said, 'I know I have Nathan's loyalty,

298

and I have enough of Dennis's to let me sleep with one eye closed. You're the open question.'

'Sir,' Nathan said, 'Celeste is cool. She killed Hurley. He can't talk about his work.'

'Well, thank you, Mrs. Brent,' Dodd said. 'You did me a great favor.'

'Allison worked for you?' Celeste said. 'Allison?'

'She and Nathan were my spies, one inside, one outside, on how Quantrill and Hurley were improving Frost. I'm sorry Allison dragged you into this situation. I assume she needed a way to hide Frost from Sorenson and she used you in that cause. It's regrettable.'

'Are you going to kill me?' Celeste asked in a whisper.

'No,' Nathan said. 'No way. She can stay quiet. Can't you, Celeste?'

'Yes,' Celeste heard herself say. 'Sure.'

Dodd flipped open a cell phone, dialed a number, waiting, and then she saw a black fury cross his face as he asked who was speaking and his chest heaved in a disappointed sigh. Dodd raised the gun and aimed it straight at Celeste.

FORTY-FIVE

The bullet zoomed a good two feet left of Miles's head and he didn't shoot back, he barreled forward, stiff armed, and jammed his gun against Wallace's throat. Wallace dropped the gun and Miles thought, *He's scared shitless, doesn't know what he's doing.*

'Stupid,' Miles said. 'Very stupid.'

'Please. Please. He told me I had to kill you.'

'Who?'

'Dodd,' Wallace said.

'You wanted me to leave with you so you could bring me to him.'

'Or to shoot you somewhere else. Not in my house. I'm sorry, I'm sorry . . . my wife is dead. I don't want to die too.' Wallace started to cry.

'Tell me the truth. Do you have Frost?'

'No. God, no. If I had it I'd have given it to Dodd immediately and I'd be a freaking hero to him, I'd be safe.'

'Be honest with me.'

'I found out Allison was dead on Wednesday. Dodd called me. I was devastated. I've hardly been out of bed the past few days; I haven't been working, I haven't hardly touched the server. I didn't know the Frost files were sitting there. Please don't kill me.'

'You didn't retrieve the files, then cover your tracks by wiping the server?'

'I wouldn't be in league with the man who killed my wife,' Wallace said. 'Jesus. I gave Dodd the server password as soon as he asked for it. He found nothing. He's coming to be sure I'm not lying to him, to check. Please.'

The phone rang.

Miles tucked Wallace's gun into his back. He picked up the phone. 'Wallace residence.'

'Who's this?' A quiet voice.

'Miles Kendrick.'

'Ah.'

'Mr. Dodd?'

'Yes. I have your friends with me. Rooms twenty-four and twenty-five at the Yosemite Gateway.'

Miles's skin went cold. 'Don't hurt them.'

'Actually, I saved them. Dennis Groote was drowning your friend Mrs. Brent in the toilet. Tell him that you're well, Mrs. Brent.'

Miles heard Celeste's voice, a few feet from the receiver. 'I'm okay. But he's pointing a gun at me.' She sounded calm.

'I don't want them hurt,' Miles said.

'Neither do I,' Dodd said. 'We need to come to an agreement. Now, Miles, I'm wondering what you're doing at Doctor Wallace's house.'

'Hunting for Frost. Same as you. Wallace says he doesn't have it.'

'Should we believe him?' Dodd sounded almost coy.

'I don't think so. But I'll give him to you in exchange for my friends and you can figure out if he's telling the truth. You know him better than I do.'

Wallace's eyes went wide but Miles mouthed, *It's okay, it's cool*, and raised an open hand to calm the doctor.

Dodd said, 'Edward's a strong scientist but not a truly strong man; I always thought Renee married him because he'd give her no trouble. I don't mean your friends any harm. Nathan—'

'—works for you. You planted him at the hospital when you got wind of Frost being tested. And you left him there to die when it all went wrong.'

'I didn't know he was in danger.'

'Bullshit. I heard your name. When Sorenson was getting ready to kill Allison. I was in her office. Hiding. I heard him on a phone say, "Dodd doesn't know."'

'That would mean that I didn't know what Sorenson planned,' Dodd said. 'I wonder who he was talking to, don't you?'

'I don't know.'

'His hired help, I suppose. I came to bring Nathan back in from the cold, and to help you and Mrs. Brent.'

'You came to get Frost and nothing else.'

'Talk to me. Face to face. I'll come there.'

No. The Wallace house was too remote, too quiet. Dodd wanted silence around Frost, around how it had been developed and tested. 'No. I want public, highly public, to meet you.' He thought quickly. Public, with limited access roads so if Dodd had backups, others with him, they couldn't easily sneak up. Distance, to thwart any last-minute plans Dodd might put into place.

Wallace seemed to read his mind. 'Inside the park. Bridalveil Falls.'

Miles said, 'Bridalveil Falls. As soon as you can. If you hurt Nathan or Celeste, I'll guarantee you never get Frost and that everyone in the press knows about Shaman. We understand each other.'

'We certainly do.' Dodd clicked off.

'Hurry.' Miles hauled Wallace to his feet. 'We're going now. Dodd could cut us off, be here in minutes.'

'But, goddamn you, you said you would help me . . .' Wallace sputtered. 'I gave up the gun, I told you what he wanted me to do . . .'

'I am helping you,' Miles said, 'do you want to stay and wait for Dodd? That doesn't make sense to me. If you're so scared of him, you should have run. You didn't.'

'I can't hide from him, not for long.'

'You were waiting to cut a deal with him, and you don't want to cut a deal with me. Allison sent Frost to you for protection. Or she wanted a scientific analysis of the work, free from Dodd. Now she's dead and you're desperate for a bargaining chip to stay alive.'

'I don't have Frost, I swear I don't!'

'I'm your best hope for walking out of this mess alive, Doctor Wallace. I can protect you. If Dodd's Pentagon, maybe he'd like to talk to my high-ranking friends in Witness Protection or a few hungry prosecutors I know in the Department of Justice; I'm one of their favorite witnesses.' He hoped this was still true – he could always tell the WITSEC inspectors and the federal lawyers that he'd lost his mind when he ran from Santa Fe and throw himself on their mercies. They still needed him to convict the remaining Barradas. But even if he was trash to the government now, and he had no official allies left to help him deal with Dodd, he needed to bluff Wallace. 'So I'm going to play good citizen, and I'm going to cut a deal with Dodd . . .'

'You're crazy!'

'That would be the problem,' Miles said.

Ten feet into the heavy growth of pines that inched down-hill from the Wallace house, the man watched Kendrick and Wallace hurry to Kendrick's car and wheel out onto the road. He lowered the listening device; the conversation between them had been about what he had expected. He flipped open a cell phone, pressed a speed-dial number.

'Yes?'

'Kendrick is taking Wallace to meet Dodd inside Yosemite Park. At Bridalveil Falls.'

'Shit. Wallace may crack. Can you handle it?' Sorenson said.

'Sure. It just got about twice as complicated. Price doubled.'

'No.'

'Your choice. I'd rather be home.' The man waited while Sorenson considered the offer.

'Agreed.' Sorenson said with a weary tone. 'Torch the house first.'

The man clicked off the phone. He broke a back window of the kitchen door, sprayed lighter fluid all over the kitchen, curtains, and office floor, lit a match, and thumbed the flame toward the puddle. He ran out back to the woods and grabbed his motorcycle. It had taken him less than three minutes.

The man got on his motorcycle and peeled off after Kendrick's car. He didn't have to hurry and catch up to them; he knew where they were going, and it was a beautiful day for a mountain ride.

FORTY-SIX

Dodd drove a Lincoln Navigator, black, spacious. Seating was difficult; no one whom Groote had tried to kill wanted to sit with him. But Groote sat in the back, with Celeste, and Nathan sat in the front seat. Dodd gave Groote a piece of pillowcase from the motel room to stanch the flow of blood from the cuts Celeste had given him.

Celeste slumped in the seat and guessed that Miles had worked out a deal with Dodd – had he found Frost? If he was trading Frost for her and Nathan, she would have told him to keep running, because Dodd, she believed, wanted them all permanently silenced about his operation.

The spectacular scenery as they drove along the winding narrow road that led toward Bridalveil Falls sickened her. Valley and rock tumbled away to their left; mountain rose on their right, studded with evergreens. The vastness of the blue sky, the sheer openness, nearly overwhelmed her. God could see her. Brian could see her. She closed her eyes, tried to calm herself. She'd made it farther than she had thought possible; she could cope. She must.

'I bet a week ago you wouldn't have thought you'd be in California, Celeste,' Nathan said. Excited now, confident, but not quiet. Manic.

'No, Nathan, I sure didn't think so.'

'The mountains, the valleys. All shaped from broken rock pushed and pulled over millions of years, under unimaginable force. Beauty out of pressure. Just like us.'

'Not like us,' Celeste said.

'If you need proof Frost fixes you, look at Celeste,' Nathan said. 'Yosemite would be an agoraphobe's nightmare, and she's holding it together.'

'You aren't the guy I believed you were,' Celeste said.

'You misjudge Nathan,' Dodd said. 'He's a hero.'

'He wants to be one and you've taken advantage of him,' she said.

'Shut up,' Nathan said. 'Frost is going to help every soldier coming back from war, for years. No more suicides. No more broken marriages, no more inability to fit back into regular life. None of what I went through. The whole country will be grateful.'

'I know, Nathan.' Celeste kept her voice steady. 'But kidnapping and threatening to kill Groote's kid, is that heroic, Nathan?'

He swallowed hard. 'He saved your life, Celeste, so you shut up now.'

Dodd said, 'I never used the word *kill*, Mrs. Brent. I'm not a monster and I resent the implication. I have no desire to hurt you or Amanda Groote.'

'You get Frost, what happens to us?'

'You can be in a testing program. A legitimate one we can make public when the drug works. And I can arrange for you to reenter public life, given your disappearance from Santa Fe. We'll say you simply checked yourself into a clinic after Allison's death. It won't be hard. If you can keep your mouth shut.'

'And if I don't, you kill me.'

306

'You were much more diplomatic on TV.' Dodd sounded amused. 'Are you going to speak out about how Frost was born, ruin it for millions of other people?'

Celeste ignored him. 'Groote.' She tapped his leg until he looked at her. 'What's wrong with your daughter that she needs Frost?'

'Like you would care.'

'I might,' Celeste said. 'She's not you.'

Groote put his eyes back to the mountains' rise, the last slivers of snow still in shadow. Celeste could not pity him, exactly, but with his broken nose, his bruised and razor-sliced face, and his frayed gaze Groote looked as if he had gone to fight a hundred wars for his child and lost them all. Such a man did not stop. He did not quit. She was afraid Groote still had more fight in him. Or perhaps he needed Frost himself, she thought with a jolt. Dodd might have forced Groote into that hinterland of sanity where she had wandered after Brian's death, lost, alone, with no map to guide her home.

Groote ignored Celeste Brent's question – he would never discuss his baby girl with these nutcases – and thought, *Dodd doesn't know. He doesn't know Allison had both the research and the buyers' list. He thinks she just stole the research. They don't know about the second auction Sorenson mentioned. They haven't put the whole picture together on what that bastard Sorenson's doing.* The two crazies didn't seem to know, either, or seem to care.

He had a trump card, value to trade for Amanda, and he knew he had to wait for the right second to play it. A deal of sorts was brewing between Miles and Dodd, and this was exactly the info that could change the deal in his favor, in Amanda's favor. Dodd was nothing more than a smug bureaucrat who thought he was running the show. Dodd was dead wrong, Groote knew, if he could just keep his nerve.

He promised himself he'd bring Amanda to this mountain paradise someday, whole and healthy. The fresh air would do her a world of good if she wouldn't be afraid of the winding roads.

Miles drove through the amazing Yosemite landscape with no eye for beauty. Rising, jutting mountains, clear sky, huge pines. Spectacular, but he wasn't in the mood to appreciate it. Wallace sat next to him.

'Tell me about her,' Miles said.

'She was . . . tough.'

'It's not what I expected you to say.'

'It's what comes to mind,' Wallace said.

Miles edged over to the right as a motorcycle drew up to them, passed them, a young man with a heavy pack mounted behind him, glancing at them as he sped past.

Wallace said, 'She grew up poor. Went to college on full scholarship, had med and grad schools fighting over her. Bright beyond belief. Great at reading people, telling them what they wanted to hear . . .'

'You didn't say anything about her helping people.'

'Did she help you?'

'Yes. I thought for a while she was the only one would could.'

'She was good at making people think she was the cure, all right,' Wallace said, staring out the window.

'She wasn't?'

'No one doctor is the Holy Grail,' Wallace said. 'But patients want to believe it of their doctors, and doctors indulge the fantasy. She liked being needed.'

A sign announced Bridalveil on their left. Miles steered the car into a parking slot.

'You stick close to me,' Miles said.

'I thought you didn't trust me.'

'I don't. But the point is to come to agreement, and all of us walk away, no problems. You included.'

They got out of the car and started to hike toward the falls. The trail to Bridalveil led up a series of terraced steps. White water cascaded in fury down a creek, topped with froth. The roar of the falls increased as they approached; the snowmelt gave way in torrents under the early May sun. Now Miles could see the top of the falls, jetting down, the mist rising from impact, the water almost dancing with the strong wind that swept through the valley.

They headed right, toward the falls themselves, walking along the raging creek of cascading snowmelt. There wasn't much of a crowd this early in the season; Miles saw a trio of Japanese tourists; an elderly couple with a decided spring in their step, leaning on each other, smiling; a young couple staring up at the falls with worshipful rapture.

He saw Nathan, smiling, jumpy, excited. Then Celeste, her lips and nose bruised, her face pale.

A tightness grabbed his chest.

Groote stood next to her – his face was a mess; the tourists passing stared at him, then put their eyes to the waterfall or the trail when Groote returned their looks – and an older man stood next to him. The man was built tall and wiry, balding, with a thin, intelligent face. He wore jeans, a black coat, boots.

They waited at a widening in the trail, a juncture where visitors could observe both the falls and the swollen rivulet that surged away from the falls' base. The roar of the falls increased and now Miles felt Bridalveil's kiss on his face, his hands; he would be soaked if he stood in the mist for ten minutes.

'Hello, Miles. It's a pleasure to meet you,' the man said. 'Edward.'

'Dodd,' Edward said, 'I don't have Frost. I've told you the truth.'

'There's a clearing where it's not so damp. I'd like to smoke a cigarette. Rocks to sit on, nature's boardroom.' Dodd started walking, as though assuming all would follow, and they did.

'Are you okay?' Miles murmured to Celeste. She nodded, squeezed his arm. He shot a look back at Nathan, who kept a worshipful stare locked on the back of Dodd's head. They followed him down the soaked stone trail, retreating from the falls, Nathan bringing up the rear. Miles glanced at Groote; Groote met his eyes, gave no expression, no reaction, as though Miles weren't there.

Dodd led them across a bridge that spanned the snow-swollen creek. A flat area, covered with boulders, was to their right and Dodd found a rock about chair height. He sat, gestured for Miles and Celeste to sit next to him. Nathan, Groote, and Wallace stood. No other visitors were within hearing and the roar of the falls drowned their conversations from any passing ears.

'A beautiful choice for a meeting place, Miles,' Dodd said. He lit a cigarette. 'Nature is so calming.'

He talked, Miles thought, as though he held every face card. 'Why is Groote here?'

'He's working for me now. Not Quantrill.'

'He kidnapped Groote's kid,' Celeste said. 'Blackmailed him into switching sides.'

'Celeste is overdramatizing,' Dodd said. 'I made a job offer, he accepted.'

'You clearly have a plan, then,' Miles said.

'Groote here goes back to Quantrill and steals Frost. I find a place for you and your friends and Doctor Wallace to lie low. When Groote's got Frost back, then his daughter – and you and Nathan and Celeste – can be in a legitimate program to test Frost and get the help you all need.' Dodd smiled.

'No strings attached?' Miles asked.

'A few. I'd prefer you not get back in touch with other . . . federal authorities. And when you're feeling better, Miles, maybe I can offer you a more rewarding life than WITSEC ever could. You're resourceful under difficult circumstances. You could come work for me.'

'What about Celeste? Her face, her name, is known. She's on the front page of the papers today.'

'I'll help her resurface. Build a back story. Interest in her will blow over in another week. No offense, Celeste,' Dodd said with a wink.

'We left a dead man behind in her house.'

'Hurley's buried,' Groote said suddenly. 'I found him, I took care of him.' He glanced at Miles – an odd look, Miles thought, full of heat.

'Hey, Groote,' Miles said. Groote looked him in the eye. 'Dodd thinks you killed his agent. Sorenson.'

Groote shook his head.

'I don't care about Sorenson,' Dodd said.

'You should. If Wallace doesn't have Frost, I'm sure Sorenson does.' Miles crossed his arms. 'What's he doing with it if he's not delivering it to you?'

'If you're so concerned Sorenson's alive and well and wishing us harm,' Dodd said, 'go hunt him down. I get Frost, I don't care.'

Miles said, 'I'm not seeing the powers of persuasion it

311

must have taken for you to talk Nathan into betraying us.'

'I didn't betray you.' Nathan's voice shook.

'Shut up, Nathan. You could have been honest with us at any point. You weren't. You delivered us to this guy.'

Nathan said, 'This was the only way for us to get Frost, be in legit testing, move on with our lives.'

Miles shook his head at Nathan. 'Are you really traumatized or you just faking?'

'Everything Nathan endured in Iraq, and afterward, is true,' Dodd said. 'He volunteered. He wanted a chance to help his fellow soldiers.'

'Don't judge me,' Nathan said. 'I'm not a criminal.'

'I agree,' Dodd said. He stood. 'Celeste, you killed a man, albeit in self-defense, but you fled the scene. Miles, I don't even want to think about how many laws you've broken in pursuit of Frost. Help me and I can make sure none of your crimes haunts you.' He crushed his cigarette under his heel.

'Or you kill us. Quantrill's not an idiot; he'll hide Frost where we'll never find it.' Miles stood now, close enough to Dodd to smell the cigarette smoke on the man's breath. 'The question you're dodging is, what is Sorenson going to do with Frost if he has it? Sit on it, take it himself, sell it back to you or to Quantrill or—'

'He's right,' Groote said. 'That would be the question.'

'Answer him,' Miles said.

Nathan said, 'Miles. Step back.'

'What, you're a bodyguard now?' Miles said. 'You were a kid too scared to know what to do in Allison's house, crying and chained to a bed in that hospital, afraid of mirrors, too scared to be honest with me and Celeste. So shut the hell up, Nathan.' He decided to test Dodd.

'Sorenson wanted Nathan dead because he was afraid Nathan knew about him. I'm curious, did Sorenson go after Nathan on your order? Do necessary housecleaning once your operation fell apart?'

The only answer was the steady roar of the falls and the delighted whoop of a hiker heading up the trail.

Finally Dodd shook his head. 'Of course not. I came to help Nathan. And to offer an arrangement to you. So you two can either help me or I can make one call and have you and Celeste under arrest and in jail for the foreseeable future.'

'Not if we tell all we know.'

'I'm talking jail in a foreign country. Shaman was highly classified. You're in possession of knowledge of top-secret government files. If you had possession of Frost, that's called treason, son. I can render your asses to Morocco or Pakistan and that's all they wrote. I don't think those are the kinds of walls you want surrounding you, Celeste.' He shrugged and offered a negotiator's smile. 'Listen, I don't want to pull out big guns. But you either cooperate or you don't. The choice is yours.'

Miles looked up at the boulder opposite him, and Andy and Allison both sat, as though they'd been hiking through the trails and needed to rest.

'Choice is interesting. Choice helps you pull and tug apart at a theory,' Miles said. 'Why, I wonder, did Wallace make the choice to stay and wait for you? Let's say he got the Frost files when Allison hid them and then covered his tracks, and he's lying about the files being destroyed. No reason for him to stay and take the heat from you. He could run and vanish. He's got a commodity worth millions.'

'Innocent men don't run,' Wallace said.

'I gave him an order to stay,' Dodd said.

'Yes, and to shoot me. He's scared shitless of you. But I think someone else gave him an order to stay and to draw you close.'

Dodd turned to Wallace, and Miles saw the blood spray first from Dodd's chest, sudden and heart-red, then from Wallace's throat, across Groote and Celeste as the booms broke through the rush of the falls. Another boom and a third bullet chocked through Wallace's chest in a puff of flesh and red.

Miles shoved Celeste, knocking her behind the boulder as two more whistling shots pierced the air inches above his head. Nathan froze in shock and then Miles barreled into him, finding cover behind a rock.

Eight more shots. Groote lay flat, caught between two boulders, and he tried to raise his head and a bullet pinged off the stone. Tourists and hikers near them scrambled in blind panic, unsure where the shots were coming from, a woman was screaming, a man seized his young daughter and retreated behind an outcropping of boulders on the other side of the walk bridge.

Then nothing. Miles counted to fifty, listening to sounds of frantic running, his own heart seeming to pound hard enough to crack bone. He dragged Wallace's body behind the boulder, raised the dead man's head.

It didn't get shot off. He eased Wallace to the ground.

Dodd lay in a dead sprawl, eyes open, his chest punctured by two rounds.

Miles grabbed Celeste. 'Come on.'

'We have to go . . .' Nathan said.

'Stay with your boss,' Miles spat.

'No, Miles, please . . . don't leave me.' Nathan pointed at Groote, who risked a dash, running toward Dodd's body. 'He'll kill me . . .'

'Come on, Nathan, it's okay,' Celeste said. But Miles watched Groote stop, search Dodd's body . . .

A gun. Dodd must have a gun.

But what Groote was pulling from Dodd's pocket was a cell phone.

'Groote—' Celeste started.

'He knows where my kid is, he called someone to move her, I got to have his call log, I got to find her,' Groote screamed. But he stuck his hand back in Dodd's jacket.

Gun, Miles thought. He knocked Groote down with a hard fist to the nose – the weak point – and Groote brayed in pain. Miles wrenched the gun free and he and Celeste and Nathan ran, Miles sure another bullet would zoom from the sniper's gun. But no more shots. The sniper was gone. Or simply waiting for them to reach the parking lot.

'My kid! Where's my kid? Nathan! Where's my kid?' Groote roared behind them.

They hurried down the now-empty path toward the parking lot, past cowering hikers, one of them screaming futilely into a cell phone, useless in the confines of the valley. The recent rainfall hadn't drained well from the parking lot and they raced through ankle-high water toward Blaine's car.

Miles started the car, peeled it out of the parking lot, revved onto the road. 'Get down, both of you,' he said; they were in the backseat. One road out; he spun out onto it, heading south, the way they'd come.

He tried to think. The gunshots had come from across the road, close to the river, where there was a stopping point to admire the grandeur of the sheer rock face of El Capitan.

Sorenson. He'd gotten Wallace to get Dodd running to

Fish Camp, probably planning to eliminate them both. And then Miles and company and Groote were pulled into the trap as well.

A motorcycle wheeled up behind them and the back windshield exploded.

FORTY-SEVEN

To Miles's left rose mountain; to his right the land fell away to valley, either precipitous rocky drops or rolling meadows down to the Merced River. The road was two lanes, one each way, and now cars on the opposite side veered to the shoulder as Miles swerved to shake the cyclist. No cars ahead of him; Miles floored the accelerator. The shooter on the motorcycle stayed close.

Miles saw the man's face in the rearview – not Sorenson, not a face he recognized. Raising a heavy pistol again.

'Stay down!' he screamed at Celeste and Nathan.

He had nowhere to go. Mountain on one side, air on the other. He couldn't shake the guy.

Then he saw a black Lincoln Navigator, powering up fast behind the motorcycle. Groote at the wheel.

The cyclist fired again and Miles heard the bullet *thwock* into the back of the passenger seat. And then in the rearview – he saw Groote nudge the Navigator into the motorcycle, hard. The cyclist fought to steady himself, swiveled his aim back toward Groote, and blasted at the Navigator. Missed. Groote didn't retreat.

As Miles hit the next curve, Groote rammed the Navigator hard into the bike, the cyclist getting airborne and landing on Miles's trunk. He scrabbled for a one-handed grip, sliding toward the frame of the back windshield.

The cycle smashed into a guardrail, somersaulted, and soared out into empty air. Groote's Navigator kissed the railing, sparks flying, as he fought for control.

Miles wrenched the car hard to the left, screeching into the oncoming lane, veering back just in time to avoid a honking pickup truck, trying to throw the cyclist clear. He glanced in the rearview. The cyclist had managed to get a hold with his gloved hand on the lip of the shattered back window. Nathan pounded his fist down on the man's grip and Miles saw the cyclist's gun swerve and take aim.

Not at Nathan or Celeste. Him. Kill him and the chase is over.

Groote thundered up fast behind them.

The cyclist fired, Miles's window shattered, and in the rearview he saw Nathan fighting with the cyclist, struggling for control of the gun. Celeste looped her blanket over the shooter's head, tried to pull him off-balance.

Then two shots boomed, in fast succession, and the cyclist screamed. A tire blew and Miles fought the wheel to keep the car from sliding into the opposite lane or into the railing and the sky beyond.

Suddenly Miles saw a sign: service area to the left. He swung hard into oncoming traffic, driving on a rim, and into a flat parking area; Groote's Navigator followed.

Nathan dragged the cyclist into the car, started pummeling him with his fists.

Celeste tumbled out of the car, falling on her back onto the pavement. Groote's car screeched up close to her. Miles got his gun, leveled it at Groote.

'Truce!' Groote yelled. 'I saved your life, man! Truce!

Don't shoot me!' And Groote dropped his gun to the pavement.

Nathan dragged the cyclist out of the car, sitting on him, and Miles could see the two shots Groote had made – neat bullet holes in the cyclist's right hip and leg.

'I saved you,' Groote repeated.

'After you've tried to kill us.'

'I thought you had Frost. My job is to get it back. But I didn't kill Allison, you know Sorenson did, and Dodd – he has my daughter. I don't know how to find her without him – without people who know him, know his operation. Please. Please, Miles. I've got to find Sorenson. Please tell me what you know. Please. My kid. I have nothing without my kid . . .' And Groote stopped. Beneath the razor slashes, the broken nose, the bruised face, Miles saw the real pain in the man's eyes. 'I have information you need to stop Sorenson. I'll share if Nathan or this bastard' – he gestured at the cyclist – 'can tell me where my kid is.'

Miles kept the gun on him, went to the cyclist. Celeste steered Nathan back against the car. 'Let him talk to us, Nathan!'

'Nathan,' Miles said. 'Total honesty. Do you know where Dodd put Groote's daughter?'

Nathan shook his head. 'No. I don't.'

'You can't trust Groote,' Celeste said.

Miles knelt by the cyclist, pulled the helmet free. 'You. Where's Sorenson?'

The cyclist closed his eyes.

'Where do we find Sorenson? Where do we find the rest of Dodd's people?'

'Dodd doesn't – have any more – people. Not in the – field.' The cyclist coughed blood. 'Why he didn't have . . . protection.'

319

'You can't help Sorenson now. Where's he at?' Groote said. He picked up his gun and put it squarely on the man's forehead. He started counting down: 'Five. Four.'

'Austin. He's in Austin, Texas.'

'Where in Austin?'

'I don't know . . . I just know Austin.'

'Is this where the auction is?' Groote asked.

'Auction?' Miles said. 'What auction?'

The cyclist ignored Miles and nodded at Groote.

'Do you know where my daughter is?' Groote asked.

'No.'

'Three,' Groote started the count again.

'I don't know . . . I don't. But Sorenson, he'd know . . . he worked for Dodd.'

'That we knew.'

'Is my daughter with him?' Groote said. The man blinked and Groote said, 'Two.'

'I don't know . . . Sorenson didn't tell me about her.' The cyclist spoke in a rush. 'I'll call Sorenson, tell him I did the hit on you all, he'll back off for a few days if you hide . . .'

'Bull,' Nathan said.

'Miles, we have to go,' Celeste said.

'You're right,' Groote said. 'One.' And he shot the cyclist between the eyes.

'Goddamn it!' Miles screamed. 'He could have told us plenty more.' He shoved Celeste and Nathan back toward the car.

Groote knelt, took a cell phone and a wallet from the cyclist's leather jacket. 'He couldn't tell us more, because we can't stay. The Forest Service will be all over this side of the park in a few minutes. We have to go.'

'What's this *we* shit?'

'Truce,' Groote said. 'We both need Sorenson. The only reason I was after you all is because Quantrill thought you had Frost. You don't. Sorenson does. Sorenson stole Frost to sell it, in a new auction. He either knows where my little girl is or I can threaten his auction to get him to give me information on how I can find her. I'm going to Austin. I don't want you getting arrested and telling the police about me. I can either kill the three of you or we can help each other, and I don't kill people on whims or for fun.'

'We can't trust you,' Miles said.

'I'm just a hired hand. You know what that's like, don't you, Miles?' Groote said.

Miles nodded.

'We have a common enemy. Sorenson. I just saved you, Miles, and you saved my life back in the hospital when you beat up Sorenson. He would have killed me after he killed Nathan. You didn't let me burn to death at that house. Your car's undrivable. We can take the Navigator. But you have to decide, right now.'

'Miles, no way,' Nathan said. Celeste took Miles's arm, squeezed tight.

'Miles. We get Frost, we part ways, not as friends, I'm sure, but we all have what we want and Sorenson goes down. He's just tried to kill all of us; he'll try again. But I couldn't let his dink call him and report in that we survived.'

Miles decided. 'Get in Groote's car.'

'No way!' Nathan yelled. 'No way, man, no, he hurt me, hurt me bad—'

'Nathan,' Groote said, 'I never tried to kill you. Sorenson did.'

'You're a sick bastard. I won't go with him, Miles.'

Miles caught Celeste's hand; shock and confusion played across her face. 'If we stay, we're going to be questioned and probably go to jail. You've just gotten out of one prison, Celeste, I don't want you in another one.'

'He tried to kill me . . .'

'You tried to slice my face open,' Groote said in an even tone. 'But we all know the truth now, and we can either argue until the police come or we can help each other. I assure you my kid matters far more to me than hurting you.'

'Get in the car,' Miles said. Celeste took a deep breath and did. Nathan jerked back from Miles.

'Nathan, I won't let him hurt you.'

'Kid,' Groote said, 'I could have killed you. I could have done much worse to you. I'm sorry. Nothing personal.'

'I won't let him hurt you,' Miles repeated.

Nathan, his jaw trembling with rage, got into the backseat with Celeste.

'You hurt them,' Miles said, 'and I'll kill you.'

'I know you will,' Groote said. They got back into the Navigator, Groote driving, easing back into the traffic. Virtually no traffic appeared to be coming from the direction of Bridalveil; Miles wondered if the road had been closed in the chaos after the shooting. Groote gunned the Navigator south, toward the park exit.

Silence as they drove.

'All that's happened,' Groote said, '– my actions were nothing personal. I just wanted Frost. For my daughter. She needs it really bad.' He told them an abbreviated story of the attack on his family, Amanda's survival, her fight against PTSD. He left out murdering most of the Duartes.

They were silent for several moments. 'The cutting,'

Celeste said. 'Frost . . . made my urges to cut nearly go away. So it might help her not hurt herself.'

'That's why you had the razor.' Groote touched at the dried blood on the shallow cuts on his face.

'Yes.'

'It really helped you. Please don't lie to me. Please.'

'It really helped me,' Celeste said. 'But I don't give a rat's ass about you feeling better. This is a truce. Not friendship. No one is forgetting what you've done or what you are.'

'I'm a shitload of things, same as you,' Groote said, 'but first I'm a father.'

Celeste didn't answer him.

'Find the registration,' Groote said to Miles. 'We may have to talk our way out if the cops have thrown up blocks.'

He was right. A roadblock had been laid near the Wawona resort, close to the southern entrance of Yosemite. The park police were stopping cars heading out of the park, checking IDs, talking to people.

'Oh, God,' Nathan said. 'What do we do?'

'Stay calm,' Miles said.

The cars fed through the line and after ten minutes, Groote pulled up to the officer.

'Good morning,' Groote said.

'Sir, driver's license and registration, please.'

'Sure.' Groote handed him the registration – not in Dodd's name, but in the name of a company called Horizon Investments, based in California, and his own driver's license. Miles supposed Horizon was a front for Dodd's operations. The officer took all this in without comment, writing down the license number and checking the registration carefully. *So much depended*, Miles thought, *on how good a description anyone gave of us, if they know we're in this SUV yet.*

'What happened to your face, sir?' the officer said.

'Fell climbing yesterday. Made a mess of myself, didn't I?' Groote said. 'Was there a problem at Bridalveil? We were coming up from Yosemite Village and a lot of cars were driving out of there like maniacs, in a damn hurry to get out, and one of them banged into me good and roared off.'

'A shooting,' the officer said.

'Holy shit,' Groote said. 'In the park?'

'Yes, sir. You folks see anything?'

'No,' Miles said. 'But that's why we need incredibly strict gun-control laws, I believe, because violence is just starting to creep into every aspect of our lives, don't you think, Officer, and if we're not safe in our national parks then we're certainly not safe in our cities and—'

The officer waved them through. 'Thanks, folks.'

Groote drove forward with a friendly wave.

'Now what?' Nathan said.

'I've got to get out of the valley, get into cell-phone range,' Groote said. He tested his phone one-handed. 'No signal. I've got to call my daughter's hospital, see if she's really gone.' Panic tinged his voice.

'If Dodd said he took her,' Nathan said quietly from the backseat, 'then it's true.'

Groote exited the park, accelerating onto the snake's back of Highway 41.

'Head for Fish Camp,' Miles said.

'We shouldn't stop at your motel—'

'We're not. We'll see if there's a copy of Frost hidden at Wallace's house, but I don't think we'll find it. He would have destroyed it rather than let Dodd get it. He was taking his orders from Sorenson,' Miles said. 'But I'd rather search than pass up the chance.'

'But Sorenson killed Allison – why would Wallace help him?'

Miles thought for a moment. The pieces were slowly, roughly, fitting together. He said, 'I think Sorenson and Allison talked Wallace into analyzing the research for them. They don't want Dodd to know what they're doing, so she doesn't use her office computer to send the files, because she knows Dodd's monitoring her system and her phone. But after she's sent the files and Wallace has given them his analysis that Frost is indeed good medicine, Allison's not useful to Sorenson anymore.'

'He killed her,' Celeste said. 'He'd always planned to, if he killed with a bomb. It's not done on impulse.'

'Without a doubt.' Miles nodded. 'And he must have wanted to keep Wallace in his pocket, so he tells Wallace that Quantrill or Dodd killed her. This is far more than Wallace bargained for. Sorenson drops off Dodd's radar. Wallace is scared, he can't let Dodd know he helped Sorenson. If Wallace runs, Dodd'll know he's guilty. Wallace can't have any evidence on his server that the Frost files were ever there. So he lied to me about Sorenson wiping the server; Wallace obliterated the files to cover his own ass.

'But he doesn't know that we've discovered the file transfer. When Nathan called Dodd, and Dodd in turn called Wallace, Wallace must have freaked. He called Sorenson and Sorenson told him to stay put. Because now, Wallace is bait. Everyone who's after Frost is rushing to Fish Camp; it's a golden opportunity for Sorenson to eliminate everyone who's a threat to him, all at once.'

Nathan paled and shook his head. 'I didn't know it was a trap. I didn't rat.'

'I believe you,' Groote said. 'You don't give info up easily. I should know.'

'Shut the hell up,' Nathan said.

'I'm still furious with you, Nathan,' Miles said. 'You weren't honest with us, you nearly got us killed.'

'Dodd said he would protect us,' Nathan said.

'Miles.' Celeste put her hand on his arm, he shrugged it off. 'Nathan thought he was doing the right thing. Dodd did save my life at the hotel. Let it go.'

'Miles, Dodd came to me, offered me a chance to make what happened in Iraq right. I couldn't say no,' Nathan said.

'If the bombing was an accident, what did you have to make right, Nathan?' Miles said. 'What on earth would you have to fix?'

Nathan stared out the window.

'Nathan. You could have told us from the beginning Dodd put you in the clinic,' Miles said. He told Groote to turn – they'd reached the road to Wallace's house.

For a normally quiet corner, traffic was heavy onto the road that led to Wallace's house. Smoke painted the sky. 'Bad sign,' Groote said.

'I promised . . . to say nothing.' Nathan put the flat of his palms on the side of his head.

'How were you supposed to report to Dodd? Through Allison?'

'I had no idea Allison and Sorenson were working for Dodd, none. I was supposed to go through the treatment and then report back to Dodd about the testing. That's all. When you got me out of the hospital – I decided to keep my mouth shut. You didn't want to deal with authority and I knew Dodd would help us, but I would have to bring you to him. I thought I was protecting the two of you.'

They reached a bend in the road. In the distance they could see fire trucks parked along the curb. Flames spouted from the shrunken wreck that was the Wallace house.

'Oh, hell,' Miles said.

'Sorenson didn't want to risk a trace connecting any of today back to him,' Groote said. 'Goddamn it.' He powered the car back toward Highway 41.

'We don't have anyplace to go,' Nathan said.

'Yes, we do,' Celeste said. 'Head for Orange County.'

'What?' Groote asked in surprise. Orange County was where Amanda had been; how would she know?

'I know a place we can go. Just drive.'

FORTY-EIGHT

Groote started calling as soon as his cell phone got a signal.

He first called Amanda's hospital in Orange, considering carefully what he would say if Amanda was truly gone, sweating, thinking, *Please let her be there, for all my sins, God, don't punish her, let her be there.*

The conversation took five minutes. Doctor Warner was not available, but the kind-voiced woman in administration told him the transfer had gone without a hitch, and she hoped Amanda enjoyed the new hospital in Phoenix.

'Gosh, I left the hospital's number at my hotel. Do you have it?' Groote said.

Of course she did.

'Phoenix,' Nathan said when Groote told them what the woman had said. 'Dodd found me at a hospital in Phoenix.'

It lifted Groote's hopes, and his hand shook as he dialed. Miles took the phone from him, dialed the number, handed the phone back to him.

Man, Groote thought, *don't be nice to me, it's gonna make it harder if I have to kill you.* He thought he had been clever in pulling them in with him, but now – the shock of battle fading – he knew they outnumbered him and he didn't like the idea that he could lose control of the group.

The Phoenix hospital had no record of an Amanda Groote, or of any new juvenile patient being transferred to them in the last two weeks.

'Please check again. Please.' Groote waited and the woman checked again.

'I'm sorry, sir.'

He clicked the phone off. 'She's not there. Dodd lied to her hospital, falsified the records.'

'You could call every psychiatric hospital in the country,' Celeste said. 'We can download a list, work the phones.'

'You'd help me, Mrs. Brent?' Groote said.

'Not you. I'd help your kid.'

'If Dodd normally lurks in a back corner of the Pentagon,' Miles said, 'he doesn't have to rely on public hospitals. He could have a secret clinic or a safe house to hide Amanda. She's not even necessarily in a hospital.'

'She's not,' Nathan said. 'Dodd couldn't risk putting her in a hospital where she might give incriminating details to another patient.'

'Give me Dodd's phone,' Miles said. 'Let me check the call log. Might help us reach someone who works for Dodd.'

Groote handed him the phone.

Miles clicked, checked, swore under his breath. 'No calls. The phone's been programmed not to record the numbers.'

Groote pounded his fist against the driver's wheel.

'Take it easy,' Miles said. 'You're no good to Amanda too rattled to think.'

'I'll take you all to Orange County, like Mrs. Brent wanted,' Groote said. 'Then I'm getting on a flight to Austin. We're square. I get Frost, I'll call you and let you know I have it. But getting it, I don't need your help.'

'Actually, you might,' Celeste said. 'I know someone who can help us find Sorenson and Amanda. A friend of mine.' She laughed, a brittle, nervous sound. 'I told him I was too afraid to go on *Oprah* with him – wait till he hears what I've been doing the past two days.'

FORTY-NINE

'Tragic yet funny,' Andy said from the backseat. 'You didn't trust me enough to tell me you were betraying my ass to the FBI, but you'll trust a guy who shot at you and chased you off a cliff and tortured Nathan and tried to drown Celeste.'

Miles made no answer, but if he could have spoken he would have said, *No, I don't trust him, not a bit, so shut up.*

Miles waited for the time to pass and for Groote to get calmer before he asked his questions. The stress of the ordeal exhausted Nathan; he'd fallen asleep, leaning against Celeste's shoulder. Celeste stared at the car's ceiling, lost in her own thoughts. Groote fiddled with the satellite radio, found a news channel, and they waited for the sniping spree in Yosemite to make the broadcast. The major news story was a bad tenement fire in New York that had killed a dozen people.

'A man came to Sangriaville asking for me,' Miles said. 'I heard you say it when you talked to Hurley.'

'Careful what you say,' Andy said. 'It got me killed.'

He watched Groote for a reaction – a tightening grip on the steering wheel, a frown that touched the mouth – but Groote's face betrayed no secrets.

'I'll bet his name was DeShawn Pitts.'

'Yeah, that was the guy,' Groote said.

'What did he tell you about me?'

'He was tight lipped. Told me you might come around asking questions. Or seeking counseling. Asked me to detain you and call him if you showed up.'

'That all?'

'He didn't tell me you were a federal witness. I figured that out myself.'

'The FBI's been very quiet in looking for me. Not putting my name, my face, on the news. That won't last. They'll do it . . .'

He stopped.

'Do what?'

Miles repeated: 'They'll do it . . .'

'You okay?' Groote asked.

'They'll do it . . . as soon as . . . we turn off the tape,' he said. He put his hands to his face.

'What tape? Miles?'

Miles fell silent, took a long, shuddering breath. 'Nothing. I'm okay. Sorry.'

'What the hell's wrong with you?' Groote asked. 'Do you need medications?'

'I'm fine. I just remembered something.' And he put his gaze to the window and said nothing more.

Then the news shifted to the shooting in Yosemite, two people dead, another body found a distance from the falls, shot at close range, but no suspects, no motive, no explanation yet.

Groote let the news run its cycle of stories and thought, *If the FBI wants you, Miles, my man, they get you. You're my bargaining chip once I get Amanda back and she and*

I need to vanish. I give you to the FBI, I blow the whistle on Dodd's operations, I get forgiven all my sins. But he said, 'The Bureau doesn't want to expose you, which means they're not giving up on getting you back as a witness.'

Miles took a long time to answer; whatever he had remembered when they talked about the FBI, Groote could see it rattled him to the bone.

Miles said in a low voice, 'You and I get them to safety, and then we go on without them. I don't want them in any more danger.'

'They'll be quiet about me – what I did?'

'Yes. I guarantee it.'

Groote nodded. It would, he knew, make his life so much easier. One enemy in his pocket was easier to manage than three. He hoped nothing was said on the satellite news about a missing WITSEC inspector; life was complicated enough right now.

FIFTY

They reached Tustin, in Orange County, late Saturday night.

Celeste could see Miles was shaken. She thought he was nervous about trusting Victor Gamby not to call the authorities on them.

'This is a bad idea,' Miles told Celeste. 'You've never met this guy face to face.'

'I know him,' she said. 'I trust Victor.'

'You know him through e-mails, for God's sake.'

'Victor has done more to help PTSD patients through his blog than anyone else I know.'

'He would be entirely in his right mind if he called the police.'

'None of us are in our right minds,' Celeste said. 'Wait.' She walked up to the doorway of the modest house in a quiet stretch of Tustin. The jacaranda trees were heavy with bloom and the breeze knocked purple blossoms settling on her head as she walked up to the front door.

Nathan said, 'I still have a job to do. Getting Frost for the soldiers.'

Miles put a hand on Nathan's shoulder. 'You do this my way, Nathan. Dodd stuck you in an illegal medical testing program, he took advantage of your disease and your guilt, and he's dead and you don't owe him a thing.'

'I'm going to find Frost.' Nathan's voice was unsteady.

'Nathan,' Miles said, 'we'll discuss it later.'

Miles saw the door opened by a fortyish man in a wheelchair. Celeste spoke to him and then the man opened his arms – one of them a prosthetic – and Celeste leaned down to him and embraced him.

They talked for ten minutes, Celeste kneeling by his wheelchair. The man listened intently; he never interrupted Celeste. Then he gestured at the car, a welcoming wave.

Miles and Nathan walked toward them. Groote hung back near the Navigator.

'Miles, Nathan, this is Victor Gamby,' Celeste said. 'Victor, Nathan Ruiz, Miles Kendrick. Back there is Dennis Groote. He's, um, shy.'

He shook hands with both of them and said, 'You boys c'mon in and we'll talk.' He motored the wheelchair around – Miles saw that his legs were missing as well, the pants legs tidily tucked in under stumps – and they followed him inside. Groote brought up the rear, glancing around as though the house were a trap.

'Thanks for your hospitality, Mr. Gamby,' Miles said.

'You're welcome. Nathan, forgive me, but Celeste says you dislike mirrors.'

'Yes, sir,' Nathan said. He hung back, staying close to Celeste.

Victor said, 'Freddy! Company!'

A young man, in his early thirties, came in from the back. Wearing wraparound sunglasses, walking with a cane. Blind. Scar tissue inched out along the edge of the sunglasses.

'You fought in Iraq', Nathan, that right?' Victor said.

'Yeah.'

'So did Freddy. Blinded by an IED outside Tikrit.'

Freddy said hi as they all shook his hand.

'Freddy, Nathan doesn't care for mirrors, which makes no sense because he's about ten times handsomer than I am. Would you go around, hang sheets on the mirrors that Nathan might see?'

'That's okay,' Nathan said. 'I can control myself.'

'No reason to be embarrassed.'

'If I'd known that,' Groote whispered to him, 'damn, I wouldn't have used the screwdriver.'

'Shut the hell up,' Nathan said quietly, 'and stay away from me.'

Miles stepped between them.

'Then when you're done with the mirrors, Freddy, if you'd make sandwiches for our guests?' Victor said.

'Sure, but the only bread we got is rye.' Freddy had a surfer boy's easy accent.

'That'll do, I'm sure. Thank you so much.' Victor waited for Freddy to leave the room, put an unafraid gaze on Miles. 'Celeste's told me the basics of the trouble you all are in.'

'I appreciate your willingness to help us,' Miles said. 'I know you run a popular Web site for people with post-traumatic stress disorder . . .'

'And you want to know if you can trust me with your secrets.'

'Well . . .'

'It's all right, Miles. I've had my site for a couple of years now. A million hits a month. I do database consulting work for the government, I'm an independent contractor. Don't worry, I'm not a fed. I'm not calling the cops on you all, because Celeste says you're after a medicine that could help every traumatized patient in the world. Including me, including Freddy.'

'Is he, um, your boyfriend?' Nathan asked.

Victor shook his head. 'No. I find me a lost lamb, let 'em stay till they're on their feet. Always a PTSDer. Like you, like me. I got my legs and arm blown off on 9/11.'

'Victor was at the Pentagon,' Celeste said quietly.

'Before Freddy I had a young lady staying with me, saw her brother and her fiancé gunned down in a gang war in Compton. Before that another soldier from Iraq. Before that a young father who lost his parents and his children, drowning before his eyes, in Hurricane Katrina. Never a shortage of pain in this world. I help 'em get back on their feet best they can and then I send 'em out to help another soul.'

'You need to help us with eyes wide open. Celeste killed a man in self-defense but we didn't report it. I'm hiding from the witness protection program. Groote helped us flee the scene of a multiple homicide in Yosemite.' Victor gave Groote a brief but appraising stare, and Miles wondered exactly how much Celeste had told him about the man. 'People want us dead. And the government, at least a slice of it no one acknowledges, is involved in a major cover-up over medical research.'

Victor Gamby pointed at his eyes. 'Wide open. Start talking.'

Miles told him the entire story, from his morning meeting with Allison and Sorenson, to arriving on Victor's doorstep. Victor didn't interrupt. Freddy stumbled through the room and noisily assembled sandwiches and salad in the kitchen. Celeste stood to go help the blind soldier and Victor grabbed her arm. 'Freddy's got to cope.

Let him be. Kindest thing in the world for him.' Celeste sat back down and Miles finished their account.

Victor frowned. 'First of all. This medicine. Frost. You understand there's ongoing research in this area – how to minimize the impact of PTSD.'

'I don't know much about it.'

'I keep up with every PTSD research angle being pursued. Most shrinks don't have the resources to deal with traumatic memory. Dose us with antidepressant meds and pray for mercy. Because PTSD's a bitch to treat, with a smorgasbord of symptoms, and onset that varies widely after the initial trauma. Rumor has it the Chinese government experimented with beta blockers and memory diminishment, on political prisoners, back in the early nineties and got nowhere. There are highly regarded teams doing legitimate research at Harvard and at UC-Irvine. But if Frost can diminish traumatic memory long after the event takes place, then Frost is much, much further along.'

'First to market,' Miles said.

'It meant millions to Quantrill,' Groote said, 'if we're looking at cold, hard cash.'

Victor nodded. 'Profits in the billions, if the research is already completed.'

'So the buyers at this auction Sorenson's staging will be very serious,' Celeste said.

'People will risk a lot for profits that big. Nice how they want to help us, isn't it?' Victor gave a low, soft laugh.

'If Sorenson is ex-Pentagon,' Miles said, 'can your connections give us info on him, or where Dodd might have hidden Groote's daughter?'

'You understand that the news is saying the Bridalveil

shootings was the work of a deranged ex-soldier. Lost his mind. Nobody in the government's going to own up to your dead friend.' Victor cleared his throat.

Celeste said, 'So someone's already covering up for Dodd and the Pentagon.'

Victor shrugged. 'I'll see what I can find, but I make no promises. I'm not a hacker. I'm not doing anything illegal to help you. I can trade on connections, on favors – it's the grease in Washington – but I may get every door slammed in my face. I'm not a government employee – my power base is dependent on my contractor connections and my fame in advocacy for PTSD patients. So I may get nowhere.'

'My daughter—'

'I'll do everything I can,' Victor said. 'But I have to tell you, Dennis, that if I were Dodd, I would have gotten Amanda out of the country on a government flight. To a safe house in Mexico, or in the Caribbean. But off American soil. Finding her will not be easy.'

'Understood,' Miles said. 'Thank you, Victor.'

'We don't have a dinner bell, but the quiet tells me that Freddy's got dinner ready. Let's eat. Then I'll start working the phone and the computers and see if I hit any lucky numbers.'

FIFTY-ONE

'We should rest,' Celeste said.

'You're right.' Exhaustion seeped into Miles's whole body. Victor had excused himself into his office, banned them from interrupting him. Groote sat on the quiet of the back porch, watching the moonlight peeking out from the clouds. Miles observed him for a minute – the first time leaving Groote alone – and followed her to the guest bedroom she had claimed, and saw twin beds.

'Nathan's sharing with Freddy. They can talk about the war. Groote can sleep upstairs, assuming he's human and can sleep. You don't mind, do you?' she said.

'Of course not.'

She lay down on one bed and he lay down on the other. They faced each other across the space – a side table, a lamp, separating them.

'Big risk to trust Groote,' she said.

'*Trust* is too strong a word. He's using us, but we're using him, so it's okay.'

'He looks at you,' Celeste said, 'in a way I don't like.'

'He's sweet on me.'

'Don't joke. He acts as if he still has a score to settle.'

'He's a hired gun,' Miles said, 'but he's off the job. Now it's personal, as they say in the movie trailers. As long as he thinks we can help him get his daughter back, he'll work with us. I know how to keep him leashed.'

'I imagine Victor coming to tell us he's found Amanda, where she is, and then Groote kills us all and goes on his merry way.'

'I won't let that happen.' Miles jostled the bed, trying to get comfortable.

'You remembered something.'

'No.'

'Miles. I don't know you that well, I suppose, but I can tell. What happened?'

He pulled his jacket close around him, as if cold.

'It's warm in here. You could take off your jacket.'

'No. I'm comfortable.'

'I noticed you don't like to take off your jacket.'

'I get cold.'

'Don't lie.'

'I keep something I meant to give Allison in my jacket.'

'What?'

He realized he had nothing to lose; he would be leaving Celeste soon enough, probably to never see her again. Truth made for a good parting gift. 'My confession. Of murdering my best friend.'

The expression on her face didn't change. 'Your best friend . . .'

'Yeah. Since I was three years old.'

'Self-defense. You have nothing to confess.'

He closed his eyes.

'It's not your fault, Miles.'

'Yeah, it is.'

'Do you really know that, in your head, your guts, your heart? Do you?' she asked.

Andy stood on the far wall, arms crossed, blood on his

shoulder, on his throat. Three bullet wounds glistened in the lamplight.

'It's not your fault,' she repeated. 'It's not your fault.'

'He told me I killed him with a word. Then I remembered. On the drive. Talking with Groote about the FBI. How I killed him.'

'Is Andy here now?' she asked.

'Yes.'

'Ask him,' she said, 'what he wants. Why does he stay?'

'He's not a ghost seeking vengeance,' Miles said. 'My head invented him.'

'Then your head's trying to tell you information you need to know.'

Miles said, 'What do you want, Andy?' He didn't feel embarrassed or stupid, talking to Andy with Celeste in the room.

Andy put his hands over two of the wounds. 'I want you to know what you did, Miles. I want you to know what you didn't do.'

Miles repeated the words to Celeste. She frowned. 'Show me the confession.'

'No.'

'Why?'

'He's my burden to carry.'

'I'm not offering to carry Andy for you. Just let me see what you remember.'

'And reading it will, what, make you respect me?' Thirty seconds of silence passed. 'I killed my best friend. What kind of person am I?'

'I didn't save my husband. I locked myself in a house for a year. What kind of person am I, Miles?' She sat up from the bed. She held out her hand. 'Give me the confession. I can handle it.'

He sat up, pulled the paper from his jacket, handed it to her. She unfolded it and began to read:

Allison:

I killed my best friend. I was working with my dad in Miami — he owned a private investigations firm. Dad died (cancer) and my friend Andy was an accountant for what I believed was an insurance company but the firm was a financial front for the Barrada crime family. Dad lost three hundred thousand on gambling and he owed the money through a Barrada bookie. When he died — I owed the debt. The Barradas threatened to take Dad's firm, which was all Dad left me, but Andy got me a deal; he told me that I could work it off by doing clandestine work for the Barradas. Andy wanted financial and logistical information on other crime rings: spreadsheets, payments, dealer networks, information on shipments into the country.

I wasn't a hit man or an enforcer. I was their personal spy and Andy gently told me that if I refused, the Barradas would kill me and he would not be able to stop them. He wept as he told me and I believed him. He was giving me a way out. The Barradas had me conduct eleven covert jobs against their competitors and I succeeded in every one of them. I believed the debt was paid. But they made it clear I couldn't walk away.

I approached the FBI in Miami. I told them I would testify about the Barradas' spying on the other crime rings if they would provide immunity to me — and to Andy. He saved my ass, so I was saving his. But Andy couldn't know, they told me, his loyalty to the Barradas ran too deep. He was engaged to a Barrada cousin, who owned the insurance front. I would have to get information on Andy, leverage over him, so that he couldn't run back to the Barradas, give him no choice but to cooperate. I had to eliminate loyalty as a choice for him.

I set up a meeting with Andy in a Barrada warehouse. The FBI gave me falsified data I could claim to have stolen from the Duarte crime ring, a group in Los Angeles wanting to expand and make alliances in south Florida. I had already lifted some minor stuff from them but this faked FBI info was designed to make Andy drool: names of dealers under their control, bank-account numbers, people on their payroll. I was to take two FBI undercover agents with me. The undercovers pretended to be guys I had recruited to be my operatives and they planned to record what Andy said about the spying operation and then immediately make the offer to him of immunity. Because I couldn't do it alone, and Andy might have to be physically handled. I told the FBI I couldn't turn without Andy. He might not want to believe it, but the Barradas would blame him for my betrayal, for bringing me into their camp and me selling them to the feds. They'd kill him, I was sure.

This was the only way to save Andy.

We're at the warehouse and this is all I remember: I introduce Andy to the guys and we're talking, we're showing him the data, I say I can get more on the Duartes but it's going to involve a substantial operation – the sting I have in mind for them, I can't do it alone, I need the two guys with me. I ask Andy, real specifically what kind of data he wants me to steal from the Duartes, and he's talking up a beauty, feeding everything into the tapes that the FBI needs, to put on the real pressure, and he asks me when can you get started and then

it's all a blank

then I see him pull a gun from under his shirt. Aims it at one of the feds' head and I've got my gun and I never use a gun much but I shoot because I can't let him shoot a man in the head.

My bullet hits his shoulder as he shoots at me and hits my chest and we both scream and fall and I raise the gun at him again

then it's all a blank again

The next time I'm aware of what's going on I'm in a safe

house in Jacksonville, and they're offering me the witness protection program and my best friend, my brother for all intents and purposes, is dead and I don't know what I did wrong, why I killed him.

Celeste folded the paper.

'You remembered something else,' she said quietly.

'Yes. The first blank. When Andy asked me when I could get started.' He stopped. 'Groote and I were talking about the FBI and when they would start naming me in the news – it brought it back, clear as day. But . . .'

'Don't shy away from it,' she said.

'He asked me when me and the guys could get started on the project and I said, *They'll do it as soon as we turn off the tape.*'

'You let him know he was being taped.'

'I said . . . yes, for that reason, but for a joke, to try and soften the blow. We all laughed. Even Andy. But then he saw my eyes, he panicked, he realized it was a bust and he pulled his gun, aimed it at the undercover's head . . . If I'd kept my mouth shut, told him a different way . . .'

She took his hands in hers. 'There's no good way to tell him, is there?'

Miles shook his head.

She gripped his hands tightly. 'But Andy drew the gun. He chose to fight. You saved a life, two lives, your own. You and I both saved lives, wow, we're in a special club.' Her voice broke and tears came to her eyes. 'If God keeps a ledger, don't you think our accounts are balanced?'

'I . . . shot to wound him, not to kill him. I still don't remember the details.'

'He shot you in the chest. Did he show you the same consideration?'

Miles opened his mouth to speak, then shut it.

'I handled it wrong. He panicked.'

'Did he expect you to work for the mob forever when you were strong-armed into service? I don't care if you knew him from when you were in diapers, he's a horrible friend.'

Miles released her hands. 'So what does Andy want to tell me, that he's sorry? He never offers an apology. What I did, what I didn't do, what the hell does that mean?'

'The tape the FBI made of the meeting – did you ever listen to it?'

'They told me the tape failed. Andy died for nothing.' He sat down again. 'God, you must think I'm a terrible person.'

She folded her legs under her on the bed. 'I told you my husband went out to get eggs and coffee. And a man I thought was a close friend, and instead was stalking me, I let him into my home and he tied me up and he waited for Brian to come home. He held a knife to my throat. He didn't gag me. He said he was going to hurt me because I hadn't loved him, I didn't appreciate him – all your standard stalker bullshit – but he wouldn't hurt Brian. I believed him. I was petrified with terror, I couldn't think two seconds into the future.' She tapped the side of her temple. 'The brain that outfoxed nine very smart people and won five million dollars – frozen like ice. I heard Brian call to me as he opened the front door. If I had screamed for him to run, he would have had a chance. He could have run, saved himself. Instead, with a knife at my throat, I didn't scream out a warning and my husband came in and the Disturbed Fan tortured him to death. In front of me. So I could see every howl of pain, every grimace, every inch of agony. A neighbor heard my Brian's

346

screams and called the police and they busted in and killed the Disturbed Fan about three minutes after Brian died. The Fan was smoking a cigarette before he started in on me and I was just lying there, staring into my husband's dead eyes, waiting to die, wondering, *Why didn't I scream and warn him? Why?*'

'Because you were afraid. Because you wanted to believe him that he wouldn't hurt Brian.'

'Well, how stupid was I?'

'I wanted to believe Andy would be happy about me getting us both out of the mob. You wanted to believe Brian would be safe if you followed orders. Do you think Brian blamed you, for one second?'

She didn't answer.

'If you had screamed, do you think Brian would have run? Hell, no. He would have run to you. Fought to save you.'

The truth of what he said crushed her. 'All because I wanted to be on a stupid TV show.' She buried her face in her hands. 'So why can't we move past all the grief?'

'Because we loved these people. You don't shed them like a skin.'

'Do you think if I kept taking Frost – I would forget what happened to Brian?' Her voice cracked. 'If I forget the terror we experienced, aren't I awful?'

'Brian wouldn't want you to carry that grief forever. He sure wouldn't want you always cutting yourself.'

She wiped at her eyes. 'Thank you for showing me the confession.'

'Thanks for telling me what happened to you too.'

The silence between them grew awkward; almost as if they'd been physically intimate and didn't know what to say, how to part, how to step forward.

She came to his bed, and she curled herself into his arms. They lay, tense, barely touching each other, and she closed her hand around his and he began to relax. Touch to touch. Her hair – she had showered after they ate, put on loose clothes Victor gave her – smelled of tangerine and he realized he had forgotten the perfection of holding a woman, the yield of skin, the beat of breath.

If he kept chasing Frost, he could be dead in a day. Or in prison. This might be the last bit of happiness, a final morsel, in his life.

He closed his eyes and slept.

A hand touched his shoulder. Miles opened his eyes. Victor sat, wheeled close to the bed.

Bad news, he mouthed. *Let's talk.*

FIFTY-TWO

Victor's office held a range of computers: two Linux-based workhorses, a gleaming Apple Macintosh, four beige-box PCs.

One monitor displayed a picture of Quantrill. The next of Sorenson, then one of Allison.

Groote stood by one screen, staring at the picture of Sorenson.

'I haven't found your daughter, Dennis, and I'm running into stone walls inquiring about government safe houses. Locations are closely guarded secrets. I'm going to have to use a roundabout approach, and that will take time.'

'If they kill her because Dodd's dead . . .'

'I doubt it. Dodd's death will freeze them up; they'll need to regroup. You have to be hopeful,' Victor said.

Groote sat, put his battered face in his hands, then stood. 'So what does it buy me? A day, two? Even if we get Frost, I'm not sure how to contact whoever Dodd works for.'

'I've put a couple of bullets in your gun, gentlemen. Or it's evidence to help you decide either no way in hell you two move forward, or you lay low, or you go to the police right now.'

'We're listening,' Miles said.

Victor gestured at Sorenson's face on the screen. 'James Sorenson. But before he was Pentagon, he was posted with the Foreign Service in Beijing. Before that, the army. Now he's no longer on a government payroll – at least not one anyone will admit. I can find nothing else about him: family, academic background, zilch – those files are sealed. He's quite the bureaucratic nomad. Usually a government lifer wriggles into a spot and holds on tight.'

'Or he's the hot potato, handed around, because he's trouble,' Miles said.

'I have contacts in the army archives and at Defense trying to find out more, but nothing yet, other than one Pentagon friend telling me Sorenson was, and I quote, "a loose cannon, crazy, difficult to deal with." Sorry, I don't have a bridge into the Foreign Service; that's a brick wall to me.'

'Okay. Quantrill.'

'I can tell you,' Groote said, 'he's a corporate spy.'

'More than that,' Victor said. 'A dot-com millionaire, moved his money before the Internet bubble broke. He owns a consulting firm that once was accused of corporate espionage, but the charges got dropped; I smell a payoff. He's also linked to a number of companies that own other companies that own specialty hospitals, both here and overseas, or have contracts with the Veterans Administration.'

'If he's illegally testing drugs at one hospital, could he be doing it at another one?' Groote said. 'Maybe he and Dodd worked out a deal, to get Frost back from Sorenson – and Amanda's at one of his hospitals . . .'

'I can check, but I don't think Dodd and Quantrill came to any understanding before Dodd died,' Victor said.

'Regarding the testing, I'm almost sure if he tested Frost at one, he might have tested it at others. His only health-care scandal was a VA hospital in Minneapolis accused of testing unapproved cancer medications on patients. Two doctors and an administrator were prosecuted. Another doctor ducked on not enough evidence. That doctor resigned from the VA and took a job with a hospital that Quantrill's holding company owns in Florida. Otherwise Quantrill sticks to the shadows.'

'Like Sorenson.'

'Has it occurred to you Sorenson's hunting just as hard for you? He'll know by now his hit in Yosemite failed – and, better for him, he'll know the government's willing to lie to the media to cover up Dodd's involvement. If you're caught by the police, you're on the news. You can wipe him out by going public.'

'Unless he can reach Amanda and she dies if we talk,' Groote said.

'Even if he doesn't, we go public, and the government shuts us up or discredits us, or we talk and we send Frost to pharmaceutical purgatory,' Miles said. 'It would kill public acceptance of the research, set it back for years. No. I have to get the formula and then get it to a company that'll develop it responsibly.' Miles stared at the photo of Sorenson on the computer screen. A nagging tugged at the back of his brain. The facts didn't click together in sweet harmony; facts didn't always; but he couldn't put his hand on what bothered him.

'This is a lot, man, thanks,' Groote said.

Victor wheeled over to Groote. 'Would you please excuse us, Dennis? I need to speak with Miles privately. Thank you.'

Groote stood and walked out the door without a word.

Victor waited until he heard Groote return to the back-yard patio and close the sliding glass door. 'You can't trust him.'

'I know. But I need him. I can't fight Sorenson alone.'

'Groote's ex-FBI. He has a private security firm. You already know he's not terribly interested in following the law.'

'Despite his rough edges, he still has that federal air. It's the only thing that gives me hope he might act decently in the end.'

'He might need Frost,' Victor said, 'more than you or I do. Now ... I know you're angry with Nathan for not telling you the truth about Dodd. But you need to know Nathan's story. A bit of careful cajoling and a promise of ten free hours of highly expensive database work got me his file via the Department of Defense.'

Miles held up a hand, stood. 'Don't tell me. I don't care.'

Victor leaned forward, tapped Miles on the knee with his prosthetic arm. 'You asked me to help you, eyes wide open. I'm telling you to listen, ears wide open.'

'Tell me.'

'Cleopatra,' Victor called to one of the computers, 'play Ruiz video file.'

Prompted by voice-activated software, the computer began to show a film. A nervous Nathan, clean, hair damp, but his nose broken, his eyes bruised, his face pitted and bandaged, sat staring into the camera.

The tape started with the interviewer identifying himself, the date, the location at a U.S. military base in Kuwait.

'Sergeant Ruiz, I want to talk to you about the events of April second.'

'Yes, sir.' Nathan wiped a finger along his bottom lip, caught himself, sat upright. 'Yes, sir.'

The interviewer summarized the approach Nathan's artillery unit had taken as the American forces rolled toward Baghdad. Nathan agreed with each point.

'And then, after you'd fired your missiles, you stopped to await further instructions.'

'Yes, sir.'

'And you performed an operational check to see if all systems were functioning properly.'

Nathan nodded. 'Yes, sir, as always.'

'And the results?'

'All was well.' Nathan swallowed.

'The infrared beacon that would identify you as American forces was working?' the interviewer said.

Nathan nodded.

'I need a verbal answer, please.'

'Sir, yes, sir, the fireflies – the infrared beacons – were working.' His voice cracked at the end.

'So then you stepped away from your post.'

'Sir, yes, sir, but just a few feet . . .'

'And during your absence the beacon failed.'

'Yes, sir.' Nathan's voice stayed steady. 'I assume so. The backup failed as well.'

'And how long were you away from the equipment?'

'Only a few minutes, sir, then I returned.'

'You didn't notice the fireflies had malfunctioned.'

Silence.

'Did you hear the question, Sergeant?'

'Sir, yes, sir, I heard you. I did not notice the beacon had failed.'

'Do you only pay attention to the equipment during operational checks, Sergeant Ruiz?'

'Sir, no, sir.'

'But you failed to notice that the beacon failed, and the appropriate alarm also failed.'

Four beats of silence, and Nathan's military impassivity faded into pure pain. He fought hard to put a calm expression back on his face. 'Sir, yes, sir, but . . .'

'But?'

'Out in the field, sir, the unexpected happens. I don't know why the system failed. It . . . just did.'

'Yet you were responsible for its repair.'

'That's true . . . sir.' Nathan swallowed; sweat formed on his bruised and battered forehead.

'And how many minutes before the friendly fire hit?'

'Nine minutes after we launched our last missile, sir.'

'Nine minutes and you don't notice the beacon isn't transmitting.'

'Sir, yes, sir.'

'Nine minutes you had to save your company.' An awful, heavy silence and Nathan blinked hard into the camera. The unseen interrogator continued: 'According to Captain Cariotis, during those nine minutes you were talking and laughing with your friends, enjoying the success of your mission. You thought your work for the evening was done, with all your missiles successfully launched.'

'Sir, yes, sir.' Nathan closed his eyes and took a long breath. 'Sir, yes, sir.' Tears formed in the corners of his eyes. 'But the fire control could have confirmed for the pilot, sir, that we were American forces . . . I don't understand how I alone—'

'You're right there, on the scene, with the broken beacon. You could have noticed it. You could have fixed it. You could have alerted fire control there was a problem.'

'Jesus,' Miles said, 'they blamed him for the entire accident.' His mouth went dry, thinking of Nathan's nightmare back in Santa Fe, crying out, *I fixed it I fixed it I fixed it.*

'Cleopatra, pause video,' Victor told the computer, and Nathan's face froze on the screen. 'Without the working infrared a U.S. pilot could think Nathan's company were Republican Guard forces. A pilot gets a bad confirmation from fire control after he sees missiles rise in the dark, he fires, and you have dead American boys all over the desert.'

'Oh, man,' Miles said. 'Those poor kids.'

'Yes,' Nathan said, behind him, standing in the open doorway. 'Those poor kids I helped kill.'

Miles stood. 'Nathan. I meant you as one of those kids. I am so, so sorry, man.'

'You don't judge me,' Nathan said. 'I went to serve. I went to protect. I'm not a torturer like Groote. I'm not a screw-up like you, Miles.'

'It was a genuine accident,' Victor said. 'They happen in war all the time.'

'I thought you were my friends. Stupid of me,' Nathan said. He wiped his nose with the back of his hand. 'I'm getting the hell out of here.'

'Nathan, you have nothing to be ashamed of – we understand what you must have gone through, why you helped Dodd. Stay with us.'

'Turn off that tape!' Nathan kicked his boot into the monitor. 'You sure are a spy, Miles, a much better one than me. No secret is safe from you.' He stormed out, through the house, through the front door. Miles chased him, grabbed his arm as he stepped off the lawn into the street.

'You can help us find Sorenson . . .'

He pressed a gun against Miles's head. Miles's gun. 'Let go, Miles. Let me go.'

'I won't. You'll have to shoot me.'

'Miles, please! Please!'

'You're not running off. Let us help you.'

'You're so full of shit. You lectured me how we had to stick together. You're dumping me and Celeste to go off with Groote, a fucking animal who . . . tortured me.'

'Nathan—'

'Shut up. Shut your goddamned hypocritical trap, Miles. He hurt me, Jesus, but I kept your goddamn name shut for hours because I thought it was the right thing to do. I wanted to do right. Be strong again.' He started to sob.

'Nathan, God, I'm sorry.'

'I lost every friend I had in the army. All of them. I thought you would understand since you lost all your friends in Florida. I thought . . . never mind what I thought.' He shoved Miles away, leveled the gun at him. 'You only want me to stay because you're afraid I'll call the cops, tell them where you and Celeste are. That I'll be the hero again. Don't worry. I'll treat you better than you treated me.' He walked backward into the quiet of the street.

'This is crazy, you don't have money, you don't have a car.'

'I'll keep my mouth shut about you and Celeste. Unless you follow me. Then I talk till my throat's sore, you got me?' Lowering the gun, Nathan walked away from him.

Miles stepped into the street to follow him and the gun came back up.

Miles watched him walk into the darkness and went back inside the house.

'I'm sorry, Miles,' Victor said.

'He might be back in ten minutes or ten hours when he calms down,' Miles said. 'He thinks I hate him. I don't. But he doesn't understand what trust is.'

'How much of your plans do you think he heard?'

'Enough to know I wanted to leave him and Celeste with you. He might have heard that in the car; we thought he was asleep.'

'Will he go to the police?'

'I don't know.'

'Well, the only law I've broken is harboring fugitives, and if I haven't had the TV on, I can't know you were fugitives.'

'I'm sorry.'

'You and Groote might need to head out. Just to be safe.'

'Can Celeste stay? I can't put her in further danger. She's been through too much as it is.'

'You better go while she's asleep. Otherwise she'll fight you tooth and nail.'

The faces connected to Frost stayed frozen on the computer screens. Except for the computer on the far left: it displayed Victor's Web site for trauma patients. He had a poll running, a purely hypothetical question, the one Sorenson had asked him a lifetime ago: *If you could forget the worst moment in your life, would you?*

Ninety-four percent said yes. That was the power, the promise, of Frost.

So if you find Frost, can you find Nathan again? To help him?

Miles watched Celeste sleep, lost in the heaviness of her own dreams. He took the confession from his pocket, left it propped against the lamp. He leaned down and kissed the top of her head.

*

'Let's go,' Miles said. Groote stood from his patio chair. Miles thought it best not to mention Nathan had left; Groote would want to hunt him down. 'Maybe we can get a late flight to Austin.'

'Actually,' Groote said, 'I have an idea. Allison stole the buyers' list from Quantrill. That'd be useful information.'

Miles saw where he was going. 'We get details on the auction from a buyer, we might get real close to Sorenson without him knowing it.'

'And we can get that list tonight,' Groote said. 'You're not afraid of alarm systems and men with guns, are you, Mr. Spy?'

FIFTY-THREE

Nathan had a dollar fifty in quarters he'd stolen from the blind soldier's room and he fed a few into the pay phone at the gas station. Stealing from a blind guy, God, he was classy. He wiped the tears and snot from his face with his sleeve. He had a wallet with five hundred dollars in cash and a photo ID Dodd had slipped him back in Yosemite, a ticket to reenter society after his mission at Sangre de Cristo. But he had had no change to operate the phone, and five hundred dollars might not be enough money to do what he knew he must do. His legs hurt, his back ached from the beating Groote had given him back in Santa Fe, and he didn't want to be alone. But he would be, until he finished his duty.

His mother answered on the third ring.

'Mama? I'm out of the hospital. I'm all fixed.'

'Sweetheart? Oh, thank God,' then a torrent of Spanish. He waited for her words to subside and he tried to laugh so she would believe he was happy.

'I need a favor, Mama. I'm not in Santa Fe. They moved me to a different hospital near Los Angeles to finish the treatments.'

'I don't understand . . .' and she started in with the questions, rat-a-tat, and he closed his eyes.

'Mama,' he interrupted her, 'I got to have money. To eat, to get home.' But he wasn't going home. No. He had to finish being a hero first.

FIFTY-FOUR

Miles picked the kitchen door lock with a special attachment on Groote's Mr. Screwdriver, not wanting to think about its being the weapon that had brutalized Nathan. The tumblers clicked into clear and Miles gave the door the barest push. Groote stood behind him, gun at the ready, and they listened for the hum of the alarm. None.

Quantrill hadn't activated the system yet; he hadn't gone to bed. Probably he was upstairs in his office, trying to persuade the buyers not to attend Sorenson's auction, assure them that all was well, that he alone had the one and true Frost.

Miles slipped the screwdriver/pick into his back pocket and followed Groote into the house. They heard the distant roar of gunfire, then a billowing blast of artillery, the scream of a jet. Then the rising pulse of an orchestra, music thundering along with the battle, all coming from a half-open doorway off the living room.

Guards, Groote mouthed to Miles. He gestured Miles toward the upstairs, mouthed, *Office*, gestured Miles to go up.

Miles went up the stairs. Groote waited, gun at the ready. If the guards stayed put in front of their blockbuster, no worries, no need to kill them.

Quantrill sat in the chair, at his empty desk, head back, a red-and-black smear on his forehead, eyes half shut.

Miles touched the dead man's throat. Still warm.

The man's computer was gone from the desk. Miles went into the bathroom next to the office, grabbed a hand towel, used it to slide open drawers, search the closet that doubled as a supply cabinet. No handheld computers that might have carried a backup of Frost or the buyers' list, no CDs or DVDs, no disks – all cleared out.

Sorenson was cleaning house, eliminating every possible interference, and they had just missed him or his hired killers.

He eased the dead man out of the chair and searched his pockets. Wallet, full of cash, untouched. He found a cell phone, folded shut. He tucked the cell phone into his pocket.

Miles came down the stairs; Groote was still in position, the movie still playing. Miles walked past him and into the media room. The two bodyguards were sprawled on the couch, a bowl of buttered popcorn between them, three bullet holes marring both faces.

'Well,' Groote said, 'I guess Quantrill won't be writing me a paycheck.'

'We just missed him. This happened about fifteen minutes ago. Sorenson just ended the buyers' option of sticking with Quantrill. Now he's the only game in town.'

Groote leaned down and took a handful of popcorn. Miles tried not to puke as the man munched. 'Assume he made efforts to contact buyers, warn them away from the auction, plead with them not to buy from a thief, or even threaten them with exposure if they didn't boycott the auction.'

Miles held up the cell phone. 'We might find a buyer he called. I get a cell number, I can find nearly anybody.'

'All we need,' Groote said around the mouthful of popcorn, 'is one.'

They found an all-night coffee shop near the Santa Monica Pier that offered Internet access, and Miles started working. After finding that Quantrill had spent his final hours on earth calling a Chinese restaurant, his landscape crew, and two numbers that Groote believed to be those of the dead popcorn-eaters, Miles hit pay dirt on the fifth number. He found it belonged to a Greg Bradley. A Google search of the man's name, combined with *pharmaceutical*, showed that Bradley owned a consulting firm based in Boston that advised Aldis-Tate, one of the largest U.S.-based drug companies.

'That's our boy,' Groote said. 'Sorenson pretended to be from Aldis-Tate when he came to the hospital.'

The call log indicated the conversation between Quantrill and Bradley had been lengthy – well over thirty minutes.

'Long conversations,' Miles said, 'suggest a detailed discussion, and that means Quantrill might have been persuasive about bucking the second auction.'

Groote frowned. 'So you think Bradley chickened out?'

'Let's see if he did. Give me a second.' He dialed Bradley's cell phone, waited.

'Don't screw this up,' Groote said in a low voice.

'Hello?'

'Mr. Bradley?'

'Yes?'

'Hi, sir, this is Corey with the credit-card security firm Ironlock. I'm checking on a charge cancellation that raised a red flag in our systems. Have you canceled an airline flight recently, sir?'

'Uh, yeah. Today.'

'A flight to Austin, sir?'

'Well, yeah . . .' Then a long, awkward pause. 'Who are you again?'

Miles spoke with hyperbrisk efficiency: 'Sir, we check any cancellation that raises a red flag as we insure the credit-card companies and we pay their charge cancellation insurance. We're investigating a couple of airlines that charge falsely, then cancel immediately so we have to pay up. But if it's a genuine cancellation, that's no problem, and I thank you for your time.' He hung up. 'I think he canceled. He got frosty when I mentioned Austin.'

'You're a good liar. Is there such a thing as that insurance?'

'I have no idea.' Miles started trying the next numbers in the call log.

He got lucky three numbers later. Quantrill had called the same number, three times in a row, the first conversation lasting forty seconds, the next two barely lasting ten seconds.

'If it's not a girlfriend,' Groote said, 'it's someone who doesn't want to talk to Quantrill.' He raised an eyebrow. 'You're good at this.'

The man's name was David Singhal and he was a former VP of research at a Swiss pharmaceutical, now running a research consulting firm based in Los Angeles. Miles searched his name using Google's Images option and found a photo of Singhal from his interview in a European business journal. Fiftyish, cultured, intelligent eyes, a graying goatee. Miles tried the number.

'Hello, Mr. Singhal?'

'Yes?' He had a clipped British accent.

Miles said with shotgun delivery, 'Hi, this is James with Excelsior Credit Card Security, we work with VISA and with AmEx, and there's a question about your account, did you recently cancel a flight reservation to Austin?'

Singhal was more cautious than Bradley: 'I'm sorry, who are you with?'

Miles repeated, adding, 'We're assisting the credit-card companies with a database corruption. The discrepancy is that one version of the credit database has you making a charge for an LAX-Austin flight, the other rebuilt database has canceled that charge.'

'It sounds like I should call my airline,' Singhal said. 'I'm not going to give you my credit-card number over the phone.'

'Uh, yes, sir, very wise, you should never do that.' He made a stab. 'I can do the database fix so there's no confusion about your ticket status. Was your flight on Southwest?'

Singhal hung up.

'Great,' Miles said. 'He'll be calling the airline directly and they'll tell him all's well.'

'Give me the phone.' Groote took the phone, dialed, spoke quietly, dialed another number, gave a clearance code. He hung up, got them both refills on their coffee, sat down. His phone rang and he listened, clicked the phone off. 'David Singhal is on the GlobeWest flight tomorrow morning to Austin. I'll get a call back if he changes his reservation.'

'How'd you find that out?'

'A contact at the Bureau.'

'The government's monitoring airline passenger lists.'

'Not a surprise, surely.'

'Okay,' Miles said. 'Now what?'

'Sleep,' Groote said.

They stopped at a twenty-four-hour megastore and bought clothes and necessities. Groote gathered cash from an ATM. They checked into a hotel near LAX, same room, twin beds.

Groote said good night and switched off the lamp. Miles couldn't sleep; he was afraid if he closed his eyes, fell toward rest, Andy would come back.

'Groote?'

'Yeah?'

'When we were driving down today . . . you never said exactly who attacked your wife and daughter.'

The silence was longer this time. 'Punks who were threatened by Bureau attention to their ring, thought I was involved in helping decapitate their operations. Misplaced revenge.'

He wanted to ask, *What ring?* If it had been someone the Barradas aimed him at . . . but the only southern California ring he'd targeted were the Duartes . . . and they were all dead now. 'Who were the punks? Drug dealers?'

'Doesn't matter.'

'So why'd you leave the Bureau?'

'I could no longer reach my career goals.'

'What goals?'

'Well-placed revenge,' Groote said. 'I don't want to talk anymore, Miles. Good night.'

FIFTY-FIVE

The next morning, the second flight from LAX to Austin soared into the crisp blue sky and Miles saw, across the row where an elderly gentleman scanned a Sunday newspaper, the headline that read FEDERAL OFFICER MISSING and below that a picture of DeShawn Pitts.

He couldn't read the article from where he sat and the gentleman read slowly, every word, never scanning an article. Groote dozed in the seat next to him. Five rows ahead of him sat David Singhal, dressed in a suit, reading the *Wall Street Journal.*

Finally the man folded the paper, tucked it into his seat pocket.

'Sir?' Miles leaned over and spoke in a whisper. 'Excuse me. Might I see your paper if you're done?'

'Sure.' The gentleman handed him the pages.

Miles read the article with chills touching his skin. DeShawn Pitts, a federal marshal – the story left out that he worked for Witness Protection – had gone missing two days ago, while on unspecified duty. The FBI was asking anyone who had information to call them.

Hurley died on Thursday. DeShawn was at the hospital that day – Miles heard him on Groote's call to Hurley – and he went missing on Friday. The day after Groote had talked to him.

Or maybe DeShawn didn't give up, kept questioning, kept looking for Miles – he would, if ordered, if WITSEC accepted DeShawn's argument that Miles wasn't capable of making a cogent decision given his disability – and he ran into Groote again. Groote was hunting Miles; so was DeShawn. Imagine they intersected. At a bad time.

Be okay, DeShawn, please be okay.

Miles scanned the rest of the article. No mention of him – WITSEC still wouldn't compromise his new name. But a mention, at the end, of it having been a difficult week for Santa Fe police: a woman had been killed in an explosion at her office (Allison); a celebrity had vanished from her home (Celeste); four high-school kids critically injured in a car crash outside town; a doctor and a tourist had also gone missing. The hospital had reported Hurley missing. Would that news – or DeShawn's sheer persistence – have brought DeShawn back to Sangriaville, closing in on a connection? Back to Groote?

Miles suddenly wanted to be off the plane, very badly.

He folded the paper, handed it back to its owner with a thank-you, got up, went to the bathroom, splashed water on his face, tried to collect his thoughts, weighed the inferences. He returned to his seat. Groote was awake.

'Airsick?' Groote said in a low voice. 'You're pale.'

'No,' Miles said, 'I'm okay.'

'Don't go mental,' Groote said.

'I said I'm fine.'

'Good. Because we're almost home free.'

If you killed DeShawn – I will kill you, Miles thought. 'Yes. I hope we are.'

FIFTY-SIX

Miles sat in the Austin Four Seasons hotel bar, Allison and Andy and now DeShawn sitting across from him, an accusing retinue, people dead from his mistakes.

He could not lose his grip now. Andy's light-switch presence – on and off, on and off – made Miles sure that his sanity was a matter of nuance and fluctuation, but now with Allison and DeShawn haunting him he knew his mind was on the verge of breaking apart, slipping into fragments that could not be easily pieced back together.

He couldn't let it show. Groote would kill him if Miles's mind broke and he became unneeded weight.

He put his gaze on the window, watching the calm of Town Lake as it stretched past downtown. Think of your favorite things, like that assortment of pleasantries Julie Andrews sang about in that old song. He summoned good memories of Austin: Miles had been to this bustling, creative hothouse of a city once before, to an Austin City Limits Music Festival with Andy – Andy worshiped Oasis and Miles was a huge fan of The Black Crowes and they'd come, drunk beer, grooved to the bands. Andy scored backstage passes and Miles remembered Andy relentlessly flirting with a beautiful girl who was the girlfriend of a major band's drummer. They got kicked out of the VIP tent and laughed about it all the way back to the Four Seasons.

'Good times,' Andy said.

'Yes,' Miles answered, under his breath. 'Now hush.' Sweat broke out along his back.

'What are you going to do if he killed me, Miles?' DeShawn said. 'I have a right to know if I can count on you.'

'Don't talk to him in public,' Allison said from the other chair. 'They'll haul his ass to a hospital, pump him full of antipsychotics, and maybe he won't listen to us anymore.'

'You don't think a pill is going to make me go away, do you?' Andy said. 'Might as well trade a cow for magic beans, Miles. You know you and I are a team forever. Permanent odd couple. I'm the original fracture in your head, these newbies are just hangers-on.'

'I'm going to kill you again,' Miles whispered, 'and this time it's self-defense.'

'It wasn't the first time,' Andy said. 'Not really. Deep in your brain is the truth.'

'Dying to come out,' Allison said.

'Shut up, shut up,' Miles said in a soft mutter. He straightened his shirt. You could appear scraggly yet hip in the Four Seasons and not attract undue attention: Austin was a film and music town and dress did not often equal actual wealth. He was dressed, unthreateningly, in clean jeans and a T-shirt that promoted a music group so obscure he might pass for Austin-cool.

Eleven minutes later, he watched a man cross the lobby, carrying a briefcase, heading up to the elevators. David Singhal, returning from a cab ride he'd taken shortly after arriving at the hotel. Groote had followed him, also in a

370

cab, then called Miles to say the guy had simply gone to a restaurant for lunch.

Groote hadn't gotten back yet and so Miles followed Singhal through the lobby. Miles got in the elevator next to the man, folded his hands behind his back; Singhal had already pressed the button.

'If you go to the Frost auction today,' Miles said conversationally, 'you're going to be killed.'

'Today,' Singhal repeated in wide-eyed shock. The doors slid open at his floor. 'I've no idea what you mean . . .'

'I'm not wearing a wire. And don't act like you don't know what I'm talking about. You're in deep trouble, Mr. Singhal, and only I can get you out of it.'

'You've made – a mistake.' Singhal walked past him. 'Leave me alone or I'll call hotel security.'

'You go ahead. Then I'll call the FDA.' Miles followed him to a suite at the end of the hall. 'You were going to buy Frost from Oliver Quantrill. Now you're buying it from someone else who's willing to take a smaller profit. It's a mistake.'

Singhal kept a poker face. 'Again, you're confused.'

Miles pulled the gun from the back of his pants, hidden by his loose shirt, aimed it at Singhal's stomach. 'Then let's talk privately and you can clear the air. Inside.'

Hands trembling, Singhal opened the suite door and Miles followed him inside. He ordered Singhal to sit on the bed, called Groote, told him to come to suite 409.

'We have two minutes. You're going to tell me where the Frost auction is. If you do, then I'll make sure your pharma client gets an opportunity to develop it for free. I'll give you the research – all I care about is that sick people get the medicine. But I have to know where Sorenson is.'

Singhal bit his lip.

'Please take my offer. If you think I'm scary, wait till you meet my . . . friend. His daughter's been kidnapped by the people running the auction.' Not exactly accurate, but it had the effect he wanted: Singhal swallowed. 'I need to know where the auction is.'

'It's an old private asylum, east side of town. Abandoned but bought by Sorenson's people a month or so ago.'

'When?'

'Six P.M.' Six hours away.

'Do you have a pass, any special way to gain entrance to this auction?'

'No.'

'I'm the nice guy. The completely ruthless man on his way up is the bad guy. Please reconsider your answer.'

A knock on the door. Miles let Groote inside.

'Who are you people?' Singhal said. 'If I know who I'm dealing with – we can agree to an arrangement.'

'Here's your arrangement.' Groote grabbed the man by the throat, pushed him smoothly up the wall. Then he started punching Singhal, precise stiff-fingered chops. Steady as a metronome, in the kidneys, in the space between ribs, above the heart, and Miles thought, *That shouldn't hurt*, but suddenly Singhal's face purpled and he said, 'My wallet. God, stop. Please.'

Miles pulled Singhal's wallet free from his jacket and found a slip of paper in the wallet: an address in east Austin and an access code: 12XCD.

'There's a fence around the property. That's the electronic code to get past the locks.'

'What kind of security did Sorenson promise?' Miles asked.

'He . . . said we'd be safe.'

'How many buyers coming?'

'I have no idea . . . please. I have a family.'

'So do I, asshole,' Groote said.

'Groote. Don't kill him.'

'Tell me about security.' Groote raised his fist.

'I was just assured . . . it would be safe . . . I don't know, honestly.'

Groote shook his head at Miles. 'He can't be calling and warning Sorenson.'

'Don't kill him,' Miles said again.

'Yes.'

'No.'

'Goddamn it, you want to walk into a freaking ambush? Better him than us.' Spittle flew from Groote's mouth.

Miles punched Singhal. Hard. Singhal's eyes rolled, the guy collapsed.

'Good idea,' Groote said. 'He might start to scream, us discussing his lack of a future.'

The blow had hurt his hand and Miles worked out the pain with a shake. 'You kill him, and we get caught, then you'll never see Amanda again. The guy in Yosemite, shooting him you saved lives, and we'd all swear to that in court. But this would be cold-blooded murder, and I'm sure you're not into that gig. It never pays.'

Groote shook his head. 'He can't warn Sorenson.'

'Then help me.' Miles tied up Singhal with the curtain cord, gagged him with a shredded pillowcase, stuffed him in the closet. He called the front desk, told them he was Singhal, he was sick with a vicious stomach flu, could they please be sure he wasn't disturbed today. No housekeeping, yes, and please put no phone calls through.

'I don't like this,' Groote said.

'We have six hours before the buyers are due,' Miles said. 'Come on.'

They got their rental car and headed for I-35.

They didn't see the car pull out after them, staying back a half mile but never losing sight of them.

FIFTY-SEVEN

Groote took the exit, three left turns, and drove along a street that held modest homes, most immaculate, a few slouching in disrepair. At the far end of the street, looming tall over the neighborhood, was a Gothic building of gray granite, forbidding. A stone sign that read YARBROUGH HOSPITAL EST. 1893 was worn with time, bedecked with graffiti. Above it, on wooden posts, a weathered, worn sign advertising a fund-raiser Halloween haunted house called 'Nightmare Hospital' was covered by another, smaller board that said HORIZON PROPERTIES NO TRESPASSING.

'Horizon,' Groote said. 'Same as the fake company that owned Dodd's car.'

'Sorenson killed Dodd and then uses his resources,' Miles said.

'Nice and efficient,' Groote said. 'You clearheaded, Miles?'

'Yes.'

'Take this.' Groote handed him a small gun and an ankle holster. He'd acquired a modest armory with a phone call after their arrival in Austin. 'Good to have if it gets ugly and you're down or your clip's empty.'

'Thank you.' Miles attached the holster, let the cuff of

his pants drop over the weapon, surprised at the gift. 'Groote?'

'Yeah?' Groote switched off the car's ignition.

'When this is done . . . we walk our separate ways. No need to hurt each other, is there?'

'I can't think of one, Miles.'

'What will you do?'

'Get my daughter where she can't be hurt again.'

'Then you should probably give up your war on the Duartes.'

Groote looked at him.

'The people that hurt her and killed your wife. It was the Duartes, wasn't it? You know they did it even if the FBI's not sure.'

'Why do you think that?'

'We don't have time for subtlety, Dennis. I don't want you putting a bullet in my back as soon as we get Frost.'

'Why would I be so rude, Miles?'

'Back in L.A. I asked you about the ring you blamed for hurting your family. You dodged giving me an answer, and it bothers me. Because there's no reason for you not to tell me. Unless it was the Duartes. Because I've got a connection to them. You know about my work for the Barradas, spying on rival crime rings, including the Duartes. You were FBI. Of course you'd know.'

Groote gave him a sidelong glance.

Miles kept his gaze steady on Groote's. 'I am very sorry for your loss, but I have never hurt your family. I stole some financial information from the Duartes, and the FBI gave me fake files about the Duartes to use in a sting against the Barradas. I didn't ever hurt the Duartes enough to bring them to a boiling point. I don't know what aimed them at your family, but it wasn't me. They were clearly already in the Bureau's headlights. You don't have a reason to blame me. So if you've got revenge on your mind, forget it.'

Groote's mouth twitched into a smile that died after a moment.

'I'm going to go back into Witness Protection, if they'll have me. I still have to testify against the Barradas, what's left of them. And then they want me to testify against other crime rings. It puts a lot of trash out of business. And it's faster and easier than killing them off, one by one.'

Groote looked straight ahead.

'I have a friend in WITSEC to call. You said you met him – DeShawn Pitts.'

'Yeah,' Groote said, his voice neutral.

Miles watched him for a sign of reaction. 'I'll tell DeShawn – since he's a good guy – where Amanda is, if Sorenson knows. So we can get her protection immediately, get her to safety right away.'

Groote said, 'That's a kindness, Miles.'

'You hurt my friends. You hurt Nathan, you attacked Celeste. I won't forget it. But I know you were trying to save your daughter.'

Groote coughed into his fist.

'I'm helping your kid, Dennis, and that evens any grudge you're thinking of carrying against me. Clear?'

'Crystal,' Groote said.

'Is there anything you want to tell me? Any reason I should have to be angry with you?' Thinking, *Did you kill DeShawn?*

'I can't think of a single one,' Groote said.

The silence hung between them like a curtain. Finally Groote spoke: 'We keep the plan simple. If Sorenson's there, we take him. If not, we take Frost if it's there, or we hide ourselves in the hospital until Sorenson shows up and then we take control.'

'Simple.'

'Most things are.'

'Come on,' Miles said. 'Let's end this.'

FIFTY-EIGHT

Miles entered the keypad number from Singhal's wallet. The lock holding the ancient iron gate beeped, disengaged, and Miles pushed the metal bars open, left it unlocked.

They ran across the overgrown grass to the hospital's front door.

'You first,' Groote said, 'since it's your idea.'

The door was locked. Miles knelt down, tested the lock with Groote's Mr. Screwdriver, worked it open. They stepped into the silence of the abandoned hospital.

Groote shut the door behind them. Both men held their guns out in front of them, pointing into the dim light. The opening foyer was dusty, scattered with junk – left-over papier-mâché monster masks; bright orange flyers, fading, that promoted the haunted-house event and other long-ago October concerts in clubs; discarded paper cups and beer cans; a tattered banner, torn in half, that said:

TO CHAMBER OF HO

They stood and listened for a long minute. The silence made Miles's ears ache.

Ho? Groote mouthed, pointing at the ripped sign.

Horrors, Miles decided. *Chamber of horrors.*

Groote tapped at his ear. *Listen.* And in the hush, he heard a quiet computerish hum from down the hall.

Miles saw Andy beckoning him along the hallway. Sweat broke out on his ribs, in the hollow of his throat, in his hair, and he realized he was more scared than he had ever been in his life. Scared of what would happen, scared of the psychopath standing next to him, scared of what he was becoming.

Groote gestured with his gun toward the hall. They went past several deserted offices. Tattered curtains, left-overs from the haunted house, hung in the windows, the rooms all empty. In the last one a laptop sat on a folding table. Miles moved to read the screen.

It displayed a PowerPoint presentation called 'Research Options on Memory and Trauma with a Beta Blocker Approach.'

All the bloodshed, all the suffering, all the millions at stake, it came down to a PowerPoint presentation.

Miles put his mouth close to Groote's ear to whisper, 'We're not alone. Sorenson wouldn't leave this behind.'

Trap us in the hallway, Groote mouthed. He gestured down the corridor. Miles nodded and followed him.

A brick propped open a door at the end of the hallway. A large room loomed beyond. Perhaps once it had been the cafeteria, or a space for socializing. Now it wore false walls, shaped into a twisty maze, a setup of nightmarish paintings on black paint, and mirrors arranged to confuse and frighten. Junk, left behind by the Halloween fund raiser, probably with a thought to reuse it next year, before Dodd bought the derelict property.

Miles could smell the dusty aroma that seems to permeate open spaces long neglected. It had hung like a perfume in the fatal air in Miami, and panic seized his chest. He could not flashback now, no, Jesus, don't lose control, he told himself, don't let your brain be a traitor.

Groote nodded at him and Miles went through the door first, gun out, arms level, afraid to breathe, to think, to see. *No Andy, no Allison, no DeShawn, please*, he thought. Groote followed him. The haunted house-scape still stood in the large room, monster faces leering at them from plywood and black paint: howling ghosts, shambling zombies, big-fanged vampires, all the playthings of manufactured, false fear.

Miles tapped Groote on the shoulder. They hadn't discussed what procedures to take if they needed to do a search. Groote jerked his head to the right, pointed to Miles, jerked it to the left. Miles nodded. He moved to the left, Groote moved to the right.

Miles walked down a twisting passage. Black fabric, hung to mask the operations of the haunted house, hung in tatters. Silence again.

Andy stood at the end of the passage, and he frightened Miles more than any fabricated monster. 'You can't do this. Sorenson will kill you. I mean, you think you're really going to stand there and shoot another person?'

Miles glanced behind him. Allison stood watching him as though to see what he would do next. He whirled back to Andy; but he was gone. He pivoted again; Allison had vanished. But the curtain moved, and there was no hum of air conditioner to sway it—

He sensed movement behind him and spun as Sorenson burst through the tatters of black fabric at the corner where Andy had stood, leveling a gun at him and firing.

The bullets needled through the meat and muscle of his arm and his leg. Miles screamed with agony and fell through the black curtain along the passageway, trying to simply put cover between himself and Sorenson. Two more bullets whistled above him, ripping holes in the black cloth. He went flat and he heard two shattering gunshots as he barreled headfirst to where a plywood wall met a wooden support pillar.

Trapped. No way to go forward or sideways.

Miles rolled back out into the passageway, bullets blazing above him as he tried to gain his footing, and he saw Groote take two shots, chest and shoulder. Groote staggered back, fell hard on the flooring, eyes wide, his teeth chomping into his own lip in pain and shock.

Miles turned.

Sorenson walked toward him, the gun locked on Miles's head.

FIFTY-NINE

Miles fell back against the fabric, a plywood Dracula collapsing on him, Groote coughing and cussing behind him, yelling at him to find his gun and *shoot the bastard*.

Miles wriggled out from the fake monster as Sorenson charged at him. Miles tried to aim but Sorenson had shot him in his shooting arm and he fired and missed. Sorenson leveled a kick that nailed Miles's wrist, knocked the gun past the curtains. Sorenson whipped his own gun across Miles's face.

'I told you in Allison's office that I'd end your pain,' Sorenson said. 'I keep my promises.'

Sorenson moved past Miles, put the aim of his gun on Groote.

Groote tried to crawl and Sorenson shot him again in the leg. He brought his gun up; Sorenson shot him in the hand.

He screamed.

'Miles,' Sorenson said. 'Who else knows about today?'

'No one. Leave him alone.'

'Where's the rest of the nut squad?'

'After Yosemite . . . they all hid. I went with Groote.'

'You mean that piece of shit I sent after you all actually succeeded in frightening you? Wow. I'll have to send flowers to his grave.'

Miles shouted, 'You knew I was a witness. You wanted my death as camouflage for killing Allison. I was supposed to die when she did. WITSEC, everyone else, would blame it on me, especially when the police found my file on Allison's computer. You tricked me and Allison . . .'

'You have to seize your opportunities when you can, Miles.'

Groote looked up at Sorenson, fighting for consciousness, blood trickling from his mouth, his nose, from his hand. 'Amanda. Amanda. God, please, help my girl. Where is . . . she? Never hurt you. Please.'

Sorenson walked toward Groote.

Miles saw himself lying on a floor, the smell of blood and concrete grit heavy as smoke in his nose and Andy lay on the concrete, bleeding.

Footsteps walking past Miles, toward Andy.

Andy, calling for Miles, calling for his mama . . . but Miles had shot him in the throat.

No. He couldn't have. Not how it happened.

Miles blinked.

Sorenson leaned over Groote. Groote moaned, spoke pleading words.

But Miles couldn't hear Groote; he only heard Andy calling, *Miles, don't let them hurt me, please. I'm sorry.* Andy clutching his shoulder where Miles had shot him.

Sorenson smiled at Miles. Aimed the gun at Groote.

The fed glanced at Miles. Aimed the gun at Andy.

Not again.

'Amanda—' Groote called to his absent child, to the empty air.

'*Miles, help me,*' Andy screamed, '*– please!*'

Miles heaved to his feet, stumbled toward the two men, the blood pouring from his leg, ignoring the agony.

384

Not again. No.

Sorenson fired two bullets into Groote. The hair puffed on Groote's head; he kicked once and lay still.

The fed fired twice into Andy's throat.

Miles screamed.

The fed looked at Miles. Tried to smile. Lowered the gun. 'He tried to kill us all. Your fault, Miles, you said the wrong thing and set him off. Your goddamned fault. You should have shut up.'

Miles fell to the floor.

Sorenson aimed the gun at Miles. 'Miles, you're going to talk . . .'

His voice was calm again, as though they were back, sitting in the plush leather chairs in Allison's office. 'I don't have to kill you. But I need to know what you know. I'll make sure you get Frost. I'll trade you treatment for you telling me everything I need to know about who's coming after us. I can set it up, no problem. I couldn't let a fuck like Groote live. But you, we can make a deal.'

'Please . . . I'll tell you.' He drew his knee to his chin, groped for the small gun above his ankle, putting a wince on his face as if pain were overwhelming him. He'd forgotten about it in the shock of being shot, of running, of Groote dying, of memory returning with the force of a bullet. 'I'll tell you . . .'

He tucked his hurt leg close to him, gripped under the cuff of his pants as though grimacing against the pain. Closed his hand around the small pistol.

Sorenson leaned forward and Miles sprang the gun up, firing, painting a neat hole in Sorenson's eye.

Sorenson fell dead.

'Uhhh,' Miles said. He started to crawl back across the

concrete, slowly, painfully, aware of the blood oozing out of his leg and arm, toward Groote.

He checked Groote's throat. No pulse. He dug in his pockets, checking for a cell phone to call for help.

He flipped the phone open, tried to make his thumb work the pad.

He heard footsteps approaching him. Sorenson had help, backup, Miles was dead now, nothing to be done. This was death; this would be peace. He crawled, waiting for the inevitable bullet to break his spine, drill into his head.

A weight slammed into his head, once, then again, and he knew no more.

SIXTY

Stone was cold and damp against his skin. Slowly he opened his eyes and sat up. Dried blood covered his face. He wore only his T-shirt and underwear. Rough bandages, fashioned from his shirt, covered the wound in his arm and in his leg. Pain pulsed under the wrappings, as though fingers had dug around in his wounds, and patched him up without care. The room was narrow, the air tasted dense and coppery in his mouth, as though fear lived and grew in the dark corners and its essence had seeped, over many years, into the stone.

The abandoned madhouse. He was still inside.

He tried to speak. 'Hello?' His voice sounded broken. He cleared his throat. 'Hello?'

Several seconds passed. He heard the clicking of locks – more than one – and the door to the room opened. A person stepped inside the dim light of the room from the bright light of the hallway. Miles blinked and his voice died in his throat.

'Hello, Miles.' Allison Vance wore a suit; her hair was lighter, styled neatly, as it had been in the pictures at Edward Wallace's house. She stayed ten paces back.

At first he thought, *My mind's still gone, snapped*, and it shouldn't be, he knew he had not killed Andy. No. But then she said, 'Hello, Miles,' again and her quiet voice echoed, ever so slightly, against the stone. Instead of echoing in his head. Then she raised a gun – the gun Groote had given him, that he'd killed Sorenson with – and leveled it at him.

'Allison?' he managed to say. 'Allison.'

'My name is Renee Wallace,' she said.

'Your . . . name is Allison Vance. You're . . . dead.'

'No. You're dead. Unless you do exactly as I tell you.'

'You – you asked me for help, you set me up.'

'Miles.' She cocked her head, offered the gentle smile she'd always used greeting him in her office as they prepared to sit and talk and she would try to pierce his past of secrets. But there was no understanding, no kindness, in her face; the concern was only a false expression painted on a mask. 'I'm not the problem. You are.'

'Sorenson said in Santa Fe . . . he didn't kill you. I thought he was lying.' He coughed. 'The auction—'

'Miles. There is no auction. Not now. I have a buyer already.'

She'd set him up again. 'Singhal.'

'Yes. I'll make you a deal, Miles. You tell me what I need to know and I'll make sure you have Frost. I'll cure you. You're a killer, and it's a better offer than anyone else will make you.'

'I'm not a killer. I remember it now. I didn't kill Andy.'

'Yes, you did. I've seen your government file, Miles, two federal officers swear you shot him . . .'

'No . . . FBI did . . . they even told me the tape was botched . . . blamed it on me . . .'

She shook her head. 'You killed him. You killed Groote, you killed Sorenson. You killed Hurley. I'll bet you even killed DeShawn Pitts.'

'That's a lie. You – you asked me for help . . .'

'Miles. All I have to say is that I told you about the Frost program, that you wanted in, Hurley said no. After all, it's designed to help the innocent victims of violence. People like Celeste. Like Nathan. But not you – you cold-bloodedly murdered your best friend.'

Miles shook his head. 'No.'

'So you snapped. You've killed everyone who got in your way. That's how the authorities will see it, Miles. A mentally broken man, denied his wish for help.'

'No.'

'You went after Frost yourself. First you wanted to get rid of me. I'll bet the bomb fragments they find at my office will be very similar in composition and design to bombs the Barrada family used in the past. You might know how to make one of those, Miles. It won't be coincidence.'

'You can't explain away . . . vanishing . . . after the explosion.'

'I was on a business trip, Miles. I didn't hear about the blast and you know I forgot my cell phone back in Santa Fe. The woman who died was looking at office space, I imagine. I can step back into being Allison Vance long enough for the story to be over with, then I just leave town again and no one cares.'

He remembered the woman's voice then, before he picked the lock into Allison's office: a woman from Denver asking about office space. Yesterday's paper mentioned a missing tourist in Santa Fe. Jesus.

'I just need to know what you know.' She held up a white pill, perfect as a pearl. 'The answer to your prayers. The cure for your pathetic madness. All you have to do is tell me who else knows about me and Frost, and tell me where I can find them.'

Celeste and Nathan. She wanted them. So Singhal's company could silence them. No one else could gut her; no one else was still alive who could hurt her.

'I – I can't.'

The awful false smile disappeared; in its place was a fury of cold resolve. 'I won't kill you, Miles. I'll shatter you. Singhal's company will buy Sangriaville from Quantrill's estate – I'll hook you up to one of Hurley's machines, play every horrible nightmare and trauma into your head. I'll break your mind so bad it can never be fixed. I'll keep you locked up in a hospital forever. No one will ever look for you. The feds will give you up for lost or dead. You and Groote's brat, I'll just use your heads as my research playground. Unless you help me. Help me and we're friends again, I'll cure you.'

Groote's daughter must be here as well, locked elsewhere in the decaying madhouse. 'No. I didn't kill Andy. I didn't . . . I don't need what you're selling.'

'You're not a hero, Miles, you're a useless punk of a head case. You'll never be fixed without this' – and she showed him Frost again, a white oval, pure as snow. 'Celeste. Nathan. Tell me where they are. Now.'

'You won't hurt them?' He clutched at the bandage on his leg as though twisted in doubt and agony.

'They want Frost too. They want to be healthy and whole. I'm sure I can reach the same deal with them as I'm offering you.'

She would have them, and Victor, too, all killed, he knew. She'd kill him as soon as they were confirmed dead; his usefulness was over, and she was gambling on his desperation, believing that he couldn't think cogently.

'I understand you a lot better than you think,' he said.

'What?'

'You said that to me before . . . I believed you died. It's true. It works both ways. I want help. Don't want to be this way no more.'

'So tell me.' She lowered her voice.

'Celeste . . . had a total breakdown. After the shooting in Yosemite. She and Nathan both. Her TV agent wired her money, they rented a house there in Fish Camp for a week. She and Nathan are still there. Far as I know.' He leaned against the stone wall. 'Hard for us . . . to be out in the real world. Couldn't cope. Couldn't.' Let her think he and the others were nothing, useless, help her put her guard down.

'Address.'

He hesitated. She knew the streets in Fish Camp; he didn't. He could hardly invent an address. Through the haze of pain he knew his only hope was that, Fish Camp being remote, whoever she sent to eliminate Celeste and Nathan would take hours to reach Yosemite, and he would be dead or free by then. 'I don't know . . . street address. There were a cluster of rental properties . . . behind a grocery. They're staying at one.'

She flipped open her phone, spoke softly into it, repeating what Miles had said. Giving him a property name to call. She closed the phone.

'You better not be lying. I've got someone calling the rental office to check.'

Mistake. He hadn't thought past the pain; their presence could be disproved with a couple of phone calls.

He might have only a couple of minutes before she got a call back telling her he'd lied. No margin for error. 'I'm not. They slowed me down.' He loosened the bandage on his leg.

'Leave that alone, you'll bleed. I want you conscious.'

'It hurts.' He stripped the whole bandage loose and grimaced at the bullet hole in his leg as though it were a picture in a book, not a wound in his own flesh. Blood oozed out. He held the strip of cloth between his hands.

'I said leave it alone.'

'You shouldn't have killed Groote.' He had to play her along, get her to come close to him, get her thinking there was another threat to her that only he could help defuse. He collapsed on the floor, as though standing drained him of all energy.

'I did the world a favor. Now. Who did Groote tell about Frost?'

'FBI . . . old buddies of his,' Miles lied. 'Helped us find your buddy Singhal. Tracked him here.'

Fear briefly shaded her face. 'I need names.'

He let his eyes go half closed, mumbled. *Come close*, he thought. *Closer. I only get one chance.*

She took two steps. And stopped. She might not believe him. But he'd put an itch under her skin. 'Miles? The names.'

Just three steps closer. He tensed to jump at her.

Then he heard a boom, rumbling, as if a tank had crashed hard into the front of the building. The madhouse shuddered.

She turned and he leaped, grabbing at her gun. It fired, powering the bullet past his head, pinging off the stone wall. She kicked him hard on his wound, whirled and fled the room. Miles stumbled after her, agony screaming in his leg. She stopped at the top of the stairs; Miles saw they were on the top floor, no more stairs rising beyond this floor.

She ran down the stairs.

'Allison! Allison!' he yelled.

And then he heard an answer, over the clatter of her feet on the stairs: 'Miles?'

Nathan.

'Nathan, get the hell out, call the police, Allison's got a gun—'

And then the awful, final crack of two bullets. Miles limped down the stairs, half falling, half running, the pain in his leg terrible, but frantic for Nathan.

In the foyer the smashed front of a sedan lay among the remains of the front door, debris and dust crowning the h   o   o   d and the starred windshield. The driver's door was open; the car empty.

Nathan was gone.

Miles heard footsteps and spun. Allison ran back into the foyer, clutching the laptop from the office he and Groote had passed, the gun aimed at him.

'Allison.'

She stopped, steadied her aim, took a step back.

'You can't run. You can't just keep . . . running. Doesn't work.'

'Shut up.'

'Running is nothing.' He could taste his own blood in his mouth. 'You'll never get out. Never escape. Never. Ever. If not me, Nathan will find you. Celeste. Any of our friends. Any of Dodd's followers. It won't end for you. Ever. You've thrown your life away. You're the crazy one.'

Rage and fear contorted her face. She fired at him and he dived through the open door of the wrecked car.

She emptied his small gun as she charged at the car. He counted every shot. She rushed the door, aimed at him, and he kicked through the open window with his good leg, catching her in the chest as her finger clicked on an empty clip. She staggered back, lost her balance, cracked her head on crumbling masonry on the floor, and went limp as she hit the tiles.

He heard his name yelled. 'Miles! Miles!'

Nathan.

'Here!' Miles stumbled to Allison, pulled the gun from her unconscious fingers.

Nathan's face appeared in the hole that had been the front door.

'Nathan, holy God . . .'

'I'm not a screw-up,' Nathan said. He steadied Miles against the car. 'I – I followed you and Groote here from the hotel . . . I didn't know what to do . . . so I waited . . . until I had enough nerve. When you didn't come out . . . I couldn't just drive away. So I rammed the rental car through the door, then I ran to get help.' He gestured at the mess. 'What the hell was I thinking . . .'

'No, you did awesome, Nathan.' He grabbed Nathan's shoulder, embraced him, pounded his back.

'I didn't do it for you, Miles,' Nathan said. His tone was cool. 'You I'm still pissed at. I did it for my friends.'

'I know. I'm just glad you did what you did. Thank you.' He didn't know what to say and the words came, drawn by his memory of Nathan's nightmare: 'You fixed it, man.'

'I did.' Nathan gave him a thin smile. The side mirror hung broken from its control cables and he carefully turned it to face the battered car. 'Is Frost here?'

'If it isn't,' Miles said, 'she'll tell us where it is. We won, Nathan.'

'I ran when she shot at me . . . to a house down the street . . . they're calling the police. The guy's a vet. Like me.'

'We need to call Victor and Celeste as soon as possible. Stay here. Don't let Allison run.'

Nathan sat on Allison's back. She didn't respond.

Miles climbed the stairs, calling Amanda's name. He heard a weak reply on the second floor.

The door was bolted shut. He opened it, saw a girl cowering in a corner, dressed in hospital scrubs, pale.

'Amanda?'

'Who are you?' She trembled at his bloodied face, the exposed wound in his leg.

'A friend of your dad's.'

'I want to go home. The sounds. The voices. This place is full of ghosts.'

'No,' Miles said. 'The ghosts are gone. It's okay now. There's nothing to be afraid of.'

SIXTY-ONE

'Does it work?' Miles asked.

'Yes,' Amanda said. She sat on the hospital's porch, letting the wind kiss her face. 'It does. The magic's all in the super beta-blockers. They kick bad-memory ass. And the therapy.'

'You think I should take the pill?'

'Yes. But I don't like the therapy part,' she said. 'Talking so much. Quiet's nicer. In the quiet I hear my mom's and my dad's voices.'

'They loved you very much,' Miles said.

'I know that.' She scratched at a star-shaped scar at the corner of her mouth and he wondered how she had gotten it. 'Are you going to take the medicine, Miles?'

'I don't know,' he said. 'Sometimes pain makes us stronger. Sometimes it makes us weaker. I'm not sure which kind my pain is.'

'You should take the medicine,' she said. 'Hurting so much it ruins your life really sucks.' She stood. 'I'm helping Nathan.'

'What with?'

She announced her project with teenager wryness. 'It's so lame. I'm painting a mirror for him.'

'Don't get attached to it.'

'No. It's a mirror for when he's ready to look in one. I'm painting all the NFL team logos on the sides. He knows if he breaks it I'll kill him. I think he might be ready soon, so I better get it finished.' She went to work on her project.

Miles watched a new arrival from the porch. A young man with the bearing of a soldier, but with haunted eyes, got out of a van accompanied by one of Victor's newly hired counselors. Sangre de Cristo had been seized by the government, as part of its investigation of both Quantrill and Dodd. Victor and his army of lawyers had negotiated a contract, after much arm twisting and gentle persuasion, to run a program to test Frost in participation with a respected pharmaceutical. Victor and Celeste began, quietly, to contact people who were active on his PTSD Web site. Ex-soldiers from around the world. Survivors of abuse, of rape, of terrorism, of natural disasters, who could not shake the trauma of their devastating memories. And two or three times a day, a new person would arrive, stepping out of a taxi or a rental car, or brought by his or her family, blinking up at the rise of Sangre de Cristo as if its walls held a final hope. Victor would bring them in for coffee and talk, explain the theory and potential and risks of Frost, and they almost inevitably agreed to be part of the testing. The government, eager to bury Dodd's and Quantrill's work and promote a legitimate drug, planned to seek a fast-track approval. Allison sat in a federal prison cell, awaiting trial.

Miles found Celeste walking on the edge of an artificial pond in the back of the property. She tossed pebbles in the water. She stood far from the blanket of walls. She lifted her face to the wind, to the sun.

'What are you thinking?' he asked.

'Remembering. Not thinking. Just . . . remembering. I have two presents for you.'

'Not my birthday.'

'Surprise, yes it is. A new start. A new life.' She pulled from her pocket the confession he'd left for her. They'd been back in Santa Fe for three weeks; she had not mentioned the confession; he had not asked for it. 'This is yours.'

'I guess it made for a rotten gift.' He stared at his feet.

'But it's not the truth. You know you didn't kill him.'

'I still screwed up. If I hadn't panicked him . . .'

'You didn't kill him, Miles, and the FBI will deal with the man who did.' She pushed the paper into his hands. 'It's not a confession anymore, it's the last chapter of your old life. I would rather focus on the new.'

He tore the confession into slow, deliberate shreds, cast the fluttering bits onto the calm of the waters.

'You mentioned two presents,' he reminded her when he was done.

She answered, 'I'm starting on the new Frost today.'

He said nothing.

'I can't bear the memories of Brian dying. I need Frost. So I can move on . . .' She put her hand to his cheek, the *we* unspoken. *So we can move on.*

Would you forget the worst moment of your life? He knew he hadn't killed Andy. His worst moment was not of being a murderer but of being helpless to save his murdered friend. He never wanted to be helpless again. Never so alone again. He couldn't have his old life back – but he would do whatever it took to have a new life.

He glanced at the opposite bank. Andy still stood there, shaking his head, frowning, saying, 'No, don't do it, Miles, don't make me go. I want to stay. Always.'

'Is he there?' she asked.

'Yeah, and mad at me.'

Celeste opened her closed fist. A white pill lay on her open palm, white as the torn shreds floating like confetti on the water.

Miles took the Frost pill from her palm. He slipped it into his mouth, put it on his tongue. Celeste closed her fingers around his.

He swallowed and opened his eyes.

'Let's go have dinner,' she said. He nodded, and walked away from the pond with her, not looking behind him, because, he hoped, there was nothing for him to see.

ACKNOWLEDGMENTS

My debts in writing *Fear* are enormous. Huge thanks and appreciation to Mitch Hoffman, Brian Tart, Lisa Johnson, Kara Welsh, Kristen Weber, Erika Kahn, and everyone at Dutton and NAL; David Shelley, Jenny Fry, Kerry Chapple, Sheena-Margot Lavelle, Nathalie Morse, and everyone at Little, Brown Book Group; and Peter Ginsberg, Shirley Stewart, Holly Frederick, and Dave Barbor for their always wise counsel.

I owe thanks to Gerald Shur, the founder of WITSEC (better known as the witness protection program). Mr. Shur answered all my questions with aplomb. His book *WITSEC: Inside the Federal Witness Protection Program* (coauthored with Pete Earley, published by Bantam) is a terrific account of how the program has worked and evolved in protecting federal witnesses.

Thanks also to James L. McGaugh, Ph.D., director of the Center for the Neurobiology of Learning and Memory, and professor of neurobiology and behavior at the University of California-Irvine; and Roger K. Pitman, M.D., Massachusetts General Hospital and Professor of Psychiatry, Harvard Medical School. Dr. McGaugh and Dr. Pitman are leaders in the research of memory and emotion, and they generously shared their insights on how we might treat or minimize PTSD. While no such drug as Frost currently exists, promising research into the use of beta blockers gives hope that we might one day be able to blunt horrific memories and mitigate the crippling affliction that is PTSD. For those interested, Dr. McGaugh's book *Memory and Emotion: The Making of Lasting Memories* (Columbia University Press) is a fascinating and accessible treatment of this complex subject.

Another round of thanks to these wonderful people who shared their time and wisdom: Lawrence Hauser, M.D., kindly offered insights on PTSD gleaned from years of practicing psychiatry. William E. Thompson shared his experiences about his time in Iraq as an army reservist and photojournalist. Heidi Mack, who runs www.jeffabbott.com like a well-oiled machine, and Jerry Saperstein, computer forensics expert (www.civildiscovery.com) and thriller fan extraordinaire, answered my tech questions. Betty Osborne, Ellen Ray, Pam Kohler, and Mark Kohler provided information and kind introductions to open doors during my time in Santa Fe. Marsha Jackson was a lovely and generous guide to Santa Fe and answered more questions than I could count. Chris McLarry of McLarry Fine Arts; Victoria Price of Price-Dewey Gallery; and David Loren Bass of Bass-Thomson Gallery all shared their expertise on the nuances of Santa Fe gallery operations. David Bailey, Chief of Fire/Arson Investigations, Austin Fire Department, and my friend and firefighter L. J. Saul, discussed explosion and fire scenarios with me. Paige Johnson of Seton Shoal Creek Hospital answered questions about psychiatric admissions and security. Maria Lima, Sandi Wilson, Joy Cocke, Cinco Cocke, and Jill Grimes, M.D., all get gold stars for helpfulness and support. Any errors or enhancements for the sake of drama are my responsibility, not theirs.

Great thanks to my longtime friend David Schmid for exploring Yosemite with me and not thinking I was crazy for plotting out a shooting and a car chase during our trip to the most beautiful place on earth, and to his wife, Jennifer, and their sons, Daniel, William, and Andrew, for their hospitality during my time in California. And finally, heartfelt thanks to my wife, Leslie; my sons, Charles and William; my mom, Elizabeth, and my stepfather, Dub, for their incredible encouragement and support.